D0760924

Mulberry Moon

Center Point
Large Print

Also by Catherine Anderson and available from Center Point Large Print:

New Leaf

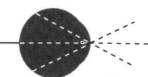

**This Large Print Book carries the
Seal of Approval of N.A.V.H.**

MULBERRY MOON

A MYSTIC CREEK NOVEL

Catherine Anderson

CENTER POINT LARGE PRINT
THORNDIKE, MAINE

This Center Point Large Print edition is published in the year 2017 by arrangement with The Berkley Publishing Group, an imprint of Penguin Publishing Group, a division of Penguin Random House LLC.

Copyright © 2017 by Adeline Catherine Anderson.

All rights reserved.

This is a work of fiction. Names, characters, places, and incidents either are the product of the author's imagination or are used fictitiously, and any resemblance to actual persons, living or dead, business establishments, events, or locales is entirely coincidental.

The text of this Large Print edition is unabridged. In other aspects, this book may vary from the original edition. Printed in the United States of America on permanent paper. Set in 16-point Times New Roman type.

ISBN: 978-1-68324-396-0

Library of Congress Cataloging-in-Publication Data

Names: Anderson, Catherine (Adeline Catherine), author.
Title: Mulberry moon : a Mystic Creek novel / Catherine Anderson.
Description: Center Point Large Print edition. | Thorndike, Maine : Center Point Large Print, 2017.
Identifiers: LCCN 2017008764 | ISBN 9781683243960 (hardcover : alk. paper)
Subjects: LCSH: Large type books. | GSAFD: Love stories.
Classification: LCC PS3551.N34557 M85 2017 | DDC 813/.54—dc23
LC record available at https://lccn.loc.gov/2017008764

This book is dedicated to Finnegan Gurnsey, a young Australian shepherd who inspired me to feature him as a secondary character in *Mulberry Moon*.

Mulberry Moon

Chapter
ONE

With the taste of tacos lingering in his mouth, Ben Sterling opened the door to leave Taco Joe's on West Main and hollered good-bye to Joe Paisley, the owner. A rush of icy pine-scented air surrounded Ben as he donned his tan Stetson and stepped onto the sidewalk. It smelled like home and reminded him how glad he was to be back in Mystic Creek, not just for a visit, but living on his ranch again.

Liquidating his business as a rodeo stockbroker hadn't been an easy decision. He'd made damned good money. But it had kept him on the road most of the time, often in flat, arid country where only a few bushy trees dotted the landscape. He'd quickly grown tired of the constant traveling, but he'd stuck it out to build a nice nest egg. Now he had finally quit, returned to his roots, and was trying to build a real life.

Because it had been sunny when he left home, he'd forgotten a jacket, so all he could do was hunch his shoulders against the frigid temperature. His new Dodge Ram waited along the curb only paces away. Against the backdrop of late-nineteenth-century storefronts that characterized

Mystic Creek, it looked futuristic in the grayish light that always bathed the town as the sun started its slide into oblivion.

The smooth soles of his riding boots lost traction, warning him that the concrete was icy. In mid-September, Mystic Creek sometimes had weather fluctuations, warm one minute and freezing the next. *Stupid not to bring a coat,* he thought. *This is high-elevation Oregon.* He guessed he'd been gone too long. Climatic habits ingrained in him during boyhood had lost their hold on him.

Walking to his vehicle, he saw his dog, Finnegan, watching him through the back cab window. Eight months old, the blue merle Australian shepherd had the mottle of black, gray, and white fur common to blues, but his markings were distinct, his narrow nose and forehead sporting a tapering white blaze. He bounced from side to side on the bench seat, acting as if he'd been alone for hours.

A smile touched Ben's mouth. A bachelor and now thirty years old, he enjoyed having a dog. When Ben first returned to live on his ranch, the big, rambling house had felt empty when he stayed there alone. He'd grown up in a large family. He preferred noise buzzing around him. Finn had provided the perfect antidote, snuggling with Ben in the recliner while he watched TV or read novels, always eager to play, barking joyously, and offering a warm presence beside him in bed at night. Hello, when a man couldn't find Miss Right, no matter how hard he searched, sometimes he had to settle for companionship from a four-legged friend. There were worse fates than being loved by a dog.

Not that Ben didn't keep company with women. He just couldn't find that one special lady he wanted to be with for a lifetime. Dating at thirty was a crapshoot with lots of promising beginnings followed by disappointing endings. He couldn't find anyone who truly loved animals, for one thing, and his life revolved around all kinds of them. He'd met a few gals that had a cat, a bird, or a goldfish, but they didn't want a dog in the house. Or they were afraid of horses. A number of them had even visited his ranch in high heels and gotten pissed if they stepped in manure. He couldn't build a future with someone like that. He needed a down-to-earth person who didn't run in terror from his free-range chickens or pick dog hair off her fancy clothes.

As he circled the truck to the driver's door, delicious aromas drifted across the street from the Straw Hat, which served Mexican cuisine, and the Cauldron, another eatery in Mystic Creek, which specialized in home-style fare. Ben enjoyed eating at the Cauldron, and apparently so did many others. Through the front windows, he could see that the place was packed. The menu offered a wide variety of homemade choices, and the prices were also easy on the wallet.

There was only one fly in the ointment for Ben where the Cauldron was concerned: the café's owner, Sissy Sue Bentley. She was a petite woman with cropped dark hair, blue eyes that dominated her heart-shaped face, and a figure that was perfection on a small scale. She'd caught his attention over a year ago, and he'd started patronizing her establishment, hoping to get better acquainted. Despite his efforts to be friendly, she'd treated him as if he had a contagious disease. After a couple of weeks, he'd started to feel like a stalker and chalked it up to bad chemistry. Now he avoided the place.

Sissy wasn't the only pretty female in the area, after all. On weekend nights, he sometimes frequented the nightspots in nearby Crystal Falls, hoping to meet someone he could relate to. So far, he'd run across several gals who were stunning, and a few intriguing enough to date for a couple of months. In the end, though, even if the sex was great, there was always something to put the kibosh on the relationship. It was just his luck that the only local woman he found attractive had taken an instant dislike to him.

As Ben pulled open the truck door, Finn leaped forward and slathered his face with doggy kisses. Ben laughed and gave the pup an enthusiastic scratch behind both ears. "I missed you, too." He gently pushed the shepherd off the driver's seat and started to climb inside the vehicle.

A familiar sound stopped him dead in his tracks. *Berk, berk, berk.* He swung around and did a double take. A white hen was strutting eastward along the street. Ben had seen some strange sights in Mystic Creek. One time a skunk had joined the participants of a Fourth of July parade and cleared the sidewalks of people with one threatening lift of its tail. More recently, a black bear had moseyed onto East Main and pushed its way through the swinging doors of the Jake 'n' Bake and devoured everything in the pastry section while Jake hid in the cooler until law officers arrived.

Now it was a chicken invading the downtown area. Where had it come from?

Just then, two more hens fell in behind the white leghorn, all three of the fowl covering ground at a pace suggesting they were late to an appointment. Finnegan barked. He was used to seeing chickens at home, but never within the city limits.

What the hell? Ben looked in the direction from which the chickens were coming and saw more feathery pedestrians appearing from behind the last building on the opposite side of the street. It housed Marilyn Fears's One-Stop Market, a small mom-and-pop shop. Had Marilyn decided to raise chickens? It was a popular hobby, and so far as Ben knew, the town had no ordinances against it.

Marilyn had space behind her building for a coop and run. A small distributary of Mystic Creek flowed behind the shops on that side of West Main, so the land back there hadn't been developed. Diverting the stream's natural course wasn't an option. In this town, nobody messed with Mystic Creek. The waterway was thought to be magical by many people, and even a narrow brook originating from it was revered.

As Ben watched, the flow of hens didn't abate. How many chicks had Marilyn ordered? As Ben stood there, dumbfounded, even more chickens appeared. Beckoning Finn out of the truck in case he needed the dog's help with bird herding, he gingerly headed toward the store. If Marilyn's chickens were loose, she'd need help collecting them. The ones he'd seen were pullets, not yet full-grown, and at an age when hens were sometimes warier of humans than they might be later. He didn't want that nice older lady to fall on the ice and get hurt.

As Ben circled the store, he noticed the dim interior beyond the front window, which sported a glowing sign that read CLOSED. It was Friday night and only shortly after six. Though a gloaming heralded the approach of nightfall, full darkness wouldn't descend for a while. He guessed the market mostly got business from nine to five on weekdays, allowing Marilyn, who lived in the upstairs flat, to lock up early.

The oncoming birds made Ben feel as if he were going the wrong direction on a one-way thoroughfare. As he turned the corner at the back of the building, his gaze followed the line of fleeing chickens to the property behind the Cauldron. *Shit.* Through the deepening gloom, he saw a tiny coop in Sissy's backyard—one of those DIY kits. Attached to it was a pathetic wire run. She probably didn't know her chickens were loose, and even if she did, the Cauldron appeared to be packed with customers. The last time Ben had eaten there, Sissy had still been doing a one-woman show, rushing to service tables, pinning slips to the order wheel, and then racing into the kitchen to cook.

Just then Ben saw her dart from behind the coop in pursuit of a brown hen. She lunged at her target, slipped, and did a belly flop on the ground. Ben winced. The lady had been unfriendly to him in the past, greeting his polite overtures with icy disdain. He owed her nothing and almost made a U-turn. But the fowl had fled in all directions, and Ben's dad, Jeremiah, had raised him to always offer his help when someone else was in a jam.

Snapping his fingers to keep the dog beside him, Ben hurried across Marilyn's lawn to Sissy's dirt yard. Finn trembled with excitement. "Do you need some help?"

Startled by Ben's voice, Sissy whirled to face him. Even with dirt smeared on her cheek and across the front of her white chef's coat, she was still cuter than a button. Her short, dark hair, which covered her ears in wisps to frame her cheeks, was tousled and peppered with wood chips. Some of the old folks in town said Sissy was the spitting image of Audrey Hepburn. Not long ago, Ben's mom and sisters had insisted that he watch *Breakfast at Tiffany's* with them. Except for the difference in eye color, Sissy definitely resembled Hepburn.

His gut tightened. He didn't get what it was about Sissy that drew his interest, but when she turned that wary blue gaze on him, he wanted to reassure her.

She gestured at the fleeing chickens and cried, "Nobody ever told me they can *fly!* What kind of hatchery sells chicks to people without telling them that?"

Ben wondered if this was a trick question. "Um, well, they are birds. Right?"

She placed her fine-boned hands on her hips. "Not all birds can fly. Penguins, for instance! And emus! Name me one time you saw a chicken soaring in the sky!"

Ben struggled not to grin. For once, she was actually speaking to him without an order tablet in her hand. Now was not a good time to pop back with a smart-ass comment. "Not often, I have to admit."

"Not often? I've never seen a chicken fly!"

Ben glanced at the hens going airborne to get over the sagging wall of the run. "That could be because all the chickens you've ever seen had their wings clipped."

"Clipped?" She rolled her eyes. "What parts are clipped? All I know is my whole flock is loose, my café is filled with customers, I have food on the stove, and—"

She gulped and her cheeks puffed out with her deep breaths.

"I'd be happy to help," he offered.

With a jerk of her shoulders and a lift of her chin, she stood tall—well, as tall as someone of her diminutive stature could manage. In her ice queen voice, she informed him, "I think I can handle it by myself."

That stuffs it, Ben thought. She hadn't even bothered to thank him for offering. His father may have raised him to be a good guy, but not a fool. Just as he turned to walk away, thinking up a rejoinder he'd never say aloud to her, a white leghorn flapped past him. Before he could stop himself, he shot out a hand, caught both its legs in his grip, and tipped it upside down, a quick, humane way to prevent all the struggling and squawking that might have ensued.

I need lessons in how to be a convincing jerk, Ben thought. *She doesn't want my help. She's made that clear. And now I've caught one of her*

17

damned hens. Angry with himself for being a pushover, he started toward her pathetic excuse for a run. The brown hen she'd been chasing now perched on the sagging wire. Ben snatched it up by its legs, turned it head down, and met Sissy at the jerry-rigged gate.

She flashed him an incredulous look. "How did you do that?"

"There really isn't much to it."

She glanced at the two birds hanging almost lifeless at his sides. Not wanting her to think his technique was abusive, Ben said, "This is how many poultry wranglers do it. All the fight goes out of the chickens, and it's safer for them."

"You're hired."

Ben nearly told her she couldn't afford him. But in good conscience, he couldn't let the hens run free all night. They might die of exposure, or fall victim to predators. He glanced at his dog, still quivering with excitement. The pup was already proving to be a good herder, and Ben had used him often to round up his chickens after a day of free range.

He snapped his fingers and pointed at a buff Orpington. "Good boy, Finn! Bring 'em in."

Finnegan leaped into action. While the dog expertly steered three terrified hens toward home, Ben dumped his captives inside the run, caught two more, and opened the makeshift gate to facilitate his dog's efforts. After Finnegan had done his part, Ben entered the enclosure, pulling the gate closed behind him. He caught all the buggers and stuffed them into the coop to prevent more escapes. The run was useless. The wire sagged so low, even chickens with clipped wings could probably hop over it.

After securing the door, he exited the run. He looked at Sissy. "How many chickens do you have? I saw at least fifty on the street."

In a small voice, she said, "Eighty."

"Eighty?" Ben studied the structure. "That coop isn't big enough for eighty grown birds. Twenty, maybe."

She pushed tendrils of dark hair from her brow. "It seemed a lot bigger when they were small. I want to increase my breakfast business, and since a lot of my customers are farmers, I thought . . ." She flapped a limp hand. "Well, you know. They dislike commercially grown eggs. So I took courses online and passed a test so I'd be legal to raise layers and sell eggs. I even know how to grade them for size."

In other words, she knew a lot of useless stuff about chickens and nothing practical. "And you think your breakfast crowd will go through eighty eggs a day?"

"There's a mortality rate with chicks." She pushed her fingers through her hair, making it spike in all directions. "I can't remember the percentage, but I ordered plenty of chicks just in case some of them didn't make it."

She looked exhausted. Even worse, an expression of utter defeat played over her face.

"But then nobody died!" Her tone was laced with frustration. A horrified expression flashed in her eyes. "Not that I wanted anybody to die." She dropped her hand from her hair to press it over her heart. "I love them. They were such cute babies. I kept them in troughs in my bedroom under heat lights like they tell you to do. And then they got pasty butt, and I had to wash all their bums every night." She gave him an imploring look. "They became my pets."

He tried to imagine washing the encrusted butts of eighty chicks every night after a hard day's work. As for loving chickens, they were just livestock, filthy creatures and so dumb they took dumps in their drinking water.

Ben went after another hen. Before he closed in, a rooster just old enough to be feeling randy grabbed the chicken by her neck feathers and threw her to the ground.

Sissy, hurrying along beside him, cried, "Some of them are getting vicious with the others. Just look at her, being so mean! It started a couple of days ago. I don't know what's gotten into her. Margie! You quit that!"

Ben realized that Sissy didn't know how to tell the difference between male and female birds when they were still so young. The ground had grown slick with a layer of ice, and his boots provided little traction. He barely managed to slide to a stop before he knocked the birds over with his shins. Startled, the two chickens parted company, the hen going one way while Margie the rooster went the other. He chased the hen, letting Margie escape. A male bird was less likely to skedaddle. No guy in his right mind abandoned a place where he could score countless times a day.

Finn had herded several chickens into the run and was standing guard at the open gate to make sure none of them tried to dart back out. It would be a race against time before they took flight over the short wire walls of the enclosure. Ben needed to stuff this hen and all the others into the coop.

Sissy ran in to help as Ben deposited birds inside the shelter. Her black work shoes, soled for grip on smooth floors, didn't perform well on ice. Just as she neared the coop, her feet shot out from under her and she landed hard on her backside, losing the captured bird in the process. With so many hens squawking, Ben didn't hear her teeth snap together, but he felt certain they had.

She scrambled erect and began helping him get hens into the coop. The first two she caught squawked, twisted in her arms, and flapped their wings. From then on, she grabbed them by the legs and flipped them upside down. *Quick learner,* he noted.

When Ben exited the run, he saw Finnegan disappear around the corner of the building. Ben guessed the dog was going out to the street where hens were running helter-skelter along West Main. Finn was accustomed to cars. On the ranch, Ben had started training him early to respect them. If the pup saw an automobile coming, he'd dart out of harm's way.

Within seconds Ben heard hens approaching, and an instant later, they came around the corner of the building, legs scissoring and wings flapping to take them airborne in fits and starts. Finn ran back and forth in a broad fan pattern behind them, blocking the way of any bird that tried to retreat.

"Wow!" Sissy exclaimed, her face even dirtier now than it had been earlier. At her side dangled a hen, its wings spread and motionless. "He's really good at this."

Ben's chest swelled with pride. "He's a great herder."

Soon at least ten chickens were racing around inside the run. Ben and Sissy wasted no time in capturing them. Once it grew dark, it would be difficult to find them.

After securing all the captives inside the coop, Ben turned to see Sissy kneeling outside the gate with her arms around Finnegan. "Thank you so much," he heard her say above the raucous cries of the birds behind him. "You're a wonderful—no, *fabulous*—dog!" She ruffled Finn's fur and planted a kiss on his forehead before releasing him. "Good boy! Bring 'em in!"

After scrambling to her feet, Sissy began chasing other escapees. Ben joined her. Finn had left to bring in more strays from the street, so they were temporarily on their own. Ben regretted telling Sissy that catching chickens was easy. Without his dog, he pretty much sucked.

Ben lunged after a black rooster that was determined to avoid capture. The male darted behind a pine and used the large trunk as a barricade. The yard was dotted with smaller trees near the back boundary. Ben wished the gump had chosen to hide behind one of them. He feinted to the right, one hand on the bark of the ponderosa to help steady his balance. The rooster shrieked and circled the other way. *This is my chance,* Ben thought. Pushing for speed, he switched direction to meet the bird head-on. His boots slipped on the ice. His legs shot sideways. All that saved him from doing the splits was his momentum, which, as he waved his arms to keep his balance, flipped him onto his back.

Ben's head hit the frozen earth with such force it stunned him, and in the second it took for him to regain his wits, he felt his sprawled body sliding at a fast clip over the ground. He thought he heard Sissy scream. The next second he plowed into something, groin first. Pain exploded between his legs. He saw stars. His stomach clenched on a wave of nausea. Blinking to clear his vision, he heard someone groaning. It took him a moment to realize it was him.

Through a reddish haze, he stared up the slender trunk of a new-growth pine. The canopy of green branches at its top seemed to swirl above him in an eerie pattern against the darkening sky. He couldn't move, couldn't cuss. All he wanted was to roll on his side and curl up into the fetal position, but he couldn't manage that, either. He'd taken a few hard blows down there over the years, but nothing had ever hurt like this.

"Oh, my God! Oh, my God!" Sissy's voice trilled above him. "Are you all right?" He felt her drop to her knees beside him. Ben blinked, swallowed back another wave of nausea, and finally got her face in focus. "There was nothing I could do!" she cried. "You sped toward that tree like a race car. I'm so sorry. This is all my fault. You wouldn't be out here if not for my stupid chickens."

She rested a hand on his shoulder and kept talking. Nothing she said made much sense to him until the pain subsided a bit. Even then, he was so captivated by the raw emotion in her voice that her words didn't register in his brain.

For the first time, Ben was seeing her without the mask of indifference, allowing him to glimpse the young woman she really was under the facade, a person with feelings that ran deep, not only for chickens, but also people. She wasn't as cold as she pretended to be.

"I can run inside and make an ice pack," she offered. "Maybe that'll help."

The suggestion startled Ben back to reality. Considering the location of his injury, he almost groaned again. Finn had returned. Opposite Sissy, the dog stood over Ben, licked his face, and whined. Ben realized that the throbs of pain under his cupped hands were growing less intense, and he was starting to see a glimmer of humor in the situation.

In a high-pitched soprano voice, he said, "I think I'm going to be fine."

Caught off guard by his joke, Sissy giggled and sat back on her heels. Ben gazed up at her pixie face, taking in her large, expressive eyes, her delicate bone structure, and the softness of her lips. The thought flitted through his mind that he wanted nothing more in that moment than to kiss her senseless. If a woman could turn him on now, when his nuts still ached, he guessed he really was going to be fine.

He dug his elbows into the ice-encrusted dirt to lever himself up into a sitting position, which prompted Sissy to scramble back to her feet.

She leaned forward with her arm outstretched.

"Here, I'll help you," she said.

Ben accepted the offer, noting that his hand nearly swallowed hers. She inched closer to the tree and braced her body against the trunk to pull him up. Her shoes slipped on the ice, but she caught her balance.

Tightening her grip, she said, "Ready? On the count of three. One. Two. Thr—"

The next instant, Ben lay flat on his back again, only this time with her weight angled across him. "Well, if this isn't a hell of a situation."

Finn gave a happy bark and bounced forward to slather the side of Sissy's face with kisses. Two humans were down and at his mercy. She sputtered and then started to giggle again. As dazed as Ben still was, he appreciated the melodious sound of her laughter. It reminded him of his mom's dainty wind chimes.

She held up her hand to shield her mouth, not seeming to mind when Finnegan licked her cheeks. "I think he's lost interest in chickens. Two people tumbling around in the dirt are a lot more fun."

"He's still a pup."

After Sissy rolled off him, Ben sat up. "I'll try standing by myself this time." He shifted onto his knees, curled his arm around the tree, and finally gained his feet. The pain had ebbed to a dull ache. Still using the pine for stability, he grasped Sissy's hand and helped her stand. The rooster, watching from a distance, cackled in dismay because his pursuer might soon be back in the game.

"Well, that slowed us down." With a glance at the sky, Ben added, "We're losing daylight. If the cold doesn't kill those hens, predators might. We have to get them inside the coop."

Just then, hungry café customers spilled out the rear door of the building. Leading the crowd was Crystal Malloy, a striking redhead about Ben's age who owned Silver Beach, an upscale salon and spa. Her coppery hair, which fell nearly to her waist, sported brilliant stripes of pink and green. She wore a fitted black jacket over a green knit top and a gathered black skirt that ended well above the knee. Spike-heeled black boots that clung to her shapely calves finished off her outfit.

"We decided to come help!" she called. "I turned off the stove so nothing will burn."

Ben wondered how she hoped to walk on ice wearing footwear more suited to a dominatrix.

In a deep voice, someone behind Crystal yelled, "It's our only hope if we want to eat before midnight!"

The speaker, Tim VeArd, co-owner of the VeArd Boat Dock on Creek Crossing Lane, threaded his way through the people on the porch. Around sixty with a thick thatch of white hair, a tall, robust build, and blue eyes that always twinkled with humor, he was still a fine figure of a man. Ben had heard that Tim had been in the navy, acquired a love of boats, and turned his passion into a thriving business. His wife, Lynda, more often called Lighthouse Lady because she loved lighthouses, was a spirited redhead with a kind heart who worked tirelessly at her husband's side. The majority of their profit came from buying old vessels and restoring them for resale.

"You know how to catch chickens?" Ben asked.

"Do horses know how to buck?" Tim's boat shoes didn't appear to slip on the ice. "I was raised on a farm, son."

Crystal stepped off the porch behind VeArd, and she, too, seemed able to keep her footing. Ben guessed the spikes on her boots acted as picks. Before Ben knew it, everyone else descended the steps, some slipping and sliding, others wearing shoes with soles made for slick surfaces. Ben saw Chuck Berkeley, a lofty young guy with black hair who'd just purchased Beer, Wine, and Smokes, a business near the town center on Huckleberry Road.

Tim pointed a finger at Sissy. "You, back to the kitchen to fix our dinners. The cavalry has arrived."

Sissy glanced at the chickens darting around the yard. Ben noted her worried expression. "I'll show everyone how to catch them. Your hens won't be hurt."

As she walked toward her building, brushing at the grime on her apron, she called over her shoulder, "I'll have to clean up before I cook. Otherwise you'll have feathers and wood chips in your food."

A rumble of approval followed her into the building.

After Sissy disappeared, Ben taught the volunteers how to catch chickens. He wondered if these people had offered to help only because they were hungry, or if they considered the café owner to be a friend. He decided it had to be the latter. Apparently Sissy wasn't an ice queen with all individuals, only with him.

After everyone knew how to catch a chicken, Ben allowed them to spread out. There followed a comical roundup. At one point, Crystal Malloy bent over to grab a hen, lost her footing, and sprawled on the ground with her skirt flipped above her waist. She flashed a red thong at every man still in the backyard. Even Ben froze in midmotion, and he'd never found Crystal to be that attractive. Her brand of beauty, as flashy and stunning as it was, did nothing for him. Even so, the sight made him momentarily forget that his mission was to rescue pullets.

When people spilled out onto West Main in pursuit of Sissy's flock, Fred Black, aka Blackie, the local pawnshop owner, slipped on the ice and wrapped himself around a parking meter like the stripe on a barber pole. Tim VeArd, while attempting to save Lynda from a spill, lost his footing and fell spread-eagled over the hood of someone's car. Chuck Berkeley nearly rammed his head through the display window of Needles in a Haystack.

When every last bird had been caught and put away in the coop, Finnegan received many congratulatory pats for being such a fine helper. After all the volunteers had reentered the building for dinner, Ben, still a bit achy between his legs, cast the pup an accusing look.

"I wanted to be hero of the day," he told the dog. "How can I catch Sissy's eye if you steal all my thunder?"

Finn barked and wagged his stubbed tail as if to say, "I'm sorry, bro. It's not my fault you can't measure up."

Ben crouched to hug his dog. "Thanks, buddy. Sissy's flock is safe for the night." He settled a thoughtful gaze on the tiny coop. "At least it soon will be," he amended. "Unless I miss my guess, it'll be really cold tonight. Without some heat, those chickens could freeze to death."

Chapter
TWO

Sissy gave the stainless steel counters a final swipe, then tossed the rag at the laundry hamper. It landed on the floor. Stifling a groan, she bent to pick it up. After the wild-chicken chase and hours of hard work, she was too tired to grumble. Her butt hurt from falling on the ice. Her feet ached from being on them for so many hours. All she wanted was to sip a glass of wine while she soaked in a hot bath.

That lovely thought was rudely interrupted by a persistent hammering sound from out back. *What now?* Curious about the noise, she removed her coverall, then groped with her fingers along the shelf where she always put her wristwatch and ring while she worked. Her ring was there, but her watch had vanished, and in its place lay a crinkled piece of foil. A tingly sensation spread over her nape. *Not again.* She had either been misplacing things with alarming frequency, or someone or something was trying to drive her crazy. She had no idea where the foil had come from. It looked like something she might have dropped on the floor while cooking.

Feeling eyes on her, Sissy whirled to look

behind her. Darkness crowded against the window, and shadows hovered in the recesses of the room. She saw nothing unusual, but she couldn't shake the sensation that she was being watched. Over the last few weeks, she'd begun to wonder if the building was haunted. Her aunt Mabel, the original owner, had died of a heart attack in the upstairs flat. Sissy didn't believe in ghosts, but there was no denying that peculiar things had been happening. She'd heard weird noises. Things clattering over the floor. Stuff being dropped. And nearly every day something went missing. *Now my wristwatch,* she thought. She was surviving on a shoestring budget to save enough money to build a new coop and run, and after that, she would reinvest her profits in the business. She couldn't comfortably afford a new timepiece.

The banging sound snagged her attention again. She hurried to the storeroom, grabbed her winter jacket, and exited the building onto the back porch as she yanked the garment on. A shudder marched up her spine. It was so cold that ice crystals had formed in the air. Standing under light coming from an outdoor fixture, she tensed as her eyes picked out a large dark-colored pickup parked near her chicken run.

Finn, barely visible in the darkness, rocketed up the steps. He danced around Sissy's feet and whined in greeting. Now Sissy knew for certain to whom the truck belonged. At least it wasn't a burglar.

As disgruntled as she felt about Ben Sterling being on her property again, she couldn't be cross with the dog. He was cute and such a friendly fellow. She loved his fur. He looked as if he'd been sponged with dabs of paint, the colors blending together to give his body a bluish hue. His lower legs were the color of curry powder. A white blaze marked his forehead. When he wagged his stub tail, his whole body wiggled.

"Hello, Finnegan!" She briskly ruffled the silky fur on his back. "You're such a good boy! Yes, you are. And a champion chicken catcher!"

The pup bathed her hand with his tongue. Smiling, Sissy lost a piece of her heart to him. It wasn't Finn's fault that his master embodied everything that she most distrusted in a man. Ben Sterling was suave, charming, and successful. The first time she'd seen him, nearly a year and a half ago, all of her inner alarms had gone off. Hair the color of honey had protruded from beneath the brim of his Stetson to lie in a gleaming wave across his forehead. His hazel eyes, deep amber flecked with green, brown, and black, had twinkled with mischief and gleamed with masculine appreciation when he looked at her. Dressed in a Western-style work shirt and leg-hugging Wrangler jeans, he'd been a country version of Mr. *GQ*. Any woman under seventy would have salivated.

Any woman, she amended, except her. According to the gossips, he'd been born into a wonderful family. He and his siblings had gotten college educations handed to them. Ben had acquired more than one degree and used them to become a successful businessman who now owned a nice chunk of arable land, a remodeled farmhouse, and several expensive horses, not to mention a small herd of beeves. He was well respected in Mystic Creek, and so were all the members of his family. His brother Barney, a recently married deputy, would probably run for office someday and become the county sheriff. Not her kind of people, not by a long shot. Sissy's father had the not-so-distinguished honor of being the town drunk, and her parents had lived in lots of towns.

When Ben first made it clear that he was interested in her, Sissy had made it equally clear that she didn't share the sentiment. Men like Ben often felt entitled to get what they wanted from a woman. They acted like Mr. Nice Guy until they gained her trust or got her at a disadvantage. She'd learned the hard way how that story always ended. No, she wanted nothing to do with him. She had her life planned, and she was determined not to take any detours that might set her off track.

Now here he was again. Last time he'd come sniffing around, it had taken her two weeks to get rid of him. He was determined. She had to give him that. *Well, watch out, Mr. Sterling. I'm not playing that game again.*

Sissy stiffened her spine and descended the steps onto icy ground. She'd closed the café at ten, later than usual because she'd been running behind schedule. Now it had to be after eleven, far too late for a man she barely knew to be on her property.

Finn, walking beside her, was having as much trouble keeping his footing on the ice as she was. She saw the beam of a flashlight bobbing inside the closed coop. Judging by the squawking, her hens were not happy to have a man in their midst. Who in the heck did Ben think he was? He had no right to be out here.

The gate to the run hung open. Sissy marched toward the coop, prepared to blister the man's ears. She twisted the door handle and barely cracked open the portal, knowing her hens would bolt for freedom if she offered them an avenue of escape.

Rawk, rawk, rawk! A bird jumped and nearly smacked Sissy in the face. She fell back to protect her eyes, but didn't open the door any wider.

"What do you think you're doing?" Finn barked as if to warn Sissy that she'd better not hurt his human. Shoving a writhing mass of feathers aside, she yelled to be heard. "This is my coop, my property, and you don't have authorization to be here."

Ben, crouched with his back to her near the right end wall, was frontally illuminated by the glow of a flashlight lying on the floor. Sans Stetson, his bangs and sideburns gleamed like a horseshoe-shaped halo around his head. At the sound of her voice, he didn't flinch, but she did see his shoulder muscles tighten under the yoke of his shirt. He shifted to look at her, his chiseled features falling into shadow.

"Okay. I get you. Maybe I should have asked before I started this."

"Maybe?" she retorted. Finn growled. "You've got no right—"

"You already covered that." He glanced at his dog. "Finnegan, back off! She isn't going to hurt me. She's no bigger than a minute."

"I'm stronger than I look!" Sissy glanced at the dog. The flashlight played over Finn's face, and she could tell that he truly was worried. Altering her tone to reassure him, she said, "It's okay, Finnegan. I won't kill him."

Ben huffed, clearly not amused. "Look. I'm aware that I should have knocked to get an okay from you. But I knew you were exhausted, and I saw no reason to keep you up even later by asking before I did this. You would've felt obligated to help, and it's really not a two-person job."

"Well, I'm out here now, and you're right; I'm so tired I postponed breakfast prep for the morning, which means I'll have to hit the deck by four." She glanced at the paraphernalia around his feet. A silver dome with prong grips shimmered against the wood chips. "Just what are you doing? Is that a heat lamp?"

"Yes. I saw that you needed one. I had an extra at home. Around here, we call it doing a favor for a friend."

Her voice dripped ice. "Since when did we become friends?"

He pushed to his feet, his ascent ending in a stooped stance because the ceiling was so low. The chickens started to squawk again.

"You're right. My bad. I'll gather up my shit and get off your property." He picked up the heat lamp, his tools, and the flashlight. "Just so you know, though, you may find all your chickens dead in the morning. The weather app on my phone predicts temps as low as twelve degrees before dawn, and that doesn't account for the wind-chill factor."

"Twelve degrees?" She hadn't had a moment all day to check her phone for e-mail, let alone to look at the weather forecast. "It's only September sixteenth!"

"It's an unseasonal cold snap. Mystic Creek

weather is unpredictable." He arced the light beam over the coop interior, sending the chickens into a brief panic. "There are cracks in the walls of this enclosure large enough to accommodate my middle finger." He held up his fist with that one digit lifted and illuminated by the beam. "As you can see, it isn't exactly little."

Sissy felt a reluctant giggle welling at the base of her throat. "Are you, by any chance, giving me the finger?"

"It's up to your interpretation. What d'ya think?"

Sissy struggled not to smile, probably because he wasn't making nice now, and she felt in no danger of getting her socks charmed off. "I think I've made you angry."

"Hell, no. I went past angry when you reamed my ass for being on your property without permission. Now I'm royally pissed off."

One arm cradling his stuff, he shuffled to the door, forcing her to step back as he exited in a rush to keep any hens from escaping. Sissy felt her shoe lose traction on the ice and thought, *Oh, no.* The next instant, she went down, hitting the back of her head so hard on the frozen earth that fire-works went off before her eyes.

She heard Ben say, "Holy fricking shit!" Then metal clanked as it struck the earth. "You'd better not be hurt, damn it. That's not fighting fair."

Finn nuzzled Sissy's cheek. She blinked to clear her vision. From her prone position Ben suddenly looked like a giant. "I *fell*. Do you think I did it on purpose?"

He crouched beside her and pushed his dog back. "Let's just say it happened at an opportune moment. How can I make a grand exit, flipping you off as I leave, if your head's cracked open?"

Sissy checked the throbbing place for injury. She felt a knot forming on her scalp, which would probably hurt like heck the next day, but she wasn't seriously wounded. She levered up on one elbow. "I'm fine. You can carry on with your grand exit." Gazing up at his bulky silhouette, she squelched a smile. "And, FYI, when you're royally pissed off, gesturing with one finger doesn't quite cut it." She held up her hand with all her fingers and her thumb extended. "Back at you times five."

A rumble of laughter came up his throat. "You've got a sassy mouth. Has anyone ever told you that?"

An unpleasant memory of her father flashed through Sissy's mind. "More than once. What I lack in size I make up for with brass."

In the silvery glow of a full moon and the canting beam of the flashlight, his firm lips shimmered as they slanted into a crooked grin. "This isn't funny, you know. I can't leave until you're on your feet and I'm sure you're all right."

Sissy pushed to a sitting position, and even as a wave of dizziness assailed her, she said, "I'm good. Flip me off and get out of here."

"I can't leave until I'm sure you're okay."

"Oh, bother." Sissy rolled over onto all fours. Her palms stung as she pressed them against the ice. She got one foot under her. "Don't try to help me. We already did that gig today."

"I changed into Western boots with studded soles. Modified them myself for conditions like this." He stood and extended a big hand to her. "I'm steady as a rock. Let me give you a lift up."

Sissy gave him a measuring look before she accepted the offer. "Steady as a rock and possibly as dumb as one, too? Any idiot knows to wear a coat in weather like this."

"I left it in the truck. It's too bulky to work in."

The grip of his hand over hers sent a shock of heat up her arm. Once on her feet, she weaved slightly. "Blood rush," she told him. "Just give me a sec." Finn whined and sniffed Sissy's leg. "I'm okay, Finnegan. Don't be worried."

Ben grasped her shoulder. "Urgent care on Red Barn Road is open twenty-four seven. It couldn't hurt to get checked out."

Sissy straightened. "See? I'm right as rain. You hit your head today, and you didn't see a doctor. Mine's just as hard as yours is."

"I've noticed."

Sissy truly did feel okay. The dizziness was all but gone. Finn nudged her leg again. She patted his head. Careful to keep her footing, she turned and studied her coop. Ben's prediction that her birds might die during the night made her heart squeeze. "I read online that chickens don't need heat lamps. Besides, I don't have electricity out here."

"I brought an outdoor extension cord that'll reach the outlet on your back porch."

"Oh." She glanced up at him. Concern won over pride. She loved her feathered babies. "Do you really think my chickens might freeze to death?"

"Nah." He rested his hands on his narrow hips and hunched his shoulders against the cold. "I just used that as an excuse to come over and possibly get lucky with a woman who hates my guts."

She tried not to laugh and lost the battle. "I don't *hate* you. You're just not my type."

"Fair enough. And just for the record, I didn't come here hoping to score. That's the most pathetic excuse for a coop I've ever seen, and I honestly believe your chickens will die if it drops to twelve degrees. They're young and they don't have extra layers of protection yet. Even if they did, that's pretty damned cold." He angled his head to peer down at her through the moon-washed shadows. "I don't doubt you read an article disparaging heat lamps, but did it occur to you that the person giving that advice may live where people seldom see snow? Chickens do freeze to death, and this is Mystic Creek, where it sometimes gets too cold to snow."

"Those hens are packed in there like sardines. Can't they share body heat?"

"Chickens are cold-blooded. They have a lot less body heat to share than mammals."

Just the thought of finding Sonya, Pearl, and the others stiff and cold in the morning roiled her stomach. "Can I borrow the extension cord? I have a lamp and the tools I need. I can hang the light myself, no big deal, and I'll replace the cord."

"I'm sure you can hang a lamp. But you shouldn't be out here working alone at night in these conditions. What if you fall and get hurt? Marilyn is undoubtedly asleep, and José Jayden doesn't live over his restaurant. Who'd hear if you yelled for help?"

"You were out here working alone. Wherein lies the difference?"

"You didn't know I was here, so if I'd gotten hurt, you wouldn't have been responsible. I've also got studded boots. If I drive off, aware that you're out here, I *will* be responsible if you fall and can't get up. Therein lies the difference."

His tone was crisp and, limned by a wash of

moonlight, his expression indicated that she was frustrating the hell out of him.

Sissy sighed. Independence was one thing, but clinging to her pride when it endangered her animals was something else entirely. "I really don't want any of my chickens to die."

Ben held up his hand. In the dim light, she saw that he had all five digits extended. "Back at you times five. Now can I hang the damned light?"

It took Ben less than fifteen minutes to install the heat lamp, and then he started running the extension cord to the coop. As he worked, he talked. "I understand that relationship-wise I'm not your type, but surely you're not that fussy about a handyman."

There had been no room for her to help inside the coop, and now she would feel silly if she tried to assist in unwinding a cord. Instead she shivered and petted Finnegan. "What's your point?"

"The coop you've got is a pile of crap. You need a new one at least four times bigger. Insulated, too. And unless you want to regularly clip the wings of eighty chickens, you need a huge run with framed wire walls at least eight feet tall."

"Eight feet?"

"Even at that height, your chickens will still perch on top of the frame sometimes. Mine do.

43

But they seldom fly away. They know where the food and water are."

Sissy bit her lip. "You're describing a very costly coop and run."

He punched a hole in the coop wall, then bent to shove the end of the extension cord through it. "It won't be so bad if a *friend* does the work."

"I don't take charity."

He stepped inside the enclosure, stirring up a chorus of cackles. Seconds after the door shut, Sissy saw a glow of light that gleamed through every crack in the walls. Ben hadn't lied; the coop was a wind tunnel, offering little protection for her hens.

When he emerged, he resumed the conversation as if there had been no lull. "If you want these chickens to survive, you don't have a choice." He walked toward her with a loose-jointed shift of his hips. "Eighty birds will get sick without more room, both inside and outside. You have two little roosts. The rest of the birds have to sleep on the floor. Maybe when they were chicks, you thought the coop would provide enough space, but now you've got to realize it doesn't. When you take on critters, you assume a responsibility to provide them with good care."

Sissy felt as if he'd slapped her. "I'm fully aware of my responsibility to my chickens, and I've gotten bids on a bigger coop and run. The prices quoted to me were astronomical. It will take every dime of my savings and then some. And I don't have the 'then some.' " She paused to catch her breath. "I ordered too many chicks. I admit it. I was an ignorant twit. And now I can't scrape up the money to give them a proper home. Maybe I should just put up an ad on Craigslist and give them away."

He shook his head. "Not a good plan. When you give away chickens, they can end up in a stewpot."

"*What?*" Sissy stared at him. "People may *eat* them? That's horrible."

"To your way of thinking. To other people, it's no different than eating a chicken from the store, except it's free." He tossed his stuff onto the bed of the truck and turned to rest his hips against the dropped tailgate. Tendrils of light from the coop bathed the area with faint illumination. "There has to be a way that you and I can strike a bargain."

Sissy bent her head. "It sticks in my craw to take charity. I know it sounds prideful, but I've got my reasons, and I just can't do it."

"There's nothing wrong with being prideful." He fell silent. Then he said, "*Damn* it. I owe you an apology."

"More than one," she informed him. "Would you like me to make you a list?"

He slanted her a look that was far from apologetic. "I count one actual offense. I'm pretty

45

damned prideful myself. If the situation were in reverse, I couldn't accept your help for free, either." He sighed. "Shit. I'm a male chauvinist and didn't even know it."

Feeling defeated, Sissy joined him to lean against the tailgate. Finn came to lie at their feet. Light from the coop bathed the run and cast a golden glow over them as well. "I've created a mess—that's for sure. Lesson learned. When you don't know jack about raising hens, don't go online and order eighty chicks."

Ben chuckled. "You did go a little overboard. But that doesn't mean there's no solution."

Sissy could see no humor in the situation, and she found herself wishing that he'd go back to being sarcastic. She felt safer when they were bristling at each other. "I can't think of one." She gestured at her crooked, tumbledown run. "It's clear I'm not gifted when it comes to construction, so I can't save money by doing it myself."

He laughed again. "You're a great cook, though, and maybe, because you are, we can negotiate a deal so you *are* paying me."

She noticed that the tailgate hit him at his hips. The metal edge touched her well above the waist, an unnerving reminder of how tall he was. And he was put together nicely as well. She fixed her gaze on the sagging wire so she wouldn't notice anything else unsettling about him. He had it right. For the sake of her chickens, she had to negotiate a deal with him. If she kept it businesslike, she'd be all right. She'd seen better-looking men. She just couldn't remember when.

"So, what kind of deal are you offering me?"

He rubbed his jaw. "I eat out a lot, so here's my idea. I get four square meals for every full day of work I put in. The way I see it, I'd pay full price if I just dropped in, and with my appetite, I'd probably drop fifteen bucks a pop. So you'd essentially be paying me sixty dollars a day for my labor."

"*Four* squares? For most people, it's three."

"I start working as soon as it turns daylight. When I'm about two hours in, I eat a big breakfast. I burn that off by midmorning and need more fuel. I normally eat lunch a little late so it'll last me until dinner." He held up four fingers. "Add 'em up, and no, that isn't back at you times four."

He'd left something out, and she couldn't let it pass. "What about materials? They must cost a fortune, or the bids I got wouldn't be so high."

"I can get a lot of stuff at the ReStore in town, the one that recycles used building materials, and I've got several rolls of wire that have been sitting at my place for years. I might as well give myself some extra storage space by using them."

Sissy shifted her gaze skyward and chuckled

in spite of herself. "I never saw this coming. Me, hiring Ben Sterling to build my chickens a coop and run. God must have a sense of humor."

"Am I *that* bad?"

Sissy shook her head. "No. It's just that you really *aren't* my type, and having you around all the time, even short term, may not be a good plan."

He joined her in gazing up at the full moon. "I get the feeling that I *am* your type, and that's why you act like a porcupine around me, because I scare you."

"Not a chance." She would never admit to him that she found him attractive.

He expelled a breath and slanted his head upward. "Well, that's good, because that's a mulberry moon."

It looked like an ordinary moon to Sissy. "What's a mulberry moon?"

"A September full moon. It's an old Native American name for it."

"That's strange. Mulberries ripen in June, so far as I know."

"True, but the American Indians fermented them and made wine, which they couldn't drink until sometime in September. They marked the fermentation time needed by watching for the September full moon."

"Ah." Sissy kept her gaze fixed on the sky. The moon under discussion was enormous and the color of churned butter with wisps of crimson and mauve ringing the bottom of its sphere.

"There's a legend about the mulberry moon." His voice pitched low and husky. "They say that any man and woman who stand together under a mulberry moon are destined to fall in love and live happily ever after."

"Really? How fascinating." She made sure skepticism edged her tone.

"Worried yet?" When she shook her head, he added, "Even riskier for you and me, we're not only standing together under a mulberry moon, but we're near a distributary of Mystic Creek, which also comes with a legend about falling in love."

"I've heard all the different versions of the one about Mystic Creek." Sissy gave him a sideways glance. "And both legends are undoubtedly a bunch of crap."

He nodded. "Yep, just BS. The way I see it, the Native Americans who fell in love under a mulberry moon were probably drunk from their wine."

She laughed. "I like that. BS with a cynical twist!"

"But possibly correct. If you drink enough wine, practically anyone looks good."

"I'll remember that and never serve you any fruit of the vine." Sissy pushed away from the truck. "Moving on to the construction of my coop and run, it's too cold out here to discuss the details. You're shivering without a coat. And, after hearing about your appetite, I'm fairly sure you're hungry by now. Does a Coney Island hot dog and fries sound good?"

"You're tired. I'll just go home and grab a sandwich. We can discuss the details tomorrow."

Sissy beckoned for him to follow her. "I've decided to do my breakfast prep tonight so I don't have to get up so early, and I didn't have time for dinner. If I cook for one, I may as well cook for two."

He fell into step beside her, one arm positioned to grab her if she slipped. "You heard my stomach growling."

"Yep. I'm not deaf."

Once inside the café, with Ben perched on a stool at the counter, Sissy wondered if she'd lost her mind when she invited him in. He had nailed it on the head; he was her type, and she was scared to death of him. Now her task was to make sure he never realized it. Bristling at him constantly didn't seem to do the trick.

As she hurried to throw together their meal, she assured herself that her salivary glands were working overtime only because she was hungry and smelled food.

"This won't take long. The fryer is still hot from dinner and will reheat fast."

"No hurry. This coffee hits the spot."

When the hot dogs were prepared and in the warmer, Sissy went to stand facing him at the business side of the counter. She propped her elbows on the stainless steel work surface, a foot lower than the service bar. It offered a comfortable leaning spot for a short person. And she liked the security of a solid counter between them.

"Like I said earlier, I don't accept charity. I've had work done here, and paying a man only sixty dollars a day to do any kind of carpentry would be highway robbery on my part."

"Ah, but that's my offer, and you really shouldn't turn it down. You could hire someone else—somebody who doesn't have my appetite and a habit of eating out—but he'd very likely know as little as you do about chickens and charge three times more."

"And you know a lot about them? Chickens, I mean."

He winked at her. "I've been around chickens since I learned to walk. I know how to design a coop and run that will work and keep them safe from predators. I've already built one for myself. If you put your chickens in the coop at night, they'll be fairly safe. You'll need a good latch, of course. Raccoons are•nocturnal and pretty clever."

Sissy nodded, trying to envision the structure.

He obliterated the picture forming in her mind

with "That wire you built your run with is deadly." He created a large O by touching his index finger to the tip of his thumb. "A hen can poke her head through openings that large. Skunks love chicken heads."

"Oh, God!"

"Exactly. I've seen chickens lying headless in their runs without another mark on them. True fact." He settled that twinkling, mischievous gaze on her face. "If you want a coop and run that's safe, you'll hire me."

Sissy toyed with her lineup of salt and pepper shakers. "I still don't think sixty a day is enough to pay you."

He winked at her. "We'll negotiate it out, fair and square. I'll want extra desserts."

Sissy shook her head. "We need to have a clear understanding now. No negotiating later. When the job is done, I don't want to feel indebted to you."

He shrugged. "So what's your offer?"

She could scarcely believe that she was about to hire him. He'd be on her property for God only knew how long, and even worse, he'd be eating at her café four times a day. The thought unsettled her so badly that she nearly changed her mind. But what about her chickens?

"Here's my idea," she said, her chest tightening with reluctance. "After you finish the job, I'll provide you with four square meals a day for an extra two weeks. Paying you with food works for me. The actual cash outlay is less than the menu price. So if I feed you for two extra weeks, your daily pay will go up to a fair level, but it won't be as expensive for me as paying cash."

"Deal," he said.

He agreed a little too quickly for her peace of mind. But just then she heard an odd sound in the kitchen. She left the bar and entered the cooking area. After she glanced around for anything out of place, her gaze settled on the shelf where she normally kept her watch and ring. Earlier there had been a piece of foil on the shelf. Now it was gone. She knew she hadn't removed it. So who had taken it? A chill ran over her skin. And, again, she felt as if someone were staring at her.

Just then, the fryer reached cooking temperature and beeped. The sound made Sissy jump. Stomach fluttering, she lifted the vat lid, lowered the fry basket into sizzling oil, and then turned the wheel to batten down the hatches. She set the timer so the fries would be cooked to a perfect golden brown.

Once back at the bar, she asked a question that she thought, until that moment, would never pop out of her mouth to anyone. "Do you believe in ghosts?"

Chapter
THREE

"Do I believe in ghosts?" Ben gave Sissy a solemn study. "I believe in spirits. The term *ghost* sounds too Halloweenish."

Sissy had expected him to laugh. Instead he'd answered her question with sincerity and conviction. That made her feel better, and less crazy, for sure.

"Why do you ask?"

Sissy shivered. "Weird stuff has been happening in this building. It's starting to creep me out."

He leaned closer, as if by proximity he could pry more information out of her. "What kind of weird stuff?"

Sissy waved her hand. "It'll sound stupid." His expression went from curious to intense. "Things are disappearing."

"What kind of things?"

"Nothing really expensive or important. Just little things. For instance, I have this candy bowl upstairs on my coffee table. I limit myself to two pieces a night because I have a sweet tooth, and I don't want to gain weight."

He lowered his gaze to take in what he could of her figure, stopping only when the counter's edge blocked his view. Her skin burned. He might just as well have said it aloud. *You don't need to worry.*

A dimple flashed in his cheek as he looked back up. "Of course. Everything in moderation." Distracted by the unexpected and tantalizing appearance of the dimple, she couldn't jerk her gaze from that spot on his lean cheek. Not a dimple, really, she decided. It was more a crease, probably a dimple when he was a boy that had been chiseled deeper over the years by sun exposure. Who was she kidding by analyzing it to death? Dimple or crease, it was sexy as hell. *I'm in trouble,* she thought. *I knew being around him was a bad idea. How do I get myself out of this?*

"Sissy?" He jerked her back to the conversation. "I hate cliff-hangers. Tell me about the candy bowl."

She hauled in a bracing breath and refocused. "My favorite candy bar is a Snickers. Only I don't dare buy regular-size ones, because once I bite into one it's history. So I get the fun-size variety bags."

He crossed his eyes at her. Then he grinned. "I asked for details about the weird shit, Sissy, not your junk food habits."

"Right. Only it's all sort of related. Mini Snickers bars come in gold foil wrappers."

The fryer timer went off. Sissy excused herself

to fill their plates. She remembered from his previous visits that he was a slow eater—unless, of course, he'd been procrastinating to hang around longer. According to the digital clock on the commercial appliance, Cinderella's coach had turned into a pumpkin three minutes ago. If he lingered over his meal, he might be in her building half the night.

Balancing plates, Sissy returned to the bar, slid Ben's meal toward him, and set her own on the lower counter at what she considered a safe distance from him. With a muttered excuse she returned to the kitchen and went into the cooler where she got three more hot dogs, which she put on a paper plate and carried out front.

"Whoa!" Ben exclaimed. "I think you're overestimating my appetite."

She shook her head. "These are for Finnegan. Is he on the porch?"

"Yes. He's already learned the stay command, and that's where I signaled him to wait."

"Well, I'd like to bring him in where it's warm to enjoy his dinner. That is, if it's okay for him to have these."

"He'll love them." Ben slid off the stool. He wore a hand-tooled Western belt, the buckle ornate and gleaming like a beacon to draw her gaze to what lay just below it. "I can go get him, but are you sure? Isn't it against the law?"

Sissy shrugged. "Service animals are allowed

in public places, and today Finn did me a great service. Besides, the inspector would never show up at this hour."

Laughing, Ben went to get his dog. Sissy gave Finnegan an appreciative pat and set the plate in front of him. By the time she straightened, the three hot dogs had vanished. Glancing over at an amused Ben, she asked if the pup could have more.

"Only three. I don't want him getting sick." He smiled at the eager canine, whose begging eyes were fixed on Sissy. "It's really sweet of you to think of him. He's still in puppy gear and eats every chance he gets. I fed him dinner earlier when I had my own, but as you can see, he's running on empty already."

She repressed a grin. "Like master, like dog?"

Ben shrugged. "If either of us starts putting on weight, I'll worry about it."

Sissy doubted he would have to worry about it for a good long while. He had a gorgeous build, slender in the right places, yet padded with just enough muscle to look robust.

She went behind the bar again and grabbed two prepared napkin rolls of flatware, then put squeeze bottles of fry sauce—a blend of ketchup and mayo—and mustard next to Ben's plate beside the salt and pepper shakers. "Bon appétit."

Ben lost no time in unwrapping his cutlery. "I never ruin a good Coney with condiments. And this one looks amazing." He flashed her a smile, and she glanced down, pretending to be intent on her dinner. "You can't distract me with food, by the way. I still want to hear about the Snickers bars."

Sissy squirted a blob of fry sauce onto her plate. "Sorry about the interruption. I have conversations in blips. Fries burn fast if you don't remove them from the oil." She salted her serving. "As for the Snickers bars, they disappear."

"Um, most things do when you eat them."

"Has anyone ever mentioned that you can be a smart-ass?"

"Sorry." He shrugged his broad shoulders. "You walked right into it, and I couldn't resist. You were saying?"

"They disappear from the bowl. The other candy bars aren't touched, only the Snickers. And, no, they aren't vanishing because I eat them and then forget. Before I go to bed at night, I now count them and write the number down. The next morning, at least one is always gone, sometimes two."

"Wow. That is weird." He hadn't waited to swallow before he spoke. His cheek bulged with a bite of food. "Do you sleepwalk? My mom's friend did, and she'd wake up in the morning with mustard all over her face."

Sissy sighed. "If I sleepwalked, I'd wake up

with chocolate all over mine. And if I were gobbling all that candy, I'd have gained ten pounds. No, someone or something is stealing them." She put another fry into her mouth. "Even weirder, the candy bars have disappeared while I'm eating them." She stabbed an index finger at him. "If you say once more that things tend to vanish while we're eating them, this story will end before you hear the good parts."

His eyes took on that mischievous twinkle again. "Well, I really want to hear the good parts, so I'll be on my best behavior."

Sissy wiped the corners of her mouth with her napkin. "So, I'll be watching TV, right? And I'll set my half-eaten Snickers bar on the end table, still partly wrapped in foil. After I've switched channels, I'll reach for my candy bar, and it'll be gone."

"Gone? Foil and all?" He sounded skeptical, and she couldn't blame him. He forked some savory ground beef and hot dog into his mouth, worked his jaw, and swallowed. "Did you look to make sure the wrapper wasn't between the couch cushions or on the floor?"

"Of course. The candy bars just disappear, either out of the bowl or while I'm munching on them." She suppressed a shiver. Somehow the whole thing bothered her more when it was dark.

He reached for another fry. It was a man's hand, blunt and capable. Burnished by the sun, his skin, dusted with golden hair, reminded her of melted butterscotch. She took a sip of water.

"That is totally freaky," he said. "Um, don't take this wrong, because I'm not poking fun, but why do you think it's a ghost?"

"I don't. Not really. It's just—well, it's been happening so much, and I can't think of any rational explanation. Can you?"

A vertical line between his eyebrows deepened. "No, I can't. But that doesn't mean there isn't one."

"Spoken like a true nonbeliever," she retorted.

"Honestly, I do believe in spirits. I just can't wrap my mind around the idea of a nonphysical being that steals Snickers bars."

The open collar of his blue shirt revealed a V of tanned skin and a thatch of golden chest hair. Warmth pooled in her lower abdomen. *Not good,* she thought. She'd spent very little time with him, yet already she felt attracted to him. What was wrong with her? She might as well develop an addiction to strychnine.

She almost jumped when he spoke again. "How in the hell can candy bars vanish like that?"

"I have no clue." Sissy's skin prickled as she thought about the many times it had happened. "Maybe I'm nuts, but I'm starting to believe this place is haunted."

He considered that for a moment. "If it's any

consolation, I'd be a little spooked, too. What else is going on? Anything?"

After months of wondering whether she was slowly losing her mind, a hint of empathy was all Sissy needed. "Yes, there's a lot more."

She broke off as Finn came to lie at her feet. She felt the warm weight of his head on her shoe. He was so young and trusting. How did he know she wouldn't step on him? She wondered, briefly, if she had ever felt that safe and relaxed.

"Well, don't stop there. What else is happening?"

She took a bite of food and spoke around it. "I have a small electric keyboard. I can't play well—I never got lessons and can't read music— but I like to bang on it sometimes, pretending the noise is wonderful."

Ben grinned. "I do the same with my guitar. I guess a lot of people have a musician inside them that the rest of the world hopes never gets out."

Sissy startled herself by giggling. "Sometimes at night, I jerk awake and hear music coming from the keyboard. Just random notes, even worse than my playing. I began unplugging it at bedtime, but sometimes I still hear the keys clacking."

He gave a low whistle. Finn lifted his head, realized they weren't going anywhere, and settled back against Sissy's ankle. "No wonder you're starting to believe in ghosts. If I woke up and heard someone plucking my guitar strings, my hair would stand on end."

Somehow it made her feel less ridiculous to hear him say that. She felt as if she were confiding in a good friend. That realization made her nerves jangle, so she decided to shorten her story. "But what *really* bugs me is that things keep disappearing!"

"Things other than candy bars?"

"Mostly small stuff," she replied. "Tonight, my wristwatch wasn't where I left it this morning before I started cooking, but my ring was still there. How does that make sense?"

She toyed with the band, making the stone, mounted in patterned gold, slide back and forth on her finger. Ben whistled. "Is that a mood ring?"

Sissy tucked her hand out of sight. "I realize hardly anyone wears them now."

"I think you can still buy them, though. I remember my mom wearing one when I was a kid."

"My mother gave this one to me when I was about twelve. I only wear it because it used to be hers."

"Did you lose her?"

Sissy's mouth went dry. She had lost her mom, but not in the way he meant. "Yes."

His expression turned solemn. "I'm sorry. You must have been really young when it happened."

"Around eighteen." Sissy sighed. "So I'm glad the ring didn't vanish. But I'm still bummed about my watch. It wasn't expensive, but I can't easily afford to buy a new one right now. Not that I'm broke or anything. I'm just trying to stay on a strict budget. Once I improve the coop and run, I'll save to remodel the café."

He fingered a fry but didn't eat it.

"You know what's really strange?" Even as Sissy asked the question, she wondered what she was thinking. Prolonging the conversation postponed the moment when he would leave. She hadn't asked him to come in so they could become best buddies. "When I realized my watch had vanished, there was a piece of foil on the shelf where the watch had been. That was when I heard you banging around out in the yard. And now even the foil is gone."

"You left a lot of people here in the café while you were outside trying to catch chickens," he mused aloud.

"Are you suggesting one of my customers stole my watch?" Sissy shook her head. "That's hard to believe. Besides, it isn't worth much. Twenty bucks, maybe."

"It's hard for me to imagine, too. I grew up here. I like all those people."

Sissy searched his gaze. "Who do you think might have done it?"

He straightened on the stool. "Damned if I

know. None of the people who came out to help us, that's for sure. Who stayed inside?"

"Nobody that I know of. Ma Thomas and Marilyn, maybe, because they're older, but they're my friends. As often as possible I treat them to a late lunch so we can visit. They tell me wonderful stories about my aunt Mabel. I never got to meet her, and they've helped me feel as if I know her. Neither of them would *ever* steal from me."

"I'm certain I saw Ma and Marilyn outside, which means the café was empty. Maybe someone came in from the street. In all the uproar, we may not have heard the door buzzer. It's a more likely explanation than a ghost playing pranks."

"Yes, and it's Friday. Or was. A lot of tourists come through town to see the legendary creek and natural bridge. Maybe it was somebody we don't even know."

He smiled. "Right. That's easier for me to swallow. As for the foil lying where the watch was, isn't it possible that a small piece jerked loose from the roll and landed on the shelf while you were wrapping food?"

She supposed it was, but how had it gone up to the shelf instead of down? "Maybe. But where did it go later?"

"The back door was opened a few times. Maybe a draft of air blew it off the shelf."

The kitchen was situated on one side of the building with a dividing wall between it and the dining area. Sissy doubted that a draft coming in the back door could be strong enough to travel through the storage area and into the café.

"It's possible," she conceded. "But what about my missing candy bars and all the strange noises I hear? And don't forget my keyboard playing all by itself."

"Well, given your passion for Snickers bars, maybe you *are* sleepwalking and eating them without realizing it. You work so hard, it's not a stretch to think you're burning off the calories."

It was an unwelcome thought, but she couldn't totally discount it. On the nights when she ate other brands of candy, she went to bed craving a Snickers bar. "Maybe." She couldn't help but smile. "It's hard to believe, though. Eating in my sleep? But I'd rather think that than blame it on a ghost. Ever since childhood I've been relentlessly rational, and it makes me uneasy when I start going off into zany land. I never even believed in Santa Claus."

Ben grinned, and then as he studied her face, the smile faded. "I thought everyone believed in Santa Claus until at least first grade."

"Not if Santa never comes."

The instant that came out, she wished she hadn't said it. Her past was private, and she'd just revealed something to him that she'd never told anyone. Maybe she was loose-tongued because of exhaustion. She'd been working without a break since the wee hours of the morning. Whatever, the sooner she got him out of here, the better. Her miserable childhood was none of his business, but there was something about him that made her forget to hold her secrets close.

This whole situation frightened her. She was telling him things she would never reveal to anyone else. With a grin, he could make her knees feel weak. He seemed so nice. But was he? She'd learned the hard way never to trust her judgment when it came to men.

Straightening from the counter where she'd been resting her elbows, she glanced at his empty plate. "Would you like any dessert?"

He shook his head and placed a hand over his belly. "No, thank you. It was fabulous, though."

"Well, I've still got breakfast prep to do, so I'd better bust it out."

He nodded. "Yep. We'll both be tapped out when our alarms go off in the morning."

"I don't mean to be rude," she heard herself say. Gently pulling her shoe from under Finn's head, she began gathering their dishes. "I'm just tired and still have a lot of work to do before I can call it a day."

"I hope you have an uneventful night," he said as he swung off the stool. "This building is ancient,

66

you know. It's bound to creak and settle. That alone might spook me and put my imagination in overdrive."

Most guys Sissy had known would never admit that a creaky old building might spook them. "It does get a little spooky here at night."

"I can only imagine. As for the keyboard pinging or clacking, maybe you have mice. The keys on some electric boards depress easily. Perhaps your guest musician has four tiny feet."

"Mice?"

"You're not afraid of them, I hope."

"No, of course not," she replied, her stomach clenching. "If the keyboard clacks, I'll cling to that thought for comfort. Thanks again, and good night."

Ben paced off the distance between Sissy's back porch and his truck with such speed that Finnegan, running beside him, lost his footing on the ice and did a belly slide. Ben bent over his dog.

"Are you okay, pal?"

The pup struggled to get back up, but his legs sprawled sideways, putting him belly down again. Ben lifted him, set him on his feet, and ruffled his ears. "Sorry. I forgot you aren't wearing studded boots." Ben straightened and cast a glance at the age-darkened building behind him. Something about the way Sissy had ended their conversation felt off to him. "I hope I didn't say or do some-thing to offend her."

Finn sat down, cocked his head at Ben, and whined. Ben decided it was a sympathetic reply in dog-speak. Snapping his fingers, he led the way, slower this time, toward his truck and opened the door so the pup could jump inside. Following behind the dog, he swung up onto the driver's seat and cranked the engine until it roared to life.

For a moment, Ben sat with his hands on the steering wheel and stared out the windshield at the trees, illuminated by headlights. Then he took a deep breath and slowly released it. Something had shifted between him and Sissy, and whatever it was had frightened her. He'd seen that in her eyes. It was going to take a lot of patience and understanding from him if he was interested in getting to know her better.

To Finn, he said, "And how could I *not* be interested? I couldn't believe she invited you into her café tonight to eat. Even sweeter, she gave you seconds. And today I never once saw her act as if getting your hair on her clothes disgusted her."

Finn went *"Grr-umph!"*

Ben grinned. "So you like her, too? I can't say I blame you. I'd bet my best Stetson that she wouldn't be scared of my horses, either, or get all bent out of shape if she stepped in cow manure."

Ben fell quiet. Then he added, "I'd never tell anyone but you this, pal, but I've got a gut feeling about her. That maybe, just maybe, I've finally found a lady who won't try to change me, someone I could build a future with." He glanced at his dog. "Remember the blonde who tried to make me ditch my Western wear and go metrosexual? That went over with me like a rainstorm during a Fourth of July picnic."

Finn barked, which made Ben laugh.

"Okay. You're telling me not to get ahead of myself, and you're right. But I can't help it. She's a hard worker. She's prideful, as she put it. When I offered her a screaming deal, she refused to pay me only sixty a day. But you know what I like most about her? She seems to like animals. I've tried meshing with women who don't, and it never works. They'd make you sleep in a doghouse."

Finn's answer to that was a low growl.

Chapter
FOUR

Ben considered himself a morning person, but when the alarm went off at four thirty he wanted to reconsider the whole thing. He hadn't gotten to bed until the early hours, and even then thoughts of Sissy had held sleep at bay. Part of him wanted to shut off the alarm and forget about it, but the other part reminded him that the person partially responsible for his lack of rest was expecting him to show up. That got him moving. A quick shower helped chase away the cobwebs, and two mugs of coffee had him ready to face the day.

He took the third mug outside with him. The frozen air burned his lungs like dry ice. According to his weather app, the temperature would rise when the sun came up, treating the residents of Mystic Creek to another day of Indian summer. He would welcome that. He enjoyed doing physical work outdoors, but given his druthers, he preferred to break a sweat right away. It somehow energized him.

As he stood on the porch, looking out at his spread, he realized again how good it was to be back. Instead of flat, barren fields as far as he could see, his view looked out over his stable, an enclosed riding arena, a hay barn, and a crisscross of white fences. Along with the rich aroma of French roast coffee, he inhaled a mixture of scents: manure, hay, grain, cows, chickens, and horses. He enjoyed the potpourri of ranch life. It was a great start to what would be a long day.

Home. He sure didn't miss being on the road to earn his living. This acreage, a half section, would provide him with enough income to live comfortably, and he could train or shoe horses for extra spending money. It was going to be a good life. All he needed was a wife he adored and kids to fill up the gigantic house that yawned empty behind him.

Careful not to spill the coffee, Ben crossed his property to feed all the animals, avoiding mud wallows and manure piles as he went. Unlike Sissy, he kept only twenty hens and one rooster, which supplied him with enough eggs to share with his two sisters and his brother Jonas when he rolled in from college. He sold any eggs he didn't use.

After going through his morning routine, he'd go to the horse barn, toss hay, fill water troughs, dispense vitamins and bran, and then exercise the three horses he hadn't had time for yesterday. He also needed to fix a section of fence. He probably wouldn't get to Sissy's place until around nine. He hoped she wouldn't turn her flock loose before he could do a temporary repair on her old run. It was still icy this morning, and he didn't relish the thought of another chicken chase.

Ben arrived at the Cauldron an hour later than he'd hoped. The bed of his pickup was piled high with posts and rolls of sturdy wire. He had no intention of telling Sissy that he had purchased the material. He suspected she was tight on money. Well, not tight, really, if she'd told him the truth, but short on discretionary dollars. He wasn't what anyone would call wealthy, but he could afford to blow a few bucks, and when the run was completed and it was time to erect a new coop, he did have a heap of extra lumber and siding left over from when he'd built his own.

His first order of business was to stretch a length of wire atop the sagging chicken mesh that she'd used to create her run. That would keep her chickens confined while he erected a new and much larger enclosure around the old one. Until the situation was under control, Ben would have Finn herd the flock back into the tiny coop before he left each night.

While loading the two commercial dishwashers after the breakfast rush, Sissy heard hammering and clunking sounds coming from behind her café. For an instant, she wished she could go out and oversee what Ben was doing, but she didn't have time. She scrubbed egg yolk off a plate. Her movements lacked their usual fluidity. She loaded these dishwashers three times a day, and she'd developed a rhythm, which had deserted her because she couldn't think how to deal with the man in her backyard.

Her first inclination, upon rising, had been to tell him she'd changed her mind about hiring him. But then she'd hurried out to feed and water her imprisoned chickens and realized that, however more comfortable she might feel if she sent Ben packing, her chickens would suffer for it. She just couldn't do that to them. Mr. Cowboy *GQ* would build them the home they deserved, and in the interim, she needed to deal with his presence.

For her, the question was, how? She had been so distracted during the morning rush that she'd missed half the funny story the VeArds had told her. Then she'd forgotten to give Christopher Doyle his usual tiny pitcher of cold water to dilute his coffee. José Jayden, who operated a Mexican restaurant next door, had asked three times for a refill, and she'd forgotten that, too. Then she'd overcooked Crystal Malloy's poached eggs.

She'd just ignore Ben, Sissy decided as she polished the stainless steel counters. By the time she reached the grill to give it a good cleaning, she was frustrated with herself. If she intended to ignore the man, why did she keep thinking about him? He was starting a job that she would pay him to do, end of story. Right? He was outside. She was in here. If she played this right, she'd see him only when he came in for meals, and even then, she could stay busy in the kitchen while he ate. On an average day, she was in the cooking area more than she liked. After prep work, she could take breaks, but normally she didn't. There were always other things to do.

"Morning!" a deep male voice called from the dining room.

Sissy jumped with such a start that she dropped the cleaning rag on the floor. She glanced at the pass-through window and saw Ben mounting one of the barstools as he might a horse. With a grin, he swept off his Stetson, a black one today, and set it on the stool beside him. On a handsome scale of one to ten, he rated at least a fifteen. She moved toward the archway that opened into the dining room.

Thrusting strong fingers through his golden brown hair to straighten it, he said, "I know I'm late. It took me longer than I expected to gather up all the stuff I needed at my place, and I had to repair a section of fence."

"I expect eight full hours of work from you. You didn't get here until ten. What kind of schedule is that?" She felt like a bitch the instant the words came out, but she didn't have an erase button.

His smile disappeared. He placed his bent arms on the service counter. "I should have warned you. Mornings at my place are busy." Those hazel eyes studied her intently for a moment. "I'll work until six. You'll get your eight hours out of me." His gaze swept slowly downward, as if he were committing every curve and indentation of her body to memory. She regretted taking off her chef coat. "I have animals on my farm that expect breakfast. Forty cows, six horses, twenty chickens, and a weanling pig."

"Won't all those animals want dinner as well?"

"Oh, yeah. But my hired man takes care of that. I do the mornings because my horses need special handling to keep them on top of their game. Today I've got an extra horse being delivered, a dun mare that's been acting up when she's ridden."

Sissy realized she was talking to him. Conversation would not come with his meals. She'd offered him food, not companionship. "What do you want for breakfast?"

Was he going to come in this late for breakfast every day? She'd be doing her lunch prep, and fixing him something special in the middle of all that would be a pain in the neck.

Ben ordered smoked ham, three eggs, a double serving of hash browns, two pieces of buttered sourdough toast, a stack of pancakes, and a carafe of strong coffee. Then he glanced up at her. "I won't be this late again. I know I'm messing up your schedule."

Sissy had to admit, as her clean kitchen grew untidy again in preparing his food, that she appreciated his awareness of her work schedule. Soon she slid two plates in front of him, along with a filled coffee carafe, silverware, and a small pitcher of warm syrup. "I think you're all set. If you need anything else, just holler. I'll be getting ready for lunch hour."

Once back in the kitchen, Sissy congratulated herself on how well she had handled him. While he ate, she would work, allowing no time for chitchat. From the corner of her eye, she saw movement outside the pass-through window. Ben had circled the dining counter to grab salt and pepper shakers. She didn't want to admire him for taking the initiative to find what he needed without interrupting her, but she did. Most of her customers *never* went behind the service counter. Sometimes Blackie would lie belly first on the surface to reach over for something, but he didn't walk around to get stuff.

Today Ben wore a red Western-style shirt, sleeves rolled back over his thick forearms, collar hanging open. She allowed herself to watch the smooth athletic way he moved, then realized what she was doing and jerked her gaze away. *You can look, but don't touch,* she told herself. *And never let him catch you at it.*

A few minutes later, Sissy was making a huge batch of biscuit dough when Ben startled her by entering her inner sanctum with his dishes. As he set them in the industrial-size sink, he said, "Delicious breakfast. You keep cooking like that, and you'll need a bigger dining area."

Warmth spread through her. She was proud of what she had accomplished with the café. Her aunt's two best friends, Ma Thomas and Marilyn next door, swore up and down that Sissy had doubled the business. "If I can ever afford to remodel, I hope to create more seating somehow."

To her surprise, he turned on the hot water and, using the green scrubber, washed his plates and utensils. "Good. You're probably going to need it."

As he bent sideways to open a dishwasher, Sissy said, "I can get that." Having six-feet-plus of handsome cowboy in her kitchen was unsettling.

"Nah." With a flash of white teeth, he grinned at her. "Your lunch hour is coming up fast. I don't want to put a hitch in your get-along."

He left and returned a moment later with his coffee cup and carafe, both of which he stowed in the dishwasher. After straightening from the task, he said, "I've got your old run reinforced so your chickens can be outside during the day while I'm working. Now I'm about to dig postholes."

Sissy tried to think of a response, but he left

before she got out a word. The scent of his shaving cologne and masculine essence lingered. She drew it in and closed her eyes.

During the lunch hour, Sissy heard the sounds of Ben working out back. The unmistakable whine of an electric saw. Hammering. And occasionally the indecipherable drone of a man uttering words, which she guessed were grumbled curses. Since he was building what would be her new run, she wanted to at least see his plan and have some input, however small it might be.

When the crowd began to thin out, she started her dinner prep, finished it in short order, removed her coat, and glanced out the front windows at the street to see if she needed to wear her jacket when she went out back. Some of her diners had commented on the crazy fluctuations in tem-perature, but nobody had specifically said whether it was actually warm today or only sunny.

Sissy decided to err on the side of caution and grabbed a lightweight jacket from the storeroom, insurance in case a cool breeze was blowing. She'd just go out for a few minutes to assess the project, see how Ben was coming along, and ask him to explain to her once more what he planned to do. If a customer came in, the front door of the café would set off a buzzer out back.

When Ben saw her step onto the rear porch, he waved and gave her a grin that would have made a lot of women melt. Sissy hesitated, assuring herself that she was unaffected. Finn, his whole body wagging, hopped up the steps. With the dog she found it more difficult to be standoffish. He greeted her with what could only be described as boundless joy. She couldn't help but smile as she bent to pet him.

"Hello, Finnegan! Are you enjoying this beautiful weather?" Sissy could feel the breeze, warm as it wafted over her cheek, and in the few seconds she was bent over to fondle the pup, the heat of the sun burned through the back of her jacket. "It feels almost like summer again."

Finn bounced around her feet like a ping-pong ball as she removed her outerwear and laid it on the porch. As she descended the steps, the dog plopped down on the garment as if to guard it. Ben appeared to be erecting a post. With the first two feet of it already in a hole, it still stood eight feet tall.

Walking toward him, Sissy noticed that he'd somehow wrapped a taller barrier of wire around the top of her old run and released her chickens from the coop. Battling a stab of guilt, she saw that even while outdoors, the chickens had scant room to move around. Little wonder that they'd tried to run away. She'd provided a horrible home for them. Watching them try to find a place to peck the dirt nearly brought tears to her eyes.

"Don't," Ben said, his voice pitched low.

She threw him a startled look.

"You did the best you knew how to do. The best that you could afford to do as well. If there's anything I've learned, it's that feeling bad about a mistake accomplishes jack shit. You have to correct the situation, and you're doing that."

Sissy felt uncomfortable with how easily he'd read her thoughts. Only for once, she couldn't think of a smart-ass comeback to hide her feelings. "They've suffered because of my stupidity."

"Yep." He bent to pick up a tool. "Join the rest of us. We've all screwed up and caused suffering. I damned near killed a horse once by feeding it inferior hay to save money. The stuff was full of foxtails, and the horse developed abscesses in its mouth and throat from the arrow-shaped weed heads burrowing deep into soft tissue. When I noticed pus dripping, I knew something was wrong. Called a vet who had to sedate the horse on-site and do oral surgery. It was a mess." He shot her a look, his eyes conveying sympathy. "That afternoon I asked my father to go with me to buy hay. He took me to see cheap hay first so he could show me what to watch out for, and then we went for quality hay. That night I stood around a bonfire while I burned the bad stuff. I learned a lesson. My horse pulled through it. Life has gone on, and I don't sucker in on bad hay anymore."

Sissy hauled in a breath, her chest so tight that expanding her lungs hurt. As she released the intake, some of her guilt exited with it. She studied the holes he'd dug, which marked the size and rectangular shape of what would become her new run.

Her resolve to be cool and indifferent to Ben had gotten lost in the wave of her emotions. "I can scarcely believe my eyes. I never expected a run this large."

Holding the post erect with one hand, he directed his amber gaze toward her. Pine boughs, dancing in the breeze, cast feathery shadows over him one moment and allowed sunlight to play over his body the next. "Eighty chickens will need every inch of the space. They like to scratch in the dirt for bugs and worms. I need to build them some dusting bins as well so they can bathe regularly."

Sissy drew to a stop about three feet away from him. As their gazes met, she could have sworn she felt invisible sparks of electricity snapping in the air between them. "Um." She struggled to collect her thoughts. *Bins.* He'd said *bins.* "What do you put in the bins?"

"I use a very fine dirt and the birds love bathing in it. Chuck, over at Ramsey's Feed and Tack, carries it in large bags—forty pounders, I think. It's cheaper to buy it in bulk. Or, if you can find powdery earth here, that'll work, too."

Sissy looked at the hens. "They bathe in dirt?"

He laughed. "You'd think they'd wash in water like we do, but they don't. Dirt works better to clean their plumage." In his hand, he held what looked like a string covered with a chalky blue substance. He shifted the post and frowned in concentration until he seemed satisfied with its position. "Can you hand me one of those boards?"

Sissy glanced over and saw a stack of two-by-fours, precut at an angle on one end. She grabbed one and took it to him.

Anticipating that he needed another board, Sissy delivered it to him before he asked. "Thanks. I don't expect you to help me, though. You've got your hands full with the café."

He resumed work, putting another post in a hole. Sissy found herself admiring the view. Ben Sterling radiated so much hearty sex appeal that not even she could fail to notice. Though she'd sworn off men and never broken that vow, a guy like Ben made her wonder what she might be missing. How would those strong arms feel around her? She imagined herself melting against his hardness and letting him kiss her.

"Do you feed your chickens scraps from the kitchen?"

Sissy jerked back to the moment and felt heat crawl up her neck. "I thought human food was bad for them."

"A few things are. Go online and get a list of

safe foods for them. I keep a chicken bucket by my back door for leftovers. Mostly I feed them whatever I eat. You must have heaps to throw away in a café. Stop wasting all the scraps. They'll love them."

Sissy forced herself not to look at him from the neck down. Not that it helped much. From the collar on up, Ben's attractiveness was still potent. She took rigid control of her thoughts and considered all the food she disposed of daily. Now she could start putting it to good use.

Hugging her waist, Sissy nodded. "Thanks for the tips. I'm taking mental notes."

He muscled the second post erect. "What's on the lunch menu today? I'm sorry about eating at irregular times. It has to be an inconvenience for you. Tonight I'll be on time for dinner, though. If I quit at six or seven, I shouldn't come in too long after your customers do."

Stomach knotting, Sissy realized that she hadn't offered him a snack. He'd specifically requested four meals a day. "Oh, God, I'm sorry. You didn't get your second square!"

He laughed. "I would have gone in and asked for something, but I was still full from that fabulous breakfast. *That* doesn't happen often. Kudos to you." He left the post teetering to turn and look at her with his hands riding his hips. She couldn't help thinking that he resembled a cowboy in a television commercial, rugged, strong, and topped off with a Stetson. "Do you make Reuben sand-wiches?"

"They're one of my specialties." She couldn't help the note of pride that slipped into her voice.

He touched the brim of his hat. "Lots of sauer-kraut?"

"Oodles."

"Well, if it isn't too much trouble—"

"It isn't," she inserted. "I'll have it done in a snap. Want fries on the side?"

"Oh, yeah."

Sissy retraced her path to the back porch. As she ascended the steps, she smiled at Finnegan, who still lay on her jacket. Only then did she realize that his intent hadn't been to guard it. He'd chewed on it, instead.

"Finn!" she exclaimed in a hushed cry, not wanting Ben to hear. "Bad dog! You weren't supposed to *eat* it!" To her dismay, she saw that one entire arm of the garment had vanished, leaving only a ragged edge just below the shoulder seam. "Oh, dear, you silly boy. I hope you didn't swallow all that." She saw bits of cloth that had drifted on the breeze into the yard.

Blocking Ben's view with her person, Sissy unseated Finn with a sharp tug on what remained of the coat. The dog, thinking she wanted to play, grabbed the remaining jacket sleeve, braced his legs, and pulled with ferocious enthusiasm.

"No!" she scolded in a stage whisper. "He'll see, and you'll be in trouble! Let go! I'm not playing!"

"What's going on here?"

Sissy jumped at the sound of Ben's voice right behind her. With a hard jerk, she got the garment away from the pup, bundled it in her arms, and turned to find her handyman at the bottom of the steps. "He, um—*nothing.* Nothing is going on."

Ben's gaze became riveted to the jacket. She glanced down and saw that the chewed armhole was poking out above her left wrist. "He didn't," Ben said. "Not your jacket. Please, tell me he didn't do that."

"He didn't mean to," Sissy rushed to assure him. "I mean, I guess he intended to, but, um, I'm a cook, remember, and the sleeve had—um —spaghetti sauce all over it. Yes, that was it, spaghetti sauce." She had a huge pot of it simmering on the stove for dinner that night. "I'm sure he started licking it off and then just got carried away."

Ben studied his dog for a long moment. Then he met Sissy's gaze, his own alight with humor. "Spaghetti sauce, huh? You aren't, by any chance, telling me a tall tale to keep him from getting in trouble, are you?"

Sissy detested lying, and as a result, she'd never been good at it. "Please don't be mad at him." A picture of her father flashed through her head in cinematic motion and color. "He's still a pup. You said so yourself." She searched for another excuse. "He's probably still teething!" She stepped between Ben and the dog.

The amusement slipped from Ben's eyes to be replaced by a crease between his brows. "Do you think I beat my dog?"

An immediate response evaded her. "I, um— no, but, um, maybe, sometimes, if he does something really bad. Only he didn't. It's a thrift-store jacket. I got it for under five bucks."

Ben held out a hand for the garment. Body suddenly stiff, Sissy thrust it toward him. He grasped the cloth. Then he ascended the steps, grabbed Finn by the ruff, and gave him a firm shake. *"No!"* he said in a loud voice, pushing the garment against the pup's nose. "No chew! That's bad, bad, *bad!*" This was followed by another shake. "No chew!"

Hanging his head, Finn slumped on the porch the moment Ben released him. Then he whined and rolled over onto his back. Ben gave Sissy a sidelong look. "That's a sign of surrender. He's baring his belly to me. In dog-speak, that means a few things. First, that I'm the alpha in our pack of two. Second, he understands that he's done a bad thing. Third, he's sorry." Ben bent to press the jacket to Finn's nose again. "No, no, *no*. You understand me, pal?"

Straightening, Ben thrust the ruined garment back at Sissy.

"That's it," he said in an even voice. "It's called puppy training, and by the time he's a year old, I'll have repeated the performance at least a thousand times. I never hit him. I don't kick him. Most dogs are sensitive animals, and rough treatment ruins them."

"I see." She had offended Ben, but she couldn't think how to undo it. "I'm sorry. It's just—" Words failed her, and she broke off.

"It's just what?" His voice carried an edge. "Don't hide anything bad that he does from me. He's still learning, and if he gets away with chewing your things, he'll continue to do it."

"I'm sorry." It was all Sissy could think to say.

Seeming to tower over her, Ben sighed and relaxed his shoulders. Then he rubbed beside his nose. "Yeah, well, I'm sorry, too. If there's anything that gets me riled, it's animal abuse. People who mistreat animals need their asses kicked, and I'd like to be first in line to do the job. Having you think I might hurt my own dog doesn't sit well. You understand?"

Sissy nodded. "I don't think that of you. I've seen how relaxed and safe Finnegan feels, and I know that's because you've only been kind to him. I—well, let me just say that I've seen dogs beaten half senseless for doing something far less serious, and I just reacted without thinking."

"If you've seen shit like that happen, you were hanging out with good-for-nothing ass-holes."

She couldn't argue that point. Her father was, without question, a good-for-nothing asshole, and nothing had ever been safe around him, including his only child.

Ben lowered his gaze to Finnegan and then crouched down. Patting his knee, he said, "Okay, buddy. You're forgiven, *again*."

Finn catapulted to his feet and threw himself into Ben's arms. Ben chuckled and administered an all-over body rub to his dog. Glancing up at Sissy with no trace of anger left in his eyes, he said, "It may be a backhanded compliment, but he only eats things that belong to people he loves. When he was little, he wasn't particular and nobody's stuff was safe. Now he ignores the possessions of other people and bestows upon me the singular honor of destroying only mine." He grinned. "Must have been the hot dogs you gave him for dinner last night that won him over. Now you're apparently on his favorite list, along with me. Aren't you lucky?"

"Should I stop feeding him?"

"That depends." He rose to his full height. "If you value your shoes, possibly. On the other hand, his breed is known for its loyalty. Now that the love bug has sunk its teeth into him, he'll probably still adore you even if you starve him half to death."

Sissy glanced down at Finn, who looked up at her with a glow of affection in his eyes. With a start, she noticed for the first time that they were mostly amber like his master's, only one of them was half bluish white. "Is he blind in one eye?"

"No, he sees out of it fine. It's a trait in blue merles, blue eyes. Some of them have one blue eye. Finn got only half of one." A rumble came from his stomach. He pressed a broad hand over the spot. "Excuse me."

Sissy took that as her cue to get his sandwich made. She turned toward the door, then hesitated. "Will you mind if I offer Finn some leftover hamburger patties for his late lunch?"

Ben threw back his head and barked with laughter. "No. But put all your good shoes on a high shelf. Last week he cropped off the tops of my best dress boots."

"Oh, no."

"Nearly four hundred bucks of *oh, no*, actually." He glanced at the pup. "Feed him at your own risk. I guess that old saying is true and applies to dogs as well as guys. The way to our hearts is through our stomachs."

Since Sissy was on her way indoors to make Ben a delicious Reuben sandwich, that adage seemed more of a bad omen than a helpful tip.

Chapter
FIVE

As Sissy slapped corned beef slices on rye bread and made sure the sauerkraut had simmered long enough, she remembered that she'd promised Finn a meal. She glanced at the end piece of the corned beef, nodded her head, and cut a few more slices. Finn deserved the best. She pulled down another plate for the dog, embellished her offering with some leftover hamburger patties, and crumbled a corn muffin over the meat for an added treat. The dog had a loving, soulful gaze that she could meet with a feeling of peace and tenderness. Not like his master's eyes, not by a mile. Gazing into Ben's gave her about as much peace as standing by the tracks when the 12:20 freight train roared in every Wednesday and Friday.

She stepped onto the back porch to offer Finn his snack, mentally reminding herself to give him a full meal after Ben ate lunch. She had a hunch that Ben normally fed him whenever he ate. Finn greeted her with ecstatic whines, wagging his tail so hard she hoped his rear end didn't come loose. Sissy granted herself a moment to simply appreciate the beautiful day.

Clumps of wispy white clouds stood out against the robin's egg blue sky. The pine trees in her yard and beyond the stream were shamrock green and swayed in the capricious wind currents like graceful dancers. All too soon, winter would descend upon Mystic Creek, and the tree boughs would bend low under the weight of snow until ice rendered them immobile. But today she could stand here, warm and happy, getting whiffs of the delicious Mexican food José was preparing next door.

Just then, movement caught her eye. Ben appeared from behind the bed of his pickup, bare from the waist up. Apparently he'd grown too hot and stripped off his shirt. Sissy's mouth, wet from imagining the taste of José's enchiladas, went as dry as sunbaked dirt. Ben's upper body was slightly lighter in color than those parts of him always exposed to the elements, but it had the same butterscotch hue, accentuated with a mat of dark gold chest hair that tapered down to the fly of his jeans like an arrow. Every movement he made set muscles rippling under his skin. His broad shoulders, toned from physical labor, were well padded. His chest, wide and mounded with what looked like rock-hard flesh, glistened in the sunlight that played over him. She tried to look somewhere, anywhere, else, but her eyes weren't getting the message from her brain.

As if he felt her staring, he snapped his gaze to

the porch. Whatever he read in her expression made him grab his shirt from where he'd tossed it over the tailgate. With quick thrusts of his arms down the sleeves, he shrugged into the garment, leaving the front hanging open. From her point of view that didn't do one bit of good. The partial display of masculine chest and abs was just as unnerving.

Just then, the café buzzer sounded, indicating that a customer had walked in. Sissy had never been so glad to hear anything. She spun around and nearly tripped over the still-chewing Finn. Doing an awkward hop-skip to avoid stepping on him, she careened through the back door and slammed it, stopping to fan her burning cheeks. What was wrong with her? Men stripped off their shirts all the time while they worked. There was nothing indecent about it. She'd seen plenty of shirtless guys, for heaven's sake. She'd never felt even a twinge of arousal, let alone a slam that nearly buckled her knees.

She hurried through the storage rooms into the dining area. Blackie, the pawnshop owner, sat at the counter, moving a set of salt and pepper shakers on the surface as if he were playing solitary chess.

Finding her voice, she said, "What'll it be, Blackie? Taking a coffee break during your walk?"

Every afternoon, the man closed his shop for an

hour to get his daily exercise. Though stocky of build, he wasn't overweight, and she admired his determination to be physically fit. He stayed mostly on pavement as he walked, sometimes circling the town center several times before reopening his business. He often stopped in at the Cauldron prior to that for a little refreshment, and she'd come to thoroughly enjoy their chats. With Blackie, she didn't worry about guarding her tongue.

His black hair glistening in the artificial light, he settled a thoughtful blue gaze on Sissy, studied her for a moment, and said, "I've got a hankering for one of your blueberry muffins and a cup of coffee."

Sissy made muffins and cakes three times a week for those customers with a sweet tooth, and, of course, she had desserts on her menu. She ordered pies and more complicated pastry creations from the Jake 'n' Bake. "One blueberry muffin with coffee, coming right up." She stepped behind the counter and washed her hands. Within seconds, she'd served Blackie his muffin and poured him a cup of coffee. "How did your outing go today?"

"Well, weather-wise it was fabulous," he said, giving her a grin, "but during my walk, Ma Thomas dashed out of her shop to grab my arm. She's in a tailspin. FedEx got some of her order wrong today and brought her two boxes of items that were supposed to go across the street to the Shady Lady."

Along with most of the town, Sissy adored Ma Thomas. Every once in a while, Sissy invited her and Marilyn next door over to her café for lunch after the crowd thinned out. It was fun, but Sissy especially enjoyed the stories they told about her aunt Mabel. How much she loved bingo nights. How she cried while watching sad movies. And how proud she would be of Sissy for stepping into her shoes and making the café even more prosperous than it had been while she ran it.

"The Shady Lady?" The thought of Ma going in there made Sissy cringe. It was an adult store targeted mostly at men and women who wanted to liven up their sex lives. Sissy had gone in once, just to check it out. "Uh-oh," she said. "Ma is such a sweetie. Whatever she found in the boxes probably shocked her to the core."

Blackie chuckled. "She made me go inside her shop and look. She wanted me to tell her what she'd been sent so she could call the supplier and get her order straightened out."

Sissy pictured some of the merchandise at the Shady Lady and mentally elbowed Ben out of the forefront of her mind. She smiled at Blackie. "So did you tell her what was in the boxes?"

Blackie lifted his muffin. "Hell, no. I pretended to be as mystified as she was. *Dildos.* Dozens of them in all shapes and sizes. I couldn't tell Ma what they were. I didn't want her to know I even knew what they were. She'd never look at me the same way again. So instead I pointed to the address labels and told her where the boxes should have gone."

Sissy giggled as she topped off Blackie's mug. The man loved his coffee. "That was probably a smart call. Now if only we could be flies on the wall when Ma goes across the street to the Shady Lady to exchange boxes with the owner!" Slipping into the kitchen to grill Ben's sandwich, Sissy raised her voice to continue the conversation. "Imagine the look on Ma's face when she sees all that stuff on display in the Shady Lady."

Blackie sighed. "I probably should have gone with her. Call me a chicken, but I didn't have the guts."

Sissy flipped over the sizzling sandwich just as a timer went off, signaling that Ben's fries were done. She hurried over to open the appliance and lifted the basket. "I don't blame you, and you aren't a chicken. Some of those gadgets are over-the-top. Maybe Ma won't know what they're for, and she'll return to her store none the wiser."

Blackie spoke around a lump of muffin in his cheek. "God bless her. She's a woman in a million. She stuck by her husband and never strayed even though he was sick for a long time. If she was twenty years younger, I'd marry her."

"You and half the population of the whole town," affirmed Sissy. "She's—"

Ben's voice cut across her words as he entered the dining room. "You kidding, Blackie? I thought you swore off marriage after your divorce."

As Sissy arranged Ben's lunch on a plate, Blackie filled Ben in on the order mistake at Simply Sensational. She heard a rumble of laughter from Ben. "Dildos? Poor Ma. How did you explain what they were?"

"I didn't! I acted as innocent as a kid and twice as dumb. There are some things that a dear heart like Mary Alice doesn't need to know, son. I only feel bad because I left her to straighten out the order by herself. Now I'm worried that she'll hotfoot it across the street and walk into that den of—hmm, I can't think of the word. But ladies of her generation don't need to know about that stuff."

Sissy left the kitchen, carrying Ben's food. Just as devastatingly handsome as he'd been minutes ago, Ben winked at her. To Blackie, he said, "I only went in once. Curiosity got the better of me. Let me just say it's not a place I'd want my mom to visit."

Sissy set napkin-wrapped silverware in front of her now fully clothed handyman and found herself still picturing him without a shirt. She set his plate down with a thump. Blackie stared at her in surprise but Ben didn't seem to notice.

"Yum!" Ben said appreciatively. "Extra kraut? Lots of sauce. You're a woman after my heart."

She was *not* after his heart, and she almost said so. But there were other things about him that were getting more and more difficult for her to ignore. The sooner he was off her property, the better she'd like it.

"Man, it's gorgeous outside today!" Blackie exclaimed. "It feels almost like summer again. It makes me want to close my shop so I can enjoy it."

Over time, Blackie had become one of Sissy's favorite customers, a friend who didn't make her feel threatened or guarded. "Oh, me, too! I daydream about closing my café and sneaking away to play hooky. Even though I know it'll never happen, I have it all planned out. I'll hang a sign on the café door saying I'll open again for dinner, climb into my aunt Mabel's SUV, and drive the curvy mountain roads until I find the perfect grassy spot to enjoy a solitary picnic. *One last day of summer.*"

Blackie laughed. "I've done it a few times. Closed up and taken off. It was wonderful. Weather like this brings out my rebellious side."

Sissy smiled. "Growing up, I sometimes hid in my parents' backyard—when they'd rented a place with one—to watch the clouds drifting above me. I often wondered where they were going. I never came up with a satisfactory answer, but one thing was certain in my mind. Anywhere had to be better than where I was. Somewhere there had to be a place where everything wasn't your fault, where no one beat your puppy to death because it barked at night, where kids felt like they were wanted instead of barely tolerated."

A leaden silence blanketed the café. Sissy realized what she'd just said and wanted to disappear. Ben sat frozen with his teeth still sunk into one half of his sandwich. Blackie had settled a saddened gaze on her.

So embarrassed she could barely think, Sissy rushed to add with false cheer, "But that's all behind me now. I'm twenty-six, on my own, and running a business. Despite the harsh winters, Mystic Creek has become my home. I have a good life here, and for the first time, I can call my own shots."

Ben had finally swallowed the bite of sandwich. Blackie looked at her as if he'd never seen her before.

"Well, honey," Blackie said, "tomorrow may be your last chance for that summer picnic somewhere beautiful. My weather app says it'll be nice for the next few days, but I never trust what it says for more than twenty-four hours. Nobody but a fool tries to predict weather in Oregon. You should close up tomorrow and take a day off."

"Oh, no, I can't. Ben's expecting his four

meals for building my new run and coop, and Christopher Doyle counts on me for his as well."

"Forget my four squares," Ben inserted. "And what you need for your hooky day is a guide who knows the area. You can drive the windy roads around here forever if you don't know where to go. Have you ever seen Crystal Falls? Not the town, but the waterfall."

"Oh, wow, it's incredible," Blackie observed. "The water is crystal clear." He glanced at Ben. "And that grassy bank? It'd be perfect for a picnic. I went once. Didn't have a picnic, but I did get hungry because it's so gorgeous you don't want to leave. You should go up there. Ben would probably love to take you."

Sissy felt as if she'd gotten stuck in a vise. "Christopher counts on me." She speared Blackie with a look. "And you count on your muffin and coffee during your afternoon walk. I can't just up and leave!"

"Sure you can!" Blackie insisted. "I can go over to the Jake 'n' Bake for a muffin and coffee tomorrow. Just close up after you feed Christopher breakfast. Tell him you're taking off and will come back before the dinner hour. Do your prep in the morning. Steal a few hours for yourself for a change. When I do it, I just say an emergency came up. People don't stop patronizing my shop. And it isn't a lie. My emergency is that I need a day to enjoy myself. Desperately."

"The waterfalls are hard to find," Ben commented. "GPS up in those mountains isn't always accurate. I'd love to drive you up there. I'll have to take Finn along, if you don't mind. He gets in a pout if I leave him and chews things, like my furniture."

Sissy felt mildly offended. "Why would I object to being around Finn? He's a sweetheart."

"So it's a plan!" Blackie slapped his palm on the counter. When he saw what Sissy knew was probably a horrified look on her face, he added, "Think of it as a favor to me and my blood pressure. I worry about you, working nonstop all day, every day."

Sissy tried to imagine taking part of a day off in the company of Ben, the cowboy who was way too sexy to go without a shirt. Apparently Ben interpreted by her expression that she was worried. "Just as friends. Finn will be our chaperone. He's still just a baby. I can't poison his mind with anything risqué."

Sissy giggled. She didn't know where that had come from, because she was totally not into this idea. She supposed her laughter sprang from near hysteria.

"So," Blackie said, "when is Christopher finished with breakfast?"

"Eight thirty," Sissy replied.

"Get your dinner prep done before then, throw his plate and flatware in the dishwasher, and you can be out of here by nine," Blackie said. "Just do it. It'll be good for my heart. You work way too hard. Money isn't everything, Sissy. Sometimes we just have to live."

Ben took another bite of his sandwich and chewed for what seemed an interminable time. "Blackie, you heard the lady. She can finally call her own shots. Stop pressuring her."

Blackie hung his head. "I didn't mean like it'd be a date or anything. Just a few hours for her to relax."

Sissy realized that Blackie now felt awful. She blurted, "I'll go. I need a few hours off."

Beaming a grin, Blackie looked up at her. "Really? Oh, honey, I'm so glad. Normally it's slow for me on weekdays, but tomorrow I'm doing a big trade with another pawnshop owner in Crystal Falls. Once we've held merchandise beyond the expiration date and it's not moving for us, we switch with each other. Otherwise I'd take you to the falls myself."

Ben said nothing and continued eating. More slowly now. When Blackie finally left, he finished off his meal in record time and then looked up at her. "Crystal Falls is beautiful beyond description. But don't let Blackie push you into going if you don't want to. If I show up at nine and you've changed your mind, I'll just go to work on the chicken coop."

Sissy's heart squeezed, and it hurt so badly it

nearly took her breath. This was Ben Sterling, one of the golden-haired favorites of Mystic Creek, the kind of man who, in her experience, felt privileged and entitled with women. They never played fair. When they got a woman backed into a corner, they went for it. But he had just offered her a way out.

"Thank you, Ben."

He slid his plate toward her. "Thank *you* for the best Reuben sandwich I've ever eaten. I'll be here at nine. Crystal Falls is truly incredible to see, and I'll bring the picnic food. If you decide against going, no worries. With my appetite, I'll empty the cooler and be hungry by dinnertime." He swung off the barstool. "Don't let Blackie pressure you. He means well, but he may not understand how you feel about some things. You're independent now. Don't let anybody screw with that."

He turned and strode toward the back area of the café with that loose-hipped stride, filled with the strength and agility that always made her mouth water. When she heard the back door close, she allowed the sharp shards of her memories to flow from her lungs on the crest of a pent-up breath and closed her eyes. Tears slipped down her cheeks. It was far too soon for her to trust Ben. Far too soon. But no privileged, well-heeled male, young or old, had ever told her that she should make her own choices and let no one else pressure her to do otherwise.

Sissy sighed. She didn't trust Ben enough to go with him tomorrow, but maybe, after a good night's sleep, she'd decide to do it anyway. Against her better judgment. Go when all her alarm bells were ringing. Go simply because he'd respected her right to make her own decision. No demands, no pressure. Maybe he really was as nice as he seemed.

Just then Blackie reentered the café. "What is Ben building out back, anyway?"

"A new chicken coop and run. I'm paying him with meals."

"That'd work for me! You've turned into a great cook." He paused at the counter. "Do you mind if I go out to have a look?"

"No, not at all."

Blackie nodded and trailed behind Ben through the storage rooms.

Sissy took that opportunity to do cleanup and find something for Finn's lunch. She had scraps of corned beef left over from Ben's Reuben and took them out to the pup, who was quickly becoming her most devoted customer, nonpaying though he might be.

Squatting beside him, she trailed her fingertips through his sun-silvered fur, thinking of his master with a troubled frown knitting her brow. Ben unsettled her, and she couldn't kid herself about why. She was attracted to him. No, that didn't describe how she felt around him. *Turned on, hot for him.* Brutal honesty was what she needed from herself, not toned-down excuses. If she intended to keep her life on course, she needed to bring these feelings to a screeching halt. And if that was impossible, she had to make damned sure he never found out.

She rested her palm on Finn's back, thinking how easily she'd come to care about the little guy. She couldn't allow herself to do the same with his master.

The next morning was summer bright with a light, balmy breeze that ruffled Sissy's hair as she tended to her chickens and turned them out into their small but reinforced run. Sissy watched them stretch their legs, noting how crowded they still were. That would be the perfect excuse for her to give Ben for canceling the drive to see the waterfall. On the other hand, the hens could survive another few hours of bumping shoulders occasionally, and an outdoor excursion on such a beautiful day tempted her almost beyond bearing. Ben had said he'd work on the run when they got back late that afternoon. He might even get it finished before dark.

Waffling back and forth about whether she should go or not, Sissy found herself doing the dinner prep when she returned to the café. She guessed that meant she was going, even though she hadn't completely made up her mind yet. Watching the clock, she felt the knots in her stomach grow tighter and tighter. At a quarter before seven, her usual opening time, she gave herself a hard mental shake. Did she want to visit the waterfall or not? Yes. So what if she felt nervous? She wasn't going on a date. Ben wouldn't expect sex, or demand it of her. Well— she hoped not, since he'd advised her to call her own shots. With a black Magic Marker, she wrote a note that read, CLOSED DUE TO EMERGENCY. WILL REOPEN AT FIVE FOR DINNER. Then, with quivering fingers, she taped the sign on her front-door window.

As always Christopher arrived at eight sharp, and Sissy greeted him by opening the door. "Ignore the sign. You're a special customer, and I'm serving you breakfast before I leave."

The old man tottered inside, using his cane to steady himself. "Well, I appreciate that. But what's the emergency?"

Sissy couldn't bring herself to lie. "I'm escaping for the day to have a picnic. I've never seen Crystal Falls—the waterfall, not the town."

Christopher seated himself at his usual booth. "Oh, you'll love it. My wife used to drag me up there once a month all summer long." He smiled with fond memories. "I enjoyed it as much as she did, but I grumped at her about it anyhow. Made her appreciate me more."

Sissy laughed. "You stinker, you." She went to the kitchen for his breakfast. After setting his food before him, she took a seat across from him to chat while he ate. "What other outdoor things did you do with your wife?"

Christopher regaled her with stories about their fishing trips. After finishing his meal, he chuckled as he struggled to get up from the booth. "Never did get her to put a worm on a hook. I had to do it for her while she closed her eyes."

Sissy ran his credit card, then walked with him to the door. "I'll be open again for dinner."

He stepped out onto the sidewalk. "Well, if you're not, I've got frozen dinners to fall back on. You go and have a good time, and if you want to linger, which I always did, do it. It's good for the soul, and my walks here are good for my heart, whether I get dinner or not."

Sissy locked up behind him. Then she lowered all the window blinds before collecting his plate and flatware to stow them in the dishwasher. She'd just finished wiping off the booth table when Ben entered from the back. "Well, are we on? Or have you chickened out?"

For a split second, Sissy almost did exactly that. He looked fabulous in a brown Western shirt, collar open and sleeves rolled back over his muscular forearms. Physically, she was at a dangerous disadvantage with Ben. Memories of how badly things had gone for her in the past when she trusted men flashed through her mind.

But she pushed those thoughts aside, remembered that Christopher had said it would be good for her, and took a deep breath to bolster her courage. "Nope. I'm all ready to go."

His burnished face creased in a grin. "Do you have another light jacket that Finn hasn't destroyed? The falls are at a higher elevation. On a day like this, it should be warm up there, but it's better to always go prepared."

"Yes, I've got another one. I'll grab it as we leave."

"Fantastic."

He followed her down the hall, pausing while she grabbed a coat off a hook and then got her keys so she could lock up. Finn waited on the porch and bounced around with excitement when he saw Sissy.

"No," she said with a laugh as she secured the building, "I didn't bring you food."

As Ben descended the steps beside her, she cast him a questioning look. "You said you'd bring the picnic stuff. I hope you remembered that three of us will be eating."

Ben chuckled. "Of *course* I remembered. While I made sandwiches, he drooled all over my boots, begging for bites." They walked toward his truck. "I made three extra for him. You'll be slumming it, I'm afraid. I stopped at Flagg's last night for deli potato salad and other stuff, nothing as good as what you whip up at the café."

"Well, I happen to like potato salad and sandwiches. Plus, it'll be nice to eat something I didn't make for a change."

Ben opened the rear door on the driver's side to let Finn leap up on the backseat. Then he arched a brow at Sissy as she circled the front of his truck. "You want a boost up? The floorboards are pretty high off the ground."

"I'll try it on my own first." When Sissy opened the passenger door, she wished she was taller. But by grabbing a handle made for pulling oneself up and jumping, she got in by herself. "Wow. It is high off the ground."

Ben smiled as he started the engine. "Running boards would help. But I use my truck on the ranch. They'd get hung up on something, sure as the world, and get ripped off."

They fastened their seat belts, and Ben drove around Marilyn's yard to reach Main Street. Sissy settled back to enjoy the ride. Her earlier anxiety had vanished. Finn, apparently accustomed to using the passenger seat, leaped over the wide console and made himself comfortable on her lap.

"Finn!" Ben scolded.

"It's fine." Sissy looped her arms around the

dog. "We're buddies now. I don't mind holding him."

"You sure?"

"I'm positive."

Ben kept his attention on his driving as he maneuvered through town. Even so, he was acutely aware of Sissy beside him, fussing over the pup and whispering things to the dog that he couldn't make out over the sound of the engine. Allowing himself one quick glance, he saw an expression of pure bliss on Finn's face. The two of them truly had bonded. It felt strange to Ben, because most women he'd dated would be complaining about all the hair Finn was getting on their clothes and flapping a hand in front of their faces because he had dog breath.

Ben smiled slightly. Yes, it felt strange, but it also felt *right.* As he circled the town center and turned onto Huckleberry, sudden inspiration struck him. "Would you mind if I stop off at my place for a second? You need a hat to keep the sun out of your eyes."

"No, I don't mind. I should have thought to grab one."

Instead of taking the Periwinkle Lane exit when he reached the man-made creek overpass, which would lead due east, he took the Bridge Road exit, which went straight to his ranch. He liked this woman. He liked her a lot. Before he allowed those feelings to deepen, he needed to see how she reacted to cows, horses, pigs, and manure. He knew for sure that she liked chickens and dogs, but if she was afraid of or didn't like big animals, it was a deal breaker for him. Being a rancher or farmer ran in his blood. He'd been raised around critters. He sometimes thought loving the smells on his ranch had been stamped on his DNA. Probably not, looking at it rationally. He only knew he couldn't change who and what he was, and though he'd thrown a wide net to find a woman who could accept that, he'd been unsuccessful.

Sissy gasped when he turned into his graveled driveway. "Oh, my gosh!" she cried. She gazed out over his land, taking in the tidy exterior of his refurbished farmhouse, the barn, the arena, and the fenced pastures that seemed to stretch forever, even to Ben. "You *own* all of this? It's gorgeous."

Ben parked beside his house. "It'll take me a while to find the straw hat my mom always uses when she comes out. Would you like to come in?"

Sissy's attention was fixed on the horses that were enjoying the morning sunlight in the paddocks outside their stalls. "I'd rather visit the horses. Would you mind? I've seen horses from a distance, but never up close."

Ben pointed. "See those last two fenced areas holding the gray and the dun? Those horses aren't mine. I'm working some bad habits out of them. All the other ones are safe. You can say hi to them through the fences if you want."

Sissy popped out her side of the truck as if she'd just been issued free tickets to a petting zoo. Finn, delighted to have one of his favorite people visit his world, ran in circles around her as she speed-walked toward the paddocks. Ben kept his gaze locked on Sissy. Either she didn't realize she might step in what Ben referred to as a poop bomb, or she didn't care. He couldn't help but grin. When she got back, she'd have to clean the shit off her shoes before he let her back in his truck.

He took his time finding his mom's straw hat. *Okay,* he admitted to himself. *This is a test, and I'm probably a bastard for not warning her to watch her step. But I'm tired of hooking up with fussy women who reject my world and want me to wear chinos with polished loafers.* Ben recalled the girlfriend who'd given him a gift certificate for his birthday to get a manicure and have his back waxed. He shuddered at the memory. He filed his nails and kept them clean. As for his back, what hair grew there had roots, and getting it all jerked out had hurt like a son of a bitch. He'd called an end to that relationship in short order.

He found the hat and moseyed back outside. He expected to find Sissy already back at the truck.

Instead she was jerking up handfuls of grass and feeding it to his horses. He walked slowly in her direction. He could hear her musical voice as she chatted away to his geldings and the red roan mare.

When Sissy saw Ben approaching, she cried, "They are so beautiful! Their noses feel like velvet." She grabbed up more grass for the mare, which was in a separate pen because she was with foal, and Ben didn't want to risk her getting kicked in the belly. Horses did that to one another occasionally. "This one's a girl, isn't it?"

"Well, now, you tell me," Ben said with a smile.

"It's a girl. She's daintier than the boys. Look at her head."

Ben normally looked lower to determine the sex of a horse, but Sissy was right. Katie did look daintier. But she was still hell on wheels when cutting cows. All the horses had been bred to be athletes and could go rump down to turn on a dime, but the mare was just a bit quicker.

"She's my best cutter," Ben told her.

"What's she cut?"

Ben suppressed a chuckle. "Cows. Only it's not like it sounds. I have forty beeves out yonder, and if I need to work on one, all I have to do is point Katie at it, and lickety-split, she separates that one steer from all the others and herds it into a chute with a head catch."

Sissy gave Katie a final stroke along her neck and turned away. "Do you have any girl cows?"

Ah, so she liked girls. Ben could understand that. He liked them, too—especially this one. He led her toward the cow pasture. He was surprised when Martha, the she-monster, ambled over to the pipe fencing and poked her nose out through the slats to get it scratched. Sissy didn't flinch. She just doled out some petting.

"She is so cute. I love her eyes."

Ben didn't ask how Sissy knew Martha was a girl. The bovine had dropped a calf last spring, and her bag, though smaller now that the heifer no longer suckled as much, was still prominent. "She's my mean cow. My hired hand calls her the She-Bitch."

Sissy didn't retreat, and that settled it for Ben. She'd passed the test. Maybe it would work between them, or maybe it wouldn't, but at least he knew she liked animals, big or small. As he had suspected, when they returned to his truck, she had to rub her sneakers clean on the grass that grew in haphazard clumps between his house and the outbuildings. Once in the truck, she tossed the straw hat he'd left lying on her seat into the back to make room for Finnegan to ride on her lap.

As Ben started the engine, she cried, "Darn it. I should have looked at your chicken coop."

"Maybe another time. If we linger here any

longer, we won't be able to enjoy the falls for as long as we want."

She settled against the seat with Finn in her arms as Ben drove back to the overpass to take Periwinkle Lane east. He knew the roads like the back of his hand and had visited the falls many times. Once out of town, he relaxed behind the wheel and enjoyed the scenery, mountain slopes of green pine boughs peppered with deciduous trees with leaves that were turning autumn brown and orange.

Then he noticed that Sissy was no longer talking. He glanced over and saw that she'd tightened her arms around Finn and that her shoulders were rigid with tension. He guessed that it had just sunk home that he was taking her into state and federal wilderness land, and she was alone with him. Judging by her stiffness, he thought she was growing nervous, possibly even frightened.

He saw a wide spot up ahead and slowed down. As he pulled over and stopped, Sissy shot a wary look at him. "Why are you stopping?" she asked in a thin voice.

"You look like you're wound up tighter than a clock. I just want to be sure you still want to go. I can turn around here and take you back to town. We can picnic on your back porch, or like I said, I can inhale all the food while I work on your run."

"How silly would that be?"

Pretty damned silly, Ben thought, but he wasn't about to say so. Something really nasty had happened to this woman. Maybe more than once. She didn't trust him any further than she could throw him. "It's even sillier to keep going if you can't relax and enjoy yourself," he settled for saying. "That's the whole point. Right? To forget about work, visit a beautiful place, and have a picnic."

She released a taut breath. "You're right. That is the whole point."

Ben expected her to add, "Just take me home." Instead she lifted her chin and said, "So let's do it. I'll relax. I'll have fun."

It sounded to Ben as if she were giving herself a pep talk. And that saddened him. She had to work at relaxing—and at trusting him. The realization made him nearly as nervous as she was. What if he said the wrong thing? Or made a sudden move that she interpreted as aggressive? Up at the falls, which were surrounded by nothing but wilder-ness, he'd have a devil of a time finding her if she panicked and ran off into the woods. Well, maybe not. Finn adored her, and he had a good nose on him.

Ben pulled back out onto the highway. To fill the silence, he began playing tour guide, pointing out landmarks. "That's Cougar Rock. I climbed it once and saw no cougar, so I don't know how it got its name."

She leaned forward, being careful not to unseat Finn. "You climbed *that?* It's nearly straight up."

Ben chuckled. "It's surprising what Mystic Creek boys will do during the summer. At least we never got bored. I went through a rock-climbing stage." A few curves later, Ben said, "That's Sky High Point. I used to hike up there as a teen. It's a great place to see wildlife. One time we boys lay on our bellies to watch a beaver dam in the creek. We were quieter than church mice, hoping to see a beaver."

"Did you?"

"Oh, yeah. A great big male with long teeth who waddled up behind us. He scared us so bad that one of my buddies wet his pants. We ran like scalded dogs, tripping over logs, running into trees. In retrospect, I think we all lost our minds. Beavers aren't known for their speed. When it was all said and done, we'd inflicted far more injury on ourselves than the beaver could have. Ah, well, you live and learn. Now I know I could outrun a pissed-off beaver at a fast walk."

Sissy giggled, and with a mental sigh of relief, Ben decided she was going to be okay at the falls alone with him.

Sissy had never seen anything so gorgeous as Crystal Falls. The creek was about thirty feet wide, and the water cascaded over a rock ledge in a magnificent rush that ended in a pool of churning foam that eddied out into depths so clear she could see the rocks far beneath the surface. Beyond that deep pool, the creek grew more shallow, calling to her to take off her shoes, roll up her jeans, and go wading— something she'd never been allowed to do as a kid and hadn't had time for as an adult.

Ben spread a blanket on the grassy bank just far enough away to avoid the mist that spewed up from the collision of water. When they sat down, he placed the picnic cooler between them and then added an oversize basket to increase the barrier. Sissy realized that he was trying to make her feel safe. Instead she felt embarrassed. Ben hadn't brought her here with nefarious intentions. On an intellectual level, she knew that. Emotionally, not as much.

As her chagrin faded, she bit back a smile. The buffer he'd created between them wouldn't stop a man with Ben's strength and agility. He could be over it and on top of her in a split second. But the fact that he'd tried to create a separation between them told her that jumping her wasn't in his game plan, if he even had a plan, which she now doubted. He just wanted her to see how spectacular nature could be and enjoy a day off with him.

"I've never gone sightseeing," she blurted. "I, um—Well, we traveled a lot when I was a kid, but it was always a race between point A and point B. We never veered off course to visit places."

Ben handed her the straw hat. "The sun hasn't reached its zenith, and you're squinting to see. We're sitting in shade, but light still beams through the boughs to blind a person. Besides, I don't want you getting sunburned."

Sissy stopped petting Finn, who'd cuddled on the blanket beside her. She put on the hat. The brim, just like the one on Ben's Stetson, cast a shadow over her face. "Much better," she said.

"It looks good on you."

"It's a Western hat, isn't it?"

"Yep. Mom's into Western."

"Oh, *look!*" She gasped in delight. "Blue butterflies! I've never seen a blue one, not ever! With the sun in my eyes, I had no idea they were here."

Ben followed her gaze. "This is the only place I've ever seen them. I think they're misfits of nature, in an area they don't belong, but they're here every summer."

"Oh, my." The butterflies fluttered near a copse of moist riparian bushes, and they were countless. "Such a delicate blue, and they are so lovely!"

Ben stretched his arms and flexed his shoulders. His sudden movement startled Sissy. She so appreciated the pathetic barrier between them. Ben had signaled a message to her by creating it, that she was perfectly safe. "Whenever my dad comes to the falls, he always says 'Never say never' when he sees the blue butterflies. It reminds me that life is filled with the unexpected, and sometimes the unexpected things are the best of all."

Relaxing again, Sissy focused on her surroundings. She loved the smells there, an intoxicating blend of pine, sun-warmed grass, and the pungent scent of creek-side moss and other plants that thrived in the moist soil. The sound of the falls was a pleasant background noise that had a certain rhythm to it that she'd failed to notice at first.

Ben began removing food from the cooler. Once it was empty, he closed the lid and arranged sandwiches and plastic tubs of other food on top of it, using it as a table of sorts. He held up a bottle of white wine. "I've even got plastic goblets. You care to join me? I've got juice and soda as well."

Sissy narrowed her eyes at him. "You once told me that when you drink enough wine, anybody looks good."

He laughed. "I did say that. But I don't plan to drink that much. I have to get us home. One drink an hour, Barney tells me. I try to space them further apart than that, just to be safe. Barney might catch me driving under the influence and toss me in the clink."

Sissy giggled. "Not really. He'd do that to his own brother?"

"In a heartbeat. He has no patience with idiots who get drunk and drive, endangering others on the road. Neither do I."

"That policy gets my vote, too." When he offered her a plastic cup filled with wine, she accepted it and took a sip. "Mmm. Nicely chilled chardonnay. Mild, slightly sweet."

"You a wine expert?"

"I wish." It was her turn to laugh. "I buy on the cheap and wouldn't know a fine wine if it ran up and bit me on the leg."

"I'm pretty much the same." He took a taste and nodded. "Cheap tastes okay to me."

He set out plates and plastic flatware. As they each selected a sandwich and dished up servings from the deli tubs, Finn stood and circled Sissy's feet. "Uh-oh, he's moving closer to all the goodies."

Ben picked a sandwich for the dog. "Made especially for him, mayo and meat, no embellishments." He laid the offering on a paper plate, but Finn wolfed it down so fast he needn't have bothered. "Whoa, boy. Good thing I fixed you three."

Sissy's was made with thinly sliced chicken, crisp lettuce, tomatoes, and slivers of onion and dill pickle on cracked wheat sourdough. Ben had added a trace of Dijon mustard along with mayo. Finn wouldn't enjoy the extras, but she did. "Delicious. So's the potato salad." She sighed and gazed at the waterfall as she ate and sipped wine. "It's so peaceful here. I could stay forever."

"I always feel the same way. Unless you decide not to open for dinner, though, we'll have to head back soon."

Sissy groaned. "It feels like we just got here. I haven't played hooky long enough yet. If I don't open for dinner, how long can we stay?"

"You serious?" He shrugged. "Until the sun starts to go down. We'll get home after dark, but I don't mind driving then. Headlights don't blind me, and actually it's safer if I can use my brights most of the way. I can see the gleam of deer and elk eyes along the road and slow down so I don't hit one."

"I could help watch for them. And Christopher, my customer that I worry about, told me he has frozen dinners at home to fall back on. He urged me to take the whole day off and enjoy the falls."

He grinned. "So, you've had fun playing hooky, have you?"

"More than just that. Being here beats getting a full-body massage, not that I've ever had one."

Ben, still nursing his first glass of wine, leaned back and braced himself on his elbows. His long sigh told Sissy that he didn't want to leave any more than she did. And she felt fairly safe with him now. That was a good feeling and yet unsettling as well. She'd felt safe many times and learned the hard way that she'd been too naive for words.

It had been a very long while since she had trusted a man she knew found her attractive. It always ended with her getting hurt, humiliated, or demeaned. In high school, boys had targeted her because of her shabby clothes and the rumor that her parents were not only transients but also low-class and crazy. But Ben seemed so different. And the attraction was mutual. She couldn't lie to herself about that.

He was looking up at the clouds. Sissy followed his gaze. After a long moment, he asked, "What do you think about when you watch the clouds drift by now? Do you still wonder where they're going?"

She cringed as she remembered the secrets she had revealed to him and Blackie yesterday. "No," she confessed. "I don't care where they're going anymore because there's no place I'd rather be than right where I am." She sent him a sharp look. "I mean that in a general way, not here, right now, although it's beautiful. I mean Mystic Creek."

He smiled. "You don't have to guard your words with me, Sissy. And I knew what you meant." He lifted his glass toward the sky. "So, let me teach you a new way to watch the clouds. Right now, I see a horse's head up there."

Sissy stared hard at the clouds and saw nothing. "Don't work so hard to see it. Use a broader scope and let the shape leap out at you."

Sissy went back to staring. "I see it!" she cried. "It's an almost-perfect horse's head." A few seconds later, she said, "Now I see a snow-covered pine forest around a small lake."

Ben searched for that and soon found it. "Wow. It's gorgeous."

After cloud watching, Ben opened the cooler again to draw out the food for a second picnic. Finn, who'd been dozing, leaped to his feet. Ben called the pup a bottomless pit, which made Sissy laugh. When they'd all three filled their stomachs again, Ben took off his hat, removed his socks and boots, rolled up his jeans, and walked into the stream to go wading. He gimped over the rocks, crying, "Ouch! Damn! Ouch!" And then, "It's *freezing*. I can't believe I went swimming here as a kid. Now it makes my bones hurt."

Finn joined Ben to play in the water. Sissy couldn't resist following suit. Ben was right; the rocks were sharp on the soles of her feet and the water was as cold as snowmelt. But they had fun, the kind of fun Sissy had never been allowed to engage in as a kid.

Finn splashed Ben first. He reacted by sharing the experience with Sissy. She gasped at the shock and threw water back at him. In seconds they were both drenched and laughing so hard that only Finn had any energy left.

As they climbed from the creek and ascended the bank, the sun was starting to set. Sissy was shivering with cold. Ben, wet from head to toe, looked as miserable as she felt.

"What were you *thinking?*" he asked her.

Instantly indignant, Sissy said, "You splashed me first!"

Ben turned an accusing gaze on the dripping-wet pup and said, "Actually, he splashed me first, so it's all *his* fault."

Sissy couldn't help but laugh. Ben came up with the idea of using the picnic blanket to dry off. He let Sissy go first. Then he took his turn before ruffling Finnegan's fur until it was only damp. Ben's hair stood up in haphazard spikes, poking every which way. His wet shirt clung to his torso, as did his jeans. Never had Sissy seen such a handsome man.

"Is my hair as awful looking as yours is?" she asked.

He gave her a long study. "Since I haven't seen mine yet, I can't really say. But don't worry. You still look damned good."

Sissy's pulse kicked and sped up. Her stomach felt as if she'd swallowed dozens of fluttering blue butterflies. Trying to hide her reaction to him, she said, "I *knew* it was a mistake to let you have a second glass of wine. Now anybody looks good to you."

Ben barked with laughter and tossed her the straw hat. "Put it on. It's the perfect cure for a bad hair moment."

Sissy put hers on. Watching Ben don his Stetson, she couldn't truthfully say that he looked better. He was perfect just the way he was, wet clothes and all.

As he loaded all the picnic gear into the bed of his truck, Sissy carried items up the hill to him, but she was too short to lift anything over the side. Soon they were in the vehicle, headed back to Mystic Creek. Oh, how she wished the day didn't have to end.

"I wish it didn't, either," Ben said.

Sissy hadn't realized she'd voiced her thoughts aloud and felt a moment's embarrassment. "It's the first time in *forever* that I've taken a whole day off. I feel as if I've been released from jail."

"No dinner crowd for you tonight. Who says the day has to end? When we get back to town, let's do dinner out. I vote for the Straw Hat. José makes some mean enchiladas."

"Looking like this? We're both a mess."

Ben kept his eyes on the road as he executed a sharp turn. "Okay, a drive-through, then. Finn will love that. He'll get to have dinner with us."

Once in town, Ben drove to the Mystical Burger Shack on Periwinkle Lane, a little place with a drive-through window that Sissy hadn't realized existed. She ordered a jalapeño cheeseburger with fries and a layered ice-cream sundae for dessert. Ben ordered two of the same burgers with extra jalapeños and a sundae as well. Finn got six hamburger patties and a small tub of vanilla ice cream. Ben circled the building and backed his Dodge into a parking slot, telling Sissy they could watch people as they ate.

"This place's bestselling hamburger is called the Heart Attack. I've never ordered one. I think in addition to two burger patties, it's got cheddar cheese, avocado slices, an egg, and bacon. It may be fun to decide which people we think are going in for a serving of coronary arrest."

Sissy laughed. "Why would anyone give a burger such a horrid name?"

"In warning?" Ben fished through the sacks and handed Sissy her burger and fries. "For whatever reason, it's a moneymaker." He fed Finn his patties and then relaxed to enjoy his sandwich. "Damn, Finn. You've got the whole cab smelling like wet dog."

"Don't be a baby," Sissy told him. "He can't help how he smells, and besides, a little wet-dog ambience lends the meal a touch of earthy elegance. It's like having another picnic"

The yard lights illuminated the cab. Ben sent her a wondering look. "You actually don't mind? For me, it's kind of like using stinky socks as a dinner napkin."

Sissy nearly choked on a fry. "It isn't that bad."

He grinned and took another bite of his burger. "Actually, the burn of the jalapeños in my sinuses is helping. I can't smell much of anything now."

After they finished their desserts, with Sissy holding Finn's tub of vanilla ice cream so he could eat it without making a huge mess, Ben drove her home. Sissy stared at her building. She hadn't thought to leave any lights on, and inside it would be blacker than smut. Thinking of her ghost—or whatever it was that played mind games with her—she dreaded going in.

"We'll escort you to the door and wait until you get some lights turned on," Ben said, as if he had read her thoughts.

"I'm sure I can handle it," she said. "I need to close up the chicken coop first, anyway. And I'm sure you're eager to get home and take a shower."

"Our showers will wait, and I'll close up the coop on my way back to the truck. It'd be bad manners on my part not to see you to the door and if my mom found out, she'd twist my ear. She'd have to stand on a chair to reach it, but trust me, that wouldn't stop her."

"Well, I wouldn't want you to get your ear twisted."

Sissy slid out of his truck, landed on ground

that seemed to be several feet down, and caught her balance. Finn sailed out behind her. Ben met them at the front bumper and kept pace with Sissy.

"Oh, drat," she said. "I need to turn the heat lamp on in the coop, too."

"Not necessary. My weather app says it won't freeze tonight. The hens will be fine."

Once on the porch, Sissy fished for her keys. Finn bounced around as if he expected to go in and be fed again. As she turned the lock and opened the door, she said, "You had six hamburger patties and at least a cup of ice cream minutes ago. How can you possibly have room for more?"

"That's not to mention the three sandwiches and the huge helping of baked beans he ate for lunch."

Just then Finn wagged his behind with such enthusiasm that he farted. Waving a hand in front of his face, Ben leaned around to flip on both of the interior light switches, which illuminated the storeroom hallway and porch. "Oh, man, Finnegan. It smells like something crawled up inside you and died." When Sissy laughed, he added, "Yeah, yeah, so very funny. You don't have to sleep with him tonight."

Sissy bent to give Finn a good-night pat. Then she turned to face Ben. "Thank you for being my tour guide today. I really enjoyed myself."

"Thank you for being such a good sport. I shouldn't have started the splashing incident."

"Actually, that was one of the highlights for me." She glanced down at the dog. "Thank you for starting it, Finn. It was fun."

Silence fell between her and Ben. Sissy had never said good night to a man on her porch, but even she knew a good-night kiss—and often far more—was normally on the agenda. Ben leaned toward her. Her body tensed. But instead of putting his mouth over hers, he plucked the straw hat from her head.

"If Mom visits and can't find her hat, she'll be pissed." He studied her face with a slight smile curving his lips. "Good night, Sissy. I'll see you in the morning, ready to get back to work. The run may be finished tomorrow."

"Good night," she called after him. "Be a good boy tonight, Finn. Don't lift the covers with bean farts."

She heard Ben chuckling as he closed and latched the coop door. Then he climbed into the truck after his dog. Sissy stood on the porch to watch them drive away. Today had been incredible. She was so glad now that she'd taken a gamble and gone with him to the waterfall. How wonderful would it be if he asked her to go again before the weather turned too cold?

The thought jolted Sissy back to reality. She had created a good life for herself. According to Ma Thomas and Marilyn, she had greatly increased the business since her aunt's death. Plus, she was starting to make a few friends and felt a little more self-confident each day. The people of Mystic Creek were embracing her with warmth and welcome, making her feel as if she was safe inside a small butterfly cocoon. Maybe she would emerge a beautiful blue like the butterflies at the falls.

She liked Ben. Today she'd managed to relax with him, trust him to a degree, and enjoy his company. But what if it was all a front? Men, in her experience, could be devious chameleons who pretended to be whatever they thought you wanted them to be until you let your guard down and gave them an opportunity to pounce. Every single time a guy had approached her with seemingly innocent intentions, the end result had been extremely unpleasant. How many times did she have to learn that lesson?

Ben seemed to be a wonderful guy. But Sissy had gleaned from experience that when a man seemed too good to be true, he probably was.

Chapter
SIX

As Ben drove toward home, he presented a question to his damp, stinky dog. "So, what do you think, pal? Does she have potential, or should I run like hell?"

Finn barked, the sound laced with excitement.

"Yep. She definitely likes you. That's a huge plus. She'd never kick you outside and make you sleep in a doghouse in the dead of winter."

Finn rumbled low in his chest.

"I know. The very thought ticks you off, but the truth is, most of the women I've dated had no great fondness for dogs, horses, or cows. Sissy's different. She truly likes you, and did you see how she acted with the large animals? And she didn't even get in a grump when she got horse-shit all over her shoes."

Ben sighed as he rounded a curve in the road. "Do you know how good it felt to spend the whole day with a woman who isn't prissy about everything? She didn't get mad when I splashed her with cold water." He fell silent. "I know. I'm a devious bastard. I shouldn't have tested her that way. But most of the gals I've been out with wouldn't have gone wading in the first place— unless they did it to impress me. And I'm tired of all the games. After the first shock from the cold water, Sissy just laughed and gave back as good as she got." He nodded as if Finn had responded. "That's an excellent point. Nobody can get doused with ice water and not show her true colors, even if it's only for an instant. She isn't putting on an act, only to reveal an ugly side later. What we saw today is the real Sissy." Ben glanced at his dog, and then reached over to ruffle his ears. "You make a great sounding board. Never mind that you can't really answer me. You help me reason my way through things all the same. I think I've finally found someone who suits me to a T. That means I need a game plan, pal, because I don't think she's looking for a man in her life."

The following morning, when Ben went into the Cauldron for breakfast, Sissy had no customers. Dumb ass that he was, he'd expected them to pick up where they'd left off last night, joking around, laughing, and enjoying each other's company. But, no. Sissy was back in her silent-treatment mode, serving him with such politeness and professionalism that he wanted to grit his teeth.

In an attempt to start a conversation, he said, "So, how's it going with your ghost?"

He hoped to get a laugh out of her, but instead she frowned. "No news on that front."

His radar pinged. Sissy was a rotten liar, which in his books was another fine trait for him to admire.

He gave up on scintillating conversation and applied himself to his meal. When he'd cleared his plate, she emerged from the kitchen to collect it.

"Seeing the falls was fabulous—a day off won't occur for me for another three years, most likely. Thank you for taking me."

Ben's heart sank. Her cool tone told him everything—and nothing. She piled the plate with his mug, napkin, and flatware. "It was a rare treat," she added.

Ben stood and reached for his wallet. Then he laughed. "That breakfast was so good I forgot I don't have to pay." He returned the bifold to his hip pocket. "Well, back to work. I'll have the new run finished by tomorrow night. I know it seems like it's taking forever, but burying wire all around it to prevent predators from digging under is time consuming."

Ben sauntered out through the shadowy storage rooms and into bright sunlight. He paused for a moment to let his eyes adjust. He felt deflated. Disappointed. He'd dated so many women. Normally, when it was over, for him it was just over. But with Sissy, he felt sad. He felt almost certain she was everything he'd been looking for, but until she gave him signals that she felt the same way, he'd be nuts to wade in over his head emotionally.

Still lecturing himself, Ben resumed work. He was stretching lengths of wire around the run when Sissy suddenly appeared. She'd pulled off the white coverall, which allowed him to see how her snug jeans skimmed over her hips and nipped in at her waist. Her top, the color of sliced peaches, revealed small, perfectly shaped breasts and slender flanks. Looking into her wide blue eyes, he decided that she had no idea how beautiful she was. She wore no makeup that he could detect. Her short hair was tousled, a style that com-plemented her delicate features and heart-shaped face. He imagined she'd look just as cute when she crawled out of bed in the morning.

"Hey," he said.

She gestured at the construction material. "I, um—What you said about mistakes we make? I've got only a couple of hours, but I'd like to help out here to correct the one I made. My chickens deserve at least that much from me."

Ben looked at her birds milling around in the tiny run with barely enough room to move. She followed his gaze. "It's awful, isn't it? I'd plead ignorance, but that's no excuse."

Ben needed to hear nothing more. "I can sure use a couple of extra hands, but I'd prefer them to be protected ones." He held up one of his, displaying a well-worn leather glove. She reached back and tugged a pair of gardening gloves from the waistband of her jeans. He smiled. "Good. You came prepared. Having someone to help hold the wire down while I cover it with dirt will be awesome."

So much for keeping my distance, he thought. But then he looked on the bright side. If Sissy helped him, she might grow more relaxed around him again.

He immediately noticed that she was observant and tried to grab things for him before he needed them. Only he didn't expect her to lift the gigantic rolls of wire and place them at strategic points around the run.

"Um, Sissy, those are way too heavy for you."

Already red in the cheeks, she huffed for breath. "Maybe I can just drag 'em."

"To drag them, you still have to lift one end." Ben figured each roll probably weighed almost as much as she did. Well, possibly nowhere close, but it was awkward weight. "I don't want you to hurt yourself," he said. "You have a café to operate."

He half expected her to argue. A number of younger women he'd met seemed to be on a mission to prove they could do anything a man could, and then some. But Sissy only dropped the wire and said, "I could figure out a way to move them without hurting myself, but that'd be a waste of time. So what can I do?"

Good on you, he thought. *That's plain common*

sense. "You can put boards down around the run. As I'm burying wire, their weight will help anchor it. When you've finished with that, I'll think of something else."

She went to work. By the time she finished, Ben was sweating, and he wasn't convinced it was from exertion. Earlier he'd noticed Sissy's stunned expression when she'd seen him out here without a shirt. Uncertain whether he'd read her right, he decided, since he was sweltering, that it couldn't hurt if he enacted a replay. He tugged off his shirt and slung it over the tailgate. When he turned to walk back, he caught Sissy gaping at him. Their gazes locked. The air between them sizzled with awareness. For what seemed like an interminable time, they both stood frozen in place.

And then Ben broke the spell by grinning. The ice queen had the hots for him. She hadn't averted her eyes quickly enough. He wanted to jab his fist into the air and let out a whoop of victory. Instead he went back for his shirt, put it on, and faced her again with the front hanging open.

"Is this better?" He hoped he looked innocent. Judging by her expression, he'd failed miserably.

Her face turned as scarlet as a candied apple. "I don't care if you parade around naked," she snapped. "It's the new millennium. Do what you want."

Ben wiped the smile from his face. He hated

people who gloated. It was enough to know that she was as attracted to him as he was to her.

Sissy enjoyed working with Ben. She just made sure she didn't look at him from his belt buckle up. Or from there down, for that matter. He was gorgeous. If he'd been an ice-cream cone, she would have licked him all over while he melted. Only he wasn't, and it was uncharacteristic of her to think about a man that way. She was Sissy Bentley, the ragamuffin girl who'd never attended the same school long enough to make good grades or any friends. As a teenager, she'd had her head in the clouds for a brief while, thinking that this boy or that one liked her. But her gullibility had died a swift death in a swank sports car parked out in the middle of a cow pasture. Now, in her mid-twenties, she had to keep her head on straight. No matter how nice Ben seemed or how attractive he was, or how much she enjoyed being around him, she'd be foolish to forget the hard lessons life had taught her.

She'd made her mistakes, and she would never repeat them. It embarrassed her that Ben had caught her staring at his body. Oh, well. She'd never make that mistake again, either.

She was no longer the poor girl who'd been the daughter of the town drunk in so many states that she'd long since lost count. Maybe she'd never mesh well with people like the Sterlings,

but she'd climbed out of the gutter and left her worthless parents far behind. After working long hours in the café, she'd taken online courses to perfect her math and spelling. Over time, she'd built up the clientele so much that even her customers noticed. She wasn't about to let a man set her off course with silly notions about an idyllic future with him.

That wasn't her dream, not because a small part of her didn't wish for true love and happy endings, but because experience had taught her that neither of those things actually existed. She had only one thing she could count on and believe in, and that was herself.

Christopher Doyle ate dinner at four thirty every afternoon. He was so punctual that Sissy knew the time without looking at a clock. Doyle was beyond being merely old. At one time, he had apparently been extremely tall, but now his fragile body had crumpled, hunching his back so that his face was parallel with the floor as he inched along, using a cane to keep his footing. He had a thick head of snow-white hair, equally white eyebrows that rested above his sunken blue eyes like hedges in need of shearing, and a skeletal face over which crepey and pale skin hung like wet, puckered chiffon to gather in a wrinkled pouch under his pointed chin. His shirt looked as if it was draped over a wire coat hanger, so thin were his shoulders.

He ordered one of three menu selections every night, and he never varied from them. On rare occasions, he'd have dessert, which had to be, without exception, apple pie à la mode. At precisely five o'clock, he asked Sissy to box what remained of his meal. He claimed that he finished the food at seven while he watched a rerun of *Bonanza*, which he seemed to believe was a recently produced series.

Sissy had become so fond of Christopher. Today he remained true to habit. He ordered meat loaf. Sissy knew he wanted the same old, same old, but she always offered him the side choices. And he always frowned in contemplation, as if he might, for once, have a salad or peas instead of corn. She believed making the choice was one of the highlights of his day, and even though she could have served him what he wanted without ever asking, she didn't want to deprive him of the ritual.

"Coffee?" she offered.

"No, dear. One cup in the morning is all I can handle. Just water, please."

Sissy got him served. He always sat in the same booth, taking up a spot that could have seated four. But he left early, so she didn't mind. She put a glass beside his plate and filled it with chilled water, making sure no ice spilled over. Christopher liked his *agua* straight up.

"What is that?" he asked, his rheumy gaze fixed on something behind Sissy.

She turned to find Finnegan behind her. The pup wagged his tail, getting his entire body into the action and looking up at her with eager expectation. "Oh, *dear*. His name is Finnegan. He belongs to Ben Sterling."

"Fine family, the Sterlings. They go way back in this town." He studied the dog. "He's a handsome young fellow. The name Finnegan suits him. But what is he doing in here?"

That was a good question. Sissy said, "Ben is building me a new chicken run and coop. I feed Finnegan scraps out on the porch, and I think he's hungry again."

Christopher treated Sissy to a wondering look. "Are the two of you sparking?"

"Are we what?"

The old man wiggled his shoulders and pumped his elbows as if he were doing the cha-cha. "Sparking. You know. Ben isn't spoken for, and so far as I know, neither are you."

"Dating, you mean?" Sissy was appalled that Christopher thought that. "Oh, *no*. I'm paying Mr. Sterling to do the work."

A frown brought the white hedges above Christopher's eyes together in an unruly line. "But Ben Sterling is well-heeled. If he isn't courting you, why on earth would he be here doing unskilled labor?"

Sissy could think of no answer, so she avoided replying by scolding Finnegan in a friendly way. "You aren't supposed to be in here, silly boy! Come away. Come on!" She seized the dog's collar. "It's against the law."

As Sissy led Finn away, Christopher called out, "Who's going to report you? Definitely not me. I like dogs. They behave better'n a lot of people."

Sissy got Finn back out on the porch and fetched him some meaty leftovers. Ben glanced up from his work. "Don't tell me he went inside," he called out.

Sissy remembered his warning about not telling him when Finn did something wrong. "Okay, I won't."

She ducked back into the building and left Ben to figure it out by himself.

Sissy set her alarm for an hour earlier than usual the following morning in order to have her lunch prep done before she opened the café for breakfast. That would free up some of the midmorning for her to work outside with Ben. It wasn't because she wanted to spend time with him, she assured herself, but because Ben's story about the horse he'd nearly killed with cheap hay had touched her, and she believed he was right about rectifying mistakes instead of feeling guilty for making them. Regrets accomplished nothing.

Over the course of the day, Sissy worked

harder and longer than she had in ages, but in the doing, she began to learn Ben's rhythm and could soon anticipate what he might need her to do next. They were a great team, and as they made progress, she was amazed by how nice the run was. Ben constructed angled walls to connect the run to the tiny coop, which would soon be four times larger.

When it was finally done, Sissy walked its perimeter, amazed by its size. "It's absolutely *huge!* And I doubt even maelstrom winds could flatten it."

Grinning, Ben opened the run door to step inside. As he ripped up T-posts and tossed the wire of the former run into a pile, her hens squawked and ran in small circles until they realized their world had just been greatly expanded. They emitted questioning sounds as they explored their new boundaries. Watching them, Sissy got tears in her eyes.

"If you put them in the coop before dark, they'll be as safe as can be. Nothing can dig under the fence, and I doubt even a raccoon can get over the top barrier."

Sissy lifted her gaze to admire the panels that sloped outward to stop any creature that tried to climb the wire. It reminded her of the barbed wire atop prison fences, only this had been constructed to keep things out instead of in. "A monkey could swing over," she said.

Ben laughed. "Thank goodness monkeys aren't indigenous to the area."

"It's fabulous, Ben." Sissy meant it with all her heart. A lot of men would have thought, *It's only a chicken run*. But Ben was a perfectionist. If he turned his hand to work, he'd do it right or not at all. "Now I can't wait to see what the new coop will be like."

"I'll have you over for dinner some night after the café is closed and turn on the yard lights so you can see mine. It's not as large as yours will be, but the construction will be similar."

Cajoled by the friendly exchanges between them, Sissy floated on the moment, imagining a quiet dinner with him at his home. In her mind's eye, she even saw lighted candles on the table between them. They'd enjoy easy conversation over the meal, and then maybe he'd take her hand, and . . .

She jerked her thoughts back to reality so fast her muscles snapped taut. A cold, hard knot took up residence in the pit of her stomach.

Ben, who apparently noted the expression on her face, cocked his head. "Did I say something to offend you?"

Sissy started to shake her head no, but then she decided to nip this in the bud before her common sense oozed out her ears and romantic idiocy took over. "It's just that you should know right up front that I'll never have dinner at your house."

He arched a golden eyebrow. "Oh? I guess you didn't like my horses and cows as much as I thought."

Sissy shook her head. "I loved meeting your horses and cows. They're delightful."

He frowned. "Okay. So why will you never have dinner at my place?"

"It's nothing personal. I just don't do men. Ever."

After Sissy went inside to cook, Ben mulled that over. What did she mean, she didn't do men? Was she trying to tell him that her preferences ran to women? What a load of crap. She sent out signals to him whenever they were together. Maybe—probably—she didn't realize that, but she did. Women who were attracted only to other women didn't electrify the air when they were near a man.

He didn't know what her game was, but he wasn't going to play. She could tell herself whatever she liked, but she was attracted to him, and the evening would come when she did join him at his table for dinner. Afterward, he'd take her for a tour of his chicken facilities. Then he would treat her to dessert—which would not be served in a dish. Oh, no. When he offered her the taste experience of a lifetime, it would be a long kiss that would curl her toes, and she would receive it while lying in his bed.

Chapter
SEVEN

Over the next week, Ben tracked Sissy's schedule and made sure his own allowed him as much time alone with her as possible. She resisted being around him, except when she helped outdoors. Even then she averted her gaze and often spoke in monosyllables. Given that he knew she found him attractive, her reluctance to be too friendly reminded him of a comment his brother Barney, who'd served in law enforcement for years, had once made about Sissy, that she possessed "old eyes." In Barney-speak, that meant she had gained wisdom from her life experiences, which probably hadn't been pleasant. Ben now agreed with the assessment. She'd been through hell at some point, and it had left her unwilling to trust anyone easily. Especially men. He couldn't help but wonder how many bad experiences she had endured to become so set on remaining single. That was a story he hoped to hear someday.

After he ate dinner each night, which he usually finished about the time Sissy's café was emptying of diners, she always came out to help him tidy up the construction site. On most jobs, Ben put away only his tools, but he couldn't leave debris strewn on the ground behind a café where customers might trip and get hurt.

Because it was now often cold after the sun went down, Sissy had started bringing out a thermos of coffee and two mugs to warm them up during breaks. Ben enjoyed those moments with her. He'd lean against the dropped tailgate of his truck, wrap his hands around a mug as if to absorb the heat, and gaze at the sky with her. The mulberry moon had cycled away to a half sphere, no longer posing any threat of love forever after, but he liked to think, since it was still September, that the shimmery light might sprinkle a little magic over them. He'd been hoping that if it got cold enough she'd invite him inside, but that hadn't happened.

Sissy especially admired the night sky when it was still illuminated by a fading sunset, streaked with frothy pink and crimson. More than once she'd wished aloud that she could duplicate on canvas the gorgeous colors and the black silhouettes of towering pine trees cast against deep indigo and starlight.

Ben, entranced by the melodious caress of her voice, wished that she'd admire the sky a little less and him a little more. He also yearned for her to talk about herself. He was curious about her aunt Mabel. Ben knew Sissy had never met the woman. But why? His folks kept in touch with relatives. It was bewildering that Sissy had grown up without ever meeting her mom's sister. And why would a middle-aged woman who surely hadn't expected to kick the bucket in her forties have already made out a will and left all her worldly possessions to a niece she didn't know?

Another thing that really bugged Ben was that Sissy rarely mentioned her parents or referred to any siblings. He knew that her mom was dead, so he assumed that her father was possibly gone as well. But that didn't explain her silence about both of them. He toyed with the idea that she'd disliked her folks, but that didn't gel for him because Sissy wore her mother's mood ring. It was clearly a possession she treasured.

One evening as he nearly moaned over the taste of Sissy's fabulous pot roast, which even Christopher Doyle ate instead of his usual order when it was available, he said, "This *has* to be a family recipe. My mom's is fabulous, but *this* is extraordinary."

Sissy's cheeks went pink. "Well, it's a family recipe, I suppose. When I first came here, I found it in Aunt Mabel's recipe box."

"Ah." Mild disappointment settled over Ben. "Well, it's amazing."

She leaned closer to whisper, "The secret is simple. I poke slits in the roast and stick in slices of garlic along with dribbles of concentrated onion juice before I roll it in flour and brown it. That's what makes the flavor pop."

Ben took heart that she'd gotten near enough as she spoke for him to feel her breath on his cheek. It smelled faintly of butterscotch, making him wonder if she'd been savoring a piece of candy. Gazing at her lips, he wished he could steal a quick taste of her mouth—just a quick, not-so-casual tongue dive into those moist pink depths.

Collecting his wayward thoughts, he said, "I'll bet your mom left you some great recipes, too, huh?"

She drew away and gave him a sharp look. "My mom's specialty was making meals on the cheap. I grew up eating canned chili soup, undiluted, mixed into noodles." Her tone was crisp, clearly indicating that the subject was closed.

Watching her walk away, Ben was left with the impression that she'd regretted telling him that as soon as she finished the sentence. Why was she so secretive about her parents? Ben talked about his own; they were an integral part of his life and came up in casual conversation.

He decided knowing more about her parents didn't matter. It was Sissy he cared about, and though it might have been wishful thinking on his part, she seemed more relaxed in his company than she had been since their picnic at the falls. She also praised his work, not effusively, but with sincerity.

Each day Ben accomplished more on the back-yard project. Now that the wing was framed in, he'd be finished soon. After that, he'd still need to build roosts, nesting boxes, and dust-bath bins, but he could finish those in short order. He tried to console himself with the thought that Sissy would still owe him four meals a day for another two weeks after the whole project was finished, but he would miss working with her out back. It was during those times that she was more likely to let down her guard and reveal things about herself.

On the evening that Ben completed the job, frustration warred with regret. He'd gotten exactly nowhere with her. Thinking hard, he bought himself two more days of working with Sissy by suggesting that she needed a leakproof storage shed, similar to Marilyn's, where she could keep chicken supplies.

"Won't a shed be costly to build? How much do I already owe you for building supplies?"

Ben had lost track of all the expenditures, and he had thrown away the receipts. He didn't want Sissy to pay for everything. Though she might never know it, the coop and run were mostly his gift to her. "Oh, I, um—well, last count, you were in for about three hundred."

"That's *all?*" She took in her chicken compound. "How much of this stuff was leftover material from your place that you wanted out of your way?"

"A lot of it. But I also got a heap of stuff at

ReStore." Ben didn't like lying to her, but he'd be even less happy about making her cough up three grand. His savings account was still in great shape, and hers wouldn't be after a drain like that. "Oh," he added, snapping his fingers. "I forgot the gravel delivery. You owe me for that, so you're in for about three fifty."

"And a shed will cost about—?"

"Oh, I don't know." Ben pretended to be mentally calculating the expenses. "If we go with a dirt floor, not that much. Maybe five hundred? Roofing material is costly, but I've got a pile of corrugated metal out at my place that I'd like to get rid of. Using it here will save me hauling it to the dump."

"A shed would be really nice. And I can afford that much more. How long do you think it'll take you?"

"Two days, max. No wiring for electricity, no insulation or interior walls."

She nodded. "So, giving you two days of free meals for every eight hours you work, I'll owe you four more days of free food."

On Ben's side, that meant four more days in her company. "It's a deal."

She smiled, held out her hand, and they shook on it.

The next morning when Ben arrived earlier than usual at Sissy's with materials to erect her shed, he couldn't tell who loved the new coop and run more, the chickens or their owner. Sissy was inside the structure when he got out of the truck, and while he was unloading supplies she toured the interior of the shelter at least three times, yelling through the walls to Ben that a family of three could live in there. When she emerged into the run, she spun in a circle, holding her arms wide. Thin early sunlight glinted in her hair, making him catch his breath.

"Seriously, I've lived in dinky houses with yards a third this size! It's amazing. These are the luckiest chickens in the world now!"

Although he worked as slowly as possible without actually stopping, it seemed to Ben that the shed went up faster than the speed of light. As he hung the door that last evening, he felt glum. He consoled himself with the thought that he could still look forward to nearly two and a half weeks of free meals at the Cauldron, but he also accepted that he'd enjoy less time in Sissy's company. Inside the café, she tended to avoid him. Sometimes he felt sure she invented tasks in order not to chat with him. She had the talent for discouraging men down to a fine art that smacked of long practice.

Sissy thanked God that Ben would no longer be working behind her café. Granted, she'd still have to see him four times a day for over two weeks when he came in to eat, but once that was over, her part of their bargain would be fulfilled. She could barely wait. Being around Ben put her totally off balance and filled her head with silly fantasies. Hooking up with a guy was not in her game plan, especially with a man like Ben.

The night the shed was completed, he came in for dinner just as her last evening customer departed. She couldn't help but wonder if he'd timed his entrance to catch her alone. She recalled seeing him without a shirt. As the image flashed through her mind, her mouth went dry and her stomach clenched. A lot of men would kill to possess a sculpted torso like that, and an equal number of women would go to almost any lengths to run their hands over it. Sissy told herself she was not one of them, but she knew she was lying to herself. Even worse, she knew she was putting herself in a perilous situation by trying to believe it. No way around it, she had a bad case of the hots for Ben Sterling, and sooner or later, the temptation would be too much for her to resist. The sooner she got rid of him, the better.

As she served him his order, a bacon cheese-burger with a jumbo order of seasoned fries, he asked, "So, how are things going with your ghost?"

Sissy wasn't about to admit that there had been countless incidents that made her skin crawl. "My ghost? It's been pretty calm around here on that front."

His amber gaze rested on her face so long that she struggled not to squirm. Whenever Ben studied her, she felt as if he looked too deep and saw too much. "Well, I'm glad. Some mornings, you still have shadows under your eyes. I thought maybe you were losing sleep."

Sissy caught the inside of her cheek between her teeth to stop herself from spilling the truth. She no longer questioned whether or not she had a ghost; she felt certain she did. Her only consolation was that no harm had been inflicted on her.

"Oops!" she cried. "It's time to take my quiche out of the oven!"

In truth, she had no quiche baking, but from where Ben sat, the wall below the pass-through window blocked his view. She grabbed oven mitts and pretended to remove a delicate dish from one of the racks.

"Boy, it sure smells good. Can you spare some for me?"

Sissy sent him a suspicious look through the opening. Did he *know* she hadn't made quiche? He couldn't possibly smell it. Thinking fast, she said, "I'm sorry. I like to let it sit before I cut it. Nothing worse than quiche that goes flat in the center."

Ben's dimple flashed. "That's fine. I wouldn't want it to fall."

He knows. Sissy took refuge in the walk-in

cooler. He *knew* she was making up reasons not to talk with him. Now what was she going to do? Her face burned with embarrassment even as the rest of her body grew chilled from the frigid temperature. She hugged herself, hoping he'd take the hint and leave if she stayed in there long enough. Soon, not even her cheeks felt hot.

After glancing at her new watch, a gift from Ma Thomas when she had them on sale in her shop, Sissy waited a full ten minutes. The walk-in was so well insulated that she could hear nothing through its thick walls. Ben had surely left by now. She finally opened the door and stepped out, only to find him loading the mountains of dinner plates on the kitchen counter into one of the dish-washers.

"There you are," he said with a lady-killer grin that she felt certain he practiced in front of a mirror. "I was about to come looking for you. It has to be colder than a witch's tit in there."

Sissy wanted him out of her kitchen, but short of bodily removing him, she couldn't think how to accomplish that. "How cold is a witch's tit? Are you speaking from personal experience?"

"No personal encounters. I try to avoid witches." He bent to place another plate in the rack. "But it stands to reason, doesn't it? A witch flies around on a broom on the last night of October. Here in Mystic Creek, parents wear double layers to take their kids trick-or-treating. How cold do you think her tits might get?"

Hiding the shivers that tried to vibrate her body, Sissy rubbed her arms. "Pretty cold." She watched him reach for another stack of plates. "What do you think you're doing?"

"Helping you out." He paused to study her face. "You've got shadows under your eyes again. If I speed things up for you in the kitchen, maybe you'll get a little more rest tonight. If your ghost keeps quiet, that is."

"I told you my ghost hasn't done anything lately."

He settled a twinkling gaze on her. "But I can tell when you're lying. Has anyone ever mentioned that you're lousy at it? There's a little spot right on the tip of your nose that turns bright red every single time."

What a wonderful compliment. He made her sound like Rudolph's twin. Sissy couldn't think what to say. She resisted the urge to cup her hand over her nose, though. That was something.

"So," he went on, "if you're lying, it follows that your ghost is still wreaking havoc and making you lose sleep, thus the circles under your eyes. And, since I don't have anything better to do, I may as well help you knock this out so you can go to bed and get a full eight."

"I have breakfast prep to do as well. You can't help with that."

"Why not?"

155

"Because it involves food preparation, and *you* don't cook."

"Where'd you get the idea I don't cook?" He lifted a bowl from the sudsy water in the sink and scratched his nose with the side of his wrist, leaving a cluster of bubbles over the cleft of his upper lip. He looked so cute that she almost smiled. "I'm actually a great cook."

"So why do you eat out all the time?"

"Because cooking for one leaves me with heaps of leftovers, and I get tired of the same thing, day after day. I grew up in a big family, and I can't master the art of making small amounts." He winked at her. "Don't worry. Just show me what to do, and we'll have the breakfast prep finished before you can holler, 'Howdy.' "

Sissy didn't need a crystal ball to see that he wasn't going to leave on his own steam. Short of ordering him off the premises, she was stuck with him, and he'd been so good about the coop and shed that she couldn't bring herself to be that rude.

"I don't appreciate being called a liar."

He winced. "You're right. It's an insult. I'm sorry. Let me rephrase that and say that you avoid telling me the truth."

She sighed and grabbed two fresh chef coats. "If you're going to handle food, you have to wear a sterile garment over your street clothes. Health regulations."

The chef coat barely fit him. But he managed to squeeze into it and tie the sash. The sleeves were tight around his muscular arms and shoulders.

As Sissy began working in tandem with him to finish the cleanup, she thought of Finn shivering on her porch. "While you're being Mr. Helpful, your poor dog is outside freezing." She set her coverall aside. "I'm going to get him."

Wrist-deep in dishwater, he called, "What about the health regulations?"

"Screw the regulations. I'm not leaving him out there. His fur isn't thick enough yet to protect him, and he's my friend."

"And I'm not?"

Sissy kept walking, pretending she hadn't heard him. Tonight he seemed determined to be pushy for the first time since she'd met him. And even if she had come to think of him as a friend—which she had, in a way—she would not, even under threat of death, admit that to him.

Later, when the breakfast prep was done, Ben jotted his cell phone number on a tablet by her cash register. "For just in case."

"For just in case of what?" Sissy didn't want his cell number. It felt all wrong.

"Well, if anything weird happens tonight, you'll know how to get in touch with me. My home number is in the book, but if you're upset, you may call my dad or one of my brothers by mistake." He gave her a thoughtful study. "It's

157

only my cell number, Sissy. Why does my writing it down upset you?"

Because he was referring to a ghost he didn't believe existed, and it felt too personal. It was another step forward in a relationship with him that she didn't want to have. She'd never had an *actual* relationship, but what she had experienced was the role-playing boys or men would resort to in order to get in her pants, an ugly term, but boiled down, only *ugly* defined it. *Hey, Sissy, you're too small to carry so many books. Let me carry them for you.* Paybacks always followed favors. And later, believing a football star, the son of the town mayor, really and truly liked her? That had been a mistake she would never forget.

Well, she wasn't that naive girl anymore. She wasn't the daughter of the town drunk now. She'd left all that behind her. She'd worked until she nearly dropped in her tracks to become *somebody*. Ben might have two college degrees, but his education had been handed to him. She'd had to scrabble her way up from poverty and educate herself. Now she could take a recipe for four and calculate, without writing it all down, how to make that recipe to feed forty. And her increase in patrons was visible proof that she'd done it right. In her own way, she had acquired an education, too, and become a successful businesswoman.

Deep down, she wanted to trust Ben. She even wished they could be friends. He was, without question, the nicest guy she'd ever met. Or at least he seemed to be. But was she seeing the real Ben? She loved this town. She couldn't gamble with the respect and position she'd worked so hard to have there. If she fell for Ben and he dumped her, she'd look like an idiot.

Tears burned at the backs of her eyes. Tears she would never let him see.

"Sissy?" He said her name softly. "What is it, honey? I can see you're upset. Can you tell me about it? Maybe talking will help."

He had no right to call her *honey,* and a master's degree in how to avoid men and sticky entanglements might help her, but nothing Ben said ever would. The males of her species were driven by testosterone, not emotion, and when it came to the life she'd built for herself there, she couldn't be an idiot and trust him. Granted, he wasn't after a quick, hard attack in the bushes or a car to get what he wanted. He wanted to play house for a while, pretending they had something special, and then end it, making her look like the stupid tramp her father had always deemed her to be. "I'm fine, Ben. Thanks for leaving your number. I'll probably never need it, but thank you for being so thoughtful." Try as she would, she couldn't make her tone gracious.

Evidently he got the message, because the soft look went out of his eyes. He circled the bar to fetch his Stetson. As he settled it on his head, he said, "It was fun helping tonight. Thanks for not giving me the boot." He snapped his fingers to awaken a snoozing Finnegan. "Come on, pal. Let's make tracks so Sissy can hit the sack."

Sissy listened to Ben and Finn leave the building. Her throat felt as though steel fingers were digging in over her larynx. The tears that she'd held in check filled her eyes, blurring her vision. *Damn him, damn him,* she screamed inwardly. *I'm in danger of falling in love with him, and I can't let that happen. He wants only one thing from me. That's all they ever want. Before I give it to him, I'll go to the Shady Lady and buy a damned vibrator.*

Sissy dashed the tears from her cheeks, snapped her shoulders straight, and lifted her chin. She wouldn't blubber over a man as if her heart were breaking. That would be too stupid for words. He couldn't change who he was, and she couldn't change, either. She had to get her priorities straight and be sensible.

The first steps toward that were to lock all the doors, turn off the lights, and go to bed. If he tried to hang around tomorrow night after her diners left, she *would* give him the boot. For the next two weeks, she'd honor her end of their bargain and feed him. But beyond that, she owed him nothing.

Ding-a-ling. Ding-a-ling-dong. Sissy moaned, pulled her pillow over her head, and wondered what insane person would ring her doorbell before daylight. She rolled, wrapping herself in sheets and blankets like a mummy. It felt so warm, and her pillow was plumped just right under her cheek after the repeated fist poundings she'd given it during the night. The doorbell fell quiet. *Oh, yeah.* She drifted happily back into blackness. *Ding-a-ling. Ding-a-ling-dong.* Her eyes popped back open. It was her cell phone, set to awaken her promptly at five each morning.

With a groan, she elbowed her way free from the tight embrace of blankets and ran to the kitchen, where she charged the device. Aching with weariness, she imagined how good it would feel to sleep for as long as she wanted. Cold air nipped under the hem of her nightshirt. She curled her toes against the icy laminated flooring. A dull ache throbbed in her temples, and she shivered.

Dimly she remembered all the loud noises that had interrupted her sleep during the night. "I hate you, Aunt Mabel!" Sissy rifled through bureau drawers for clean clothing, dashed to the bathroom to turn on the shower, and then ran to the living room to turn up the thermostat. To save money on power, she always turned the heat down to fifty at night. "You're a mean, cantankerous ghost! I'm not surprised you're hanging around here. I know where you're going now! Hell, that's where! I'd be postponing my journey there, too, if I were you!"

While brushing her teeth, Sissy grumped at her dead aunt each time she rinsed and spat. "You know how long my days are, you old biddy!" Swish, spew, scrub. "Why are you doing this to me? I'm exhausted! And it's all *your* fault!" Sissy wrenched off the tap and fumbled for a towel to blot her mouth. "I'll go bankrupt if I can't work. Your precious café will be sold during foreclosure and turned into a"—she paused to think of the worst scenario possible—"an adult sex store! How does *that* grab you? Porn magazines! Kinky toys. Sleazy movies with no plots! Instead of dining booths, there'll be soundproof closets where men will watch videos of female three-somes. Your bingo and church friends will jaywalk and risk being struck by cars rather than walk past the front door! And think of poor Marilyn! If people won't walk by this place, they'll stop shopping at her store. I know she was one of your best friends. *Everyone* likes Marilyn. If you don't leave me alone, you're going to be responsible for destroying her business and ruining her life!"

When Sissy checked the shower temp, it was still barely warm. She tapped her bare toe, impatient for the hot water to finally make its way upstairs. Then she stood under the spray and started to feel better. At least her head didn't ache now, and she could think straight. *I didn't mean it,* she apologized silently to her aunt. *You'll never know how grateful I am to you.* She gave herself a quick wash, rinsed, and grabbed her red bath towel from its hook. With a few quick rubs, she was dry.

Once downstairs with only the kitchen lights on, she went into the cooler and started grabbing items for lunch prep. Over the last week and a half, she had acquired the habit of doing that before breakfast rush so she could spend her midmornings helping Ben.

Ben. Her hand froze on a large bag of romaine lettuce. The work outside was finished now. She didn't need to make salad. Putting on her soup of the day could wait. No sandwiches had to be made in advance, so they'd be ready for the grill. She could resume her regular schedule and do this after the breakfast crowd left.

Sissy stood shivering, her mind riveted on how cozy and soft her bed had felt. She could have slept for another hour. Ben would be coming by today only for meals. Her routine at the café could return to normal.

With a sigh, she exited the cooler, her skin now ice-cold and clammy. Glancing around the kitchen, she made note of a half dozen chores she could do before breakfast. She'd let a few things slide while working with Ben. Her cupboards could stand to be reorganized and wiped clean. She could choose to be in a grump because she'd gotten up too early or be in a happy mood because the extra time could be put to good use.

The first thing she wanted to do was feed and water her chickens, mostly because she couldn't wait to see how they liked their new home now that they were settling in. She'd paid for the remodel and worked to make it happen as well. She went to the storage room, slipped on rubber boots, threw on her jacket, got her flashlight, and grabbed the treat bucket she now kept just inside the back door. Cold air blasted her in the face as she stepped out on the porch. Sliding her foot back and forth over the wooden planks, she tested for slickness and determined that, as frigid as it felt, the temperature hadn't dropped to freezing. She needn't worry about slipping and falling.

Torch beam bobbing, she walked to the chicken coop. Sissy smiled as she stepped inside the structure, the ceiling of which was now high enough for even Ben to stand erect. A heat lamp suspended from the ceiling held the chill of predawn at bay. The light didn't make it hot in the front area, which was good, but it did keep it pleasant.

This was the original coop area, barely recognizable now. Ben had installed gravity feeders. All Sissy had to do was top them off with fresh pellets each morning. In fact, Ben claimed that once Sissy invested in automatic waterers, she'd be able to leave for as long as three days without hiring anyone to feed her flock. More feeders graced a wall in the large wing addition.

Sissy filled the first bank of feeders, chatting with her hens and calling each by name. Well, with so many birds, she couldn't always tell for sure who was who, but she doubted the pullets took offense. As if the birds knew she was talking to them, they preened on their roosts and cackled back at her.

Sissy noticed a new layer of feathers littering the floor. Did all chickens lose that many when they weren't in molt? Studying the lineup of hens clustered abreast on the three horizontal roosts, Sissy noted nothing alarming. They looked healthy, if a little sleepy and disgruntled about having their rest disturbed, but she'd felt the same way when her alarm jerked her awake.

She moved into the huge new wing. The illumination of the ceiling heat lamps cast a soft golden glow over the large area. Sissy smiled as she trailed her gaze over the birds perched on the roosts, pleased that they now had plenty of space. *So beautiful,* she thought. She'd ordered a variety of breeds and loved the colorful assortment of plumage.

In her peripheral vision, she saw a black lump lying on the floor near the feeders. She turned, thinking Ben had forgotten a tool bag. But, no, it was a chicken.

"Silly you, still sleeping on the floor! You have a mansion now." Sissy walked over to the hen and bent low to give her a pat. Her fingertips met with cold, stiff hardness. Her heart caught. With a light push, she rolled the bird over. Its feet, frozen in death, remained flat against its breast. "No! Oh, no!" With a choked sob, Sissy drew the chicken into her arms. "What happened to you, sweet girl?" Tears filled her eyes. "Did you get sick? Did it get too cold in here?"

Sissy saw another lump on the floor, a reddish brown one. Then another—a white one. Still clutching the dead hen to her chest, she turned in a slow circle and saw possibly eight or a dozen other lumps on the floor. *Dead chickens.* She couldn't bring herself to count them. Dimly she registered that it wasn't cold enough to have killed the hens.

She screamed, dropped the dead hen, and ran, not allowing herself to look for more casualties.

Ben tipped the glass coffee carafe to refill his mug a second time. He enjoyed the quiet peacefulness of predawn. It was a span of minutes when the world around him hadn't yet awakened to greet the new day, and it gave him an opportunity to just *be*. He liked to sit at his kitchen table and let his mind wander as he sipped coffee.

Drawing in the steam from his coffee, he relaxed on the spindle-back kitchen chair and resumed staring at the darkness that huddled close against the window over the sink. *My time,* he thought, flexing his shoulders to awaken his muscles for the work that awaited him. He had no idea what the day might bring—and he didn't care. For now, he wanted to enjoy the sensation of being in a suspended dimension where no one existed but him.

His cell phone rang. The sound obliterated his sense of isolation. He briefly considered not answering. Who in his right mind dialed someone up at this hour? An automated telemarketing computer, possibly, but he was in no mood to interrupt his morning ritual by listening to a recorded message about a trip he'd just won.

Still, it could be important. A family emergency, maybe. Sighing, he drew the phone from his pocket and stared at the lighted screen. He didn't recognize the number and almost sent the call to voice mail. Then he remembered that his mom had gotten a new phone. She might have changed her number.

"Hello, this is Ben," he said.

"They're dying!" a woman shrieked.

Ben winced and moved the device an inch from his ear. "Who is this?"

"They're *dying,* Ben! I did something wrong! I fed them something bad. *Something!* At least twelve are dead!"

"Sissy? Is that you?"

He heard a sniff and gulp. "Yes. Yes, of *course* it's me! Who else do you know with chickens?"

"You need to calm down, honey."

"Calm *down?*" A strangled noise came over the air. "My babies are dying, right and left, and you tell me to calm down?" Her voice was so shrill it sliced through him like a well-honed knife. "Please, will you come? Please, Ben. Maybe you can do something before all of them die!"

Ben wasn't as confident in his ability to save the day as she was, but he could tell she might soon bypass mere panic and move into full-blown hysteria. "Of course I'll come. Are you in the coop?"

"No! I ran back into the café to get your cell number. Thank God I forgot to throw it away last night. Please hurry!"

She'd intended to throw his number away? That stung. "Listen, Sissy. Stay out of the coop. I'll be there as soon as I can. It's unlikely, but it could be avian flu." Ben had read recently about an isolated incident of bird flu in Crystal Falls, and off the top of his head, that was one of the things he could think of that might kill a number of chickens suddenly. Housed in that new insulated coop, the chickens couldn't have frozen to death, and they'd all looked fine to him yesterday. "I'm not familiar with avian flu—whether it's contagious to humans or not. Just to be safe, stay away from the flock until I can assess the situation."

"Oh, God! What's avian flu? Hurry, Ben. Please, please hurry!"

Chapter
EIGHT

Ben sent his truck hurtling through the predawn darkness, gripping the wheel so tight his fingers hurt. Ignoring stop signs on the deserted roads, he kept a sharp eye out for other vehicles. With any luck, if a cop spotted him bending the speed limit by over twenty miles an hour, it would be his brother Barney, and he could talk his way out of it. *As if.* Barney went by the book.

By the time he parked next to Sissy's coop, dawn was sending pale fingers over the mountains and lighting the valley. In the dim glow of the porch light, he saw Sissy waiting outside for him, her compact body huddled in a puffy jacket with her arms crossed over her chest. Her shoulders jerked with what he guessed were sobs.

He swung out of his truck with Finn trying to follow close on his heels. "Hey, Sissy!" he called out. "You stay there, okay?" Nearly shutting the door on the disappointed dog's nose, he started toward the coop and then stopped dead in his tracks as something occurred to him. "Did you pick up any of the dead chickens?"

She answered with a nod. He was too far away to see her face clearly, but he felt certain she was crying. *Damn.* It wasn't smart to love chickens. Sometimes they died young, the victims of predators, egg binding, and other things.

"Then go inside," he yelled. "Throw your jacket straight into the washing machine. Then scrub all your exposed skin with antibacterial soap. Okay? I know you're upset, but you have to protect yourself just in case they've got something contagious."

"Oh, Ben!" she wailed. "What if I fed them something that's killing them?"

"Chickens normally won't eat things that are bad for them." Ben's chest squeezed at the raw pain threading through her words. And what he'd just told her was mostly true, with his chickens, at least. "Whatever it is, I'm almost certain it isn't your fault. Go on, now. Clean yourself up, and hurry. Don't forget the antibacterial soap."

Sissy nodded, swiped her sleeve across her nose, and vanished into the building. For a second, all Ben could think of was the germs that she'd just rubbed against her mucous membranes. Then he forced himself to head toward the coop. With luck, whatever was killing the chickens wasn't contagious to humans.

In the front section, all the chickens looked fine. He stepped close to the roosts to get a better look. They still appeared to be in good health to him. Then he stepped into the new wing and stopped in his tracks. He counted fourteen dead chickens, and another one, huddled near the feeders, looked as if she might be dying. *What the hell?* Ben bent over a dead hen. He studied it and then rolled it over with the toe of his boot. *Nothing.* No sign of injury.

He quickly exited the coop and strode across the yard to the porch. Inside the building, he found Sissy in the laundry room, which was located in the back storage section. Drying her arms, she turned toward him. Her eyes looked red and swollen. She sniffed, swallowed hard, and asked, "Well, what killed them?"

Ben tried to ignore the quaver in her voice. "I don't know. I need some disposable gloves and a plastic garbage bag. I'm going to take one of the dead ones to the vet and let him make the diagnosis." He saw her soft mouth twist and quickly added, "Sissy, this isn't your fault. Trust me. If it was something you fed them, a whole lot more would be dead."

She walked to the kitchen, her posture stiff and her movements jerky. She plucked two disposable gloves from a box with a dispenser opening at the top. Then from under the sink she fetched a white garbage bag. Handing the items to Ben, she said, "It's so early. I doubt the vet's office is open."

Ben nodded. "It isn't. I'll seal the"—he nearly said *specimen,* but decided it was too impersonal —"the dead hen in the plastic bag and put her in the bed of my truck where she can't contaminate the cab. Then I'll go home and get my chores done before I go in. I'll call before eight and let them know I'm coming." He puffed air into a glove before stuffing his fingers into it. "I'm surprised you have these in my size. My mom says all the guys in our family have bear paws for hands."

"I keep boxes in all sizes." She shrugged her shoulders. "I bought them when I was still thinking about hiring help." A crease appeared between her finely drawn, dark eyebrows. "I should have had you wear some last night."

Ben drew on the second glove, wondering if she was in a mild state of shock. Her worrying right then about health regulations seemed off-kilter to him. "Next time, I'll be sure to ask for some. I did scrub up good, though, before I handled any food."

She stared at the plastic bag he held. "Wh-what should I do with all the other d-dead ones?" Her lower lip trembled, and it yanked his heart out.

"Look, don't worry about it. I'll take care of that. There's plenty of food and water for the rest of the chickens, so don't go back in there until we know what we're dealing with."

Tears welled in her big blue eyes. "But, Ben, I want to give them a proper burial. They're my little friends."

Ben thought of reminding her that the ground

beneath the surface was undoubtedly frozen and any grave would probably have to be chiseled out with a pick and shovel, but he took another look at her stricken expression and changed his mind. Aloud, he said, "Okay. If the vet says that's safe, I'll help you get it done."

At eight, Ben's truck was parked in front of the Caring Hands Veterinary Clinic. Because the vet tech, Cassidy Peck, didn't yet know what disease the bird might be carrying, Ben was admitted through the back door of the clinic and ushered into an examining room with all speed. An attractive young lady with black hair and gorgeous blue eyes, Cassidy greatly resembled her brother, Chris, who co-owned Peck's Red Rooster with his wife, Kim.

"I can bring you a cup of coffee," she offered before exiting the room.

"I'm fine. I already got my morning jolt of caffeine. Thanks."

After the door closed behind her, Ben laid the plastic bag on the examining table and sat on a straight-backed chair in the corner. He half expected to be left waiting for at least thirty minutes, but Jack Palmer surprised him by entering the room almost immediately. Ben stood.

A tall guy with light brown hair, gray eyes, and a winning smile, Jack wiped his palm on his white scrub coat and greeted Ben with a handshake. "When I did course work at university to treat birds, I thought I'd probably never need the knowledge." He laughed and jerked his head toward the lumpy bag on the table. "Living in Mystic Creek proved me dead wrong. I get parrots, canaries, and finches on a regular basis. No chickens, though. Most farmers around here just wring their necks if they get sick."

Ben nodded his understanding. "Could it be avian flu?"

Approaching the table as he pulled on a pair of gloves, Jack went from guy-next-door to professional and businesslike. "Let's not get ahead of ourselves. Have Ms. Bentley's chickens been exposed to wild waterfowl?"

Ben stepped closer. "I don't think so. There's that stream from Mystic Creek at the back of her property. I've been building her a new coop and run—been working on it for a couple of weeks. I haven't seen any ducks or geese, and this is the time of year when they're migrating. I don't think there's enough water to attract them." Ben paused. "A case of avian flu was reported in Crystal Falls. Do you think that's it?"

"Well, let me have a look to see what we're dealing with."

Tapping her toe, Sissy watched Blackie through the pass-through window as he finished his lunch with painstaking slowness. Ben had texted her to say that the death of her hen hadn't been her fault, the problem could be treated, and he'd fill her in on the details later. Blackie was the only midday diner left in the café, and she was eager to dash outside. She'd seen Ben's truck parked near her coop earlier when she'd gone into the storage area, so she knew he had returned from the vet and hopefully could tell her what was wrong with her feathered babies. It took all her self-control not to ask Blackie to hurry.

After what seemed like weeks, he pushed his dish away and drew out his wallet. His wavy black hair glistened in the overhead light. "That sure was a good burger, Sissy, and I'd love to know your seasoning secret for those fries."

Sissy hurried into the service area behind the counter. "I'd love to tell you, Blackie, but I have an emergency out back. Maybe tomorrow?"

His deep blue eyes filled with concern. "What emergency?"

"My hens are dying. I'm not sure why. Ben took one of the dead ones to the vet. When he texted me, he didn't tell me exactly what's wrong, only that it's treatable and to get out there to help him as soon as I can. I'm frantic to find out what's wrong."

"Oh, honey. I know how you love those pullets." He handed her his credit card. "Let me settle up with you, and I'll go out back, too. I've never raised chickens, but that doesn't mean I can't try to help."

Tears burned in Sissy's eyes. She'd grown so fond of Blackie. Apparently the feeling was mutual.

"I think I'll put up my CLOSED sign and lock the door." Sissy's voice twanged because her throat had tightened with the urge to cry. For her, tears were a sign of weakness, and she would be mortified if Blackie saw her lose control. "I don't know what we're dealing with, but your help will be appreciated."

After running Blackie's credit card, Sissy headed toward the kitchen to put his dishes into the machines. Behind her, she heard him say, "I'll head on out to see what Ben's up to."

"I'll be right there," Sissy called over her shoulder.

Minutes later when Sissy reached the backyard, she saw that Ben had already dug fourteen holes. The remains of her feathered friends lay in the depressions, as yet not covered with dirt. Ben wiped his sweaty brow with his shirtsleeve as he turned to face her. Even with dirty hands and dampness spotting his blue shirt, he looked fabulous, his sharply hewn features shiny with perspiration, his eyes, normally a shimmery amber, darkened with sadness for her.

"I figured you might want to say some words over each of them or throw the first handfuls of dirt, so we waited to fill in the graves." He bent his head, which was hatless. Normally he didn't remove his Stetson. She guessed that he had worked up such a sweat that he'd wanted to protect the felt. "The ground's frozen right beneath the surface, so it was hard digging and I didn't go very deep. But the vet says a few inches of dirt over them will do the trick."

"He used a pick and dug all the holes by himself," Blackie inserted.

Sissy avoided looking closely at the hens. "Thank you, Ben. It was thoughtful of you to wait until I could say good-bye." In truth, it was so thoughtful that it alarmed her. How could any woman in her right mind resist this guy? "I, um—I've been worried half to death. Has anyone else died? What does the vet think it is? And how do we treat it?"

Ben nodded, which didn't tell her much because she didn't know which question he was addressing. Then he cleared his throat. "When I checked a few minutes ago, no other chickens were dead, but a couple look mighty sick. It's a lice infestation, Sissy, the worst Jack's ever seen."

Her heart jerked. "*Lice?* But I try to keep the coop clean. It *was* my fault, wasn't it? Did they get it from overcrowding?"

"It was nothing you did. For now, can you just hold on to that thought and let me give you the details later? We've got to thoroughly dust all sixty-six remaining chickens with lice powder, and also treat their coop and run. It's going to be one hell of a job."

Blackie, standing just behind Ben, angled his neck to meet Sissy's gaze. "I'll help." He scratched behind his ear. Then he raked his nails back and forth over his scalp. "It's usually slow at my place now. People don't drop by to pawn anything until they get off work." He shrugged. "I planned to watch the Ducks game I recorded this weekend, but it'll wait."

Blackie was such a huge fan of the Oregon Ducks that he often wore hats and coats bearing the team's logo. Sissy forced a smile. "I hope they win."

Blackie scowled. "They didn't. Charlie Bogart came in and told me the score. He knows I have to record the games because I'm busy on weekends and that telling me who won always ruins it for me when I watch a game, but he does it every chance he gets! I wish I could gag him."

Ben laughed and then sobered, flashing Sissy an apologetic look. "Charlie does love football. Maybe that's why he started a sporting goods store."

Normally Sissy feigned an interest in football so Blackie could enjoy telling her about the plays, good or bad, made by his favorite team. But today she could muster no enthusiasm.

"Ben, did the vet say that all of my hens are—in danger of dying?"

Ben bent his head and kicked the dirt with the toe of his scuffed boot. He usually looked straight at her when he spoke, and that he wasn't doing so now warned her of what was coming. "The lice suck blood, and all the hens are severely anemic. A lot more of them could die. Maybe even all of them. The sooner we get these dead ones buried and start dusting hens, the better."

Sissy nodded and stepped over to the row of graves. She wanted to tell each hen good-bye and make up a silent prayer, but worry over her surviving pullets pressed her to hurry.

She felt a big hand settle over her shoulder. Warmth seeped through her shirt to penetrate her skin. She knew without looking that it was Ben who touched her. Ben, whose phone number she'd intended to throw away. Ben, who hadn't laughed when she told him about her ghost. Ben, who had worked so hard to create a proper home for her chickens. Tears filled her eyes. She decided one must have slipped over onto her cheek, because the grip of his fingers tightened a little, not enough to hurt, but just enough to say, *I'm here. I understand.*

"They're only chickens," she pushed out. "It's dumb to make a big fuss over this when the others need treatment. Just cover them with dirt."

"They were your pets," he replied, his voice gone gruff with what she suspected was emotion, not because he had loved the birds, but because he knew she had. "We at least need to say something over them. That won't take long."

Sissy had never learned to pray. Her father was agnostic or atheist. Her mom was a believer, but she'd never stood up to her husband and insisted on going to church. Sissy had never attended a single worship service. "I, um, don't have a clue what to say."

Ben kept his left hand on her shoulder and placed his other palm over his chest. "That's fine. I'll do it for you." He cleared his throat. "God, we know you love all the creatures you created, and Sissy particularly loved these birds. They had names, and they were her friends." He coughed, which made Sissy want to laugh and cry both at once. How many guys would try to pull off a reverent burial for a bunch of chickens? "Anyway, it's really hard for her to say good-bye. But we know there'll be a wonderful place for them in heaven where they can enjoy free range and lots of sunshine. And someday, when Sissy passes over, please let them be waiting for her at that—um—bridge. The bridge where pets wait for the people they love."

"The Rainbow Bridge," Blackie supplied from behind them. "It's a real place, honey. Those chickens will be waiting there, mark my words.

Just don't take off to meet them anytime soon. I'd miss your cheeseburgers something fierce."

Sissy did laugh then, even through tears. "Good-bye, little friends. Be happy until I get there." For Blackie, she added, "But that won't happen for a long, long time."

Ben and Blackie, manning shovels, filled in the small graves with dirt. Sissy stood at the end of the row, wishing she knew the words to a prayer. Instead, her silent plea was, *Please, God, love them for me. They were sweet little hens.*

Sissy checked to make sure she'd locked the front door of the café. Then she rushed upstairs to change into a long-sleeve cotton shirt that would protect her arms from the insecticide dust. When she went back outside, Ben and Blackie, with the sleeves of their shirts rolled down and buttoned, already wore white dust masks, which she guessed Ben had purchased somewhere. On the dropped tailgate of his pickup sat numerous white containers.

Blackie seemed nervous. He kept rubbing his shoulder or arm. Then he'd scratch his head. Ben apparently noticed it as well. "Blackie, I'm sorry. I forgot to tell you these lice don't stay on humans. Jack Palmer says we don't have to worry."

Blackie released a whoosh of breath that made his mask billow. "Now you tell me."

Ben turned and met Sissy's gaze as he handed her a mask. With the lower half of his face covered by the band of pleated white, his eyes seemed even more intense without his handsome features to detract from them. As she started to loop the elastic bands over her head, he added, "Cinch it in tight and make sure you squeeze the metal band over the bridge of your nose The less of this dust we breathe, the better."

Sissy had never dusted chickens, and she felt certain that Blackie hadn't, but Ben, shooing chickens back from the door, led the way into the coop and set the white containers on the floor. He turned to give them both instructions. Holding a container of dusting powder, he grabbed an unsuspecting hen from the upper-most roost and flipped her upside down. She shrieked and cackled. This sent every other hen in the front section airborne.

Blackie ducked and cried, "Holy shit!"

Sissy barely missed getting struck in the face by a terrified, feathery missile. Plumage flew as alarmed hens began squawking to one another about the invasion of two-legged marauders intent on committing murder and mayhem.

"It isn't going to be a walk in the park," Ben yelled, trying to be heard over the raucous cries. "But this is how it's done." He gave a quick demonstration.

Blackie, still dodging chickens in flight, was

dropping f-bombs as rapidly as a crazed fighter pilot during World War II. "How are we gonna know which ones we've dusted? We got lots of the same colors here."

"They'll look powdery," Ben yelled back. "When in doubt, dust again!"

Sissy led the way into the back wing, where countless other birds had flown into a panic. Ben had warned that dusting the hens wouldn't be easy, but Sissy had not envisioned a game of football tackle. The frightened chickens flapped. They squawked. They tried to hide. Blackie sprawled on his belly twice to catch his first two, and Sissy wasn't sure for whom she was more concerned: the man or the poor birds he was attacking.

Then she forgot everything but the job, catching and dusting her little friends in an attempt to save their lives.

She made a grab for Gizmo and missed. Gizmo sped for the other section of the coop with Sissy in hot pursuit. As she charged through the archway after her, Ben stepped into Gizmo's escape path. Sissy missed grabbing the chicken by the legs and rammed her head into Ben's belly. He went *oof.* The impact knocked Sissy to her knees. She lost her grip on the dust can, and it rolled across the floor to be lost in the floor-to-ceiling fog.

"Are you all right?" Ben grasped her shoulders

and lifted her to her feet. Stunned by the collision, Sissy couldn't focus on the question and
instead found herself marveling over his
strength. He'd plucked her up as if she weighed
no more than the feathers floating in the air.
"Sissy, talk to me. Did you hurt your neck? That
was a hard hit."

She blinked, trying to see him. She knew his
face had to be up there somewhere. All she saw
at first were impact stars, and then dust and
floating feathers. When she finally located his
features, she smiled behind her mask. He was
white. Even his hair was covered. He looked
like a snow sculpture of a cowboy who'd lost his
hat.

"I'm fine." She drew back a step. "Did I hurt
you?"

The corners of his eyes crinkled, making
shadowed creases in the powder. She knew
without seeing his mouth that he was grinning.
"Not a bit." A bird flapped past his shoulder.
"I'm just thinking that now I know how you'll
look when you get old and your hair turns white."

He would think of something like that. She
probably looked like Whistler's mother's mother.
"Oh, yeah? How will I look?"

"Absolutely beautiful."

After the chickens had been dusted, Sissy, with
all her muscles aching, sat between her two

helpers in the shade of a sturdy ponderosa. They had removed their masks, exposing the only flesh tones left on them, except for under their clothes. As comical as they looked, Sissy, dragging in fresh drafts of clean air, figured that she probably looked just as funny.

"So, tell me something," Ben said. "Did you buy any used feeders that came from someone else's coop?"

"Yes," Sissy replied. "I got a used grain tub and some feeders on Craigslist. Why do you ask?"

"Because the vet says a flock of chickens from a hatchery almost never get infested with lice unless they're introduced."

Sissy's muscles tensed. "So it was my fault, after all."

"No," Ben said. "You had no way of knowing the equipment was contaminated."

Blackie, who had apparently gotten his second wind, pushed to his feet. "Well, my friends, the fun's over. I'm headed home to shower. I think I've got that danged dust on my tonsils."

"Be sure to throw every stitch of your clothes in the washer," Ben advised, "and cycle them on hot to kill the lice and larvae."

Blackie laughed. "I got a better idea. I'm sealing them in a garbage bag and throwing them out. Right now, I'm a walking, talking lice killer covered with all this crap."

"Yes," Ben agreed, "but we want to stop these lice dead in their tracks. The larvae in Sissy's coop and run will hatch in about ten days, and we'll have to dust all her chickens again."

Blackie scratched his white head. Dust filtered upward. Winking at Sissy, he walked away, calling over his shoulder, "I may be busy in ten days."

Ben chuckled. "I'd make sure of it if I were you."

Sissy gazed after her older friend as he vanished around the corner of Marilyn's building. What a thoroughly good and decent man he was.

"I can't go home like this, Sissy. I could infect my chickens with lice."

Sissy's danger radar went on immediate red alert. "What're you saying?"

He met and held her gaze. "Jack Palmer says we have to strip off in front of the washing machine, throw all our clothes in, and wash them in piping-hot water while we jump in the shower and scrub ourselves from head to toe."

Was it her imagination, or had he put the slightest emphasis on the word *we?* He was interested in her, but she didn't feel that way in return. Well, okay, she did, but she'd learned from experience not to let her feelings overrule her common sense. Besides, she had only one shower, and that was in her upstairs bathroom. Surely he wasn't suggesting that they strip off and race upstairs naked together. Only, she had a very bad feeling that he was. *No way, mister,* she thought. *No freaking way, no matter how much help you gave me.*

"That isn't happening," she said firmly. "You can go home and do your stripping at your house."

A twinkle of devilment slipped into his hazel eyes. "No can do. If I go home like this, I may drop larvae inside the cab, and Finn could get them on him. If I take that larvae to my farm, all my chickens will be in danger of getting infested. Before I knew it was lice, I already went to the farm and got in my truck. Doing it again doubles the risk."

An image of her coop and dead chickens danced across her mental TV screen. Sissy would go to *almost* any length to prevent Ben's flock from getting infested, but getting naked and showering with him wasn't one of them. *Think, girl,* she ordered herself, *and think fast, and it had better be good because I have a hunch he's going to do everything he can to outmaneuver you.*

Chapter
NINE

Standing with Ben in the laundry room, which was sectioned off from the storage area, Sissy scrabbled for inspiration. What should she *do?* Did he really expect her to shuck off her clothes with him standing three feet away? *Not happening, Mr. Sterling, no matter how persuasive you are.* She had a hunch he understood the conflict raging within her. His dimple flashed as he bit back a smile. With the mask gone, he resembled a very handsome clown who'd forgotten to stick a red ball on his nose.

"There's more than one way to skin a cat," he told her, his tone laced with suppressed laughter. "I'll turn my back while you strip off and put your clothes in the machine. You can run upstairs and shower. I'll wait here. When you're clean and dressed, come downstairs, holler at me, and go into the kitchen. If you promise not to peek, I'll strip off, start the washing machine, and go upstairs to grab a shower myself."

It sounded like a workable plan, except for one detail. "But after you shower, you'll have nothing clean to put on. You won't fit into anything of mine."

"Got it covered. I'll call Jeb and have him drop off a set of clothes for me. When he gets here, you can take them upstairs and put them on the floor just inside your apartment door."

Sissy considered her options and realized she had no others. "And I'm supposed to feel certain *you* won't peek?"

The corners of that distractingly sexy mouth twitched. She suspected he was making a huge effort to control a guffaw. "I give you my word that I won't look while you undress. I guess it's a question of whether you trust me, Sissy."

Sissy's mouth popped open to tell him she'd learned as a teenager never to trust any guy, no matter what he said. She shut it again immediately. The word *trust* always did that to her. She'd made only a few exceptions during the years since high school. Except for Gus, her last boss, who'd tutored her over the phone while she learned to cook in a commercial kitchen, and a couple of guys she'd worked with who hadn't done her dirty, nearly all her personal encounters with men had been disasters, and she wasn't going to add Ben to the list. No way in this world.

Deep down, though, she knew that wasn't fair. He'd worked hard for her and he'd been paid with only food. Before burying her chickens, he'd shown her a depth of compassion and caring that had touched her heart. And honestly, with her covered from head to toe in lice powder, what man in his right mind would make a move on her?

This one, something inside her insisted. *This one.*

"All right," she agreed. "Turn your back. All the way around."

He turned to stare at the wall, which bore hooks for drying clothing on hangers. "No threats? I figured you'd tell me that if I look, you'll drown me in bleach or shove my head through a wall."

Sissy felt a grin tug at her mouth. "No violent threats. You're on your honor. You said you won't peek. I'm trusting you to keep your word. If you don't, you've had your last piece of green apple pie with cheese."

"Damn. I can't risk that." He sighed, spread his booted feet, and put his hands on his hips. Even dusted pure white, he cut a fabulous outline. Now she knew for sure where the old adage *broad at the shoulders and narrow at the hip* had come from. "I *hate* it when a woman trusts me. It spoils all my fun."

Sissy jerked open the door of the front loader and began tossing in articles of clothing as she undressed. "Don't move," she reminded him. Okay, she felt nervous. And jumpy. It felt all wrong to be getting naked with him in the room. What if he suddenly turned on her? She doubted anyone would hear if she screamed for help. But, of course, he didn't turn, and she silently scolded herself for thinking he might. She'd been around Ben enough to know he wasn't like that.

"Okay, I'm going up to shower," she told him, glad that she'd locked the front door of the café and put up the CLOSED sign. "I'll let you know the minute I get back downstairs."

"Leave your shoes," he said. "While you're showering, I'll give them a hot rinse to remove any larvae."

"Okay."

Sissy darted from the storage room area and took a sharp right to race up the stairs. Once in her apartment, she released a pent-up breath. She'd kept her eye on him, and he'd never once turned his head, not even slightly. Imagine that: a guy who honored a promise.

She wasn't sure if she was pleased or disappointed. For her, the bottom line was that Ben's trustworthiness made him all the more tempting, and she wasn't sure how much longer she could resist him.

Ben felt better after showering. His brother Jeb had dropped off clothes for him. He and Jeb were of the same height and build, so the borrowed threads fit him perfectly. His boots were still damp from the good rinse he'd given them, but he could live with that.

As he finger-combed his hair in front of Sissy's bathroom mirror, he sniffed and grinned.

He smelled of lavender, probably from her soap. Oh, well, he'd shower again before bed.

Ben had never been given to snooping, but Sissy's bathroom was so tidy that he couldn't resist opening the medicine cabinet. His was a mess; hers was the epitome of neat and organized. He turned, taking in her neatly folded red towels, which hung on a chrome rack. One felt slightly damp, telling him that she'd used it to dry off after her shower. He'd rented motel rooms less tidy than this.

On his way from the bathroom, he surveyed her bedroom. Again, all he saw was orderly and neat. Her small living room impressed him, too. The surfaces of her coffee and end tables shone as if they'd recently been polished. Her entertainment center, also dust-free, sported an assortment of organized DVDs, all in their cases. He leaned closer and thought, *Yep. In alphabetical order.* He always left his remote sitting on his recliner, but hers lived next to her TV, perfectly lined up at the edge of the stand. *Hmm.* He had to face it; he was extremely attracted to a neat freak.

She was also one of the sweetest individuals he'd ever met, and the better he got to know her, the more convinced he became that he'd finally found Miss Right. Today she had struggled not to cry, but she'd forfeited the battle by allowing one tear to slip down her cheek. When she looked at Blackie, her eyes reflected her fondness of him. She was a person who felt things deeply yet tried to hide that fact. She worked her tail off in that café, and yet he'd never once heard her complain. After so many hours of standing, her feet had to hurt at night, but she never grumped about it.

For a little gal, she had a lot of pride and strength of character. He admired those traits in almost anyone. In short, he admired Sissy. It had pleased him earlier when she'd trusted him not to look while she undressed. He was making headway with her. *Slow and steady wins the race.* The problem was, he wanted to step up the pace. Considerably.

The café was filled with customers when Ben went downstairs. Before trying to find a seat at the counter, he went to the laundry room and threw the freshly washed clothing into the dryer. As he turned the knob to start the machine, he decided to *forget* his clothes. That would give him an excuse to come back one extra time, and he'd be sure to do it when her business was slow so he could spend a few moments alone with her.

Shit. He was in trouble.

Back out front, he found one vacant stool at the bar next to the street-side window. He was glad to be tucked away where Sissy might not notice him at first. She had been through a long and trying day, both physically and emotionally. He intended to stay after she closed to help her clean up and do breakfast prep. She wouldn't like it. But if he left her to do all the work alone, he'd like that even less.

When she spotted him at the counter, she missed a step, almost coming to a stop. Their gazes locked. For an instant, the loud hum of voices around them seemed to disappear, making Ben feel as if he and Sissy were the only two people in the café. He could have sworn that the air between them was charged with some weird electricity that no one but them could feel.

Then, as if it never happened, the moment was gone, and she reached the counter. "What'll it be tonight?"

He wanted to say, *You. Nothing else but you.* But he knew she wasn't ready. That felt weird to him, too. Nowadays women quite often went to bed with men they barely knew. "What do you recommend?"

"The meat loaf is getting rave reviews, and a number of people are saying the beef bourguignon is the best they've ever tasted."

She pronounced it *bur-gey-non,* definitely an English butchery of the French word, but Ben didn't care. Sissy's knowledge bank, though different from his own, enabled her to cook like few other people he'd met. She had her talents, he had his, and all he wanted was to meet her somewhere in the middle.

No *maybe* to it—he was falling hard for her.

And that scared him. What if she could never return his feelings?

Two hours later when Sissy argued with Ben about him staying at the café after closing to help her, he said, "Think of training me in the kitchen as a form of insurance. If something ever happens and you need help, I'll know your routine."

"Cooking for yourself at home is *not* the same as cooking in an industrial kitchen. If something happens, you can't take over running this place for me."

Ben enjoyed it when her eyes sparked with indignation. They grew as blue as laser beams. "You might be surprised by how much I know about industrial kitchens."

"Don't tell me. You flipped burgers at McDonald's in high school."

"Um—have you seen a McDonald's in this town? We're talking about Mystic Creek, where chains never set foot."

"You're changing the subject. If not at McDonald's, where did you get experience cooking with commercial equipment?"

"As a rodeo stockbroker, I helped cook at large ranches with industrial equipment during events. Granted, I don't know how to make your menu of dishes, but if I had recipes, I think I could manage. Besides, I'm not cooking tonight.

I'm just helping with cleanup and breakfast prep. Relax. Go get my poor, freezing, abused dog and feed him some dinner."

Sissy went to get Finn. Before returning to the café, she stepped inside the lighted coop to check on the two hens that had looked weak that afternoon. She half expected to find them dead, but instead, though still huddled near the feeders and looking listless, they were alive and appeared to be no sicker. That lightened her heart.

"The two listless hens are still alive," she told Ben as she joined him at the prep counter. "Maybe I won't lose any more chickens."

"Maybe," he agreed, but there was a note of doubt in his tone. "Just don't bank on it, okay? You may lose several more. I hope not, but we've done all we can, and some of the sicker ones are up against bad odds."

"If you're so sure more of them are going to die, why don't you just go out and dig several extra graves then?" Sissy knew she sounded waspish and wanted to call back the words. "I'm sorry. I shouldn't take it out on you. It's just— *damn* it. Life is so unfair. One time—just one time—why can't I be lucky?"

Ben stopped chopping onions. "You've never gotten lucky, not even once?"

"Well, Aunt Mabel did leave me the café.

Sissy felt ashamed for not counting her blessings. "I did get lucky then. But that's the only time."

"I'm sorry," he said, his voice so low it moved over her skin like a caress. "Life hasn't been easy for you, has it?"

Dangerous ground, Sissy thought. But for once, she didn't care. "No, it hasn't. I know it's crazy to love my chickens so much, but they're the only pets I've ever had for any length of time."

"Then don't give up," he said. "They could all pull through. As long as you understand the odds, there's no harm in hoping."

"Oh, yes, there is. Every time I hope for something, I get kicked in the teeth."

He said nothing more, and Sissy regretted everything she had said, so she took refuge in silence as she grated hills of cheddar cheese. As the minutes passed, the tension slipped from her body. Ben brought a huge package of bacon from the cooler and began laying out slices on stackable racks so they'd be easy to access during breakfast rush. With a start, she realized they had developed a rhythm while they worked together and that she had come to enjoy it. What would she do when her debt to him was paid and he no longer came for meals? She would miss seeing him.

Finn, satiated and drowsy, fell asleep on the floor at the end of the kitchen. When Sissy had to step around him, he didn't so much as twitch. That told her a lot about his master. Finn trusted Ben never to hurt him. He'd grown from puppy-hood in an environment of kindness and caring. Maybe she'd finally met a man who was as nice as he pretended to be.

Don't even go there, she told herself.

Over the next week and a half, Sissy's hens began to recover. She wondered if it was some sort of omen. Maybe her luck was changing.

Ben continued to stay after closing to help her in the kitchen. Every night after he left, Sissy told herself that would be the last time and she would put a stop to it the following evening. But she didn't. Slowly they moved beyond merely working in tandem with each other. Before she knew it, Ben began taking the initiative to start tasks on his own during breakfast prep, which allowed her to do something else. That resulted in the work getting done in half the time it took her to do it alone.

And somehow, without her even realizing it was happening, she began to relax around the only man who had ever made her feel that he had the power to break her heart. They joked. They laughed. He entertained her with funny stories about his childhood, even though she never shared any of her own. Sometimes she was tempted to make something up. He had to have noticed that she didn't reciprocate with personal information, but thankfully he hadn't made an issue of it.

Sissy dreaded the night when he would come in to eat the last dinner that she owed him. *Silly,* she told herself. She'd still see him every now and again. But it would be different when he came to the café as a paying customer. And she couldn't continue to let him help her without paying him. She couldn't afford that if she intended to remodel the café. Because of Ben, she hadn't depleted her savings that much, and she could dream about the changes she wanted to make. Penny by penny, she was determined to make it happen.

Ben startled her from her thoughts. "You know how you detest feeling indebted to someone? I'm like that, too. But I've got a problem. I've been banging my head against a wall for weeks, and I can't figure it out. Are you any good with computer accounting software?"

Sissy used a version that worked well for her. "I'm fair, I guess."

Ben told her what software he used, and Sissy said, "I'm your person, then. That's the program I use."

"Pay dirt!" He smiled broadly. "If I send you my files, will you have a look? I know it'll be time-consuming."

Until now, Sissy had been the recipient of favors

from Ben. It felt good to have him ask her to do something for him in return. And it wasn't a small request, which made it even better. Depending upon how badly he'd screwed up, it could take her hours to get it straightened out. "I'd love to take a look."

He sighed. "When I get home, I'll send you the files, then."

When Sissy got upstairs later and checked her e-mail, she saw that Ben had tried to send her his records. Only, they wouldn't open. She called him on his cell. "You e-mailed me a dud." She stayed on the phone with him to walk him through the correct steps to send her the file. When she got it and could open it, she said, "Oh, God."

"What? You still can't open it?"

"No, it opened."

"So what's wrong with it?"

Sissy bit back a laugh. "Just at a glance, every-thing. Taking a guess, I think you screwed up the settings or something. Even your bank deposits are red."

"What's that mean?"

"Red is an expense and deducted from your balance." Sissy scrolled to his last entry. "According to this, you're over seven hundred K in the hole."

"Shit!"

She did laugh then. "Ben, don't worry. I under-

stand this program. I'll get it all fixed for you."
And I may never let you touch it again, she thought with a smile.

The days passed in a relentless cycle. For an hour each evening, Sissy worked on Ben's books, trying to get months of bungled entries repaired. His last night to receive a free meal arrived all too quickly. Sissy had little to say as they worked side by side in her kitchen for the final time. She didn't trust her voice or her heart.

Just as they were polishing the counters, Finn, snuggled on the floor in his customary spot, came suddenly awake and began to snarl. His ferocity startled Sissy. Normally Finnegan was a sweet, playful little fellow.

"Whoa, buddy. Did you have a bad dream?" Ben asked the dog. "It's okay."

But Finn continued to growl, all the fur on his back bristling. He stared up at the kitchen shelves—or at something Ben and Sissy couldn't see in front of them. The hair on Sissy's arms stood up as straight as Finn's ruff. The pup's body drew taut, as if he were bunching his muscles to attack.

"What do you see, Finn?" Ben asked, turning to study the shelving.

Something that isn't visible, Sissy thought. *Something that only a dog with keener senses can tell is there.* What she considered to be "the

201

ghost incidents" in her building had not ceased. There wasn't a day that went by that something weird didn't happen.

"There's something up there," Ben said.

Brilliant, absolutely brilliant, she almost said. But her tongue was stuck to the roof of her mouth. Of course there was something up there, and Finn knew what it was. Unfortunately, all he could do was sound the alarm.

Unlike Sissy, Ben was tall enough to reach the top shelves without standing on a stool, and reach them, he did. He began pawing through canned goods on one shelf and spices on a lower one. Sissy winced. She kept everything organized, and he was scattering stuff with every sweep of his hands.

"You won't find anything," she told him.

Ben looked down at her. A tawny eyebrow arched over one eye. "Of course I will. Finn says something's up here."

She didn't want to sound like a complete flake, but if she let him continue to mess up her shelves, she'd be working for hours to reorganize them. "Finn is telling you there's something there, but not something we can see."

Ben turned toward her and rested his lean hips against the counter's edge.

"Are you talking about your ghost? You said all the weird stuff stopped happening."

Sissy mentally squirmed. "Okay, so what if I

did? Do you know how crazy I sound when I talk about my ghost?"

With a concerned look on his face, Ben resumed his search of her shelving. Sissy knew he would find nothing, and in the end, after she was proven to be correct, her supplies would be all out of order. Ben sighed, looked at his dog, who'd settled down and gone back to sleep, and said, "Hell, I don't know. Maybe you do have a ghost." He winked at her. "On the other hand, maybe I nailed it on the head from the get-go, and you've got mice."

Sissy wasn't amused. "Pest control says I haven't."

Together, they resumed polishing the counters, and all too soon, the job was finished. This was it, the very last time they would work together. She tried to think how to tell Ben good-bye.

As she tossed her towel into the hamper, she said, "My chicken coop and run are fabulous. I could never have built anything that wonderful. I don't know how to thank you. Especially after all that you did when my hens got sick, digging graves and dusting chickens for hours. You've—"

Ben touched a fingertip to her lips. His mouth slanted into a crooked grin, and his eyes delved so deeply into hers that she felt as naked as she'd been the day she stripped off her clothes in the laundry room.

"A thank-you isn't necessary," he said. And

then, before she suspected what he meant to do, he planted a quick kiss on her forehead. "It's been fun. We've had a lot of good times together."

As if to second that vote, Finn emitted a happy bark. Ben stepped away from Sissy, gifted her with a dazzling grin, and then left the kitchen. Beyond the pass-through window, she saw him collect his Stetson from where he'd left it on a stool, settle it just so on his head, and then pat his thigh to call his dog.

She flinched when she heard the back door of the building slam closed. Forcing her feet to move, she walked through the storage area to lock up. Then, cloaked in the semidarkness, she touched the spot above her brows where Ben's lips grazed her skin. It still tingled.

He's gone, she told herself. *Your debt to him is paid in full.* She wanted to feel happy about that. No, she wanted to feel relieved. Only, instead she felt sad, so very sad, as if she'd lost her best friend.

Four days passed, and Ben never once visited the café. Sissy missed him in a way she'd never expected. There was an ache in the center of her chest that wouldn't go away. Silly things, like loading a dishwasher, made her think of him and feel lost. She wished—oh, she didn't know what she wished. She just had the awful feeling that she'd been so determined not to get entangled in a relationship that she might have blown her only chance to have something special with someone.

Late on the fourth night, right after she'd finished breakfast prep and gone upstairs to her apartment, her cell phone rang, startling her when it vibrated in her jeans pocket. She got heaps of calls during the day from suppliers, but her phone rarely rang this late. She had no close friends. She'd moved too often before coming to Mystic Creek to develop relationships with other women, and since inheriting the café, she'd had little time to socialize. She occasionally lunched with Marilyn and Ma Thomas, who'd gifted her with countless stories about Aunt Mabel, and she'd grown fond of a few customers, but none of those people would dial her number just to say hello.

She pulled the phone from her pocket and stared at the number on the screen. The caller ID didn't show a name. She swiped her finger over the ANSWER button and said, "Hello?"

"Hey."

She knew that deep voice. It flowed over her like syrup on a hot flapjack. "Ben." It was so good to feel connected to him again that her heart did a happy jig. "Hi. How are you?" She barely stopped herself from asking where he'd been. "Burned out on restaurant food, are you?"

He laughed, and the sound sent warmth flowing

through her. "Hell, no. I've been out of town. I had some rodeo stock that finally sold, and I made a haul to Montana. I just got back this afternoon. Long drive. But I saw some beautiful country."

Sissy wanted to say something witty—a reply that wouldn't reveal how much she'd missed him. Only she couldn't think of anything.

"You there?"

"Yes! I'm here. And so I don't forget, I've gotten the accounting mess fixed for you."

"That's awesome! I really appreciate it, Sissy. I'm no good at it, period."

That wasn't a news flash for her. "You missed out on beef bourguignon tonight." She said it the way he once had and felt proud of herself for pulling it off even though she'd gotten to practice all evening. "It got rave reviews."

"Damn! If you have any left over, save it for me. I'll eat it tomorrow. You do know what tomorrow is, don't you?"

Sissy frowned. What was special about tomorrow? "Um, no, not really. Saturday."

"It's the tenth day, chicken-dusting day. Did you think I'd let you do it all alone?"

Sissy had put a reminder on her phone calendar, but it wouldn't show on her screen until morning. "Oh, that's *right*."

"How are they doing, by the way? The chickens."

"Good! Nobody else has died. I think their

combs are getting pinker. Maybe it's only wishful thinking, though."

"Nah. If they're still alive, they've survived the anemia. You got lucky, after all." He muttered something she couldn't catch. Then he said, "That's great. At least one of us did."

"One of us did what?"

He sighed, the rush of his breath whooshing against her eardrum. "Sorry. I shouldn't have said that."

Sissy's face went hot. She guessed what he might have said. Again, she wanted to say something witty, but the only thing she could think of was "Um." What was this? For most of her life, her mouth had been her strongest weapon. "It's okay." She winced, thinking how lame that was. "You really don't need to help me dust hens, you know. I can handle it."

"I wouldn't miss it for the world. I'll get to see you with white hair a second time. Besides, the powder will kill all the newly hatched lice on contact. We won't even have to get naked together again."

She giggled. "We didn't get naked *together*. You kept your clothes on until I left."

"True. But it's something I can tease you about until your hair actually goes white from old age." He cleared his throat. "Um, Sissy, I have to tell you something. Five of your hens are going to start making weird noises soon. When that happens, don't be worried. It's absolutely normal, because they're roosters."

Sissy remembered hearing odd sounds coming from some of her hens. "Roosters? Margie is— oh, man, how dumb of me. I thought maybe she had food caught in her throat."

Ben chortled. "Margie should be named Marvin."

"Why didn't you tell me I had roosters? The hatchery sent me *five?* They're supposed to be ninety-nine percent accurate in determining the gender of chicks."

"Yeah, well. Someone must not have known what he was doing, because you've definitely got five roosters. That's not a bad thing. One school of thought is that fertilized eggs are healthier for us to eat." He paused. "I'm excited about seeing you tomorrow."

Sissy smiled. "I'm excited, too."

"What time will work for you?"

Sissy thought about her schedule for the next day. "Can you be here at two thirty? I can get up early and do both my preps so I'll be free as soon as the noon rush is over. I'll close the café so I can work all afternoon."

"How about if I show up around six in the morning to help so you don't have to get up so early?"

"I don't want you to do that."

"Why? You just got my books all straightened

out. It's a fair exchange. We have fun working together. Finn loves it. I don't see a downside."

"What about your farm animals?"

"I'll have my hired hand do all the feeding. See you at six?"

Sissy sighed. "Okay, but this is the last time I can let you help me in the kitchen without paying you. It just isn't right."

"You can always pay me with free meals. You'll never hear me complain about that. Or you could be my bookkeeper."

After they ended the conversation, Sissy stared down at her cell phone, unable to force the smile from her lips. Ben was coming in the morning. It was almost like having a date. She wanted to bounce around with excitement.

Instead she rushed into her bedroom to decide what she was going to wear. She wanted to look extra nice when he first saw her. That made no sense, because after lunch, she'd be covered in white powder. An alarm bell tried to jangle in her mind, but she switched if off. There was nothing wrong with wanting to be at her best when he came.

It meant nothing.

Chapter
TEN

It seemed to Ben that the chicken dusting went faster when he and Sissy did it a second time. For one thing, the hens didn't grow quite so panicky, and for another, he and Sissy performed together like a well-oiled machine. He couldn't resist com-menting on that.

"We do work well together," she agreed as they exited the coop together and she yanked off her mask. "It's as if we can anticipate each other's next move."

"With that going for us, we'd be dynamite on a dance floor," he replied.

Sissy shot a startled look at him. Then she smiled. "I don't dance. But we could be dynamite doing other things."

"Well . . ." His voice trailed off into silence. "I need to head home to take a shower."

"Yeah, me, too." She plucked at her long-sleeve knit shirt, a pretty blue one that had matched the color of her eyes before it got coated in white. He'd never seen her wear it. But, then, he'd never seen her wearing a touch of makeup, either, and she had been when he arrived. Not much—just a hint of mascara on her lashes, a trace of blush along her cheekbones, and some lip gloss. Now her lashes looked like white spikes. "I sure hope this is the last time they need dusting."

"It should be," he said.

Ben noticed how tired she looked. It bothered him. His farmhand did his evening chores, so Ben could relax after he got home. Sissy had hours of labor yet to do. He couldn't help but wonder how one small woman managed to hold up under that workload. He guessed maybe that was why she had such a wispy figure.

Ben knew the way home by heart, which gave him time to think—about Sissy, the lady who had laid claim to his heart almost the first time he saw her and still held him at arm's length. Why? He didn't have the balls to ask her.

He pulled into his paved driveway and parked beside the kitchen porch. "Okay, Finn, we're home. Wanna go help round up chickens and put them in the coop for Brett while I grab my shower?" Ben glanced over at the passenger seat. No pup sat there. He peered over his shoulder, thinking Finn might have decided to take a nap in back. "*Damn.* I can't believe I'm so wrapped up in that woman that I forgot my dog!"

Ben decided to look on the bright side. He could grab a quick shower, drive back to the Cauldron, and lend a hand during the dinner hour. If Sissy objected, he'd tell her that she could repay him by comping him his evening meal. If she argued, he had a perfect comeback. He couldn't get his dog from her apartment when customers were there. Yeah, that would work—unless Sissy had hidden Finn in a storage room.

Ben went inside, grabbed a quick shower, and had just gotten halfway dressed when someone pounded on his door. He loped through the house to answer the summons and found Brett on the porch, his face red with anger.

"That horse you brought in last week with behavior problems has gone fuck-shit crazy!"

Ben buttoned his Wrangler jeans. "What d'ya mean, crazy?" Ben had been working with the mare. She'd been bucking when her owners tried to ride her, and it was his job to tame her back down. "She was fine when I rode her last week."

"Well, she ain't fine now! She went to buckin' on me, slammed me against the arena wall, and damned near dug a hole to China with her nose to throw me from the saddle!" Brett, hatless, which was uncharacteristic of him, raked a hand through his red hair. "When I hit the ground she came after me. I jumped a stall gate to get away from her. So then she went after my goddamned Stetson. She stomped it. She bit it. And then the bitch *pissed* on it. I'm tellin' you, that mare is nuts!"

Brett wasn't a trainer, but he was a damned good rider. When he climbed into a saddle, he rode as if he had superglue on his ass. Any mare that managed to throw him had to have gone berserk.

All Ben could think to say was "I'll be right out, and I'll buy you a new Stetson."

Sissy was racing around her café kitchen, getting ready for an onslaught of dinner customers, when she tripped over Finn, lost her footing, and almost did a face-plant against the refrigerator. Once she regained her balance, she didn't know what surprised her more: that she'd caught herself from falling or that Finn was snoozing in her kitchen. Or had been. She'd jostled him awake.

She hunkered down to love on him, thinking, even as she did, that she'd have to change chef coats. Her customers wouldn't appreciate dog hair in their food. "What are you doing here, boy? Your dad must have forgotten you." That puzzled her. Ben and his dog seemed to be attached by an invisible string. "I don't mean to be an ungracious hostess, but you can only be in my kitchen when the café is closed."

Finn, who seemed to realize she was rejecting him as her kitchen buddy, looked up at her with sad eyes.

"But it's okay!" Sissy stood, opened the fridge, and found leftovers from breakfast. "I can sneak you upstairs and serve you a feast! Let me see. Oh, wow, I've got bacon. I'll bet you like that! And a leftover omelet. *Oooh-yum.* I cooked too many hamburger patties, too."

Piling food on a plate, she realized that she'd long since stopped feeding Finn on a paper one. The health inspector would probably fine her for that. If he ever caught her. "Come on, sweetness. Lucky you! Nobody gets to visit my private living quarters. Well, your dad did once—but only to take a shower. So aren't you special?"

Finn leaped to his feet and wagged his whole body. Sissy was a little surprised. She knew how much the pup loved Ben. Surely Finn felt lost without him. *Who wouldn't?* She led the young canine upstairs. Once in the apartment, she set his plate on her kitchen floor, filled a large bowl with freshwater, and then found a spare blanket to make him a bed.

She couldn't stay to familiarize Finn with her residence. That was fine. Ben would realize he'd forgotten his dog and be back to collect him in no time.

Only, Ben didn't return to get his dog. Hours went by. Surely he realized at some point that he'd forgotten Finnegan. She worried about the pup, alone in an unfamiliar apartment. He was still quite young, not even a year old yet. And he was so accustomed to being with Ben. What if he freaked out and tried to chew his way through her door? Sissy yearned to go check on him, but she was far too busy.

After the dinner rush ebbed away, only Tim and Lynda VeArd occupied a booth. They'd come in late and were barely halfway through their meals. Sissy knew they adored animals because they had, according to them, the most spoiled cat in history. Sissy crossed the café to stand over them.

"Can I share a secret with you guys?"

Tim grinned. "Unless it threatens national security, you can trust me, but my little redhead is a blabbermouth."

Lynda threw an unused straw at her husband, nailing him in the chest. "I never break a confidence, and you know it."

Tim laughed and threw the straw back at her, missing by a foot.

Sissy smiled. "Well, I have a guest upstairs, Ben's pup, Finnegan."

"The chicken herder? He's an amazing little fellow," Tim observed.

"Yes, he is," Sissy agreed. "My chickens got lice. Did you hear about that?" Both the VeArds nodded. "Ben came by to help. With so many chickens, it's a job. And somehow when Ben left, he forgot Finn. I tripped over him doing dinner prep." Sissy lowered her voice. "It's against the law for dogs to be in a restaurant—unless, of course, they're service animals—so I hid Finnegan in my apartment. He's been alone for hours. Would you mind if I ran up to check on him?"

Lynda grinned. "What we'd mind is if you didn't check on him. Tim and I have everything we require. Go for it, and no need to hurry."

When Tim nodded in agreement, Sissy raced for the stairwell. She found Finn napping on his bed. It had been hours since the pup had been outside. As Sissy scratched him right above his docked tail, his favorite spot, she gnawed her lower lip. Then, reaching a decision, she walked over, opened the apartment door that led to the stairwell, and yelled, "He needs to go potty! If I bring him down and take him straight outside through the storage area, do you promise not to narc on me to the health inspector?"

She heard Tim guffaw. "We promise," he bellowed back. "And bring him by our table. I can't eat all my steak, and Twinkie won't eat beef."

Twinkie was their spoiled cat. Sissy grinned, patted her leg to beckon Finn forward, and led him down the stairs. The instant Finn appeared in the café area, Tim snapped his fingers at the dog, and Finnegan raced over to renew their friendship. Tim fed him bites of steak, and Lynda offered him popcorn shrimp, battered pieces of cod, and French fries dipped in ranch dressing. Finn's snubbed tail did double time.

"You guys are the best," Sissy told them.

"Aside from the fact that some people are allergic to dogs," Tim observed, "I think it's a stupid law, anyway."

"Me, too," Lynda agreed. "So many service

dogs are allowed. What do they do, spray them with something to make them hypoallergenic? It's ridiculous."

Sissy wanted to hug them both. "Well, dogs do shed. I don't think it's unreasonable for people to prefer food without dog hair in it."

She took Finnegan out back for a short outing, during which he baptized every post of her chicken pen and ran next door to pee on Marilyn's shed. After relieving himself, the pup returned to Sissy and looked up at her with a bewildered expression.

"I know. You're wondering where your dad is. Something happened. He realizes by now that he forgot you, and he'll come for you as quickly as he can. He loves you to pieces." Sissy wished that she'd had a father half as wonderful as Ben. Maybe then she would have matured into a different woman. "But until he gets here, you have to go back upstairs until the VeArds leave. You'll be okay. Right?"

Sissy's concern for the dog ended the moment she led him back inside the café. Tim yelled, "I turned the sign to read CLOSED and locked the front door. Before doing that, I stepped outside and looked both ways to make sure no gestapo were on the sidewalks. We've decided that we each want a hamburger patty for dessert, and we're going to need Finn's help to eat them."

Sissy's chest went tight. For the first time in

217

her life, she had friends. She grinned and said, "Two hamburger patties coming right up."

Ben reached Sissy's place so late that he feared she might already be in bed, but he could see lights still on in her apartment. He was pleased to find that she'd left the back door unlocked for him and a light on in the storage room.

"Finn?" he called softly, thinking she might have left the dog closed up downstairs so it would be easier for Ben to collect him. "Finn?"

He heard no sound to suggest the pup had heard him. He strode up the hall and swung right to ascend the stairs. Once on the landing, he tapped on the door.

Sissy answered the summons almost instantly. "I was starting to think you'd been in a wreck."

She stepped back to allow Ben entry. He removed his hat as he stepped inside. "I'm really sorry about this." He gave her a brief account of what had happened. "I almost texted you, but it was smack-dab in the middle of dinner hour. So I thought I'd wait, and then things got so crazy, I couldn't text."

Finn, snuggled down on a folded blanket, leaped to his feet and ran to Ben, whining a joyous greeting. Ben bent to ruffle the dog's fur. "Did you think I'd forgotten you?"

Sissy gestured toward the table where a bottle of wine and one half-filled goblet sat. "Grab a chair. If you're as tired as I am, a glass of wine may hit the spot."

After tossing his truck keys on her end table, Ben accepted the invitation and took a seat across from the half-filled goblet. He put his hat on a chair next to him. "I'd love a glass of wine."

He turned the bottle to see the label. "Uh-oh, a lady who likes to live dangerously. This is mulberry."

"After you told me about it, I wanted to try some, and Flagg's Market cooperated by having it on sale. I refuse to pay more than ten dollars a bottle." She smiled as she retraced her steps to the table and handed him a glass.

As she resumed her seat and took a sip of the wine, Ben wondered why she didn't see how perfect they were for each other. "Maybe some of the September magic rubbed off on us."

Her blue eyes grew shadowed. "And you are reminding me why I vowed never to serve you any wine."

Ben laughed and poured himself about four ounces. "No worries. I could guzzle the whole bottle and not get so snockered that just anyone would look good to me." He didn't add that he needed no help to find Sissy attractive.

"It's delicious," she observed. "I may have to raise my buying bar to fifteen. It normally costs that much."

Ben nodded in appreciation as he rolled the

purple vintage over his tongue. "Worth every penny." Studying her, he decided she looked as exhausted as he felt.

"I bought two bottles. Maybe I'll go wild tonight and have three glasses. I'll never make it through tomorrow if I don't get some sleep. Last night I barely got a wink."

"What kept you awake?" he asked.

Just then, Finn, who'd settled near Ben's chair, lifted his head and snarled. The dog's gaze was fixed on the sofa. Bewildered, Ben walked into the seating area. "He's such an easygoing dog. Now this again? He sees or senses something. His hackles are up."

"Just sit back down and drink your wine. Whatever it is that Finn senses, the human eye can't detect it."

He joined her at the table again and gave her an inquisitive look.

"After last night, I no longer care if I sound crazy. This building is haunted."

"What happened last night?" he asked.

"After I went to bed, a canned good toppled out of a closed cupboard. My small nonstick skillet, which I'd left in the dish drainer, went airborne and clattered onto the floor. While I was unwrapping a new roll of bathroom tissue, the chrome rod vanished. I set it on the edge of the vanity, and in a blink, it was gone."

Ben didn't discount the possibility of ghosts,

but he couldn't help but think that there had to be another explanation. "Do you mind if I go look for it?"

She lifted her glass to him. "Not at all, and good luck. You're not going to find it."

Ben went to search Sissy's bathroom. He even checked inside the waste receptacle and vanity cupboard. He found no chrome rod.

Once back in Sissy's kitchen, he eyeballed her counters and cupboard shelves to make sure they were level. He could offer her no rational explanation for the flying skillet and canned goods.

"So you believe me?" Her voice quavered as she asked the question.

"Well, of *course* I believe you. Why would you make it up?"

She sighed. "Well, I'm glad you're taking my word for it. I was afraid I might have to show you the dent on my stove to convince you that it all happened."

Ben stepped over to the range and studied the gouge in the white enamel, musing aloud, "For a can of food to inflict this much damage, it must have fallen from the cupboard and landed on its edge."

Sissy shrugged. "All I know is that the can ended up on the floor. I was in bed when it happened, and the noise in here scared me out of ten year's growth."

Ben sighed. "Something must have pushed the

can from the cupboard. If a *ghost* picked it up and tossed it, the can would have bypassed the stove and hit the floor."

Just then the keyboard in Sissy's living room pinged. Finn sprang up, raced to the living room, and leaped at the window curtains. The next instant, the dog jumped on the sofa and began digging feverishly at the cushions until Ben, fearing damage to the upholstery, called him off.

"That settles it. He's after something real." Ben pulled off all the couch cushions and found nothing. Still convinced Finn had seen something, he even went so far as to move the piece of furniture to make sure nothing had hidden under it.

A *ghost?* Ben wanted to discard the notion, but he'd *heard* that keyboard play. Something had struck the keys—something he hadn't seen and couldn't find. Without permission, he walked through the apartment, convinced that the culprit had to be a small creature. He looked under the bed. He moved the nightstands and dresser.

"Have you noticed any rodent droppings?" he asked.

"No. With this being a food service facility, I have pest control come on a quarterly basis, and after you suggested my pianist might be a mouse, I called the company and asked for an extra visit. The guy said he found no evidence of mice anywhere."

Ben finally gave up on finding anything and resumed his seat at the table. "Why didn't you tell me weird shit is still happening?"

She pushed at her dark hair. "Because it makes me sound loony."

"Well, I'm about to sound even loonier. I don't want you staying here alone at night."

Sissy laughed. "Ben, whatever it is, it means me no harm. My only issue is that all the noise disturbs my sleep."

When she rubbed her arms and shivered, Ben knew the unexplained incidents were also giving her the willies. And he couldn't fault her for that. Hearing that keyboard chime had made his skin prickle, too.

"You could stay at my place. I've got four extra bedrooms, and I guarantee you'll sleep like a baby."

She shook her head. "I appreciate the offer, but a simpler solution is to get earplugs. I'm not in any danger." She tipped her head and arched her brows. "Moving on to another topic, did you get the berserk horse settled down?"

He raked a hand through his hair. "Actually, something didn't feel right when I rode her." He took a sip of wine. "She didn't act up with me, but as I picked up speed as I rode her around the arena, I *really* felt it. A tension in her. Something wrong with her gait. So I called Jack Palmer and asked him to come out."

"Ouch. That must have cost a pretty penny, especially after hours."

"The owners authorized the call, and they'll pick up the tab. And, man, I'm so glad I did. Jack palpated her, and he detected some tenderness. He believes she has a uterine or ovarian cyst. He took her to his clinic. I have faith in Jack. He'll figure it out, and we'll soon have a horse that's fine again."

They chatted while Ben finished his wine. Then he glanced at his watch, realized it was past bedtime for both of them, and went to retrieve his keys from the end table.

"Um—" He looked at Sissy. "I *did* put my keys there. Right?"

"Oh, no," she said. "Were they shiny?"

"My remote fob isn't, but the key sticking out the end is. I didn't retract it, and yes, my key chain is shiny. I have a special one, a miniature Western belt buckle."

Sissy shook her head. "Good luck finding them, then. Shiny things vanish around here."

Ben couldn't accept that as an answer. He had an extra set of keys in a magnetic case attached to his truck, but the missing fob would cost him over a hundred dollars. He searched between the sofa cushions. He moved the couch and the end tables. He was about to give up when he heard a horn blaring outside, that honk-stop kind of blare a vehicle emits when the alert button on a key fob has been pressed.

He hurried over to Sissy's living room window. Sure enough, there sat his truck near the coop, the lights blinking on and off, and the horn blaring.

"Damn! How in hell am I going to turn that off without the fob? My extra one is at home. All I have is a spare key in a magnetic case under the fender."

Sissy started to laugh and then clamped a hand over her mouth. Through spread fingers, she said, "I'm sorry. It isn't funny. It's just such a relief to have this happen to someone besides me!"

Minutes later, after getting inside his vehicle, Ben managed to get the horn to stop blaring. He saw that Marilyn's upstairs lights had come on. Then she leaned out what he guessed was her bedroom window.

He lowered the glass on the driver's side of his truck. "I'm sorry if that woke you."

"I was just worried that someone had broken into your truck!"

Ben noted her mussed hair and the furry robe she wore. He'd woken her from a sound sleep. "False alarm. I had trouble making the horn shut up, though."

She laughed, waved farewell, and closed her window. Ben noticed Sissy standing on her back porch as he drove away. He gave the horn a final toot to tell her good night.

"Ghosts do not steal car keys," he muttered to himself. "There *has* to be a rational explanation for all this."

Whenever Ben felt troubled, he always sought out his father for advice, so he wasn't really surprised when he found himself driving toward his childhood home on East Sugar Pine. He bypassed Barney's farm and noted that the lights were still on. Ben could only hope that his parents were awake. Sometimes they watched television later at night, and his mom loved to do crafts. Jeremiah was semiretired now and no longer got up earlier than the chickens. He had a farmhand to do the morning chores.

Ben was pleased when he saw light coming through the windows of his parents' ranch-style home. The place looked small in the darkness, but somehow his folks had managed to raise six kids there, and Ben couldn't recall ever feeling cramped.

He left Finnegan asleep on the passenger seat. The pup had worn himself out, probably pacing in Sissy's apartment. When he tapped on his parents' front door, he heard the patter of quick footsteps and knew his mother was answering the summons. Kate was a small, energetic woman who still looked and acted a decade younger than she was. When the portal swung inward, Ben took a moment to study the surprised expression that passed over her delicate features. Then sheer delight brightened her coffee brown eyes.

"Ben!" she cried. "It's so good to see you."

He tried to remember how long it had been since he'd darkened his parents' doorstep. After hugging his mom, he followed her from the entryway into the spacious family room that opened onto a formal dining area and then a country kitchen, large enough to accommodate a second table for casual meals. In the overhead light, Jeremiah's tawny hair, the same color as Ben's, glistened with more silver than Ben remembered. It saddened him to realize that his parents were getting older.

"Hey, Ben," Jeremiah called from the table. "I didn't think you stayed up this late unless you were skirt chasing in Crystal Falls."

Ben winced. His dad enjoyed taking jabs at his sons for choices they made that he deemed to be mistakes. "Not funny, Dad."

Kate swept into the kitchen, flapping a hand at her husband. "If he's skirt chasing, I don't want to hear about it." With a smile at Ben, she said, "Your father is having decaf. I'm having hot cocoa. Name your poison."

"Cocoa," Ben replied. Then he quickly added, "Please." His mom was a stickler on manners. "Can I have mine with marshmallows?"

"May I," Kate corrected. "And, yes, Ben, you may."

Ben had removed his hat when he stepped onto the porch. He set it on the kitchen bar and sat next to his dad, remembering all the noisy breakfasts he'd eaten at this table over the years. Kids slurping. He and his brothers kicking or pinching one another when a parent wasn't watching. His sisters always tattling on them.

"So, what's up?" Jeremiah asked. "You rarely show up here unless you've got a problem."

Ben winced again. "I've been busy liquidating my business. I recently got home from Montana, where I dropped off the last of my livestock."

Kate, heating something in the microwave, glanced over her slender shoulder. She wore faded jeans, riding boots, and a pretty plaid Western shirt that sported turquoise and pink with sparkly stuff in the pattern. "Barney mentioned you were out of town. I hope you found good homes for the animals."

Ben nodded. "I made sure of that, Mom."

Jeremiah inserted, "I know you've been busy. But rumor has it that you've been especially busy helping out the young lady who owns the Cauldron."

Ben knew whenever his father said "Rumor has it" that one of his brothers had blabbed. "True."

"Is it serious?" Jeremiah asked.

"On my part, yes. If I could convince her to let it be serious, I would. But she's taking her time warming up to me."

Kate set a cup of cocoa, laden with melting marshmallows, in front of Ben, and then resumed her seat where her own serving was cooling. "There's nothing wrong with a woman taking some time. Smart, if you ask me."

Before his mother could get off on a tangent about all the divorces taking place among the younger set, Ben said, "And you're right, Dad. I do have a problem. Well, not really a *problem*. It's more a mystery, and I need a sounding board."

"Shoot," Jeremiah said.

Ben told his parents about the strange things happening in Sissy's building, ending with the disappearance of his remote fob and key chain.

Jeremiah frowned. "You've witnessed Finnegan snarling and barking at something you can't see?"

Ben explained how he'd searched for something real each time and found nothing.

"That is strange," Jeremiah observed. "I believe in the existence of spirits, but I don't think they steal things. A dog might sense the presence of one and raise a fuss, I suppose. They can sense things we can't. But the missing objects—apparently a lot of them—sound crazy to me. Ghosts have no bodies. They can't pick things up, and they certainly can't throw canned goods from cupboards."

"Um," Kate inserted, "a poltergeist could—if poltergeists actually exist."

Jeremiah studied his wife. "What is a poltergeist?"

"A mischievous and sometimes dangerous ghost," Kate replied. She fell quiet for a moment. "Do you know what these stories remind me of? One time, this happened to my grandmother."

"It did?" Ben stared at Kate. "My great-grandmother had a ghost?"

Kate laughed. "Well, for a while she thought she did. She'd set aside her crocheting, and her hook would vanish. Jewelry, wrapped candies, or change she left in a dish." A distant look entered Kate's eyes. "Then there came a rainstorm, and the roof sprang a leak in her bedroom closet. Daddy went right over to fix it. While working inside her closet, he found a hole in the wall at a back corner. He shone his light inside and saw dozens of items. Earrings, bracelets, crochet hooks, candy bars, the wristwatch Grandma had lost, and even an heirloom necklace that she believed she'd misplaced."

"*Mom.*" Ben leaned toward Kate. "What took the damned necklace?" He caught himself too late. "I'm sorry, the *danged* necklace."

Kate sent him a scolding look. "A pack rat."

"A *what?*" Jeremiah asked.

Carefully enunciating each word, Kate repeated, "A—pack—rat."

Ben went limp against the back of the chair. "Of *course*. I considered mice, but they aren't

230

big enough to steal stuff. Pack rats can be fairly big. Right? Big enough to alarm Finn and make him growl."

"Oh, yes," Kate confirmed. "Some are small. Some are bigger than we want to imagine. But *all* of them are attracted to shiny things. Daddy found every single item Grandma had supposedly misplaced in that rat's nest."

"I *knew* it couldn't be a ghost!" Ben said. "Now what'll I do? Find the nest and bait it with poison?"

"I read somewhere once that pack rats won't eat the stuff that kills mice and other rats," Jeremiah said. "Instead they carry it away from their nests, and other animals or birds eat it. The best way to get rid of them is to keep your property and outbuildings free of debris. Until they move on, ratproof the building by plugging all the holes that may provide ingress with steel wool."

Ben sighed. "Behind those buildings, it's like one huge backyard. Everyone has sheds, small garages, and business debris lying around. Maybe I can just catch the rat and relocate it."

"Worth a try, I guess," Jeremiah said.

Chapter
ELEVEN

Sissy jerked awake. She lay still under the blankets and comforter, thinking her ghost was paying her another visit. *Silence.* She was about to fall back asleep when a knock snapped her to attention again. Someone was pounding on her downstairs back door. She jumped out of bed, ran to her window, and pushed it upward.

"Who is it?" she yelled.

"Ben! I'm sorry it's so late, but it's important."

"Um—okay." Her mind still muzzy with sleep, Sissy patted her hand over an oversize T-shirt. She couldn't go downstairs like this. "I'll be right there!"

She closed the window and raced to her closet for the robe she rarely used. She began flipping on lights as she hurried through her apartment.

When she got downstairs, turned on her porch light, and opened the door, Ben loomed at the threshold. He held what looked like a large wire box in one hand.

"What's that?"

"A live trap." He stepped forward, forcing her back three steps. "Your ghost may be a pack rat."

"A *what?*" That woke her up fast.

232

"It may be living with you. And tonight we're going to catch it and get it out of your building."

"Oh, God. A rat has been playing my keyboard and making me think I'm nuts?"

"Possibly."

As Ben led the way upstairs, he told her about his great-grandmother, who'd had a pack rat that stole things. "If her roof hadn't sprung a leak, my grandfather never would have found the nest."

Sissy's skin crawled. Once in her apartment, Ben set the wire thing on her kitchen counter, and then, without explanation, he began sifting through her drawers, messing everything up. Her measuring cups, always nested together in a stack, went flying in all directions.

"What are you doing?" she cried.

"Looking for bait," he said. "Shiny things." He tossed her silver quarter-cup measurer onto the counter. That was soon joined by a metal bottle opener. "This is a live trap. Once the rat goes in and steps in the right place, the door slams closed and latches. It won't be able to get out." He paused and glanced over his shoulder at her. His eyes, a blend of whiskey and gold dust, fixed on her face. "Can you handle waking up to find a rat inside this cage? If not, I can stay and deal with it."

Sissy pushed at her hair. Waking up to find a hissing, big-toothed rat in that trap didn't sound fun. But as much as she'd come to like—and

trust—Ben, she wasn't quite ready to have him stay all night with her. The rat would be caged. Ben was a whole different kettle of fish.

"I can handle that," she said. "I, um—I'll just stay out of the kitchen and wait for you to come in the morning." She stared at the cage. "Do you really think it'll get stuck in there tonight?"

He cast her another look that threatened to make her forget all her other worries. *Oh, Sissy,* she thought, *you are such an idiot. You're falling in love with him.*

"I'm almost certain of it," he said. "Do you have any of those little Snickers bars? That's what it seems to like best."

Sissy sighed and slumped her shoulders. "I quit buying them when my candy bowl got knocked off the coffee table. Now I just go next door and buy regular-size Snickers from Marilyn." The lie settled in her chest like a rock. "Okay, the truth is, when I crave a Snickers so bad I can't stand it, I buy one of those extra-large ones and eat the whole thing. That's why I always got little ones. It helps me control myself."

Ben laughed, the sound deep and wonderfully soothing to her somehow. "Sweetheart, if that's the worst thing you ever have to confess, you're amazing." He gave her a measuring look. "Has it ever occurred to you that maybe, just *maybe,* you're eating Snickers bars because you're actually wanting something else?"

Sissy blinked at him. She probably looked like an owl that was having a bad hair day. "What else would I be wanting?" she asked, and immediately regretted the question as a possible answer popped into her mind.

He placed more shiny things inside the cage. "Never mind me. I'm all mouth and no brains." He fiddled with the mechanism. "Okay. Baited and all set."

The Western wear hugged his frame, showcasing a body that screamed "man." And looking at him did make her want a Snickers bar. For the first time, Sissy could admit, if only to herself, that she wanted to have sex with the man standing before her. She wondered how a woman went about telling a guy something like that.

He turned toward her. "If you hear the trap slam closed, call me. I'll keep my cell on my nightstand. I don't want you trying to deal with this. I'll come take care of it."

"How will you take care of it?" she asked, hating the fact that her voice went shrill.

Ben stepped closer. Too close. He cupped his hands over her cheeks and thumbed her chin up so she had to look at him. "The animal won't be injured. I'll just relocate it."

"So no matter how big and awful it is, we don't have to hurt it?"

"Nope. We'll just move him to a nice place where he can build a new home."

He sneaked in and kissed her on the forehead again. With him being so tall, so broad at the shoulders, and so wide across the chest, she felt cocooned in masculine warmth for an instant. Then he stepped away. When he reached the door, he stopped. "Um—I can't lock up. You want to follow me down?"

Forehead tingling, Sissy trudged down the stairs behind him. At the lower back door, she stood well away while he let himself out, and then as the latch clicked, she yelled, "Good night, Ben. Thanks for bringing the ratcatcher."

After engaging the dead bolt, she cinched the sash of her robe tighter, wishing she could go next door and wake Marilyn to get a Snickers bar.

Ben wrapped his arms gently around her and drew her close against his hard, warm body. Sissy wanted to be even closer. She was too short to press her face against the hollow of his throat, too short to intoxicate herself with the scent of his cologne. She stepped onto his boots to make herself taller and nestled her cheek against his shoulder.

"Kiss me," she whispered. "Not on my forehead this time. I need you to kiss me, Ben."

He bent his head. Her heart started to pound. His lips shimmered in the faint light. His breath smelled pleasantly of coffee.

Ker-whack!!!

The loud noise jolted her upright. Accustomed to weird sounds that disrupted her sleep, she didn't feel alarmed. Instead, disappointment washed through her. She had rolled herself up in the comforter and the tight embrace wasn't Ben's. *Only a dream,* she thought. *But, oh, what a nice one.* She sighed and lay back, surrounded by warmth and her own scent of lavender.

Then she heard something go *Wheek!*

It was a shrill, peeping noise charged with fright. She struggled free of the blankets. What on earth *was* that? Dimly she recalled the loud sound that had awakened her. Then she remembered the live trap Ben had baited and set on her kitchen counter.

"Oh, God," she whispered. "We caught it."

Ben had told her to call him, but she always charged her phone in the kitchen overnight, and she hadn't thought to grab it before returning to bed. That meant she couldn't call Ben without going into the kitchen where the rat, now squeaking incessantly, was trapped in the cage.

Sissy pictured it—a big, hairy, ugly thing with dangerous fangs. She didn't want to go anywhere near it. But the sounds it was making would keep her awake all night. She had to call Ben so he could get it out of there.

Sissy slipped from the bed and crept to the doorway that led into her living room. She leaned around the jamb to flip on the wall switch. Light flooded the living room. *It's trapped in a cage, you silly goose. What are you afraid of? Just run in there and get your phone.* Feeling as if her feet were weighted to the floor, Sissy walked through the front room and flipped on the kitchen light.

It was the cutest little thing, golden brown in color, with round, erect ears lined in pink, a nose bracketed by whiskers that twitched like a rabbit's, and a sweet face. Far larger than a mouse, it still wasn't gigantic, about the size of a young kitten. It didn't seem at all afraid now that she'd shown herself. Then it peered at Sissy with shoe-button eyes bright with curiosity. The next squeak it emitted had a different tone, almost as if it were saying, *Oh, hi! Thank goodness it's only you.*

"You know me," she said softly. Then she laughed. "Well, of *course* you know me. We've been living together for months."

It squeaked as if in reply. A huge grin spread over her mouth. For some reason, it looked like a boy to her. A very cute little guy. She touched her finger to the side of the cage. He just scurried close, sniffing as if to identify her scent. Then he squeaked again, and this time she felt sure it was in friendly greeting.

"You little stinker," she said with a laugh. "You're the one who stole all my Snickers bars."

Tensed to jerk her hand back, she let the rat sniff her finger. His nose tickled her skin. Emboldened by his curious and gentle approach, she slowly inserted her finger all the way in. "Oh," she said, her heart almost melting. The rat nudged her. He wasn't aggressive. "You are so cute. Who was the idiot who decided to call you a rat? You're as cute as any chipmunk I've ever seen. What you need is a nice name. How about Snickers? Would you like that?"

Snickers picked up the measuring spoon. He used his front paws much like people use their hands.

"Are you hungry or thirsty?" she asked.

Snickers gave her an intent look, which she took as a yes. Only, what did pack rats like to eat? She got her laptop from the drawer of her entertainment stand and looked it up. Minutes later she returned from the downstairs kitchen with some wheatgrass and pine nuts. The cage had a side access door. She opened it and put her offerings on the floor of the enclosure. Snickers hurried over to sniff the food. He sampled a nut. Then he proceeded to eat a blade of grass, holding it like people do an ear of corn.

Ben slapped at the clock radio on his nightstand to make his alarm shut up. Then he sat on the edge of the bed, fumbling with the slide switch to turn the damned thing off. Slowly coming awake, he noticed his cell phone sitting on the nightstand. Sissy hadn't contacted him. Raking both hands through his hair, he wondered why. He'd been certain the pack rat would get caught in the trap overnight. But he guessed it hadn't. Sissy would have freaked out and called him.

Ben staggered into the adjoining master bathroom and stood for a good three minutes under a pulsing jet of warm water to wake himself up. Mixed in with the steam, the faint scent of freshly brewed coffee teased his nostrils. *Ah.* He'd remembered to prepare the coffeemaker and set the timer. When he got downstairs, a wonderful cup of java would be waiting.

After making quick work of his morning ablutions, Ben threw on clothing and stuffed his feet into his favorite work boots. Once downstairs, he enjoyed one mug of coffee in silence, wanting to enjoy at least part of his morning ritual. While sipping his second cup, he called Brett and asked him to take care of the morning chores. Ben had no clue why, but he felt uneasy about Sissy and wanted to check on her. Once he made sure she was okay, he'd be able to focus on his day.

Ben parked in Sissy's backyard shortly after six. Sunlight peeked over the mountains that ringed the east side of the valley, washing the pine-covered slopes in misty gold. Glancing up at the sky, now a deep gray streaked with rose, he decided that it promised to be a beautiful day. Once on the porch, he rapped on the door, hoping Sissy would hear him. Whether she was still upstairs or in the café kitchen, the acoustics in the old building weren't the best.

Soon, though, he heard the light, rapid pat of her footsteps. He guessed that she was hurrying down the stairs that led from her flat. Smiling slightly, he envisioned her face and wondered what she was wearing today. A knit top that hugged her torso like a second skin would be awesome. Not that she ever wore tight tops— but, hey, a guy could wish.

The door flew open so fast it almost startled him. Sissy's appearance finished the job. Though she wore her usual jeans and running shoes, the T-shirt that finished off her attire was so over-size that the hem hit her just above the knees. It was faded, thin with wear, and sported a hole in one sleeve. Her hair, normally tousled, but in a cute, attractive way, stood straight up in spikes at one side of her head. The other half lay flat. He wondered how in the hell she could still manage to look beautiful. Her face glowed, and twinkles of happiness danced in her eyes, reminding him of one of those rare midsummer nights when early stars glistened in a still blue sky just before full darkness descended.

"I caught him!" She whirled away and

vanished, calling back to him, "Hurry and come see, Ben. He's too cute for words!"

Cute? Ben wondered if he had wax in his ears. No rat was cute. But he followed Sissy as she sprinted up the stairs. After entering her apartment, she left the door standing open. As Ben stepped inside, his gaze shot to the kitchen counter. There was indeed a critter caught in the trap.

"Well," he said as he strode into the kitchen, "my idea worked."

"I've named him Snickers. You know, after the candy bars he stole. I was afraid of him at first, but he wasn't the least bit nervous of me. But, then, why should he be? We've been roommates for months!"

Ben drew up beside the cage just after Sissy did. After studying the small creature, he decided, *Nope, it isn't cute.*

Then Sissy made his pulse escalate by opening the side door. "Um, I wouldn't do that," Ben rushed to say. "He could bite you, and though we don't have many cases in central Oregon, rabies is always a concern."

"Oh, how silly. He doesn't bite." After making that pronouncement, she reached inside the cage, gently lifted the rat, and drew it out. Ben nearly had a heart attack. Cuddling the nasty little creature in her cupped hands, she tucked it against her neck just under her chin. "See? We're best friends! He already loved me. He's been hanging out with me, so to him I was a friend. And almost the first instant I saw him, I felt the same way. It's fate."

"Sissy." Ben stopped with her name and longed to say *um* for a full minute until he could think his way through this. "Rats can and do bite. They also carry diseases that are dangerous to humans. In fact, just breathing the air is probably a threat to your—and my—health."

Her eyes went bright with tears. "But he looks perfectly healthy!"

"That doesn't mean he isn't carrying viruses. You need to let me relocate him ASAP." Ben saw more tears gathering in her blue eyes. He rushed to add, "He's a wild creature. And no matter how cute he is, he needs to remain wild. I promise to find a good place to drop him off, someplace where he'll be happy, build a new nest, and make friends."

She looked up at Ben as if he'd just told her he was an ax murderer. "But that would be so cruel! It's turning winter. The nights are dropping below freezing sometimes! Snickers already has a cozy nest! If he's moved, he'll have no home, no shelter from the elements! He couldn't build another nest quickly enough to protect himself."

Snickers nuzzled Sissy's chin and then crawled up her shirt to snuggle against her ear. It gave

Ben the creeps. The rat turned to peer at Ben. In that moment, Ben had to admit, if only to himself, that the little guy was pretty damned cute—or would be, if he weren't a rat.

Even so, he could see love written all over Sissy's face. He decided that he had two choices. He could let her figure this out on her own, or he could take the necessary steps to protect her.

"Okay," he relented. "You want to keep him. I get it. But if you're going to do that, you should at least let me take him to the vet. Maybe Jack can run tests to make sure he isn't carrying anything dangerous, and there may even be vaccinations to protect Snickers from catching stuff." He paused to let Sissy assimilate that. "Will you at least let me do that much?"

She finally nodded. "I've never had a real pet as an adult, but I've read that responsible people always take them for checkups and inoculations." She returned Snickers to the cage and glanced at her watch. "I'm closing the café to go with him. Christopher will miss his special breakfast, but it can't be avoided. Snickers isn't afraid of me, but he may be of you."

Ben couldn't help but smile. He didn't get how she could have become so attached to anything so fast, but he could see it in her expression. "The world won't end if you aren't open for a day."

She sighed and smoothed her hair. It sprang erect again the moment she lifted her hand. "No, but I need to get cleaned up before I take him in."

"Do you mind if I go along?" Ben feared that Sissy might hear only what she wanted to hear while talking with the vet. "I can take notes on my phone while you and Jack talk. If you're going to keep him, Jack will recommend a good diet for him and stuff like that."

"Okay. I may be upset if Jack says I can't keep him. Two sets of ears will be better."

Ben glanced at his watch. "I'll call and make the appointment for eight sharp if I can. While you get ready, I'll go downstairs and fix us some breakfast."

She nodded and hurried to her bedroom. She stopped at the door. "Don't bring Finnegan up here. He may snarl at Snickers and terrify him."

The dog might frighten the rat. Give me patience. "I didn't think about that. Finn is in the truck, and he might go into ferocious mode when he sees Snickers. How about if I put him in the laundry room? He'll be fine in there with a bowl of water while we're gone."

Sissy nodded. "That'll work."

After Ben got Finnegan settled in Sissy's laundry room, he went into the café kitchen to fix their morning meal. He quickly learned how the appliances worked, and he chose to make a simple offering of eggs, bacon, hash browns, and toast. When he thought of Sissy upstairs, his chest panged with sadness. He felt pretty sure that Jack would not agree with Sissy's idea to make a pet out of a pack rat. He also felt certain that it would break her heart. For reasons beyond him, she'd fallen instantly in love with Snickers.

That told him so many things about her—mainly that she was lonely and needed something small and cuddly to love. *Damn.* Why couldn't she choose someone big and cuddly, like him? Ben smiled to himself, understanding in a way someone else might not that loving an animal was totally different from loving a person. People are complicated. Creatures aren't. Finnegan loved Ben unconditionally. Ben's horses loved him unconditionally as well, even though they weren't little. A special bond with an animal could be forged in only minutes. Ben had experienced that, and now apparently so had Sissy.

Ben wished he knew how to give Sissy the uncomplicated love that she needed. But wasn't he doing that right now? If she wanted to keep a wild rat, he'd go along for the ride. *Shit.* He wasn't just attracted to Sissy. He'd fallen head over heels in love with her.

Ben burned his finger on the grill as he flipped bread. He stopped cooking to shove the digit in his mouth. *I'm in love with her.* He didn't know why the hell he felt so shocked. The first time he ever saw her, he'd been captivated. And ever since the night he'd helped catch her chickens, she'd been carving out her own special place within his heart. The way she'd responded to his cows and horses. Her exclamation of delight over the blue butterflies up at the falls. How she always pampered Finn and was aware of the pup's needs, sometimes before Ben thought of them himself. He'd persisted in thinking of his feelings as a strong attraction.

He remembered the single tear that had slipped down her cheek as she stood over her dead hens. How glad he'd felt when he heard her voice after getting home from Montana. Hell, he'd even been excited about helping her dust chickens. It went on for hours until he could barely breathe. And yet he'd been so eager to see Sissy again that he'd volunteered for the job. What had he needed to realize he was falling in love with the woman, a neon sign flashing before his eyes?

Ben, still sucking his finger, stared down at the grill. He had incinerated the toast. He quickly flipped the hash browns so they wouldn't meet the same fate.

Ben felt like a whore in church while he sat with Sissy in the vet clinic waiting area. No, worse than that. He felt as if he were wearing a sign across his chest that read, WEIRDO. DON'T GET

TOO CLOSE. Other people with ordinary pets stared first at Snickers and then at Ben and Sissy. Clearly it wasn't often that anyone brought a rat in for a checkup.

"I thought pet rats were white," a blue-haired old lady, holding an equally old gray poodle, commented.

Sissy stiffened beside Ben. "No," she said. "They can come in different colors."

"I believe that's mice you're thinking of," Ben inserted, attempting to inject into his voice a tone that would stop the old woman from saying more. It didn't work.

"Well, I believe *most* pet rats are white," she informed them. "I've seen a few that were dappled color but I've never seen a *brown* pet rat."

Ben gazed at Snickers, who sat up on his haunches worrying his hands. *No, not hands, paws.* But the creature was dexterous, even so. He felt indignation welling inside him, and he also sensed that Sissy was getting upset. For reasons he couldn't clearly define, he felt as defensive of her new friend as she did. Using his French, he said, "He's a *spécial miel brun.*" In English that meant Snickers was a special honey brown, but the lady didn't know that.

"Oh, *my*," she replied. "He's an exotic rat, then?"

Sissy inserted, "Why does it matter? He's my pet, and he's here to see the vet, like your dog. You're sounding a bit racist to me, frowning upon my beautiful rat because he's not the color you think he should be."

"Oh, yes, he's special," Ben added. "They have them in France." That wasn't a lie; Ben felt certain France was just as infested with pack rats as the United States. "Getting him was no easy feat." Again, that was the truth. "We're bringing him in for a vet check. He has a delicate constitution." *Disease infested* might have been a better term. "Your poodle isn't sick, I hope."

The old gal drew her dog closer to her chest. "He has a cough."

"Oh, *no*." Ben pushed to his feet, grabbed the handle of the cage, and pulled Sissy along behind him as he moved to sit where there were fewer people. "The *spècial miel brun* should never be exposed to ordinary pets." Ben felt sweat trickling down his spine. He gave the office receptionist behind the counter a pointed look. "Can you ask one of the vet assistants to get us into a room? This extremely expensive rat may have a com-promised immune system."

The receptionist, a plump brunette with tortoise-shell glasses, nodded and hurried into the back of the building.

Sissy giggled and whispered to Ben, "A *French* rat? And extremely expensive as well?"

"Trust me," Ben replied. "When you pay the vet bill, Snickers will be extremely expensive."

A moment later, Cassidy Peck appeared. Ben noticed a glint of laughter in her blue eyes as she said, "Mr. Sterling, Ms. Bentley, will you please follow me?"

Ben was so grateful that he wanted to hug the girl as he followed her into a hallway. "Thank you. I was afraid panic might break out if someone realized a pack rat was in the waiting area."

Cassidy giggled. "The receptionist told me it's an exotic French rat. Where did that come from? On the chart, it says you caught a pack rat in a live trap."

"I never said he came from France," Ben replied. "I told the lady what color he is in French and said they have them in France, which I'm sure they do."

Once inside the room, Ben set the cage on the examining table. Cassidy smiled at them and extended her hand to Sissy. "I don't believe we've met, although I've eaten at your café. I'm Cassidy Peck."

When Jack Palmer entered the examining room, he was grinning from ear to ear. Rubbing his hands together, he said, "I can't wait to hear this story. I mean, it could make headline news. Ben Sterling, a rough-and-tough rodeo guy, falls for a pack rat."

Ben arched one eyebrow. "I am *not* in love with a pack rat." He gestured at Sissy. "My friend is, however."

"Yes, I definitely am in love," Sissy affirmed. "I brought him in to have you check him over and possibly vaccinate him against any diseases he may catch and treat him for anything he may already have. I'm keeping him as a pet."

"Aw." Jack's gray eyes shimmered, and his grin dimmed slightly. He introduced himself to Sissy and then said, "Keeping this rat as a pet isn't an idea that I can recommend."

Sissy tried to protest, but Jack held up a hand. "That isn't to say it can't be done. But studies show that being caged can shorten the rat's life span. They're very social creatures."

Sissy's shoulders slumped. "Shorten his life span? But why? I'd love him to pieces and give him everything he needs."

Ben and Jack exchanged a loaded look. Jack scratched his temple. "Well, if that's what you decide to do, no one can stop you. But if you love this rat, you need to realize that he won't be happy in a cage, and no matter how hard you try, you can't give him *everything* he needs. Plus, pack rats can carry diseases that are harmful to humans and other pets."

Sissy wasn't going to be so easily discouraged. "Can you test Snickers to see if he's carrying any of those diseases?"

Jack leaned his hips against the table and crossed his arms. "First of all, I don't recommend caging this animal, so in the spirit of full disclosure, I can run a blood panel to check for certain stuff, but why bother? If you allow the rat to come and go as it pleases so it'll be happy, testing it for diseases would cost you a small fortune and do absolutely no good. Snickers—cute name, by the way—might test negative on all counts one day and then catch a disease—or virus—the next." It was Jack's turn to arch an eyebrow. "Are you following me?"

"I'm following you, but I really want to keep him."

Jack's grin faded entirely. "I'm sorry, Ms. Bentley. It's my professional opinion that trying to domesticate a pack rat will end in failure. If I search, I may find some tests I can run on a wild rat, but I think most of them are done on dead ones in a lab. Bottom line, I can clean out your wallet, but unless you keep the rat confined, it'll be a useless expenditure. About all I can really do is recommend a healthy diet for him."

"Can you at least check him for fleas?" Ben asked.

Jack sighed. "I can even treat him for those. But if he returns to a flea-infested nest, he'll only get more."

Ben held Jack's gaze, longer this time, trying to convey to the man without words that he was breaking Sissy's heart. Apparently Jack got the message. He hopped up on the counter by the sink and smiled at Sissy.

"Let's look at a couple of alternatives," he said gently. Pulling a prescription pad and pen from his pocket, he jotted notes and handed the page to Sissy. "Here are some websites I suggest that you visit. You can read about the ramifications for Snickers if you keep him in a cage. But, after reading about them, if you decide the kinder thing is to release him back into the wild, it doesn't mean you must end your friendship with him." He nodded toward Ben. "Maybe with his help you can find Snickers's nest. Then you could visit him every day, taking him and his friends little surprises. You'll need to plug all the holes in your building, though, so Snickers can only see you at his nest. He truly may carry diseases, so that will be safer for you and your other pets."

Sissy looked to Ben as if she were about to burst into tears, and Sissy wasn't one to easily reveal her emotions that way. "I have no other pets, not even *one,*" she said, her voice shaking. "Only my chickens, and I learned the hard way not to let myself love them too much. Now I've found Snickers. And it won't be the same, visiting him at his nest."

"But you *could* have another pet," Jack stated. Arching a brow, he asked, "Would you mind leaving Snickers here for a moment while I introduce you to someone?"

By now, Sissy's body was so taut with emotion that Ben feared she might shatter like blown glass. "I don't need or want another pet. Snickers and I are fated to be friends."

Jack nodded. "I understand that, but what if there's a little creature who needs *you?* A sweet little someone who may die in the morning if he isn't adopted. Won't you please take just a moment to meet him?"

Sissy's rebellious expression vanished. "Die?"

Jack hopped off the counter. "Yes. Please, just spare him a moment. He's a very special little fellow."

Sissy glanced over her shoulder at Ben. Her pleading gaze obliterated all his objections to her keeping Snickers. If it mattered so much to her, he'd do everything in his power to make it happen.

She surprised Ben by saying, "Of course I'll spare a moment. Why will he die if he isn't adopted?"

Jack opened the door and beckoned for them to follow him up a long hallway.

Chapter
TWELVE

Jack led Sissy and Ben to a large room lined floor to ceiling along each wall with cages. Sissy felt almost claustrophobic and struggled to breathe. This vet wanted her to turn Snickers loose into the wild and try to love another animal. Well, she had news for him. She owned a café. A dog would be all wrong. She heard them whining all around her, with an occasional, pathetic meow of a cat to change the tune.

Most of the cages contained animals that looked as if they'd undergone surgery.

"Is this your recovery room?" Ben asked.

"And holding area." Jack stopped at a sink to wash his hands. Then he went to the far end of the cages stacked along the right wall. He opened a chest-high wire door. "This is who I want you to meet, Sissy."

She stepped closer. Inside the cage, she saw a fluffy gray kitten missing both front feet. The amputated limbs appeared to be almost healed, the stubs grown over with pink skin.

"This fellow got left outside by his owners," Jack explained. "When the man got home from work, it was cold outside, and the kitten sought warmth under the hood of his car. It happens too often. A recently used engine puts off heat, and a small creature gravitates toward the warmth. When the man's wife told him he needed to make a grocery run for dinner, he went back out to the car, started the engine, and heard yowling."

"Oh, my God," Sissy whispered.

"The kitten's front legs were mangled by the fan belt. I performed surgery, and he's healing nicely. He could live to a ripe old age if he were given the chance."

"What do you mean?" she asked.

"His owners have been waffling about what to do, and today, they decided to have him euthanized because he will require special care. This little guy can never go outside unless he's in a safe enclosure. He'll never be able to climb a tree or defend himself against other cats." Jack paused. "I'm supposed to put him down in the morning."

Sissy couldn't see how this poor kitten related to her dilemma with Snickers, but her heart was already aching for the little guy in the cage. "That's *horrible*" was all she could think to say.

"Especially when there's a fabulous no-kill shelter next door where the kitten could possibly be adopted and go to a wonderful home," Jack said. "If I could get authorization from the owners, I'd put him in the shelter. I work over there pro bono. I'm confident he'd get adopted. But the owners don't share my certainty of that, and they don't want the kitten to live over there for years in a cage."

"Well, that wouldn't be a good life for him," she agreed.

Behind her, Ben said, "Well, heck, of course he'll get adopted. I'd take him if I could, but I have barn cats. If the kitten ever got outside, he'd be toast."

Just then the kitten hobbled over to its food dish. Jack winked at Sissy. "See? He's already walking. I'm sure his stumps are still tender, but over time they'll toughen up, and he'll be running all over the place. Or he will if he gets the chance." He gave her a solemn look. "If only someone would offer to adopt him today and convince the owners that he'll have a wonderful, loving home, I wouldn't have to kill him in the morning. Unfortunately, a vet is required by law to comply with the owners' wishes in regards to an animal in his care. If this kitten were a stray, I'd have more control over its fate."

Sissy felt her fists bunch at her sides, as if of their own volition. That kitten was every bit as adorable as Snickers, and his owners had consigned him to death. "I could give him a wonderful home." She looked up at the vet. "He deserves to live. It's not fair that his owners have that kind of power when he is perfectly healthy, except for having no front feet!"

Jack sighed. "I feel the same way. Do you really

want to adopt him? He'll never be able to be an outdoor cat. He may occasionally hurt his stubs and need them to be medicated and wrapped. He won't be that much trouble, really, but he won't be as easy to care for as a regular kitten."

Sissy feasted her gaze on that adorable little fluff ball and instantly decided that she'd do anything to stop him from being euthanized. "I'm sure. I want him."

Jack nodded. "But then you have Snickers to think of as well, Sissy. If you keep him caged, this kitten should be able to share the same home with him. But if you let Snickers return to his natural environment, which is my vote, you can never allow Snickers to be in your residence, just in case he has caught a disease that may compromise the health of the cat."

With a decision like that to make, Sissy resisted her urge to reach past Jack to pet the kitten. He would be dead by this time tomorrow if she didn't take him. But in another room of this clinic, Snickers, all trusting of her, waited. She couldn't decide his fate without researching the ramifications of domesticating a pack rat.

As if he read her mind, Jack said, "We have some time. Maybe you should go home and read online about pack rats. Then, if you wish to release Snickers and take the kitten, you can call me. I've thrown a lot at you all at once."

Sissy stared at that sweet bundle of gray fur. This kitten, with no front feet, was defying all the odds and walking. She had defied all the odds, too. "But if I keep Snickers caged and checked often by you, I could still have the kitten?" she asked.

Jack nodded.

That settled it for Sissy. "Then I'll adopt him. He'll have a wonderful home with me."

With a slump of his shoulders, Jack said, "It may not be that simple. The owners of the kitten may still insist on euthanizing him even if I call them and sing your praises." He pulled the prescription pad from his pocket and jotted something down before handing it to her. "You can also call them to reassure them that you'll give the kitten a good home. Their last name is Miller. But be aware that they are, as pet owners go, a little odd. I think they're way over-the-top about his disability. But ultimately it will be their decision, not mine."

Sissy gaped up at him. "You mean, even if I want to adopt him, they may still reject me as suitable and have him euthanized?"

"Pretty much, yes." Jack sighed. "By law, it's out of my hands. It's one of the saddest things for me as a vet. Sometimes when I know an animal can be saved, the owners, for whatever reason, decide otherwise."

Sissy struggled to see through a red haze of

anger. "I'll do the responsible thing for Snickers," she pushed out. "Now I'll ask you to do one outrageously responsible thing for this kitten. If I call these people and tell them what a wonderful home I can give this kitty and they reject me as an adoptive owner, can you accidentally leave the back door of your clinic unlocked tonight?"

A stunned expression crossed the vet's face. Then his Adam's apple bobbed in his throat as he swallowed. "I do occasionally forget to lock the back door and set the security system."

Sissy nodded, certain he understood her intentions. It crossed her mind that she was once again trusting a man. Her common sense seemed to have leaked out her ears. "Great. Just in case, be forgetful tonight. *Please?*"

Sissy knew that she was putting the vet in a horrible position, but if it was within her power, she would *not* allow that precious kitten to be killed in the morning. She didn't wait for Jack to agree. That would make him complicit in the execution of a crime she intended to commit. She could only hope he left the clinic unprotected that night. It probably wouldn't be necessary for her to carry out her backup plan, but if the kitten's owners proved to be difficult—well, Sissy would intervene.

She turned and ran smack-dab into Ben's chest. To his credit, he acted perfectly normal, saying farewell to the vet and helping her to collect Snickers and leave the clinic. It wasn't until they were in the truck that he reacted.

"What the *hell?* You just asked Jack to leave the clinic unprotected tonight so you can *steal* that kitten if the owners won't let you adopt him."

Sissy, holding Snickers's cage on her lap, stared with burning eyes out the windshield, seeing almost nothing. "Yep."

"Are you out of your mind?"

Sissy took a deep breath and slowly released it. "No. I've lived under the radar all my life, always keeping my head down. I know you don't understand. But this is one time, only one time, when I'm going to stand up for what's right, no matter what. Normally, I don't commit crimes, but to save that kitten, I will. If I offer to adopt him and his owners still insist on killing him, I'm going in there tonight and stealing him."

Ben didn't start the truck. He stared for a long moment at Snickers. Sissy saw emotions she couldn't read cross his handsome countenance. He swallowed hard, just like the vet had. Then he said, "Well, sweetheart, if we're going to commit a B and E, we need something more than a half-baked plan."

Sissy gaped at him. "*We?* I don't expect you to do it with me."

Ben started the engine. "I know. But I'll be damned if I'll let you do it alone. I'm in love with you. Any man worth his salt stands by the woman he loves."

Sissy tried to assimilate that, but none of it computed in her brain. She'd held him at arm's length. Sometimes she'd even been rude to him.

Ben said, "Don't overthink it. I'm sorry I told you like that. I guess *romantic* isn't my middle name. But damn it, Sissy, I care about you. If you're dead set on rescuing that kitten, you're not doing it alone. Too much could go wrong."

"Your brother is a deputy!" She realized she was shouting and struggled to calm down. "You are a *Sterling,* not a Bentley. Sterlings don't commit crimes."

"This one will." He flashed her a broad grin. "Actually, I think you're bringing out my wild side. It sounds kind of fun. Bonnie and Clyde stealing a kitten. Whether you like it or not, you're not alone anymore. You've got me. We could both do time for this, but I'm not going to chicken out at the last minute. Are you?"

Sissy hadn't actually thought about the serious aspects of what she meant to do. She swallowed hard. Then she thought of that kitten, the victim of two crazy people. She'd been there once. And nobody had been brave enough to rescue her. "No, I'm not going to chicken out. If those people deny me the right to adopt that kitten, I'm going to go get him tonight, with or without you."

"With me," he shot back. He sent her a burning look. "I don't want to make you get all skittish. I know you don't *want* me to care about you. But if I can't control how I feel, you sure as hell can't."

Sissy couldn't bring herself to address his feelings or her own right then. "So, what's our plan?"

Ben pulled out of the parking lot. Moments later he headed south on North Huckleberry toward town. "Well, if you don't get the kitten, I think Jack probably makes his night rounds well before ten. So I think we should leave for the clinic at that time."

Sissy's stomach knotted. It was scary to think about committing a criminal act, no matter how important it was. "Ten sounds great. I'll be finished with closing and have breakfast prep done. I think we should wear black so we'll blend in with the darkness."

"Good idea. And we shouldn't be seen together. I won't come in for dinner tonight."

She nodded. "Should we meet somewhere, then?"

"I'm afraid someone might see our vehicles together. By ten Main is mostly dark. Meet me at ten sharp in front of the café. Stand against the building in the shadows."

"Okay," she agreed. "Douse your headlights as you come onto Main. That way, your truck won't be as visible. Come to a stop in front of my place, and I'll run out to get in." She sighed. "I just hope those stupid people don't turn me down."

"Me, too."

He drove into Sissy's backyard. She understood why he didn't offer to exit his truck and go inside. "Set the cage by the stairs and let Finn outside. I'll call him. He'll just load up if I have the door open."

Sissy, cautiously balancing Snickers's cage, opened her door and slid to the ground. "The owners work, so I'll let you know what they say sometime after five when they should be home to take my call."

Ben inclined his head at the cage she embraced. "Don't forget to visit those websites to read up on pack rats kept in captivity."

Her heart squeezed. "I won't. I think I'll keep the café closed for lunch so I have time to do that. I can also get a head start on breakfast prep for tomorrow. If the kitten's owners are unreasonable, it may be a really busy night."

After finishing dinner prep, Sissy carried Snickers upstairs. The moment she entered the kitchen, she set the live trap on her table, opened the side door, and lifted the rat into her cupped hands.

"Hi, baby." She giggled when Snickers touched her wristwatch and tipped his head, clearly mesmerized by the shiny crystal. "You already stole one once. No repeat performances."

Cuddling the rat close, Sissy got out her laptop and sat on the sofa to boot up her system. While the computer loaded, she ran her fingers over Snickers's fur. He smelled of flea powder, but she didn't care.

"We're going to surf the Internet," she said. "It'll be a lot of doom-and-gloom nonsense, mind you, and nothing I read will change my mind. From here on out, we're going to be friends always, and if the kitten grows up with you, he won't try to hurt you as he grows larger."

Within minutes, tears were running down Sissy's cheeks. She set aside the laptop and returned Snickers to his cage. Then she drew her cell phone from her pocket and dialed Ben's number.

The familiar sound of his deep voice brought more tears to Sissy's eyes. "It's me," she said, her throat tight. "I visited the websites. They say Snickers may have a shortened life span if I keep him in a cage. And that he needs to hang out with other pack rats to be happy and healthy."

"I'm sorry, honey. I wish it were different."

Sissy squeezed her eyes closed. "I can't keep him, Ben. Why can't I have just one little friend to love?" She sniffed and wiped her nose on her shirtsleeve. "If I can't get the kitten for whatever reason, setting Snickers free will leave me alone again."

"I know. But Jack Palmer says I can ratproof your building so Snickers can't get back inside if you set him free. Once we know where his nest is, you'll be able to visit him every day. So you aren't saying good-bye. You can still have Snickers as your friend."

"I worry that it may frighten the other rats if I go near their nests."

Ben laughed. "Well, you may give them a startle the first time you visit. But once they realize you bring gifts, they'll probably look forward to seeing you."

Sissy felt a bit better, not quite so sad. "It won't be the same, though."

"No," Ben agreed. "But you won't have to say good-bye to Snickers and never see him again. And there's a huge possibility that the Millers will love the idea of you giving their kitten a wonderful home. And if they don't, we move on to plan B."

"True. And if something happens so that I can't steal the kitten, I suppose I could adopt one the ordinary way. I'm sure there are lots of kittens at the no-kill shelter who need good homes."

"That's the spirit."

"But another kitten will never need me as much as the injured one does."

She heard Ben sigh. "No. His circumstances are unique. And because of his problems, you'll probably love him more than you might a perfectly healthy cat."

Sissy appreciated his understanding. Some men might not have.

"So," he said, "have you decided what the better choice is for Snickers yet?"

She also appreciated that Ben wasn't pressing her to make the decision he hoped she would. "It's pretty clear that keeping him in captivity isn't better for Snickers." She heard her voice go thin. "I have to turn him loose."

"It won't be easy," Ben warned. "The two of you bonded pretty fast."

"Doing the right thing is often difficult. Maybe I'll wait until I have the kitten before I turn Snickers loose."

"Great idea," he agreed. "You'll have the kitten for comfort. And don't forget that you'll be able to visit Snickers at his nest if I'm able to find it."

"Knowing that helps." Sissy could think of little else to say on that topic. "I'll try to reach the Millers around five thirty. I'll call you immediately after I talk to them."

She heard Ben clear his throat. "Just in case it doesn't go well, have your cat burglar clothes laid out."

"Cat burglar clothes?" She pushed aside her sadness over Snickers and laughed. "That's apropos."

"Pun intended." After a moment's silence, he said, "I'll be waiting on pins and needles for your call."

The Cauldron was packed with diners. All the counter stools were taken. The booths were full. Sissy had people standing by the front door, waiting to eat. Normally she would have been pleased, but tonight all she wanted was to chase everyone out of her café, lock the door, and wait for the Millers to call her back. At five thirty, they hadn't answered their home phone, so she'd left a message.

"It's the coach's fault," Blackie yelled as she walked by his place at the bar. "Why did he allow that stupid pass? He had to know the other team's offense might intercept!"

Sissy nodded and pretended to care, but pulling that off while both her arms were laden with plates was nearly impossible. Just as Sissy reached Chris and Kim Peck's table, her cell phone vibrated. It was the Millers calling. It was almost six. They would have listened to her message by now.

Sissy couldn't answer the call with both hands full. And she didn't like talking on her phone while serving customers. *Damn and drat!* Gritting her teeth to keep from saying those words out loud, she forced her lips to curve into a smile.

"Here you go," she said, injecting warmth she

didn't feel into her voice. "The shrimp for Kimberly, and the pot roast for Chris." She set the heaped plates in front of both restaurateurs. "I hope you enjoy your meals, but I've got to add that you're slumming it by eating here. Nothing I serve can compare to the gourmet creations at your place. All my stuff is ordinary."

Kimberly laughed. A petite natural blonde with gray eyes, she radiated friendliness. "That's why we're here. We're craving ordinary."

Chris, a tall, slender man with jet-black hair and merry blue eyes, took a bite of roast and moaned as if he'd just tasted ambrosia. "Oh, man. I heard it was fabulous, and it is."

"Thank you." Sissy appreciated the compliment, but her phone was vibrating in her pocket again. "Please, enjoy your meal, and if you need anything more, just signal me. I'll be right over."

Sissy refused to run in front of her customers, so she speed-walked back to the kitchen and darted into the pantry. She checked her recent calls, and sure enough, the last two had been from the Miller residence. Sissy quickly dialed them back.

A woman answered. "Ah, Ms. Bentley. Irene Miller at this end. I was hoping you'd get back to me quickly. I hated for you to get your hopes up only to have us dash them."

Sissy stiffened. "Dash them? I'm the perfect person to give your kitten a good home. I live alone. I have no other pets. He'd be so happy with me."

"Yes, but as we understand it, you own a café and live above your business. Stairs aren't a good fit for this kitten. Going up and down steps will always be painful for him."

"But he won't be on the stairs, and even if he ever were, according to the vet, his stubs will heal and toughen up."

"I'm sorry," the woman said. "But my husband and I both agree that stairs are a huge problem. We wish you luck in finding a kitten more suited to your living arrangements."

Before Sissy could reply, the woman hung up. Sissy immediately dialed Ben.

He answered with "Did you get him?"

"No!" Sissy said, unable to keep the outrage she felt from her tone. "And I'm swamped in here, so I'll spit it out fast. My living arrangements are unsuitable for their kitten because I have stairs. So we're on for tonight. Meet me out front at ten sharp."

"Maybe I can call and ask to adopt him."

Sissy shook her head even though she knew he couldn't see her. "You have barn cats and a dog." Because he'd offered an alternative to meeting her later, she asked, "Are you wanting to back out? There could be serious ramifications for both of us if we're caught, and I'll certainly understand if you've had second thoughts."

"No second thoughts. By midnight, you're going to be a kitten mama."

Sissy giggled nervously. "From your lips to God's ear."

Sissy's heart was pounding as she returned to the café dining room. She and Ben were actually going to commit a B and E. It was a crime. If she had any sense, she would stop this nonsense right now. She took a deep breath and thought of the poor kitten, consigned to death. She didn't have a lick of sense, she guessed, because she intended to do it.

Sissy stood in the shadows of her building, shivering with cold. West Main was empty of cars. A few upstairs lights glowed through apartment windows, but otherwise, the town had rolled up the carpet. The streetlamps shone in the darkness, illuminating the fog that had descended over the town.

Foggy is good, Sissy told herself. *With both of us wearing black, we'll be harder to spot.* From the town center, she heard the clock tower bong the hour. The repetitive sounds seemed eerie tonight, not as soothing as they usually were. Just then she heard a noise and realized it was hard rubber tread grabbing at asphalt. A second later, a long blue shape, almost indiscernible in the darkness, rounded the street corner.

When the truck stopped in the right lane, Sissy

dashed from her hiding place and darted into the thoroughfare. As she drew closer to the vehicle, she could barely make out Ben's hulky silhouette through the driver's-side window. She circled the front bumper, tucked her frozen fingers under the lift-up door handle, and jumped inside.

"Wow. The lady has springs on her feet tonight."

Sissy closed the door with as little force as possible and started to buckle up. *Safety first,* that was her motto. But what they planned to do tonight was far from safe, and if they hoped to succeed in their mission without getting caught, she had to get into the proper frame of mind. "I'm a criminal. Criminals don't worry about stupid things like seat belts."

"What?" In the yellow-green glow of the dash lights, Ben, wearing his Stetson, looked like a cowboy with faint firelight casting his features into sharp relief. "You sound pretty nervous."

Sissy hadn't realized she'd spoken aloud. "I'm just doing mental prep."

"Breakfast prep, followed by mental prep. I get you. Only, mental prep for what?"

"Breaking and entering, for one. And theft on top of that. We could get into serious trouble."

"Well, it's not grand theft auto," Ben reminded her. "It's a mutt kitten that's scheduled to be euthanized."

"True, but it's still theft, plus breaking and entering."

"If Jack left the back door of the clinic unlocked, we'll at least know he's supportive of what we're doing."

Sissy stretched her neck and shoulders, trying to make her muscles relax. "That's true. If he paved our way, he'll be in on it with us."

"Well, I can't say he's in on it, exactly. He's making it easier, but that's all. He won't go down with us if we get caught."

Sissy stiffened again. "But if he left the door unlocked, we're not really breaking and entering. Right?"

Ben drove around the town center and took North Huckleberry. The instant they cleared the city limits, he flipped the headlights on. "Whoa. Resume your mental prep for criminal activity. Just because a door is left unlocked doesn't mean we have authorization to enter the building. And Jack will have to file a police report, just as if an actual crime has been committed. With the kitten missing, it would look strange if he didn't. He'll have to play it as if it's for real, or he'll be at risk of getting his license revoked. If we get caught, Jack won't step forward. This was our idea. Well, yours, actually, but I'm in. So it's our risk to take." He sent Sissy a questioning look. "If you're that nervous, you can stay in the truck and I'll do it."

The tension zinged straight back into Sissy's body. "I said I would go, and I'm going. My kitten's life is on the line. So what's our plan?"

She saw him smile as he returned his attention to the road. "Well, I'm going to park well away from the clinic, so we'll have to walk. It's darker than hell out on Hurricane Road at night. No streetlights, only a few houses. I brought a little penlight, but I don't want to use it unless it's necessary. It'll draw attention to us. We know which cage the kitten's in. I want to sneak in, not turn on any lights, find his cage, grab him, and run like hell."

Sissy nodded. "I can't see very well in the dark."

"Well, our eyes will be adjusted to it by the time we reach the clinic. And maybe inside there'll be some sources of faint light, like digital screens on equipment." He glanced at her again. "Can you see in here with the dash lights on?"

"Yes."

"Well, then, there you go." She heard him chuckle. "I've never done anything like this, either. I'm not worried that we can't pull it off. I'm more concerned about my brother Barney seeing the police report and then meeting the kitten later. Two missing front feet are identifying marks that are pretty uncommon."

"True." Sissy was starting to relax again. Ben didn't seem worried, and there was something about him that always soothed her. "But it's very unlikely that Barney will ever see the kitten.

He does eat at the Cauldron sometimes, but he'll never go upstairs."

"It's my motto never to say never," Ben replied. "Barney's a cop. I don't know what he'd do if he found out we stole a kitten to save it from being killed. The cop in him would feel obligated to press charges against us, the regular guy in him would be glad we saved the kitten, and he'd feel conflicted. Especially since I'm his brother. I honestly don't know which part of him would win."

"Well, let's just hope he's never put to the test."

It seemed to Sissy that Ben was pulling off to the side of Hurricane Road in only seconds. The instant he cut the engine and the headlamps blinked off, an impenetrable darkness blanketed the vehicle. Sissy leaned toward the windshield to peer out. In the distance, she saw a house with some lights still on, but it was otherwise as black as a cave out there.

"You can hold my arm," Ben told her. "I'll come around to your side and help you out. No tumbles into the drainage ditch allowed. You might scrape your face, and tomorrow everyone would wonder what had happened to you."

She grabbed blindly for his arm before he got out of the truck. "Before we do this, I want you to know that there's nobody on earth I'd rather do time with."

Ben chuckled and gave her a quick hug.

"Same for me." His voice sounded thick. "But I don't think any Oregon prisons have unisex cell blocks."

"Oh."

Ben got out and came around the truck to help Sissy out. In moments, she was holding his arm. For every sure-footed stride he took, she stumbled over something. She couldn't walk with confidence until they stepped onto asphalt. She still wasn't able to see where she was putting her feet, but at least she was traveling over a level surface.

When they rounded a curve in the road, she saw the clinic. Yard lights illuminated the area all around the large building. "Oh, God. How can we stay hidden when we get there?"

"We can't. It'll be time to do the fastest one-hundred-yard dash on record. One thing's in our favor, though. The no-kill shelter next door to the clinic is home to a lot of dogs that bark and howl all night, so only one home has been built near there. It belongs to Hutch and Sue Mulder. They own Hutch's, a little fast-food joint by the high school at the end of the road. Kids go off campus to eat there. The Mulders get up early to offer breakfast, so they're probably in bed."

"Where does Jack live?"

"Just this side of the clinic."

"Oh, no."

Ben laughed. "Sissy, he doesn't want to

euthanize the kitten. If he left the back door unlocked, I doubt he's going to peer out his windows, hoping to catch us."

When they got close to the clinic, Sissy noticed that the house right next to it had no lights on. "Is that Jack's place?"

"Yes. And over on the right, catty-corner from the clinic, is where the Mulders live. Only their porch light is on. Nobody is awake there, either."

When they reached the huge circle of illumination created by the security lights, Sissy's heart started to race. "I don't think I can break any records doing a hundred-yard dash," she whispered. "My legs are short."

Ben gave her hand a squeeze and then didn't release his hold. "Just in case you trip, I don't want you to fall down."

She took a deep breath and had barely expelled it when Ben broke into a run, pulling her along beside him. He stayed on the asphalt byway that went past the building to an equine-care facility.

Once they circled the clinic, the roofline cast shadows to hide them as they raced toward the back door. Sissy was about to chuff out a sigh of relief when her feet hit a patch of ice. One of her legs shot sideways. She felt herself start to go down. Ben, still holding her hand, caught her from falling.

As she got her balance, she whispered, "Studded boots?"

"And thank God I'm wearing them."

They reached the porch. Ben let go of Sissy's hand. He chafed his palms together and stared at the doorknob. "Well, this is it, the moment when we'll find out what Jack's made of."

"If it's locked, what then?"

"We break in. We haven't come this far to let a stupid door stop us."

Ben grasped the knob. When he turned it, the door swung inward. A breath that Sissy hadn't realized she'd been holding whooshed from her lungs.

Ben drew her inside the dark bowels of the building. She heard the door close softly behind her. "Jack's the man," he whispered.

Sissy nodded, but she was too scared to speak. *I'm committing a crime,* she thought. For a moment, she felt paralyzed. Then she pictured the kitten they'd come to save, and an adrenaline rush, the likes of which she'd never experienced, sent thrills of excitement coursing through her body. "Let's *do* this!"

Ben said, "You've got mettle."

"What's that?"

"Guts. Nerve. What it takes to go the whole nine yards."

Sissy grinned as he drew her along a dark corridor. "Thanks. This is starting to be kind of fun."

Ben chuckled as he pushed open another door.

"This is it, the recovery room."

Sissy heard a dog whine off to her right. Then the sounds of animals wanting comfort erupted from all around them. Cats meowed. Puppies began to bark. Large dogs started to not only bark but also howl. "Oh, shit, oh, shit," Sissy cried. "We are so *screwed*."

"Yep," Ben agreed as he pulled her off to their left. "A built-in natural security alarm." He drew to a sudden stop. "He's here, at the end, second cage from the top. Right?"

"Right." Sissy realized he was almost yelling so she could hear him. "*Shh!* Don't talk so loud!" she yelled back, and then the absurdity of it hit her, and she started to giggle. "Get him. Quick. We have to get out of here."

She heard a cage door clank open. The next moment, Ben said, "Got him. Now is when we run like our lives depend on it."

He grabbed her hand with an unerring aim that told Sissy he could at least see something in the void of blackness. He broke into a run. At this point, his trusty studded boots put him at a disadvantage on tile floors. While Sissy's athletic shoes grabbed for traction, his footwear slipped on the slick surface. But they made it to the back door and out onto the porch, and then huddled in the shadows to hide until the animals inside the clinic finally quieted down.

"We did it," Ben said with a note of pride in his

voice. "You are one hell of a partner in crime. We should do this more often." She felt him press the backs of his knuckles against her chest. "Here you go, Mama. Your new baby. He's a cutie."

Sissy felt with her hands. In the dim glow of the yard lights, she could barely make out the kitten, but by touch, she could tell he was just as beautiful as she remembered, with dark, fluffy fur and a warm little body. Her heart felt as if it were melting as she cupped his weight in one hand and trailed the fingertips of her other hand over him.

"Ben?" she whispered, unable to keep the urgency out of her voice.

"What?"

Sissy had a hysterical urge to giggle. "It's got front feet."

"What?"

"Front feet. We grabbed the wrong kitten." A horrible thought hit Sissy. She searched by touch and felt a stitched incision on the kitten's belly. "I think this one's a girl. And, oh, God, fresh out of surgery. She's just been neutered."

"Jesus." Ben, a dark, looming hulk, turned toward her. "Spayed, you mean?" He muttered under his breath. "Be gentle. Shit! Shit, *shit!* I know I got the right cage! What the hell?"

Beyond the glow of the yard lights, a male voice boomed, frightening Sissy half out of her wits. "Why the hell didn't you turn on the lights, Sterling? My techs shift the patients, putting the recent surgery patients at that end. The kitten with the amputated legs graduated to light care today."

"Well, now is a fine time to tell me," Ben boomed back. "You could have texted me!"

Sissy recovered her senses and struggled not to laugh hysterically.

"Electronic evidence," Palmer shouted. "I never saw you. I never talked to you. I know nothing about this. Got it? Same side, six rows down, third cage from the top. And for God's sake, turn on the lights so you put that kitten back in the right place. She's still loopy from the anesthetic. Handle her with care."

Sissy heard receding footsteps and knew Jack Palmer, apparently disgusted with their ineptitude at kitten stealing, was walking back home.

Ben slumped against the side of the building. "Am I dreaming this?"

"No," Sissy replied. "Because I'm having the same nightmare." She gently cupped both hands over the kitten and held her protectively against her chest. "Poor little girl. We'll put you back in your bed. You're going to be just fine."

Ben led the way back into the building. This time, as they passed from room to room, he flipped on lights with the back of his hand. "Shit, I forgot. We should be wearing gloves. We've left our fingerprints all over the damned place."

"I guess I'm not such a good criminal. I should have thought of that."

"My fingerprints aren't on record. Are yours?"

"No. I wasn't even born in a hospital. I doubt that my parents took me in after my birth to get my footprint, either. Mama went right back out the next morning to pick apples." Sissy wanted to call back those words the moment they shot from her mouth. "They, um, had an apple orchard to care for then."

Sissy assured herself that she hadn't lied— not really. But she hadn't told the exact truth, either, and she felt horrible.

"Damn. I just remembered. I got fingerprinted in school. I can't remember when, exactly, and I have no idea what they did with the prints. It may have been only a teaching process. But if they're filed electronically anywhere, and they dust this clinic, I'm screwed." They entered the recovery room. The moment the lights came on, pandemonium broke out again, with each of the animals letting loose with a noise common for its species. "Did you?" Ben asked loudly. "Get fingerprinted in school, I mean?"

"No. Maybe I was sick that day." Sissy thought it more likely that she'd been out of school on fingerprinting day because her parents had been moving again, but she didn't wish to tell Ben that. He had grown up in a different world, a normal world where he'd gotten to attend school in the same town all his life.

Ben took the kitten from her arms and returned

it with great care to its cage. Then he turned to Sissy. "We've got to wipe down everything we touched. Maybe your prints aren't on file anywhere, but mine may be."

Sissy wished they could just get her kitten and leave. But Ben could go to jail for this if they left any prints behind. They found a stack of white cloths on a counter in one corner of the room. Ben dampened two at the sink located in the same area.

Shoving aside all her thoughts about the kitten, Sissy wiped down the first kitten's cage to make sure Ben hadn't left so much as a partial print on the door. While she did that, Ben rubbed both sides of the recovery room door, making certain he cleaned every inch he might have touched. Then he walked down to the sixth stack of cages, and, using the same rag to prevent himself from leaving his fingerprints behind, opened a cage, and drew out the darling, fluffy gray kitten that Sissy had already come to love.

"Oh, Ben." She barely heard the clamor of the other animals now. Her entire attention became focused on the kitten. "He is so precious! And he's much smaller than the other one, still just a baby."

"He'll be your baby if we can get out of here without any trouble," he said as he took her rag and tossed it in a laundry hamper. Walking ahead of Sissy, he led the way to the door, then used his cloth to turn the doorknob and switch off the light. "Keep both hands on the kitten. I'll rub down surfaces we may have touched earlier as we walk out."

Hugging the kitten to her chest, Sissy led the way, falling even more in love with her new baby as she walked, yet acutely aware of Ben behind her making swishing sounds as he cleaned away any possible fingerprints.

Once they were outside, Sissy opened her black hoodie, tucked the kitten inside, and drew the zipper tab back up. "You're safe now." To Ben, she said, "He'll stay warm this way."

"Yep. His last home sucked, but now he'll have a good one."

Sissy held the kitten between her breasts as she and Ben made the long trek back to the truck. Ben gripped her arm to steady her in case they encountered more ice. When they reached his vehicle, he helped her to the passenger side, opened the door, and grabbed her at the waist to lift her onto the seat. When he leaned across her to fasten her seat belt, she didn't know of whom she was more acutely aware: the helpless kitten curled against her breasts, which Ben so cautiously avoided smashing with the strap, or the man. His body heat wafted over her, tantalizing her with the scent of his cologne. His hands brushed against certain parts of her anatomy that she'd never given another man permission to touch. Ben might be the one person for whom she would break that pattern.

Chapter
THIRTEEN

Once they were in the apartment above the café, Sissy felt all the earlier tension of the evening fall away, and her muscles relaxed. They had committed a crime, but they'd made a clean getaway, and even better, the kitten could now look forward to a long and happy life. Sissy couldn't help but smile as she crouched to set the little guy gently on her kitchen floor.

Admiring the gray ball of fur, Sissy noticed two white patches on the kitten's left hip. "Oh, Ben, look. He's not solid gray. He has two spots of white."

Ben stepped around to look. "His whiskers are white, too."

Sissy's grin broadened. "He makes me think of a kid whose mom sewed patches on his jeans. Wouldn't that be a darling name? Patches, I mean."

Ben crouched beside her, his mouth also tipped in a smile. "It's cute, for sure, and it suits him."

The kitten decided to check out his new home and hobbled over to sniff a cupboard door. "Just look at him walk!" Sissy cried. "He's a tiny miracle."

"He sure is," Ben agreed.

When the kitten sniffed a second cupboard, an awful thought occurred to Sissy. "Oh, my God. I'll have to roust Marilyn out of bed. I have no cat food, no litter box, and no litter to go in one! Flagg's Market is closed by now."

"After I agreed to help you break him out of jail, I went shopping," Ben said. "I knew you wouldn't have time. I've got everything he'll need in the back of my truck. I'll run out and get everything."

While Ben was gone, Sissy remained hunkered down to watch Patches explore the kitchen. The thought that he would have been dead in the morning if not for her and Ben brought tears to her eyes. Ben. He was such a rare gem. How many guys would risk going to jail in order to save a kitten's life? Not many, she decided. And that decision was quickly followed by another one. It was time for her to stop holding Ben at arm's length, and take another huge risk. He was a wonderful man, truly one of a kind, and she was going to lose him if she didn't let him know that she'd come to care about him.

She jerked with a start when Ben pushed back inside. His arms were laden with two bags, one of dry kitten kibble and the other of litter, plus a cat box filled with items she couldn't identify without standing up. She watched as he began unloading purchases onto her countertop. She saw ceramic dishes with paw prints. Two toys appeared, one a gray mouse and the other a clutch of feathers attached to what resembled a miniature fishing pole. Then Ben set out a box of rice pabulum and some small jars of pureed meat.

"What's the baby food for?"

"My mom starts kittens with pabulum mixed with pureed meat, powdered milk, and warm water. They love it, and according to her, it's healthful for them. I didn't get powdered milk. I figured you probably have some."

"I do." Sissy pushed erect.

As they worked, mixing a small amount of starter food for Patches in one bowl and filling the other bowl with freshwater, Sissy felt tears welling in her eyes again. *What's wrong with me?* Then she thought, *What a dumb question. This man is one of the most wonderful people I've ever known.*

After Patches ate, Sissy made him a bed in the corner of her living room and put his filled litter box nearby so he wouldn't have to walk far when he needed to relieve himself. She gently settled him on his blanket. He immediately tucked himself into a little ball and fell asleep. She gazed down at him for a long moment, unable to stop smiling.

"This is the best present anyone ever gave me," she told Ben.

"Don't thank me. You're the one who decided

to break into the clinic. I was just your backup."

Sissy hugged her waist, unable to resist glancing at Snickers, who sat up in his cage watching her. He needed to go. If he had a disease, Patches might catch it.

"Well." Ben shrugged and pushed at the brim of his hat. "It's super late. I'd better head home. Someone may spot my truck in your yard, and Finn will be in a dither. I normally take him everywhere. I decided he might not be a very good partner in crime, though. Can you imagine how excited he would have gotten with all those dogs and cats sounding off?"

"Pretty excited." Sissy followed him to the door. "I'll walk you down so I can lock up."

"Good plan."

He descended the stairs two at a time. Sissy's legs weren't long enough to manage that unless she jumped. At the back door, she gazed up at him. A tender, shadowy look clouded his eyes. She knew he wanted to kiss her. Recalling her wonderful dream of being held in his strong arms, she was sorely tempted to encourage him. Only nervousness made her hesitate.

"I'll never forget tonight."

He chuckled. "Like I said, you're bringing out my wild side."

"I'll never regret rescuing him. He's so precious." Her throat tightened. "You're the best, Ben."

"You're not bad yourself." As he stepped out onto the porch, he said, "Try to get to bed at a halfway decent hour."

"I'll do that."

After the door closed behind him, Sissy listened to his receding footsteps, first the click of his studded bootheels on wood and then the softer thud of leather soles on packed dirt. She sighed and walked back into the café. After turning out all the lights, she went upstairs. When she entered her apartment, Snickers perched on his hind-quarters to look at her with bright, beady eyes filled with interest and expectation.

As Sissy approached his cage, she said, "It's time to set you free, little guy." She opened the side door, cupped him in her hands, and held him to her cheek for what might be the last time. Then she lowered the rodent to the floor. "Good-bye, little guy. I'll come visit you if Ben can find your nest."

Snickers scampered to the edge of her kitchen linoleum, then stopped and sat up to look at her with what she could have sworn was a happy grin. Then he let loose with a chirp and raced away, stopping only to check her coffee table to see if the candy bowl had reappeared. When he found nothing, he ran into the bathroom and vanished.

Sissy released a taut breath and turned to scrub her hands and face with antibacterial soap. Then she walked through the flat, spraying all surfaces with disinfectant.

Sissy caught movement from the corner of her eye. Patches had awakened from his nap and was batting his toy mouse around on her carpet with his front stubs. Smiling, she sat cross-legged on the rug to watch him play. She wondered if the mouse was the kitten's first toy. He seemed to take it all very seriously, acting as if the stuffed gray felt might run away or turn on him. Sissy couldn't help but laugh at his antics.

Patches tired quickly. When Sissy noted a decrease in his enthusiasm, she picked him up and cuddled him close. "Hey, little guy. I'm your new mom. Do you know that yet?"

She sat on the sofa, got comfortable, and lightly stroked the kitten's fur until he began to purr, his body vibrating against her breast. Sissy felt as if her bones were melting. She settled back, closed her eyes, and listened to the sounds he made, which were fairly loud. Earlier Sissy had tried to thank Ben for the kitten, and he'd waved aside her gratitude. She doubted that he fully under-stood how much she'd needed this kitten to love.

Finally, Patches fell so deeply asleep that his purring stopped. *Ben.* Sissy drew her cell phone from her pocket and dialed his number. *It's time,* she thought. She had to tell him how she felt or risk losing him, and she couldn't imagine not having Ben in her life.

"Hey, you," he answered. "How are you handling your first night of motherhood?"

Sissy laughed, which startled Patches awake. He immediately started to purr again. "It's gone well." She fell quiet. "I just wanted to call and thank you again. You'll never know how much having the kitten means to me. I set Snickers free right after you left."

"Uh-oh. I know that must have been a bitch."

Sissy saw no point in sugarcoating the truth. "It was. But then Patches woke up and started playing with his mouse. He was so cute. Watching him play helped me stop feeling sad about Snickers. And it isn't as if I'll never see him again."

"Nope," Ben agreed. He hesitated. "Is that the kitten purring? Dear God, he sounds like a John Deere tractor."

Sissy grinned. "Pretty impressive. Tiny kitten, huge motor." She cupped her hand over the feline's soft warmth. "I'm so thankful to have him. I can give him a good life, and he'll fill mine with joy for years to come. If it weren't for you, I might have chickened out. I'd be here all alone. I'm tired of being alone."

"I know what you mean. I traveled so much that I never realized how completely alone I was until I gave it up and came home. Boy howdy, did it ever hit me then. My house is big. It was only me, wandering from room to room. Sometimes I'd actually talk to myself, and I swear my voice bounced off the walls. Now I talk to my dog."

It was so like Ben not to try to capitalize on how mushy she was feeling. Instead he was sharing his experiences with loneliness. That meant the world to her. "Is that what convinced you to get a puppy? The loneliness?"

"Yes. I was so lonely at night I was tempted to move back in with my parents!"

Sissy burst out laughing. "Honestly?"

"Well, feeling tempted and actually doing it are two different things. I love my parents, but my mom is a nurturer, and though I enjoy being fussed over when I visit, I don't think I could handle it full-time. And my dad—well, he's the salt of the earth, but he doesn't always approve of my lifestyle."

Sissy's smile deepened. Though she didn't have a social life, she understood that other young people did. A man as handsome as Ben didn't take a beautiful woman out on a date and then kiss her good night on the doorstep.

Her smile vanished, and an awful, clenching sensation attacked her stomach. The thought of Ben in some other woman's arms made her feel nauseated. Her only consolation was that he'd been at her place so much lately that he probably hadn't dated anyone for a while.

"So rather than do something totally crazy, like live with my parents, I got a dog. I'm still a little lonely sometimes, but mostly not. Finn is great company. I don't know how you've lived alone without a pet for as long as you have."

Sissy stroked Patches's fur. "Me, neither." And then, before she could reason her way through it, she blurted, "You probably date a lot of women."

Silence. It lasted so long she was going to ask if he was still there when he finally said, "I did."

Past tense. Sissy couldn't help but focus on that. "What made you stop?"

"I found you."

Sissy felt her larynx bob up and down. Her throat knotted as tight as a beggar's fist around a quarter. "Me?" she whispered.

She heard Ben cough. "I told you how I feel this morning. I know you've given me no signals to hope for anything in return. And, trust me, I've even lectured myself about acting like a fool. But for the first time in my life, my brain has gone on vacation and I'm leading with my heart."

"Oh, Ben."

"I know, I know. You're not ready. Maybe you'll never be. If that's how it turns out—"

Sissy cut him off. "Ben? I'm in love with you."

"What?"

"You heard me."

"With me? You're in love with *me?*"

She smiled at the incredulity in his voice. "Why do you find that so hard to believe? You're a wonderful person. Honest, trustworthy, caring. How could I not fall in love with you?"

He cleared his throat. "Hold on. *Shit.* I'm not all that honest, Sissy. I've lied to you a few times."

Her eyebrows shot up. "About what?"

"For starters, about the coop and run. I got a few supplies at ReStore, but most of it, I bought new because ReStore was low on inventory. I could afford it and I knew you couldn't."

"You played me." Her mouth curved in another smile. "Shame on you." Then, "Uh-oh. Exactly how many free meals do I owe you now?"

He chuckled. "I don't know. I threw away the receipts. You're not mad?"

Sissy took a bracing breath. "You're not the only one who's lied, Ben. Everything about me is pretty much a lie."

"What do you mean?"

"I need to tell you about it, need to tell you everything, but it's a long story, and it won't be easy for me to get it out. Tonight probably isn't the best time if we hope to get any sleep."

"Probably not," he conceded. "And nothing you tell me is going to change how I feel about you, anyway. So it doesn't really matter."

"Yes," Sissy pushed out. "It does matter. I can't move forward with you until you know everything about me." She sighed. "I'll warn you now that I'm going to have to gather my courage before I can talk about it. For me, it'll be like standing naked on the courthouse steps."

"No rush," he assured her. "I'm not going any-where."

"Promise?"

"Yes. It's enough for me right now just to know you have feelings for me."

"I like knowing that you have feelings for me, too," she said.

"So, how about if we end this conversation with those three words? I need to hear you say them again."

"I love you, Ben."

"I love you, too."

She waited for him to hang up because she didn't want to do it first. He finally started to laugh. Oh, how she loved the sound of his laughter. "Okay, this isn't going well," he said. "How about if we hang up on the count of three?"

"Or we could talk a bit longer."

"Better idea," he agreed.

She got up and carefully put Patches back on his bed. "I, um, had a dream about you kissing me."

"Aw, shit. Was I awful?"

She giggled. In her wildest imaginings, she couldn't picture Ben being bad at kissing a woman.

"No, wait. Let me guess. We bumped noses. Our teeth got stuck. I stepped on your foot while I was kissing you?"

"No! It was a lovely dream. I'm just—well,

nervous about me being the one who's awful at it."

"Well, that isn't going to happen. You have the most kissable mouth I've ever seen."

"I do?" Sissy heard the thin edge in her voice and wanted to punch herself in the shoulder.

"Oh, yeah, and please don't tell me a dozen other guys haven't told you that."

Sissy bit back a grin and then wondered why she bothered. He couldn't see her. "Okay, I won't."

"Good. I hate false humility."

Sissy figured he'd hate hearing the truth even more.

"So, here's how we'll handle tomorrow," he went on. "I'll show up. We'll see how things roll. And just so you won't get all nervous, I won't kiss you unless you ask me to. Deal?"

Sissy wasn't sure she'd ever find the courage to ask him to kiss her, but she said, "Uh . . . okay. Deal."

Sissy crawled into bed, exhausted from a long day of work and an exhilarating evening of crime, with Patches tucked under her chin and part of her pillow providing him with a bed nearly as soft as a cloud. As she fell asleep what remained of her conscious thought centered on how utterly at peace she felt. Finally, she had someone who was really *hers,* a kitten who needed her as much as she needed him, and a wonderful man who said he loved her.

Best of all, she'd found the courage to tell Ben she had feelings for him, feelings that went deeper than friendship. And he'd understood her hesitation, if not the reasons behind it. She felt like one of the luckiest women in the world.

Her alarm clock clamored at five in the morning, jerking her from the soundest sleep she'd enjoyed for a long while. Patches awakened more slowly, blinking and yawning as he sat up. Sissy grinned and picked him up as she swung her legs over the side of the bed.

"You are so stinkin' cute!" she told him. "But not so cute that I want you to pee in my bed."

Barefoot and wearing only a T-shirt that nearly reached her knees, Sissy carried the kitten to his unused litter box. She wondered if he already knew how it went, a question that was soon answered when Patches pushed aside litter with his pink stubs and squatted over the spot to pee and do number two. Afterward he used his back feet to cover the mess.

"And smart, too!" Sissy cried. The not-so-sweet smell of cat manure drifted to her nose. "Ugh. That's going to be a new daily chore for me, cleaning your box and giving it squirts of odor eliminator."

She allowed the kitten to make his way to the kitchen. Babying him too much would not help the ends of his healing legs to toughen up. He needed to walk a little. Not too much at first, because he'd been confined to a tiny cage after his surgery. She hoped to avoid raw spots or blisters. But some walking would be therapeutic.

In what felt like only minutes but was actually over an hour, Sissy had a café filled with customers. For reasons beyond her, the Cauldron seemed to be drawing more people. That made her feel fabulous. As Sissy raced back and forth to cook and serve, she faced the inevitable. She had no choice but to hire some help. One person couldn't deal with so many customers alone. Her patrons expected three things: quick service, tasty food, and friendly conversation. Sissy was still managing to provide the first two things, but she had little time to chat, even with her favorite diners. She felt a stab of regret that she couldn't sit for a moment with Christopher while he ate breakfast. And Blackie was clearly feeling glum because she hadn't stopped to hear him describe the new Oregon Ducks football helmets.

When Sissy arrived at the VeArds' table, Lynda glanced up and smiled. "You look absolutely radiant this morning."

"I had a fabulous evening and got a great night's sleep."

Sissy wanted to chat with them, but she heard someone clanking a spoon against a coffee mug, a sure sign of impatience. "I'm so sorry. Duty calls. Maybe you can come in for lunch and it'll be slower."

Lynda waved her away. "You have a business to run. We understand."

Sissy was exhausted when her last breakfast diner left. But she couldn't afford to take time for even a short break. Mountains of dirty dishes awaited her. She also needed to spend at least a few minutes upstairs with Patches. It would be unkind to leave him alone for hours on end.

As she put plates into the dishwasher, Sissy heard strange noises coming from outside the back of her building. *Ben,* she decided. She'd become familiar with the sounds of construction. What on earth was he doing now?

When Sissy had her cooking facility tidy, she busted out her lunch prep, wiped the counters, and then dashed upstairs to fetch her kitten before going outside to see what Ben was up to.

"Hey, you!" he said when she stepped out onto the porch. "And you brought my step-kitten, too! That's dangerous. A customer might drop in and see him."

"If I hear the buzzer, I'll hide him under a light jacket to take him upstairs."

Ben crouched on the steps over countless boards and a gigantic roll of wire that he'd propped against the deck. "What on earth are you going to build now?" Sissy asked.

"An outside kitty playground. Wire tunnels. My

step-kitten needs some outdoor time, especially during our good-weather months."

Outside kitty playground? Sissy sighed. "What if someone sees him?"

Ben smiled. "The heat will die down. Something else will soon have everyone's tongue wagging. We'll wait a few months before we let him out-side."

He planned to install a cat door in the wall of her building, through which Patches could enter a wire tunnel that would lead to a kitty platform where he could sunbathe or crouch under a small roofed area that would protect him from the snow and rain. "My biggest concern is how to design climbing ramps for him. He has no front claws to pull himself up. It'll take some pondering."

Sissy, who'd always prided herself on being a person who rarely cried, now found herself battling tears. *Again.* It was becoming a habit with her, and she didn't like it. Was he real, this man? He wasn't asking for or expecting anything from her for doing this. He was building Patches a playground out of the kindness of his heart.

"Oh, Ben, no wonder I love you."

"Keep it coming, sweetheart. I love hearing you say it."

"I love you. I love you. I love you."

He stared down at the boards near his feet. "I had a plan. Now I'll be damned if I can remember what it was."

That made two of them. She'd even forgotten what the main dish for lunch was. "I'll leave you alone so you can collect your thoughts." Sissy rose and stood a step above him. "After lunch hour when I've finished dinner prep, I hope to close the café and spend time with Patches upstairs. He loves the toys you got him. Maybe you can find time to come up and join us."

His eyes twinkled with amusement. "That's an invitation I won't turn down. Wow, our first date!"

"Nope, it's our second."

"It is? How'd I miss the first one?"

Sissy grinned. "You didn't. It was our second chicken dusting day. I wore a special top and I even put on makeup. It was a date whether you knew it or not."

He moved his gaze over her face. "You sure looked pretty when I got here that morning. That touch of mascara really set off your eyes."

"You noticed? The makeup, I mean."

"I notice everything about you."

For Sissy, the lunch shift dragged by, every minute seeming like an hour, and then when her customers finally dwindled away to only an occasional drop-in, she still had dinner prep to do. Blackie stopped by for his afternoon coffee and muffin. Sitting at the counter just beyond the pass-through window, he finally got a chance to describe, in precise detail, the new design on the Oregon Ducks football helmets. Sissy made all the appropriate noises and responses, but she was actually thinking about Ben and their "date" that afternoon.

Blackie kept talking. *I should wear something special,* she thought. *Maybe just a touch of makeup, nothing too obvious.* Then she tried to imagine what she and Ben would talk about. She decided it wouldn't matter. She enjoyed all their conversations. Getting to know him, teasing him —heck, she was starting to feel as if she was almost normal.

You're not, she reminded herself. But somehow Ben made her feel good about herself, anyway.

As she went up the stairs to her flat later, she could still hear Ben working. He hadn't even come in for lunch. After she had given Patches a cuddle, she was going to put on a special top. Maybe she'd even try to do something different with her hair. A little makeup was definitely on her agenda. *I notice everything about you.* Well, she wanted to look different enough that she'd be worth noticing for once.

Ben stretched his tape measure along a board and marked the spot where he intended to cut. Without Sissy there to keep him company, he'd opened the driver's-side door of his truck and turned on the radio, selecting the only local station, which interrupted the country music with important announcements—weather warnings, news, or to tell anyone listening that someone in town needed help. Today the main news topic was the break-in and robbery that had occurred the night before at the veterinary clinic. *No suspects yet.* Ben was glad to hear that. *No apparent motive.* Another bit of good news. *Everyone should be on the lookout for a gray kitten missing both front feet.* Ben was not glad to hear that. Until the furor died down, Patches would have to stay in Sissy's apartment. That sucked.

"Oh, my *stars!*"

At the sound of Sissy's voice above him, Ben jumped with a start. He turned to see her leaning out an opened living room window. Even at a distance, she looked so beautiful that she nearly took his breath away.

"Oh, *Ben.* It's going to be the greatest kitten run *ever.* I love it. Patches is going to love it, too. You're absolutely amazing."

She was the amazing one. Her top, the color of mulberry wine, clung to her figure. Instead of tousling her dark hair every which way, she'd tucked it behind her ears and somehow spiked her bangs. And he was pretty sure she'd put on makeup, because her lips looked nearly as rosy as her top.

"Is it kitten-watching time?"

"It is, and I even made food. My version of a Super Bowl party."

Ben pulled off his leather gloves. "I'll be right up."

Minutes later, Ben stood on the landing with Finn. When Sissy answered his knock, she cast a worried glance at his dog.

"He's good with cats. They're everywhere at my place."

"I need to visit there again. After I close up here, of course. I'd love to have dinner there, as you once suggested, and then tour your chicken facilities."

Ben winked at her. "Definitely dinner. For once you won't have to eat your own cooking."

"That sounds nice." She closed the door behind him, her attention on Finnegan, who noticed the kitten and bounded toward it. "Are you sure—"

"I'm positive. It'll be fine."

Finn surprised even Ben. It was as if the dog sensed Patches had been hurt. The pup got on his belly and inched toward the kitten. Then they touched noses. Finnegan saw the toy mouse and went to grab it. Patches took a flying leap and covered the stuffed felt with his body.

"He's saying it's his," Sissy said. "I told you how much he loves it."

Wonderful smells drifted to Ben's nostrils. "Did you make pizza?" he asked, even though the question he really wanted to ask was what kind of perfume she was wearing. It wasn't lavender.

"Man, now my stomach's growling." And his blood pressure was rising. The mulberry sweater skimmed her breasts and clung to her torso until the ribbed hem flared over her hips. "That's a pretty sweater."

Her cheeks went pink, and she plucked at the scoop neckline with nervous fingers. Ben had never in his life wanted to kiss a woman so badly. He'd dated plenty of gals whose clothing left little to the imagination. Yet Sissy, in her shy attempt to look pretty, was sexier than all of them put together.

"Thank you."

Ben wished he could dress her, starting with undies and bras from Victoria's Secret, with her modeling everything for his appreciation. Not that she'd ever agree to that, but he could dream.

"Grab a seat. I'll bring the food."

Ben sat on the middle sofa cushion, hoping that Sissy would sit beside him because the coffee table would probably be where she laid out the food. *A guy could scheme as well as dream.*

Sissy set a giant-size pizza on the coffee table. "It's a meat lover's. I slapped it together during the lunch hour and slipped it into the oven up here afterward."

Ben's stomach was gnawing at his backbone, but he had eyes only for the neckline of her sweater and the scant two inches of cleavage it revealed. It provided a breast lover's view, and he was far more interested in that than the food.

As she straightened, she caught him looking. Her eyes went laser-beam blue, and for a second, he thought she was pissed. Only then he saw her blush, a telltale sign that it wasn't anger that had her eyes sparkling. She circled the table to sit beside him, keeping a precise six inches between their hips. Ben bit back a grin. A half foot wasn't much distance for a man to cover.

He leaned forward to grab one of the plates and a slice of pizza. As he did, his arm brushed against hers. "Napkins." She leaped to her feet. "I forgot."

"Paper towels are fine," he told her.

She returned with two store-bought paper napkins with flowers at the corner. Ben figured his would be soiled after he wiped one hand.

They finally got settled against the cushions and ate as they watched Finn and Patches play. Finnegan continued to be gentle. Occasionally he would steal the mouse, Patches would launch an attack to get it back, and then the game would start all over again. Ben laughed. Sissy giggled. He was surprised at how much fun it was. He'd dropped a lot of money on dates in his day, and he'd never enjoyed one as much as this. Of course, it wasn't so much the visual entertainment as it was being intoxicated by the essence of the woman beside him. He'd told her that he wouldn't kiss her until she asked him to, and he regretted it now. Dumb mistake.

When he saw Sissy glancing at her watch, he realized that the dinner hour was approaching. "Did you notice that your buzzer never went off?" he asked. "Normally you have people drop in during the afternoon."

"I put up the CLOSED sign. Blackie already came in for his coffee and muffin. Now that I have Patches, I've decided I need to take breaks in the afternoon to spend time with him."

"And maybe do something outrageous like rest for a while, or go somewhere fun with me?"

Her smile made her whole face glow. "I'd love that. Where would we go?"

"A late lunch and a matinee would be fun. And there's a great park outside of town with a covered pavilion with picnic tables. We could have a snow day, and eat while it snows all around us. If you hired some help, maybe we could do something really crazy, like go out at night, maybe for a nice dinner and dancing."

"I don't know how to dance. But maybe I can learn. And I do need to hire help. It's getting to be too much for one person."

"It's been too much for one person ever since you opened the café."

"I know. But I'm saving, remember. The longer I can tough it out, the quicker I can afford to turn this place into a dream café." She picked up the dishes. Ben was surprised to see that all the pizza was gone. He couldn't remember eating that much, let alone how it had tasted. "I'm getting there, though," she continued. "With money, I mean. It's time to hire help even if it slows me down."

Ben followed her into the kitchen to rinse the dishes and stash them in her dishwasher. As they worked together, she gave him a questioning look. "I'd love it if you'd stay long enough to come in for dinner this evening. Afterward maybe you could help me clean up and do prep so we can actually go out. Seeing a movie would be huge for me."

Ben searched her dainty features, trying to read her and failing. "It's a date. I'll see what's playing at the theater."

He kissed her on the forehead, wishing as he did that he could trail his lips over every inch of her skin. Then he slapped his thigh to summon his dog, straightened his hat, and walked to the door. "What's on the menu tonight?"

"Beef bourguignon, minced pork sliders, Italian sausage lasagna, and—"

"Stop!" he cut in. "I was sold when you said *beef bourguignon*. Save me two servings."

"Two servings, on the house. It's my way of repaying you for all your labor today."

As Ben strode down the stairs, he wished she would reward him with a long, deep kiss, and to hell with the beef bourguignon. But beggars couldn't be choosers.

Chapter
FOURTEEN

Sissy couldn't believe how packed the Cauldron was for dinner. It was standing room only again. Glancing around as she rushed between the kitchen and the tables, she juggled ideas along with dishes. When she remodeled, she'd need to add benches at each side of the door so people could sit to wait for a table. As she shoved potatoes into the oven to bake and snatched two steaks off the grill to deliver to a couple celebrating an engagement, she tried to think what it was that had started to draw so many people in. She had experienced a few sparse months when she first reopened the café, but after she learned not to scorch all the food, business picked up fast. Never quite to this degree, though.

During a brief respite, Sissy gazed out the pass-through window, trying to determine what she was doing differently. Nothing, so far as she could tell. It was as if the Cauldron had become a community gathering place where everyone wanted to eat because they knew good food and great company awaited them here.

Raised in Mystic Creek, Ben knew nearly everyone, and he enhanced the feeling of camaraderie. He moved from table to table, sometimes even taking a seat. He emanated sincerity and warmth. He made people laugh or grow serious over a topic of conversation. After he moved on, those individuals turned to chat with people who sat nearby.

Sissy heard a timer buzz and raced back into the kitchen to take three racks of hot lasagna from the main oven. It smelled wonderful, so she knew that much of her newfound success was due to her cooking. But the rest of it was because the café had become an informal gathering place.

While cleaning the service side of the front counter, Sissy chatted sporadically with Blackie as she worked. She tensed when he asked, "Did you hear about the break-in at the vet clinic last night?"

Sissy hadn't *heard* about it; she'd committed the crime. So she wasn't really lying when she replied, "No, I haven't heard about that from anyone."

"Well, someone got in. Jack forgot to set the security system and says he may have left the back door unlocked. The cops are saying that the perpetrator could have used a credit card to jimmy the lock. What's really weird is, the only thing stolen was a kitten that had its front feet amputated. Who'd steal a kitten? Hell, you can get one for a few bucks at the no-kill shelter, and it'd have all four feet."

Ma Thomas, who owned a perfume-and-soap shop on East Main, sat one stool over from Blackie. She had more silver in her short hair now than natural blond. Her smile always made Sissy feel warm. "Well, I heard the *real* story. I can't say who told me, but the owners of that kitten decided to have it put down just because it lost its front feet! Jack tried to tell them the kitten would adjust and could live a long and happy life, but they—they're new in town, last name Miller—wouldn't listen."

Blackie sobered. "They were just bent on killing it, no matter what?"

Ma nodded. "Somebody even offered to adopt it and give it a wonderful home, and they still wouldn't let it live."

"Huh." Blackie polished off his chocolate cake with an enormous last bite. Cheek bulging, he said, "So it wasn't really a theft. Somebody rescued the kitten."

"That's what I was told," Ma replied. "And I have it on good authority. The way I see it, the woman who stole that kitten deserves a medal." She winked at Sissy. "I'd collect money to have one made for her if it wouldn't get her in trouble."

Sissy's stomach dropped. She shot a frantic look in Ben's direction, but he was busy chatting with Christopher. At the edge of Sissy's mind, she was startled to see that the old man had come in so late, undoubtedly to enjoy socializing. But

311

mostly all she could think was *People know.* Sissy felt a little dizzy as the realization sank home. Gossip traveled fast in Mystic Creek. If Ma Thomas knew who'd taken the kitten, it wouldn't be long before everyone in town did.

"In trouble?" Blackie echoed Ma and slapped his palm on the bar. "If our county sheriff objects to a kitten rescue and some woman does get in trouble, I say we organize a protest! We'll march to the sheriff's department and make our voices heard." He swiveled on his barstool. "Ben!" he roared. "Come here!"

Sissy, heading to Christopher's booth to deliver his order, met Ben halfway across the room. "I'm screwed," she whispered as they passed each other.

The volume in the restaurant dropped. People watched Ben. He grinned broadly at Blackie. "You look fit to be tied. Did somebody eat all Sissy's chocolate cake?"

Blackie slapped his hand on the counter again. "Hell, no, she always saves me a piece. You heard about that kitten that got stolen from the vet clinic last night?"

Sissy had just returned to the counter. Judging by Ben's expression, he felt the same way Sissy had when she was asked that question. "Um— I heard something about it today on the radio." He flicked a questioning look at Sissy. "What's up? Did they figure out who did it?"

312

"What's up? I'll tell you what's up," Ma interjected. "Our sheriff dusted the whole joint for fingerprints and is hot on the trail of whoever stole that kitten."

"What a waste of our tax dollars!" Blackie complained. "All over a kitten the owners decided to have put down because its front feet were amputated! So some woman decided to rescue the kitten and broke into the clinic to steal it. Now, ain't that the crime of our new century? Heinous! Punishable by God only knows how much jail time. Lots more important than murders and stuff."

Ben lifted an eyebrow. "I think the last homicide here was about seventy-five years ago."

Blackie snorted. "It's still foolishness if you ask me. Does your brother Barney know about this?"

Ben frowned. "I don't really know, Blackie. We haven't spoken today."

"Well, I'll be the first to tell him I hope he's not involved in that stupid investigation. Trying to locate and arrest a kitten rescuer is a waste of everybody's time and tax dollars."

It seemed to Sissy that her diners would never leave, but a few minutes before nine o'clock people paid their tabs, collected their coats, and began walking out. When everyone but Ben was gone, Sissy locked the front door and turned her sign to read CLOSED.

"There went going to see a movie," she cried as she turned to face him. "I couldn't focus on the screen. We are so screwed! Who could have known it was me? What if I go to jail?"

Ben closed the distance between them and drew her into his arms. Sissy had been held tightly by men, but never had the sensation made her feel safe. "Sweetheart, you won't go to jail. If anyone gets arrested, it'll be me, the idiot who did it."

Sissy pressed closer to him, needing to feel his strength. "You aren't an idiot. You're wonderful. And it was my idea, not yours." She glanced up. "Where's Finn?"

"I sneaked him upstairs to your apartment so he could hang out with Patches."

"I hope nobody saw him pass through the café."

"I don't think so, but note to self: When you remodel, we need to create a walled-off area at the bottom of the stairs so you don't have to worry about people seeing Patches if he comes downstairs to go outside."

Just then a loud knock came at the front door. Sissy hadn't yet turned off the street-side lighting or dimmed the interior ceiling fixtures. Ben dropped his arms from around her. Sissy sprang away from him. They both turned to see who was standing outside the glass door.

"Well, shit," Ben said. "It's Barney."

Sissy knew Ben's brother. The deputy didn't

come in to the Cauldron as often since he'd gotten married and started a family, but he still dropped in occasionally. "You know why he's here," she said, her voice shaking. She pictured herself getting cuffed and stuffed. "Oh, God, Ben, what should I do?"

"Well," Ben said, "I think you should start by opening the door."

Sissy hurried over to do just that, only her voice crackled as if it came from a radio with air-wave static. "Hi, B-Barney. Wh-what a surprise."

Barney stepped inside and closed the door. "Hi, Sissy." He removed his dark brown Stetson and inclined his head at his brother. "Ben."

"Hey, Barney," Ben replied. "What brings you in? The coffee's still fresh, and Sissy makes fabulous chocolate cake."

Barney, dressed in uniform, strode to the counter, found a clean spot to place his hat, and said, "I'm not here to eat, and you know it." He turned to look at his brother. "What the hell were you thinking? Breaking and entering is a class-C felony, burglary in the second degree, potentially punishable by up to one hundred and twenty-five thousand in fines and five years in prison!"

Sissy grabbed hold of the bar to steady herself. Ben hadn't stolen the kitten for himself. She couldn't allow him to take the blame. "It was me, not Ben. I did it!"

Barney, whose eyes were the same gold-flecked

315

hazel as Ben's, gave her a long look. "I know you were probably with him."

Ben folded his arms and shifted his weight to one foot, looking far too relaxed for a man who was about to be arrested. "Come on, bro, get on with it and stop with the lecture. If you were here to throw me in the slammer, you'd be hanging your head and apologizing."

Barney's badge flashed on his khaki shirt as he lifted his hands, palms up. "The phones are ringing off the hook at the department. Half the populace of Mystic Creek is up in arms about Sissy getting into trouble for rescuing a damned kitten!"

Anger surged through Sissy. "Patches is not a *damned* kitten. He's a sweet, darling kitten who deserves to have a life! And how on earth did anyone find out it was me that entered the clinic to rescue him?"

"A clinic receptionist blabbed," Barney replied. "She'd gone back to use the ladies' room and overheard you and Jack talking. She told only one person, and in strictest confidence, but her friend blabbed to someone, and so it went."

"And in Mystic Creek, word travels faster than the speed of light," Ben finished for him.

Barney nodded. "Now Jack's in trouble, you guys are in trouble, and Sheriff Adams is in a jam as well. The law is the law. He should arrest both of you and cite Jack Palmer for over-

316

stepping his bounds as a vet. But the people in this town—the voters who'll reelect Adams as sheriff—don't feel that a crime has been committed, and they aren't going to vote for any jackass, including me, who throws two heroic kitten rescuers into jail and files charges against Jack for aiding and abetting."

Ben spread his feet. "I'm sorry for causing a political shit storm. I just couldn't let the owners kill the kitten for no good reason."

Barney thumped his chest. "*I'm* the one who brought most of the stray animals home when we were kids, not you! When did you suddenly become the softie?"

Ben huffed. "I rescued just as many critters as you did. You off duty?"

Barney nodded.

Ben glanced at Sissy. "Can you open a bottle of wine, Sissy? My treat."

Barney groaned. "I'm not having a drink with you. No matter what people in town think, you committed a crime."

Ben strode over and swung a leg over a bar-stool. Sissy circled the counter. "You want mulberry?" she asked. "I picked up a few bottles. My customers love it."

"Sure," Ben agreed. "Maybe some magic will rub off on Barney and make him forget his tough-cop image."

Barney took a stool beside his brother. "I don't

have a tough-cop image. And having a glass of wine will not negate the fact that you've caused a lot of serious trouble for me, my boss, and the only vet we've got in town."

Sissy poured three glasses of wine, passed two to the men, and kept one for herself. She wasn't quite so nervous now, but she was still on edge. She glanced at her watch. Patches and Finn had been alone in her flat for hours.

She excused herself and ran upstairs to check on her furry friends. Finn needed to go outside and pee. Patches rubbed against her ankles, begging to be picked up. "Well," she told the animals, "in for a penny, in for a pound. Let's all go down-stairs."

As Sissy descended the stairs with Patches in her arms and Finn taking two steps at a time in front of her, she wondered what Barney might say. Probably something about conforming to the health codes. *The law is the law.*

But when Barney glanced toward the stairs and saw them, he said, "Aw, come on! Have a heart, Sissy. Don't show me that kitten."

"Show him the kitten," Ben said. "He'll melt into his boots."

Sissy led Finn through the storage area and let him outside for a whiz festival. When the pup returned, she made her way back to her place behind the counter, where her mulberry wine awaited her. Barney stared hard at Patches, snuggled in the crook of Sissy's arm. She saw his gaze drop to the kitten's pink stubs.

"Son of a bitch." He took a gulp of wine. "Can the poor thing even walk?"

Ben answered. "He can not only walk; he can romp and play with Finn. It's really something to see."

"So why did his owners insist on putting him down?"

Ben tasted his wine. "I'm sure they felt they were doing the right thing, but in truth, they weren't. Jack tried to tell them the kitten would adjust, but they firmly believed they were making the kinder choice for him."

Barney sighed. "It would have been sad if Jack had euthanized him." He angled a glare at Ben. "That isn't to say you did the right thing. You committed a B and E. You catnapped that kitten!"

Ben shrugged. "Guilty as charged. And if you arrest me, no hard feelings. Do the crime, do the time." He met his brother's gaze. "But just between you and me and a fence post, if you'd known about this kitten, wouldn't you have been tempted to swipe him to save his life?"

Barney shot him a glare over the rim of his wineglass. "Unfair question."

"I'll take that as an affirmative."

Barney tipped his head back and flexed his shoulders. "You can take it however you want, but I would have figured out how to do it legally. You could have called an animal rights group."

"We didn't have time. It's a great idea, but we had only a matter of hours."

Finishing his wine with three gulps, Barney swung off the barstool and went to collect his hat. "Well, for what it's worth, I'm glad you saved him. I just don't approve of how you went about it."

"So what's going to happen?" Ben asked. "Are Sissy and I going to be arrested?"

"Sheriff Adams went to see the owners of the kitten this evening. I wasn't there to hear what he said, but I think he warned them that they need to keep their heads down and their mouths shut about the kitten if they hope to have any friends in town. Jack called the department and told Adams that he deliberately left the clinic door unlocked for you, so technically you entered the clinic by his invitation."

"I never expected Jack to take the heat for this," Ben mused aloud.

"The only way he'll get in trouble is if the kitten's owners file a complaint against him. And I don't think they'll do that, not unless they want to be run out of town on a rail. People are riled up. Last I heard, Blackie and Ma Thomas were planning a protest march and they got so many volunteers that they had to hold their first meeting at Dizzy's Roundtable. Half the town could gather there."

Ben chuckled. "And of course you knew all this when you came in here to chew my ass."

Barney grinned. "Somebody's got to keep you in line. I still can't believe you snuck into that building and stole a cat." He drew open the door, paused, and glanced over his shoulder. "Wish I could've been there, but future sheriffs miss out on all the fun stuff. Next time be a hell of a lot more careful. You left one print. We didn't run it for a match, but it was too large to be Sissy's."

"People come and go in the back of that clinic all the time. How can you possibly figure the fingerprint is mine?"

"Well, now," Barney said, tapping his temple. "There were *no* fingerprints on the kitten's cage, none on the door handles or on the doors themselves. So someone wiped all those surfaces down. But he missed that one telltale print."

"Shit," Ben said. Then his eyes narrowed on his brother. "Wait a minute. Maybe I missed one print, but that doesn't mean I missed one of my own. It could be Jack's, or a kennel keeper's."

Barney grinned. "Had you going for a minute, though, didn't I? It works on most perps, and I'll tell you why. They're dumb as buckets of rocks."

"Are you implying that I'm dumb?" Ben asked, but his brother had already walked out.

Sissy and Ben worked together in the kitchen to clean up and then do breakfast prep. Then, both too exhausted to go anywhere, they took their pets upstairs. This time Sissy sat cross-legged on the carpet to watch the pup and kitten play. Ben decided that the sofa had lost its appeal without her on it, so he joined her.

"How soon will you hire help?" he asked. "I'm looking forward to that movie—and other outings. Maybe a stroll along Mystic Creek so we can fall madly in love."

She fixed those guileless blue eyes on him. He saw pain in those depths. "I thought we already had."

Ben's heart caught. Was she really that insecure? "Sweetheart, I was just joking about the legend of Mystic Creek."

"Are you sure? If you don't love me, tell me now."

"Sissy, it was a *joke*. Of course I love you. I've never told another woman that, and I mean it from the bottom of my heart."

She relaxed and resumed watching the animals romp. Ben wished she would open up. Something had made her feel horribly insecure, and he wanted to know what it had been. He guessed she'd tell him about her past when she felt ready. Until then, he had to be patient. Instinct told him that pushing would get him nowhere and might cost him the ground he'd gained.

"So, tell me about your remodeling plans."

She smiled dreamily. "I want quality plank

flooring, reclaimed barnwood if I can afford it. And new booths with a rustic look. I hate those chrome-and-formica things I have now. They're so sixties. And I'm thinking about some faux overhead beams as well. It's an old building. I think rich wood wainscoting will look fabulous. You may not have noticed, but a large percentage of my clientele is older. I'd like to draw in the younger set as well."

"You need more seating," Ben observed. "Most people come in alone or in pairs."

They discussed ideas on how to maximize the dining area space.

She turned her gaze on him. "You're very observant. I didn't realize you were thinking about my renovations."

"Well, sure, I have. It's hard not to notice when your café is packed that the people still waiting could be seated if you changed the booths and tables to accommodate two instead of four."

"And my café is approved by the fire marshal to hold more people already, so creating more seating would work great."

"And if we wall off at the bottom of the stairs, you could even put in a gas log fireplace there."

She scrunched her shoulders and then relaxed them with a sigh. "Oh, a fire would be perfect, especially on snowy winter evenings. It'd make the whole place seem cozy." She nodded. "We've come up with some great ideas!"

Ben got the fishing-pole toy out and dangled the feathers in front of Patches. The kitten leaped for them and so did Finn. Ben jerked the bait right out from under their noses. Both he and Sissy laughed as the game continued. It was a nice way to end the day.

Knowing how early Sissy had to get up, Ben decided not to overstay his welcome. "Well," he said, pushing to his feet, "I think it's about time for me to go home and hit the sack."

She nodded, her expression revealing regret. Ben wished she would invite him to stay longer, maybe even for the night. With other women, that was the norm. With Sissy, it wasn't. She hadn't even asked him to kiss her yet.

Sissy walked downstairs with Ben and Finnegan. She told herself it was only because she needed to lock up after them, but she had other reasons as well. Ben had promised her that he wouldn't kiss her until she asked him to, and though the thought jangled her nerves, she wanted to do that tonight.

When they reached the back door, Ben paused and turned to look at her. She could tell by the tender expression in his eyes that he yearned to take her into his arms.

Gathering all her courage, Sissy said, "Ben, will you kiss me? Not on the forehead. A real kiss this time."

He'd put his hat back on. With the bent knuckle of a forefinger, he nudged up the brim. "I've been thinking about that, and I've concluded it might be better if you kiss me."

That was the last thing she had been expecting. "Me, kiss you?" Her knees started to quiver. "No, no, that won't work."

"Why not? It doesn't matter who takes the initiative, just as long as it happens."

Sissy couldn't think what to say. She settled for "I don't think I'll be very good at it. I, um, don't know how."

Ben looked stunned. "Pardon me?"

"I don't know how," she repeated. Heat rose up her neck and pooled like fire in her cheeks. "I, um—it's a long story."

His dimple flashed in his lean cheek. "How can that be possible? You're twenty-six. Young, smart, and beautiful. Dozens of guys must have kissed you."

"Not dozens," she forced herself to say. "Only a few, and they were—well, so rough and forceful that I was so busy trying to get away that I didn't learn much about kissing."

Sissy knew that she'd just opened a door, inviting Ben to ask questions she wasn't ready to answer. But instead he clenched his teeth, treating her to a spectacular display of rippling jaw muscle, which told her the information she'd just revealed made him angry. But almost before she registered that, his expression went tender again. He murmured something she couldn't quite catch, and then, ever so gently, he trailed his fingertip over her features, tracing the arch of her brows, the bridge of her nose, and the bow of her upper lip. His touch made her feel beautiful and cherished.

"Sweetheart, kissing is sort of like dancing. All you have to do is follow my lead."

"I've never danced, either, remember. Not with a partner, anyway. I'd probably mash all your toes."

His lips quirked in a quelled smile. "You're not heavy enough to mash my toes."

Then he bent his head, his gaze holding hers. Sissy didn't know what to expect. Ben feathered his lips over hers, the touch so gentle and airy—and so tantalizing—that she found herself leaning her head farther back to experience more of the same.

And he delivered. His kisses were as light as the flutter of a butterfly wing.

When he finally withdrew, her heart was pounding and her breathing had gone shallow. *That's it?* she wondered. He'd never even put his arms around her. He winked at her and pressed a quick kiss to her forehead.

"Good night, Sissy," he said in a gravelly voice. "Have sweet dreams."

The next instant, the door closed behind him.

She listened to the rhythmic thumps of his boots as he descended the porch steps. Then she heard him call out to Finn. Trembling with aftershocks from the sensations he'd sent spiraling through her, Sissy locked the door behind him and leaned against it because she felt weak in the legs. Then a dreamy smile curved her lips. She had never been kissed like *that!* And, oh, wow, she hoped he'd do it again, only maybe with a little more pressure next time.

Hands knotted over the steering wheel, Ben drove home with his teeth clenched with such force that his molars ached. Sissy had never learned how to kiss because she had always been too busy trying to escape. What kind of jerks treated a woman like that? Thinking about it made Ben wish he could take those guys apart. Now he understood her former aloofness. His brother Barney had pegged her right. She'd had some really lousy experiences.

Once parked by his house, Ben cut the engine of his truck. Finn, who couldn't see much scenery during a drive at night, bolted upright from his snooze. Clearly the pup was waiting for Ben to exit the vehicle as usual to take a quick stroll around the ranch proper to check on the animals, Finn's favorite part of getting home. But Ben needed a moment to just stare out the windshield at nothing and breathe slowly. It wasn't often that he felt this angry.

Slowly, his heart settled into a normal rhythm, his jaws stopped throbbing, and he was able to flex his fingers until his urge to make fists ebbed away. Sissy. He already missed her, and with only a limited knowledge of what she must have been through, he felt his affection for her deepen.

"I love her, Finn. She's everything I ever wanted: sweet, pretty, honest, caring, and responsible. But what if I make a wrong move with her and mess this up?"

Finn tilted his head, peered at Ben, and then let loose with a growl-bark noise that he'd never made before. Feeling as if his skin might turn inside out, Ben opened the driver's-side door, leaped to the ground, and called to his dog.

"Yes, Finnegan, we'll take a walk. God knows I need to burn off these feelings somehow."

The next night Ben returned to the café just before closing time to help Sissy do after-dinner cleanup and prep. Afterward he turned to Sissy and said, "Let's go next door to the Straw Hat for dinner and then take in a movie. Patches and Finn will enjoy playing while we do the same."

She fiddled with her hair. "I look a fright."

"You look fabulous. Come on. Just say yes."

She smiled and nodded. Within minutes they were sitting in a booth at José's, keeping him open later than usual, but he didn't seem to mind.

"What a rare treat to see you here, Sissy," he marveled aloud. "Normally, you order takeout and I walk it next door."

"I'm playing hooky," she replied with a dimpled grin. "And afterward we're walking over to the Mystic Players Theatre. They have a late movie playing. We don't care what it is."

José laughed. "I hear it's an oldie but a goodie. Most films last only ninety minutes. You should still get a fair night's sleep."

Both Ben and Sissy ordered enchiladas with green sauce, filled with minced chicken, cheese, and rice. While they waited for their meals, they gazed at each other over flickering candlelight. It reminded Sissy of her imagined dinner with him at his house, and she smiled. She no longer felt threatened by the thought of her and Ben being an item. *Sparking,* as Christopher had called it. She'd told Ben she loved him, and she'd meant it. She just hoped he would still love her after she told him the sordid details of her life and parents.

"What?" he asked, as if he read in her expression that something was troubling her.

Sissy refused to lie to him. "I'm just thinking of all that I need to tell you. You have no idea where I come from."

"It doesn't matter. I'm just glad you're here."

It did matter, but Sissy didn't want to spoil the evening by worrying about it. After enjoying their meal, they walked to the town center and took the cobbled path that circled the city park. It was a crisp night, but when Ben took hold of Sissy's hand, his touch chased away the chill. When they reached the natural bridge, an amazing archway of stone created by the creek tunneling through it for hundreds of years, Ben let go of her hand to lock his arm around her shoulders. From across the stream, lights from Peck's Red Rooster glistened upon the churning water like gold nuggets that had rained from the starlit sky.

"Next time, I'll take you to eat there," Ben said, his deep voice vibrating lightly against her shoulder. "I'll reserve a table that overlooks the stream."

Sissy hoped there would be a next time. Just as she looked up, he lowered his gaze, and as if a powerful magnet drew her toward him, she was suddenly gently cocooned in his strong embrace. The next instant, he kissed her. Not a light, nearly nonexistent feathering of his lips over hers, but still more of an invitation than a demand. Sissy wanted to accept the offer, only she wasn't certain how.

"Slow and easy," he whispered against her lips. "Relax against me and let your lips go soft. I'll take it from there."

He felt so thick through his arms, shoulders, and chest. So deliciously warm, with the night air still nipping at her back. As she had in her dream, she stepped up onto his boots to gain enough height to place her hands on his upper arms and press her nose against his throat to intoxicate herself with the scent of him, a delightful blend of male musk, cotton, a faint scent of soap, and a tantalizing masculine cologne. Being held in his arms made parts of her she hadn't acknowledged start to ache and then burn with need.

He ran the tip of his tongue along the seam of her closed teeth, prompting her to open for him. When she did, she moaned with pleasure. This wasn't a slobbery and brutal rape of her mouth, but more a shy hello, with him cautiously dipping deeper for a better taste of her, and in the process, she got her first taste of him. She felt his body shudder. Drawing his lips from hers, he murmured against her cheek.

"I've wanted this for so long." His voice sounded different, coarser, deeper, and tighter. "If you want me to let go, just tap my arm. No need to feel trapped or try to escape."

Sissy already knew that. Ben was different from any man she'd ever met. He resumed kissing her. Sissy wished it might never end. She had never wanted to be with a man. The experience was so new to her that she wasn't even certain what she actually yearned for from him. She'd watched films, she understood the nuts and bolts of sexual intimacy, but she wasn't quite certain how a couple went from heady kisses to actually doing the deed.

When he finally lifted his head, he smiled down at her. "You are incredible," he whispered.

Sissy felt like a flower that had just opened its petals to the sun. "So are you."

Keeping one arm loosely encircling her back, he glanced at his watch. "Well, as incredible as we both may be, we're late for the movie."

They decided to go regardless. Ben bought a large tub of popcorn and a soft drink for each of them. Sissy didn't think she had room for a single bite, but she munched on the popcorn anyway. When a film scene cast relative darkness over the small theater, Ben licked the buttery salt from her lips and then dipped his tongue into her mouth. When light splashed over them, he ended the kiss.

Ben whispered, "If my folks are here, my dad will tell me to go find a room."

Sissy giggled. "So when do you plan to take me to a room?"

He grinned at her. "When you're ready."

"What if I'm ready now?"

His grin broadened. "Oh, no. I'll know when you are, and now isn't it."

As they walked home, Sissy asked, "What was that movie about?"

Ben, back to holding her hand, threw back his head and laughed. "It beats the hell out of me."

· · ·

That evening became the template for the nights that followed. Ben worked on the cat tunnels, went home to clean up, and returned to the café around a quarter after eight, smuggling Finn up the stairs to spend time with Patches in the flat. Sometimes he ordered a meal, always sitting beside Blackie at the counter to chat while he ate, and other nights, when he didn't eat, he flirted outrageously with Sissy with only his eyes. Either way, when the last customer left, he helped Sissy in the kitchen and then he sometimes took her out for a meal or spent what was left of the evening with her upstairs, their only entertainment being kisses in between light conversational exchanges.

Their time alone together became almost as important to Ben as breathing and nearly as automatic. Every second while Ben was with Sissy, he was acutely aware of her. He loved the smell of her even when she wore no perfume. The faint lavender scent of her soap, the clean, sweet smell of her hair, the velvety softness of her skin when they accidentally touched. He wanted her so badly that he often lay awake at night, aching with need.

He struggled not to ask Sissy about her past. If he got her to talk about it maybe he'd know how to move forward without fucking things with her up. But Ben hated it when people tried to make him share personal stuff before he felt ready, and he wouldn't do that to Sissy. She would talk about it when the moment felt right to her, and until then he could only wait and love her with all his heart.

He'd finally found that one special woman—a woman he wanted to stay with for the rest of his life. He instinctively knew that he would never grow bored with her. He'd learned during their evenings together that she was a witty conversationalist and had a quirky sense of humor. In a debate over whatever topic came up, she was quick on her feet and presented a well-conceived argument, but she never seemed resentful if he could convince her he might be right.

So, as much as he longed to lose himself in her physically, Ben found satisfaction in other ways. With each passing day, she seemed more relaxed with him. That was a good sign. She became more spontaneous and laughed more often. When she sat beside him on the floor to play with Patches and Finn, she'd sometimes lean against him, inviting him to drape an arm around her and follow up with a deep, lingering joining of their mouths. She no longer stiffened and tried to pull away when he touched her. Instead she went limp and pressed closer, comfortable with him, and sending him signals that she yearned for more.

Ben felt it was wiser to wait. He'd know when

Sissy was truly ready, and when she was, he'd linger over her for hours while he made love to her. But the time wasn't right yet. Sometimes when he caught her off guard, he saw in her eyes a bewilderment and pain he couldn't understand. During those moments, he knew an awful memory had slipped into her mind. He wanted no unpleasant memories to come between them when he made love to her. None.

One night, Finn, who'd worked cattle all morning and afternoon, crashed on the bed Sissy had made for him beside Patches's sleeping pad. Snoring softly, the dog was totally out of it, allowing Sissy and Ben to tussle gently with the kitten. Patches, who didn't seem to realize he had no front feet, played as any kitten might, grabbing at a toy or their hands as if he had paws.

"He's got mettle," he told Sissy, lifting his arm slightly. "Look at him hug me tight. I think playing with Finn has been good for him. If he ever accidentally runs into a cat with claws, he'll bypass all the swatting maneuvers and jump in for a bear hug. Then he'll be able to use his teeth and his back feet to fight."

Sissy's eyes glowed with pleasure. "He's so smart. His stubs are still a tiny bit tender. But the other day he slipped out the door and tried to run down the stairs in front of me. When it started to hurt, he flipped around and went down backward."

"He's going to grow up and be a gorgeous tomcat."

Just then, Ben felt something crawl onto his lap. Finn was sacked out on his bed. Patches had a death grip on his wrist. Ben glanced down to see what the hell was on him—or, more precisely, on the fly of his jeans.

"Holy mother-fricking *shit!*" Ben shook Patches loose from his arm, shoved Snickers off his lap, and leaped to his feet. It took everything he had not to scream like a girl. "You little bastard. You bite me there, and you're one dead rat!"

Snickers sat up and worried his hands. *No, damn it, his* paws, Ben reminded himself. Snickers looked up at him with bright, beady eyes, his expression inquisitive, as if to say, *What's your problem, man? I was just saying hello.*

"Oh!" Sissy said softly, with that same mama tone she used with Finn and Patches. "My sweet boy." She scooped the rat up in her hands and cuddled him close.

Ben watched, struggling not to say, *Don't let him near those gorgeous breasts. He could scar them for life.*

She glanced up at Ben. "Don't be afraid, Ben. He won't hurt you."

Okay, now Ben *felt* like a girl—and not just any girl, but a scaredy-cat girl who reacted to anything slightly alarming by shrieking, stomping her

336

feet, and turning in circles. Sissy was probably surprised he hadn't jumped up on the coffee table.

"I'm *not* afraid of him. He just startled me, is all."

"Oh, good." Cupping Snickers with one hand, Sissy patted the carpet beside her. "Sit back down and make friends. He is such a sweet thing."

Ben would have preferred to have a wisdom tooth dug out of his gum without Novocain. But, damn it, a guy had to do what a guy had to do. He crossed his ankles and sat down. "If he bites me . . ."

"Oh, you big silly. Look at him! I've only ever seen his teeth when he was eating a blade of wheatgrass."

"Trust me, he has teeth. And Jack says he'll have to be quarantined for ten days if he bites. He could have rabies."

Sissy giggled. "Does he act like he has rabies? Look at him. And you? You're so big and strong. I can't believe you're afraid of a tiny guy like Snickers."

"I am *not* afraid of him." *Okay,* Ben thought, *so I'm afraid of something. Big deal.* "Let him go. I'm fine with it. Come here, Snickers."

Ben waggled his fingers at the rat, hoping against hope that the rat would think he was waving good-bye.

Snickers did not read body language well. He scampered from Sissy's lap and leaped onto

Ben's again. Ben stared down at the rat sitting atop the most valued part of his anatomy. The rat reared onto its haunches, worried his hands again, and wiggled his whiskers. Ben's arms felt knotted and frozen. But he forced himself to cup his hands around one of the last creatures on earth he wanted to touch.

To his surprise, Snickers felt soft and warm. When he curled his front feet over Ben's thumbs, it was a friendly touch, nothing about it aggressive. "Hi, little guy," Ben said. "I forgot to plug up all your ingress holes." *Little bastard.* "I'll be sure to do that soon. You really shouldn't be around Patches. He might catch something from you."

"Oh, my God, you're right." Sissy scrambled to stand, sounding so distressed that Ben felt guilty. Well, almost. It was absolutely true that Snickers might be carrying diseases. "I need a gift for him. Something special. And then he'll leave to go put it in his nest!"

"Scrunch up a piece of tinfoil," Ben said. "He'll love that."

While Sissy rummaged in the kitchen, Ben ran his fingertips over the rat's fur. Maybe Sissy had it right and rats weren't so bad. Just then Finn awakened and came up off his bed as if someone had just torched his tail. Teeth bared and hackles raised, the pup lunged across the floor.

"No!" Ben said.

Finn stopped dead.

"This is Snickers," Ben told the dog. *"Friend. No!"*

A hangdog expression settled on Finn's mottled face. He sat down, curiously eyeing the rat. Ben would have urged Finn closer to touch noses and become acquainted, but Snickers was an animal that might be carrying diseases the pup wasn't vaccinated against. The sooner Snickers left, the better. That thought was followed by inarguable fact: Snickers had already contaminated the flat with any dangerous germs he might be carrying, and neither the pup nor the kitten had gotten sick.

"Don't let Finn hurt him!" Sissy cried.

"I won't. It's fine. Finn realizes now that even rats are welcome here." Ben rolled his eyes at the dog. In a whisper, he said, "Next she'll fall for a black widow."

"I made it into a nice small ball for Snickers," she called from the kitchen. "I pressed it tight. I don't want him to eat any foil."

"Good idea," Ben said, smiling to himself. Snickers actually was cute. And he didn't seem at all inclined to bite. This rat wasn't a demon from hell. He was a little mammal with a cute face, inquisitive eyes, and a gentle nature. He was a key thief, though. It had cost Ben over a hundred dollars to replace his remote.

Sissy returned and placed the shiny ball of

foil in front of Snickers on her upturned palm. "What do you think, Snickers?"

The rat grabbed the ball and leaped from Ben's hands like a flea off a dog's back. Then he was off. Ben turned to watch him leave. "He's coming in and out through your bathroom."

"Yes. But he's entering the building somewhere downstairs. I hope, after we ratproof the place, that we can find his nest. It was good to see him again. He's so sweet and dear."

"Tomorrow, I need to get that done," Ben told her. "The ratproofing, I mean. I've been so caught up in you that I forgot all about it."

Ben had to admit, if only to himself, that he could now tolerate the rat. But *sweet and dear* was carrying it too far. He joined Sissy in the bathroom to wash their hands with antibacterial soap. As they both scrubbed, Ben fantasized about getting her into a shower and running his hands all over her soap-slick body. If success were measured by a football field's standards, he figured he was stuck on the ten-yard line. Showering with Sissy was so far off in his future that he couldn't even see the goalposts.

Ben forced his mind to mundane matters. He needed to put a reminder on his phone to buy mountains of fine steel wool and fill every point of ingress in Sissy's building with the stuff. Then he needed to follow Snickers back to his nest so Sissy could go there to visit him.

"So, how's it going with your bookkeeping program?"

Ben almost groaned at her question. "Don't ask."

She laughed. "Give me your bank username and password, and start bringing me all your receipts. Then I can download all your transactions. You do so many things for me, I certainly don't mind taking over your books. I'll just do yours when I do mine."

"Really? I *hate* doing that crap."

Sissy laughed. "I kind of enjoy it. Scan me copies of your checkbook register each month, too."

A few minutes later, Ben decided it was time for him and his dog to head for home. "When are you going to hire some help downstairs? You won't have to get up so early then, and we can stay later."

"A perfect reason to get an ad in the paper as soon as I find time."

Normally, Sissy followed Ben and Finn downstairs to lock up after them, but tonight she said, "I'm going to spray with disinfectant just in case Snickers left germs. Do you mind saying good night up here? I'll run downstairs in a couple of minutes to lock up."

Ben shook his head. "No, I don't mind."

Ben stepped in close, drew her gently into his arms, and kissed her good night. He ignored that *good night* felt more like *hello, baby*. He heard her breathing quicken and knew she was

341

aroused. Restraining himself was one of the most difficult things he'd ever done. But even though he still didn't know the story of Sissy's life, he did know that the greatest gifts he could give her were time and the privilege to decide when she wanted their kisses to take them to a deeper level. She'd give him a sign when she got there.

He stepped away, touched his hat, and said, "Good night. Sleep tight."

Once outside on Sissy's porch, Ben took a couple of minutes to stand and breathe deeply. Sissy hadn't been alone in growing aroused during that kiss. He felt as if his dick had turned into an ear of field corn. And, damn it, his testicles ached like a son of a bitch. He needed a woman, but it couldn't be just any woman. His carousing days in Crystal Falls were over. He thought he heard Sissy come downstairs. Then he heard the lock click and knew for sure she had.

"Okay," he said to his dog. "I can finally walk straight now."

Ben set off toward his parked truck. He'd just unlocked the doors with his remote when a shrill scream came from Sissy's building. Before Ben could turn around, the scream came again. Fear such as he'd never felt in his life slammed into him.

Sissy. Something horrible had happened. As he ran he could only pray that he could bulldoze his way through the back door.

Chapter
FIFTEEN

Ben hit the porch with a flying leap, struck the door with all his might, and then nearly fell to the floor in a tangle with the stout frame and planked portal.

Scrambling to keep his balance, he yelled, "Sissy! Where are you?"

She screamed again, apparently in too much agony to speak.

The stairs. Oh, God, Ben thought, *those damned steep stairs.* He raced along the hallway through the storage rooms, veered right once inside the café, and nearly fell over Sissy, who lay sprawled on the floor near the bottom step. She'd tripped, he guessed, which, unless she was on ice, was so atypical of Sissy, so nimble and quick on her feet. Ben knelt beside her. Her face had drained of color and turned chalk gray.

"What happened? Talk to me, honey. Where are you hurt?"

She bared her clenched teeth. He watched her struggle to speak. "Right—leg. Be-low kn-knee."

Ben grabbed his phone and dialed 911. He perused Sissy's leg. No blood had seeped through her jeans. *Good sign.* But he knew that the bone had to be fractured. One thing he'd learned about Sissy over the last month was that she didn't get dramatic when she got hurt. He remembered when she'd slipped on the ice, landed hard enough on her butt to crack her tailbone, and then smacked the back of her head on the frozen ground with enough force to knock some people unconscious. Never once had she so much as shed a tear, let alone screamed.

"This is Ben Sterling. There's an emergency at the Cauldron!" he half yelled into his phone. "Get here fast! Sissy Bentley. Fall on the stairs. I think she's fractured her right tibia."

He thrust the phone back in his pocket as soon as he knew help was on the way. "It's okay, honey. The paramedics are on their way."

She'd stopped screaming as soon as she saw him. It was one thing to scream for help, but she'd clench her teeth until they chipped before she reacted to the pain in front of an audience. She turned her head sideways, closed her eyes, and bit down on her lower lip.

Ben heard sirens, but damn it, they sounded distant. Sissy was hurt, really hurt. *Hurry the hell up,* he silently urged them. Why weren't they here? The fire station was at the edge of town on North Huckleberry. What was taking so long? Ben knew the wait seemed like an eternity to Sissy. In that moment, he would have given almost any-thing to take her place. She was such a little gal and fragile. Never should she have to endure pain like this.

After what seemed like hours Ben saw headlights sweep over the wall. The sirens went quiet as the screech of braked tires sounded on the street. "I gotta go let 'em in. I'll be right back. Just hold on, sweetheart."

Ben dashed for the front door, turned the key in the lock, and swung the glass barrier wide. Tyler Ryder, the fire chief, spilled out the driver's side of the red ambulance. The rear doors opened, and Sheryl Moses leaped out onto the asphalt, a large medical bag clutched in one hand. A petite blonde, she didn't look strong enough to be a firewoman and paramedic, but she performed as well as any man, sometimes better.

Ryder sped through the opening, acknowledging Ben with only a jerk of his head. Having dined at the café, he didn't need directions to the stairs. Talking on his cell phone, he raced to the back of the restaurant to crouch over Sissy, with Sheryl close on his heels. Cody Charles, a young Mel Gibson look-alike who'd been riding shotgun with Ryder, reached the door last, steering a folded gurney ahead of him. Ben began shoving chairs and tables out of the way to form a wider path for Sissy to be ferried out.

When he got back to the woman he loved, he couldn't get close enough to let her know he was there. Sheryl was palpating Sissy's body to check for other injuries. Then she grabbed scissors from the bag and cut the right leg of Sissy's jeans open from hem to thigh. Sissy's shin had already turned bright red with a blue tint, telling Ben that blood welled beneath her skin.

"Horizontal, but stable," Sheryl said to Ryder. "That's my guess, anyway."

Sissy began to breathe fast, each intake shallow. Sheryl pushed her bag open wider. "Nitrous. Authorization to administer. Great deal of pain here, Chief."

Ryder echoed Sheryl's words into the phone and gave his paramedic a thumbs-up. Ben decided the fire chief was talking with medical personnel at St. Matthew's in Crystal Falls, the closest facility that could handle anything serious.

Sheryl put a mask over Sissy's mouth and nose. Seemingly from out of nowhere, Chandler Oliver appeared with a portable tank. Within seconds, Sissy was breathing the gas, and the rise and fall of her chest slowed. Her dark lashes swept up and down over her glazed blue eyes.

Next, Sheryl slipped an uninflated neck brace under Sissy's head, fastened it at her chin, and started squeezing an oval-shaped rubber pump. The brace billowed quickly to stabilize Sissy's cervical spine. Then Sheryl and Chandler slid a body board under Sissy, both of them taking as much care as possible not to move her. Ben's knees felt as if they'd turned to jelly. After a fall like that, Sissy could have other broken bones, or even have a spinal fracture.

Ben was forced back when the crew of three lifted Sissy onto the gurney, which Chandler had unfolded.

"I'll insert the IV en route," Sheryl barked. "Let's go. Move it, guys. Let's go."

Ben ran after them. He stood on the sidewalk and watched as Sissy was put into the ambulance. She seemed to be in less pain now. Sheryl jumped in back with her patient. Tyler Ryder met Ben's gaze as he strode the length of the vehicle to get back in the driver's seat.

"You can follow us," he said. "No room for you in there. They'll be in close contact with the hospital and working on her as I drive. She'll get some intravenous analgesic on the way. My guess is, she broke only the leg. But we won't know for sure until they take X-rays."

Ben stepped up to the door as the chief climbed inside the cab. "Tell her—" He broke off and swallowed. "Tell her I love her and I'm right behind the ambulance."

Just as the ambulance left, a county sheriff's truck sped around the corner and parked at an angle at the curb. Barney jumped out and slapped on his Stetson as he leaped onto the sidewalk. "I was way out on Seven Curves Road when I got the call. What happened?"

"She fell on the stairs. I was about to leave when I heard her scream."

Barney strode inside and went straight to the stairs with Ben right behind him. His trained gaze swept the scene for clues. Then he jabbed a finger and asked, "What the hell is that round, silver thing?"

Ben scanned the risers. On a step below the apartment door, he saw the foil ball that Sissy had given Snickers. "Oh, God. It's a sparkly thing she made for a pack rat. After she locked up, she must have stepped on it going back up the stairs. Look, I'll explain later, okay? I'm out of here. I'm following the ambulance." Ben stepped into the hall. "I busted down the back door. That has to be fixed. Her place can't be left wide open all night." He stopped midstride. "Finnegan is around here somewhere. The kitten's upstairs. Can you take care of them until I make it back here?"

Barney nodded. "I'll call in the troops. Just go. Got it handled. Keep your damned foot out of the carburetor."

Ben knew *the troops* meant his family. His heart welled with gladness that he had such a great support system, but only for an instant. Then all he could think about was Sissy, how bad her injuries might be, and how he would manage to take care of her without everything at his ranch going to hell in a handbasket.

It took bloody forever to reach St. Matthew's. Ben had to find a slot in visitor parking while the emergency vehicle circled in under the ER portico. By the time he reached the automatic sliding doors, Sissy was nowhere to be seen. At the front desk, Ben identified himself as Sissy's brother. He knew he'd never get information about her condition unless he lied. He learned that she'd been taken into the bowels of the emergency care section.

"I'm glad you're here, Mr. Sterling," the receptionist said. "She's got no ID on her. The paramedics from Mystic Creek knew her name, but we need a lot more information. Can you go to admitting and fill out some paperwork for her, please?"

Shit. Ben knew so many little, personal things about Sissy that, collectively, they'd become huge, but he was sadly lacking in knowledge to fill out admittance information for her. A stern-looking woman gave him a clipboard to which were attached forms. He went to sit on a black vinyl chair. Filling out the paperwork was a bitch. He lied and said his parents were her mother and father. He guessed at harmless answers, but when he got to medical history, he couldn't make things up.

Why in the hell had he never asked Sissy if she'd undergone any surgeries, or if she was allergic to anything, especially medications? He couldn't even get online and try to hunt down her parents. She'd never told him their names.

Ben got up and approached the desk. The harassed woman gave him an unsmiling look. Ben handed her the clipboard. "Uh, this medical history? I can't fill it out. She left home at eighteen, so for the last eight years we haven't been in close contact. Plus, brothers and sisters don't talk about health stuff much."

"That's fine," the woman said as if she'd heard all this before. She grabbed the clipboard. "When she comes back around, a nurse can ask her questions."

Relieved, Ben resumed his seat. That lasted ten seconds. He paced. He sat. He paced. He didn't want to go to the john for fear a doctor might come out and not find him. If not for that damned rat, Sissy wouldn't be in the hospital. Deep down, Ben knew it was more his own fault than it was Snickers's. If he had only ratproofed the building when he should have, none of this would have happened.

Finally, a doctor in pale green scrubs entered the waiting room. They sat in a quiet corner to talk. The man was taking Sissy in for surgery. He explained to Ben what he planned to do, saying something about a metal brace and bolts in the bone, but none of the words sank into Ben's brain. His stomach bunched into knots.

His heart felt as if it was pounding hard enough to crack his ribs.

After that one-sided conversation, all Ben could do was wait. It seemed to him that hours passed before the doctor entered the waiting area again, and once more Ben could barely register what he said. All that stuck in his gray matter was that no invasive surgery had been necessary. The horizontal fracture of the tibia was stable, what-ever the hell that meant, and over time it would heal.

After what seemed like forever, Ben was informed by a weary-looking CNA that Sissy had been moved from recovery to a private room. Family members could see her there now.

"She may be asleep," the assistant warned. "She came out from under the anesthesia fine, and now we want to let her rest as long as possible."

Ben found the elevators and went up to locate the room. As he stepped inside, he could barely make out Sissy's small form on the hospital bed. The lights had been dimmed. She lay with her arms at her sides and her injured leg elevated on pillows. Through the sheet and blanket, he could detect the unnatural angles and shape of either a brace or a cast.

A beige chair that looked as if it reclined was positioned at the far side of the bed. Ben, taking care not to let his boots rap on the tile, circled to take a seat. He'd just gotten settled when a plump older woman with faded red hair entered the room. She checked Sissy's IV tube, giving it a flick with her middle finger. Then she glanced briefly at the digital screen to check Sissy's vitals.

"So, you are Ms. Bentley's—brother?"

Startled by the question, Ben said, "I was told to be quiet."

The woman chuckled. "Our talking won't disturb her. She's still sleepy from the anesthesia, and I just added some analgesic to her IV, a nice, slow drip of la-la land to keep her comfortable. A horizontal fracture that goes clear through the bone is extremely painful."

Ben tried to swallow. His throat was parched. "Did the doc put bolts in her leg? I remember him saying he might. But when he talked with me later, my brain took a vacation."

"It wasn't necessary. It's a stable break."

"What does that mean?"

The nurse smoothed Sissy's hair back from her forehead, something he'd longed to do himself. "Well, it means that although the bone is broken all the way through, it was forced only slightly out of alignment. With stable fractures, a surgeon will sometimes apply a metal brace on the outside of the leg to support the compromised bone. He secures that brace by drilling a bolt into the bone above and below the break."

A swirling grayness overtook Ben's mind. Bolts in her bone?

"This young lady was very lucky. Her tibia remained almost aligned, and the surgeon was able to shift it slightly. He decided that a boot brace will temporarily work to support it. When the leg stops swelling, he'll apply a regular cast." She pulled up the sheet and blanket to reveal the large red boot on Sissy's leg, which reached to hug her thigh. "I'm going to unfasten the straps on this to have a peek. If her leg is swelling, I'll need to make adjustments. The trick is to keep the bone firmly supported while allowing room for swelling, so every hour I need to check on her."

Ben thought he had a strong stomach, but he battled against an urge to gag when he saw Sissy's discolored and swollen leg.

"It's not pretty," the older woman observed. "But open fractures are worse. The bruising and swelling will slowly dissipate."

That wouldn't happen fast enough to suit Ben. "What'll happen if the leg swells more than you expect before you return to check on her again?"

"We can watch her on the monitors and know if she gets uncomfortable. Plus, I'll be checking once an hour until we get through the rapid swelling phase." She smiled as she refastened the boot. "For a brother, you're very devoted."

Ben met the woman's gaze. He'd always been a lousy liar, and he saw no point in testing his talent now. "Please don't kick me out of here. I'm the closest thing to family that she has."

"Boyfriend? Significant other?"

"Friend, aiming for lover."

A broad grin moved over the woman's mouth. "She has an aunt and an uncle out in the third-floor waiting room."

Ben's heart leaped with hope. "She does? Thank God! Maybe they know her medical history."

The nurse chuckled. "I suspect they're just more friends who love her so much that they'll lie to see her. The uncle's name is Fred Black."

"Blackie's here?" Ben sighed. "If Sissy could pick an uncle, he'd be it."

"And her aunt is a woman named Marilyn Fears."

"Aw, Marilyn." Ben dredged up a smile and gave the nurse an imploring look. "Please don't give them their walking papers. Sissy needs people who love her right now."

The woman shrugged. "I'm old-school. You say you're her brother. They say they're her aunt and uncle. Until she wakes up and tells me differently, you're blood relatives as far as I'm concerned."

Ben wanted to hug her. "Are there visitation rules? I mean, like, are you going to chase me out of here at the stroke of midnight?"

"Visitor hours end at ten." She glanced at the wall clock. It read ten minutes after twelve. "A few CNAs will come in throughout the night. I'll tell them it is in her best interest to have one family member in the room with her in case she wakes up." She held up a rigid forefinger. "*One.* Tell the aunt and uncle that they can come in separately, and not to wake her. The longer she sleeps, the better. When she does wake up, she'll be in a lot of pain. We'll be on it. Only one person can sit with her all night. I'm assuming that will be you."

Ben nodded. Damn straight, it would be him, even if he had to arm wrestle Blackie. He wouldn't leave Sissy unless he was carried out of there, and he figured, with a little ego to make him feel invincible, that it would take four men and a stun gun to accomplish that. "I appreciate your breaking the rules to let me be with her."

The nurse grabbed the clipboard, jotted some notes, and then turned to leave the room. "I never break hospital rules."

Ben detested leaving Sissy, but he wandered up the hall to find Blackie and Marilyn. While they each took turns going in to sit with Sissy, Ben found a john and then went downstairs to the cafeteria, where free coffee was kept in large pump carafes. Chilled sandwiches and salads were available in a vending cooler. Ben considered eating, but his stomach roiled. He filled a couple of coffee cups for Blackie and Marilyn.

Blackie had tears in his eyes when Ben joined them in the waiting room.

"She's awake, sort of. Throwing her head, mumbling. They're giving her something to ease her up."

Ben handed over the coffee, then gave Marilyn a hug and Blackie a strong handshake. "Now that you've both seen her, you need to go home and get some sleep. I'm staying. I'll remind her you were here. Thank you for caring so much. I'd stay and chat with you—"

"But you can't stand not to be with her," Marilyn interrupted. "We understand. Just go."

Smiling his appreciation, Ben pivoted on one foot and headed for Sissy's room, hoping to get there and speak to her before the pain medication sent her under again. He had no idea what he meant to say. He just wanted her to know he was with her. He had a bad feeling that Sissy had never really had someone always in her corner.

Ben resumed his seat in the chair beside Sissy's bed. A CNA had just given her a dose of something in her IV tube, but even when only half-awake, she tossed her head on the pillow and mumbled under her breath. She was so pale. Then, as if an alarm had gone off inside her head, her eyes popped open.

"It hurts. It *hurts.*"

Ben got up and leaned over her. "I'm here, honey."

Her blue eyes, glazed and unfocused, melded with his. "Help me, Ben. The pain. Bad."

Ben had been kicked once by a bull and fractured his femur. He'd never forget the agony of it, and his break hadn't gone clear through the bone.

He grabbed Sissy's patient remote and pushed the red button. When the old nurse bustled into the room, he said, "She's hurting. She's not a complainer. It's bad. I know they gave her something, but she needs more."

The nurse bent over Sissy. She didn't ask questions. "You're right." She left the room and returned moments later to administer Sissy a dose of something through the IV. "That'll do the trick. Lights out for at least four hours. Judging by how you look, I'd say you'd be wise to grab a nap while she does."

After the woman left, Ben watched Sissy until the medication took hold. He saw her grind her teeth. He counted the creases that sprang forth on her sweet face as her body tightened to stifle a scream. His heart felt as if it were being ripped apart. But as much as that hurt, her agony was worse.

After the medication took effect, she drifted to sleep, and he slumped in the chair, tipped his hat low over his eyes, and tried to rest. It was four in the morning. He needed a couple of winks, because he suspected Sissy would need him when she resurfaced. And he would be there for her, no matter what.

Sissy's hospital stay became a blur for Ben. He slept when he could, ate when she was fast asleep, and became almost robotic with exhaustion. Sometimes she jerked awake, worrying aloud about Patches being alone. Ben assured her that the kitten was being well cared for by members of his family. Another time, she came wide-awake, concerned about her restaurant. When Ben told her that he would operate her business until she was able to work again, she told him how Crystal Malloy liked her eggs.

And suddenly it hit Ben that Sissy wouldn't be able to run the café for a long while, and that it was her only source of income. He soothed her back to sleep. Then he slipped from her room to call Brett, telling him that he'd have to take over at the ranch until otherwise notified.

Brett was a good man. Great with horses. But he wasn't a trainer, and Ben was boarding two horses that needed behavioral modification at his place. Leaning against the hallway wall, he hung his head, trying to think of someone who could take over for him.

Ben thought of his dad. Was he still in good enough shape to work with difficult equines? Ben straightened out of his slump, drew his cell phone from his pocket, and dialed his father's number. It was only seven thirty in the morning, but Jeremiah answered quickly, sounding bright and chipper.

"Hey, Dad. I've got a question for you. Are you still able to work with problem horses?"

Jeremiah laughed. "Well, I'm not using a cane yet, and I still ride every day. Besides, it's been my experience that working the quirks out of a horse requires more intuition and good sense than it does muscle."

Ben couldn't have agreed more.

"So?" Eagerness rang in Jeremiah's voice. "Don't get me all excited and then disappoint me."

"You're excited about working with horses again?"

Jeremiah laughed. "Hell, yes. I wouldn't want to do it full-time, but I'd love the opportunity to work with horses every once in a while. Your mother has me making Christmas tree ornaments, for God's sake."

Ben smiled. "Say no more. I'd be going nuts." Ben gave his father the rundown on the horses he had in his care. "Brett can handle all the grunt work. All you'd have to do is work with the two problematic horses. Three hours a day, tops. They lose their focus if I work with them for more than an hour and a half each. I let them rest two days a week. Are you interested?"

"I'm so interested that I'll go today!" Jeremiah muttered something Ben couldn't catch. "It's not like you to jump ship in the middle of a training stint. Did you get kicked or something?"

"No, Dad, I'm fine." Ben explained about Sissy's accident. "I don't have it straight from the doctor yet, but I'm guessing she'll be unable to work for at least two months. If she has to close the doors that long, she'll lose customers. I can't allow that, so come hell or high water, I'm going to run the café."

"I knew she got hurt. Barney called your mother about a cat, and she went right over there. But you, run a café?"

"I've worked a lot in the kitchen. I may hit rough spots, but I think I can do it."

Jeremiah sighed. "You must really love this woman."

"With all my heart."

"I'll let your mother know when she gets home. She used to wait tables years ago. She'd probably love trying her hand at that again. I can help you nights with the cleanup if you tell me how. Barney said he's got the door fixed."

Tears burned in Ben's eyes. "You guys are the best. Whenever I need you, you're always there for me."

• • •

Ben grew so exhausted that he often wasn't sure if it was night or day. He programmed his brain to focus on only the important stuff, such as doctor visits and instructions the nurses gave him for Sissy's home care. Otherwise the routine of the hospital played on the screen of his mind like a film on fast-forward. He wasn't even sure how long Sissy had been a patient there. He slept as often as he could to sharpen his senses, ever aware that when Sissy got better, he'd be the one who had to chauffeur her home.

Chapter
SIXTEEN

At six o'clock one morning, the doctor stopped in during rounds and startled Ben erect. "I'm sorry," Ben said. "I must have nodded off."

The surgeon smiled. "Most of us do when we've slept in fits and starts for over forty-eight hours." He bent over Sissy. "Ms. Bentley, how are you feeling this morning?"

Sissy opened her eyes. "My leg hurts." She stifled a yawn and struggled to focus. "But all I really want is to go home."

The doctor, a stocky blond who looked to be in his mid-forties, nodded. "I think we may arrange for that to happen today. But first I'd like a set of X-rays to check your tibia. If all looks in order, I'll put in for her release."

Ben sat alone in the room while Sissy was taken downstairs for X-rays. When she was wheeled back in and her bed was returned to its former position, the nurse grinned at Ben. "You ready to take this young lady home? I've been told you plan to be her caregiver. That means you have to go through all the instructions for her care with me and sign a paper. You up for that?"

"Absolutely."

Ben listened intently to everything the nurse told him. Then the surgeon returned. "X-rays look great." He smiled at Ben. "It's your job to keep them that way. No weight on the leg. She must take sponge baths until I see her again. Under no conditions should the boot be removed. No showers, no matter how creative you think you can be to keep the boot dry. One slip, and she'll be in the OR getting bolts in her bone. No sex." He sent Ben a pointed look, making Ben wonder if the entire hospital knew he wasn't Sissy's brother. "If she isn't using the restroom, I want her elevating the leg above her heart. She can sit up occasionally with it elevated below the heart to eat, but for short periods of time at first. I'll let her know when she's allowed to do it longer. The therapist will fit her for crutches. They are to be used only while she has assistance for as long as she's on pain medication. The stuff I plan to prescribe is what I fondly call 'happy juice.' Easy on the stomach, great for pain relief, but she may get dizzy. It's a narcotic, so you must take the script to a pharmacy to fill it. Choose one near you, because she may need refills." He tapped his pen on the clipboard. "That's it from me. The nurses will tell you the rest, and my PA will be getting in touch to schedule appointments."

Ben nodded and gave him his phone number, a favor the doctor returned. "Get my number on her phone as well," the surgeon said. "If anything happens or if you have questions, I'll get back to you as quickly as I can."

Ben expected checkout to be simple. It wasn't. Sissy's jeans had been destroyed with scissors the night of her fall, and she'd puked all over her top. Sissy told her attendants to trash the clothing. A nurse supplied her with a pair of overlarge, bile green scrubs to wear home, one leg hacked off to ride above her boot. He had to sign papers. It seemed like hours passed before Ben had her on the passenger seat of his truck in a reclining position with her injured leg resting on a pillow on the dash.

The ride back to Mystic Creek was a nightmare for Sissy. The stiff suspension under the Dodge made it a rough ride. Sissy didn't complain, but Ben could tell by her pallor that every bump in the road hurt her. Before he even got her out of Crystal Falls, he was rethinking his plan of action.

"Maybe I should just fill the script here so the trip home won't be so awful for you," he told her.

"It'd be too far to drive back for refills, which I believe I'm going to need," she replied. "Besides, the new guy, Drake Mullin, who bought the Pill Minder, can use the business. The older people think he's too young to know what he's doing."

"Fresh out of pharmacy school, he probably knows a lot more than the old fart that sold him the place."

"Ahhh!" Sissy cried when one tire hit a pothole in the street.

Ben's heart hurt for her, but there was no way he could make it a smooth ride. Whatever speed he drove, every jiggle brought Sissy pain.

They made it to Mystic Creek without mishap, but not without a great deal of discomfort for Sissy. Ben wanted to take her straight to the café, get her settled upstairs, and then get her prescription filled. Sissy countered him on that idea.

"I'm going to need a slug of that happy stuff *before* you help me out of this truck and I try to climb the stairs on crutches."

Ben parked along the curb on East Main and raced across the street to the Pill Minder. When he pushed open the door, a bell jingled. Except for the dark-haired, broad-shouldered young man behind the counter, there wasn't a soul in sight. Ben decided Sissy had it right; the guy needed customers.

Ben strode to the counter. "I'm Ben Sterling. I don't think we've met."

"I'm Drake Mullin, the idiot that wanted to get out of the city, live over his pharmacy, and connect with his customers. It never occurred to me that I might have no customers. It's the only pharmacy in town. I don't get it."

Ben didn't have time for a chat, but he did feel sorry for the guy. "I'll get my mother on it." He slapped the script onto the counter. "I need that filled fast."

"You'll get your mother on what?" Drake asked, his brown eyes filled with bewilderment.

"Getting the old fools in this town to stop driving to Crystal Falls to get their prescriptions filled. They think you're a pup who'll make mistakes with their medications."

Drake picked up the paper but didn't look at it. "A *pup?* I'm thirty-one years old! Better for me to fill their prescriptions than the last pharmacist. At least I can see."

Ben forced a smile. "I hear you. The old people in town are being silly. But for right now, that concern goes on hold. I've got a lady in my truck in so much pain that she's about to scream."

Drake looked at the script and whistled softly. "Well, this'll take care of it. For Sissy Bentley, huh? I heard she got hurt."

Ben leaned over the counter. "Drake, just fill the goddamned script. I promise to drop by as soon as I can to visit. I'll bring coffee and donuts from the Jake 'n' Bake, and we'll talk until you can't wait to be rid of me. But right now, Sissy is in horrible pain and every second seems like an eternity to her."

Drake turned away and strode into an aisle. "I hear you, and I'll hold you to the donuts and coffee. Plus, you're in luck. This stuff comes in a bottle. No measuring. All I've got to do is label it, and off you'll go."

Ben tapped his knuckles on the counter. He already had his credit card out to pay when Drake handed him a small white sack with the pharmacy's logo on it. "Just go. The machine takes forever to get card approval. Come back and pay when you can."

Ben felt a newfound respect for Drake. "Thanks. That's kind of how Bill did business."

Ben shoved his card back into his wallet and said over his shoulder as he headed for the door, "My mom knows everybody. She'll get on the horn and have half the people in town convinced you walk on water, and the other half will stop by to see if they can watch. I swear, she could sell monkeys to a banana grower."

The moment Ben got back to his truck, he read the dosage and opened the bottle of happy syrup to pour some into the supplied measuring cap. Sissy, now looking green around the gills, took the tiny cup in a shaky hand, tipped her head back, and swallowed the cherry pink liquid. Then her arm flopped down at her side. Ben plucked the cup from her tightly clenched fingers.

"I'm just going to sit here," he told her. "Let's give that stuff a few minutes to take hold."

"Amen." She let her head loll on the reclined seat. "I've never had anything hurt like this."

"Just hold on, honey. The liquid should get into your bloodstream fairly fast."

He glanced at his watch. It was ten after three. The next time he checked, only another minute had passed. "How are you feeling?"

"No relief yet. Call the doctor to see if he can prescribe something stronger."

Ben, who'd given Sissy his jacket to wear, lifted a hip to fish his phone from his back pocket. He knew she wasn't a wimp when it came to pain. He got an answering service and left a message for the surgeon.

Sissy, still pale, said, "He told us to just call him. Like it was a hotline straight to his ear. Instead we get his answering service? It could be twenty minutes before he calls back!" She sank against the seat again, too short to utilize the headrest. "I need another dose."

Alarm bells went off in Ben's mind. Another entire dose didn't sound like a smart idea. "Honey, this may be powerful stuff. Let's not overdo it."

"I'll take my chances!" she cried. "Give me that bottle!"

Ben tucked the sack between his hip and the driver door. "Not until I call Drake and ask if you can safely take more."

"Drake, the pharmacist nobody trusts?"

Ben was already dialing the Pill Minder. Drake answered and said, "Pill Minder. I'm sorry. Can you hold for a minute?"

Ben shot a wondering look across the street. He could see the pharmacist at the counter, holding the phone. There wasn't a single customer in the store. "Hell, no, I can't hold for a minute. This is Ben Sterling. I was just in there."

"Oh." Drake laughed. "I just started saying that. It's my new plan so anyone who calls will think I'm busy. Busy draws customers. It's been proven in a study."

"Well, I hope your new tactics work, but for the moment, there's an immediate problem. Sissy's still in horrible pain. She's wanting a second dose of syrup. I just want to make sure it's safe."

"No!" Drake said. "You didn't already let her take it, I hope?"

"No. I called you first."

"Well, don't let her. Somebody twice her weight, maybe, but there isn't much to her, and that's a powerful narcotic. It'll hit her in a blink."

Ben glanced over at Sissy. She was gazing out the windshield and smiling slightly. Her body now looked almost limp. "Uh, yeah, I can see that. I think the pain crisis is over now."

Ben saw Drake at his front window, peering out at them. "Getting her upstairs to her flat will be challenging. You want some help?"

Ben hooked a thumb at the druggist. "Like you said, there isn't much to her. But thanks for offering."

• • •

Ben took a page out of the paramedics' book and parked in front of Sissy's café so that she would have a straight shot as she moved toward the stairs on crutches. After he cut the truck engine, he glanced over at her as he probed his left front pocket for the key to her place. *Still there.* He shifted to dig it out. Then he exited the truck to unlock and open the front door of her restaurant. Seconds later, he had drawn her new crutches from the backseat and opened the passenger door, and was studying Sissy, who was now giggling.

Barely able to contain a grin, he asked, "What's so funny?"

"Oh, I was just thinking about John Wayne. Remember that movie? He and Maureen O'Hara were still married but estranged, only somehow they got stuck with each other again. And he got drunk. She was trying to help him up the stairs, he started to go over backward, she couldn't hold his weight, and down they went."

"I won't let you fall back down the stairs."

Sissy giggled again. "Oh, yeah? I think this thing on my leg weighs almost as much as I do. I've never used crutches. The law of averages says that as I try to swing my body up, I'm going to lose my balance and fall over backward."

Ben was pleased to note that she was still reasonably alert.

He steadied the crutches on the pavement with

one hand and reached out to her with his other one. "If you're wobbly on these things, I'll carry you."

"I don't think that'll work." She flashed him a grin, mischief twinkling in her eyes. "For the first time in my life, I may not fit into a space large enough for most adults." She gestured at her elevated leg, which was only slightly bent at the knee inside the brace. "I suppose you might manage if you go up sideways."

Ben realized she was right. "Okay, sideways it may be." He'd definitely decided to carry her and come back for the crutches later. He could tell just by looking that she was drunker than a lord. After balancing the crutches against the truck, he leaned in to unfasten her seat belt. Then he slid his arms around her, one behind her back and the other beneath her legs. "One, two, three, up!"

She was so relaxed that her butt sagged, and he nearly dropped her. The only rigid place on her was the brace. He left the door open, stepped up onto the curb, crossed the sidewalk, and turned sideways to get her inside the café. He'd have to carry her upstairs the same way.

"Too bad we're not on video," she chirped. "The Duke was good, but we may outperform him."

Not if Ben had anything to say about it. Holding her close against his chest, he carried her through the café and found solid footing on the first step with his right boot. Then he lifted his other foot. And so it went, all the way up to her flat. Once at the top, he decided Sissy would have an additional cost when she remodeled. These narrow steps were going. It was a miracle she hadn't killed her-self when she fell.

Once inside the flat, he deposited her on the sofa, gathered pillows from her bed to place at one end, and then carefully lifted her hurt leg onto the billowy softness. Patches bounded across the living room carpet, proving that missing two front feet would never slow him down. He leaped onto Sissy's chest, pushed his whiskered nose against hers, and said hello with a mournful meow.

"Oh, Patches. How are you, sweetness? Did you miss me?"

Ben decided to leave Sissy wearing his jacket while he trekked back down to get her happy juice and crutches, along with the white plastic bag of stuff that the nurse had sent home with her.

When he got back upstairs, Sissy, wide-awake but smiling, held Patches on her chest. Ben's oversize jacket had slipped off her right shoulder to reveal the borrowed scrub smock. Ben looked down at her and decided she was the only woman on earth who could look beautiful in bile green.

"Hi," she said. "Where'd you go? You missed our family reunion."

Ben dropped the bag on the floor. Patches, he

noticed, had already tucked himself into a ball and fallen asleep. "He missed you."

"He missed you, too. Where's Finnegan?"

Ben didn't think a rambunctious dog would mix well with a woman on crutches. "Finn is at Barney's house. They have a golden retriever his age. It's pup heaven over there."

"That's too bad. I'll miss him tomorrow during breakfast prep."

Surely Sissy didn't think she could work tomorrow. He decided to leave that topic shelved. "He'll be back soon."

She stroked the kitten. "Don't avoid the subject. I have to reopen the café in the morning. I can't let everything I worked for get flushed down the toilet just because I broke my leg."

Ben sat on the coffee table. "Well, there's a pickle, because cooking takes two hands. Maybe with practice, you could learn to get around with only one crutch, but you'd still be a hand short."

She went from happy to sad. "I can't keep my café closed until I can walk again. I overheard a nurse say it might be as long as six weeks before the doctor gives me a walking cast."

Ben drew in a steadying breath. "The café will reopen in only days. I've made arrangements at my ranch. I won't be needed there." He paused to let her absorb that. "Remember when I told you teaching me how to do kitchen cleanup and

373

meal prep was sort of like insurance? If something happened, I could take over for you?"

She fixed an appalled gaze on him. "*You* can't run the Cauldron."

"Why not? I know how to operate the cooking appliances. I sure as hell have the prep work down pat. I can do it, Sissy. Maybe not as well as you can, but your customers don't come here *only* for the food. They come because they love you. You're their friend. You make them feel important. Take Chris Doyle. Plenty of people say hello to him and ask about his day, but you know what he wants for each meal and you plan your daily menus around his eating preferences. You go out of your way for him."

Tears slipped down her pale cheeks. "He's the grandpa I never had."

Ben's brain snagged on that. Didn't everyone have at least one grandpa? "He's pretty special," he said. "He loves you, that's for sure. And that's my point. Christopher is worried about you. He'll come here to eat, and while I'm trying to juggle your load, I'll remember his menu choices. I may not make each meal as well as you do, but I'll give it my best shot."

"You have your own business to run. And you love it. I don't want to be responsible for you going under while you try to keep me afloat."

She had a point. But he had something going for him that she didn't, a supportive family.

"Let me do this. At least give me a fair chance. I know it'll be hard to run the café with the same efficiency you do. But while you're laid up, you can advise me. I'll have your brains and my brawn to keep things going here."

"Maybe it'd work. But it's not easy." She smiled faintly. "At least I'll still be able to do the books for both operations."

Ben felt a wave of pure pleasure move through him. In the past Sissy would have objected to him helping her out. But, with him, at least, she'd moved beyond her fear that any man who helped her would expect paybacks. It also told him that their relationship had reached a new level.

"Never said it will be easy. But you'll be just upstairs. I can call you on my cell. I can send you pics of the food. You can direct me." Ben leaned close to her, got a whiff of her hair, and still smelled lavender. "I can pull it off. Won't you at least let me try?"

She smiled and said, "Why not? Even if you hit a few rough spots, at least the café will still be open, and you have a way with people. As soon as I get used to crutches, I can come downstairs and supervise." She shrugged and grinned more broadly. "We're a great team."

"Yeah, we sure are." Ben finger combed her hair, thinking of how smoothly she'd slipped into his life, accepting him for who he was and what he was. Hell, she even loved his dog. Even in the hospital, she'd worried aloud about Finn, and today she'd been disappointed that the pup wasn't present for their reunion. "Have I told you today how much I love you?"

She beamed another smile at him. "No, and I've missed hearing it."

"Well, I love you." He bent to kiss her forehead. "The best thing about that is, I thought I'd never find you."

She laughed. "You found me, but I chased you away. I'm glad you didn't run this time."

Ben studied the expressions that flitted over her face, every line of which he felt certain had been engraved upon his heart. What was she thinking about? He saw tenderness warm her eyes. Then a deepening of her smile. He had never wanted to be a mind reader—until just now.

"Ice," he said, jerking Sissy's attention back to him. "Thank God you've got a good ice maker downstairs. I remembered to elevate your leg, but I forgot to ice it."

"I hate icing it. I get so cold!"

"It's probably because you don't have much meat on your bones. I'll double-layer you up top." He reached down to draw his jacket over her shoulder. "That sheepskin lining will help, and I'll turn up the thermostat." He strode toward the door. "I'll be only a minute. If you need to use the restroom or anything, tell me now. I don't want you trying to maneuver by yourself."

"I'm good," Sissy told him. "And I promise not to move."

As he ran downstairs, she listened to the sharp reports of his riding boots on the steps. Moments later, he returned, carrying a large, black garbage bag partly filled with ice. He gently packed the cubes around her leg, making sure the sack was knotted tightly enough not to leak and get her boot wet as the frozen chunks melted.

Then he stood back and studied her. "How's your pain level?"

"It's definitely there. A five or six, I think."

He inclined his head and glanced at his watch. "Well, the directions say that you can have another quarter of a dosage if you don't have total relief in thirty minutes. It's been that long."

Sissy nodded. As he went to collect the bottle of medication, she admired his backside. He returned with the carefully measured liquid and put the cup to her lips. "Down the hatch. There's no point in being uncomfortable unless it's necessary."

Sissy swallowed the syrup. "It tastes *awful*."

Within thirty minutes, Sissy was chattering and giggling as if she were drunk. She'd study Ben for a moment and then burst out laughing. After ten minutes of the odd behavior, Ben began to get worried and called the Pill Minder. No pain medication he'd ever taken had made him feel happy and energized.

Drake answered with, "Hi, Ben." Then he chuckled. "Sorry. I now recognize your number. No one else calls here. Well, rarely, anyway."

"Hell, man. That's bad." Ben heard Sissy giggle and glanced over his shoulder. She was now engaged in a conversation with Patches, which he normally wouldn't have found strange, but Sissy was saying both her lines and the kitten's, making her voice squeaky when it was supposed to be the cat talking. "I'm a little worried. Sissy's laughing and talking a blue streak, and right now, she's—" Ben broke off. The pharmacist didn't need to hear details of Sissy's behavior that might embarrass her later. "I'm a little worried."

"Is she still in pain?" Drake asked.

Ben asked Sissy and she giggled at the question. "She doesn't appear to be."

Drake chuckled. "I can hear her. She's as happy as a flea in a dog kennel. That particular narcotic can cause euphoria. As long as the medication is controlling her pain, which is undoubtedly considerable, it's okay for her to feel happy."

"Are there any warning signs of overdose that I should be looking for?" Ben explained that he'd given Sissy an extra one-quarter dose, just as it said on the bottle.

"Well, if she falls asleep in the middle of a sentence, call me. Or if she floats in and out and her speech becomes slurred, I might worry a bit. But it sounds to me as if she's pretty alert. Maybe get some food in her stomach."

"Good advice."

Ben got off the phone and fixed Sissy a small meal—beef vegetable soup with a slice of toast. He discarded the half-melted bag of ice, helped her to sit up on the sofa, pillowed her braced leg on the coffee table before serving her. "I let it cool a bit, but still be careful not to spill it."

She filled her mouth with some meat and vegetables. Then she began waving the spoon as she chattered between bites. A blob of beef flipped off the flatware and landed on the front of her scrub top. She dimpled a cheek at Ben and giggled.

Oh, boy. Ben couldn't help but smile. His little neat freak had vanished. After getting her tummy full, she allowed Ben to position her on the sofa in a prone position again, and then promptly fell asleep. Ben gazed down at her, thinking she looked as innocent and sweet as a young girl. He didn't feel that she'd blinked out with abnormal swift-ness. Her last words had sounded fairly rational.

Taking advantage of the downtime while Sissy napped, Ben stepped out onto the stairs to call all the members of his family with whom he hadn't yet spoken, the only exception being Jonas, away at university. Everyone was happy to help Ben out. When he finished making phone calls, he felt as if someone had just given him a bear hug. He was so blessed in his family. Nobody had questioned him about his relationship with Sissy, even though everyone had to be curious.

After making sure Sissy was still fast asleep, Ben went down to check her kitchen supplies. He had never made out an order for a café, so he called Joe across the street.

"Unlike Sissy, I cook the same stuff day after day," Joe told Ben. "It's not dinner hour yet. I'll come over and have a quick look at her weekly menu."

Seconds later, Joe appeared at the door. He was around six feet tall, with deep brown hair and eyes that matched. Ben walked over to let him in. "I really appreciate this, Joe."

"Well, don't be too overcome with gratitude until I actually help you out. My operation is nothing like Sissy's."

Joe perused Sissy's menus, helped Ben find the names of her suppliers on invoices in her file cabinet, and made out a list of things Ben would need to order for the first week.

"I'm really grateful for your help," Ben said as he escorted Joe out. "She's your competitor. A lot of people would rub their hands together and hope she went under."

"We're not competitors," Joe corrected. "Sometimes people want a taco, sometimes they don't. Sissy doesn't steal any of my business. Same goes for José next door at the Straw Hat. We all offer different stuff."

Joe saw a woman and small child enter his building. He shook Ben's hand. "Gotta go make tacos and fill soda cups. I don't open for breakfast at my place, so I'll come back in the morning to help you make out your first order. You won't have to call it in until you're ready to roll."

"You're a good man," Ben told him.

"Not a big deal. Tell Sissy everybody in town is keeping her in their thoughts."

After locking up, Ben returned to the flat to find Sissy awake again, her face drawn and pale. He glanced at his watch and realized he'd spent more time downstairs than he'd intended. Her second full dose of pain medication needed to be administered.

"Damn, honey. You should have called me."

"I don't have my phone." Her voice rang taut. "Haven't seen it since before I fell down the stairs."

Ben made a mental note to find the phone and get it charged. But first, he needed to get her pain under control. He gave her a dose of medication. Within fifteen minutes, she was euphoric again. Ben found her phone in the kitchen, spotted her charger plugged in by a toaster, and got the phone hooked up.

"Your cell will be charged in about an hour," he told her as he sat on the coffee table. He couldn't help but grin. Her eyes, glazed over only a few minutes earlier, now looked clear and danced with merriment. The next time he felt depressed, maybe he'd ask a doctor for some of that syrup. "How you doing?"

Ben was surprised when she reached out to clasp his hand. "I need to tell you some stuff— things I've never told anyone about myself."

Ben thought, *Uh-oh.* He'd yearned for this moment, ached for her to open up, and now he didn't want her to say a word. He pressed a fingertip to her lips. "Sweetheart, you should wait to tell me later when you aren't on a narcotic that's loosening your tongue."

"I've wanted to tell you this for a long time."

And now she had a good measure of false courage. "I understand," he assured her. "But if it's waited this long, it can wait a couple more days."

"No." She shook her head, making her hair flash in spots like dark gold in the light coming from the kitchen. "It's about me, my childhood. The story won't change if I wait to tell you." She caught her lower lip between her teeth. "My parents never stayed in one place."

Ben nearly groaned. She'd regret this once she

sobered up. He needed to stop her before she got started. "Sissy, this really isn't the time."

"I *want* to tell you the truth about myself."

Ben had a bad feeling about this, but he couldn't shove a sock in her mouth. "Okay, but tomorrow remember that I tried to postpone this conversation."

"I was born in an old travel trailer at an apple orchard in Hood River."

Everyone in Oregon was familiar with Hood River, renowned for its apple production. "No wonder you're so sweet."

She gave his fingers a soft squeeze. "My mother went into labor at the top of a ladder, picked apples until she couldn't continue, and went inside the trailer to have me. The next morning, she made a baby sling for me out of a pillowcase and started picking apples again."

Shock burst through Ben. "You weren't taken to a hospital?"

"No. My father was, is, and always will be an insane alcoholic. My mom lived in poverty because he drank away almost every dime they made, and she continued to do that until I left home. She married him against her family's wishes. I guess they must have disowned her and are all as loony as she is. Not even at the very worst times did she ever try to contact any of her relatives for help." She expelled a long breath, as if those words had been pent up within her for years. "They moved, on average, about four times a school year, and at least once every summer. I rarely got to attend the same school for more than two months. It was difficult to make friends." She closed her eyes and tightened her grip on Ben's fingers. "When I did manage to make a friend, my parents moved again. It wasn't long before I realized that trying to forge relationships with other girls wasn't worth the bother.

"Keeping up academically was nearly impossible. Sometimes a new school would be behind me in some subjects, but the next school might be way ahead. If I got lucky and found a teacher willing to spend time with me, my parents moved again before I got enough help to make a difference. When I graduated, I had barely passed most of my classes. I excelled only in English, because I always escaped from reality by reading books from the school library. Even though I could decipher words and guess their meanings, I was a rotten speller." Her mouth twisted with bitterness. "My folks often moved in the middle of the night. They owed rent. They hadn't paid for their utilities. They sneaked away under cover of darkness and never warned me ahead of time. I'll bet I took thousands of dollars in books from school libraries over the years."

Ben tried to think of something to say. "Well,

you were just a kid. It's not as if you deliberately stole them."

"Spoken like a man who always got to return his library books." Her mouth twisted again, this time into a smile laced with fond regret. "Librarians are special. They enjoy when kids haunt the library, looking for wonderful books to read." Her dark lashes swept low over her cheeks and then fluttered upward. "They don't judge children by their covers, so to speak. They never seemed to notice that my clothes were bargain bin specials or that my hair had been hacked by my mother. I never owned a hair dryer or a curling iron until I ran away from home."

Ben had moved beyond wanting to silence her. He was fascinated. Sissy was peeling away all the layers and revealing to him who she really was. His heart hurt for the little girl she'd once been.

She looked deeply into his eyes. "The school librarians were always my friends. By the time I was ten, when I arrived at a new school, the first place I wanted to go was the library. I knew I'd make a new friend there, if only for a short while."

Ben wanted to hug her up in his arms. "Hey, you," he said, aiming for a teasing tone. "I think you may be spilling beans tonight that you'll wish you still had in the pot tomorrow."

She shook her head. "I need to get all this said." Her aching blue gaze locked on his. "You need to know who I really am, Ben. Otherwise, I can't move forward with you. Do you get that?"

His stomach knotted. "Sure. I get that. I don't think I've kept any secrets from you. I'm glad you're not going to keep any from me."

"My teens weren't fun. The girls picked on me, and so did the boys, only in a different way. The poorer girls called me names, laughed at me, shunned me, and sometimes beat me up if they caught me alone. I was beyond poor, and I think it made them feel good to finally be able to look down on someone instead of being the ones who were looked down upon. The rich girls, with professionally employed parents, treated me like I had a contagious disease. It wasn't only my awful clothes and haircuts. I couldn't get good grades, no matter how hard I tried, so they thought I was a dummy as well as a scumbag."

Ben winced.

"The boys saw me as easy picking. I had no friends. They probably knew I was lonely. The first time I got targeted, a boy offered to carry my books. I'd gotten to the school in spring, and there were no empty lockers, so I had to lug everything around all day. My parents couldn't afford to buy me a book bag. Translate that to mean my father wanted the money for booze. This boy shared two classes with me, so in between those two periods, he'd carry my books to our next class. I thought he was so nice. He was cute and popular. I think it was about a week and a half before he demanded paybacks."

She paused and swallowed. Ben's heart hurt. "Paybacks?"

"Yeah. He coaxed me into an empty classroom and wanted sex. When I refused, he threw all my books at me." She touched a tiny white mark above her eyebrow that Ben had never noticed. "A corner of one of them cut me and made me bleed."

"Dear God. Did you go to the office and report it?"

She burst out laughing. "You really don't get it, do you? If I had done that, the principal would have called my folks, and then my dad would have punished me for drawing attention to myself. He isn't just a drunk; he's crazy. He did jail time for car theft and assault. He jumped parole. He owed people money in every town we lived in. He stayed under the radar as much as possible. Before I finished high school I'd lived in thirty-six states." She took a deep breath. "At the next school, a boy noticed that I had nothing to eat for lunch several days running. He bought two lunches in the cafeteria, found me, and handed me a tray. I was wary. I was starting to realize that nobody did anything nice unless they expected a payback. But he'd already paid for it, and I was hungry, so I sat with him in the cafeteria to eat. That guy waited until after school. There, if you lived within a half mile, you had to walk, and I was one of the unlucky ones who couldn't take a bus. He| waited. He'd been watching. He grabbed me off the sidewalk and dragged me into some bushes. He said I was his, bought and paid for. I curled my hand over a rock and bonked him in the face. I ran like a rabbit for home and never told my parents."

Ben felt sick. He remembered when he'd tried to hang a heat lamp for her, and he finally understood why she had so adamantly refused, why she'd rejected his offer of friendship at first, and also why she never wanted to be indebted to anyone.

"I'm so sorry," he murmured.

She flapped her hand. "I'm not finished. Now I'm going to tell you about my first boyfriend. And trust me, your story about your first romance won't be similar to mine, period."

"Oh." Ben tried to think of something he could say.

"He was actually my *almost* boyfriend. When I got to that new school, I was—hmm—sixteen, I think. I definitely knew the drill. Kept my head down. Didn't stay in the bathrooms any longer than necessary because that was where other girls might draw on me with lipstick or beat me up. A hobo is what they called me there."

Ben's muscles jerked. "A *what?*"

388

Sissy giggled. "A hobo, or sometimes a scum-bag or transient. Your childhood, compared to mine, was likely a walk on easy street," she said with no trace of resentment. "Anyway, back to my story. I arrived at this new school. I thought I'd learned to be invisible. Watched my feet when I walked. Sat outside in a hidden place to eat my sack lunch if it was warm enough, or sneaked into an empty classroom to eat if it was winter. I went to a water fountain if I wanted a drink. Kids could leave campus if they had transportation, but some of them stayed to eat in the cafeteria. I didn't want them to see what my mother had managed to make for me—or, most times, what I'd made for myself because she'd started working nights a lot by then.

"Anyway, I'd been at the new school for about a week when a guy cornered me out in the hall during lunch hour. He was very nice and said all the right things. 'You're so pretty, blah, blah, blah.' And he asked me out to the movies. I about fainted. He was a very popular football star, and I couldn't believe he'd even noticed me. His dad was the mayor and owned a huge ranch." Tears pooled in Sissy's eyes. "That boy was so out of my league, but I thought he actually liked me. So I said I'd go out with him."

Ben felt her fingers loosen their grip on his and start to tremble.

"Instead of taking me to the movie theater, he

drove out onto his dad's property where he knew nobody would happen along. By then, I was nervous. No, actually, I was scared. I tried to get out of the car, but it was a fancy one, with door locks that the driver could control. He tried to rape me." She lowered her gaze, her attention focused on the beef stain on the green scrub top. "He picked on the wrong girl. I was a nobody, but I sure as hell wasn't going to be a victim because of that. So I fought him with every ounce of my strength."

"Good for you." Ben heard his voice. It sounded like a boot being dragged over gravel. "I hope you kicked his ass."

"Not really. Mostly I just pissed him off. He called me a piece of white trash and said I wasn't good enough to lick his feet. When I scratched him, he punched me in the face. At that point, I knew I had to outsmart him, so I went limp, pretending he'd knocked me out, and then I waited for my chance. He dropped his pants and straddled me, giving me a perfect target for a knee jab, and I gave him a good one. Then I punched him with an upward slam to his nose. While he cried like a baby, I crawled over him to release the door locks, and then I ran."

"Oh, sweetheart. I'm so—"

"I'm not finished. That's only the start of my story. It was darker than smut out there. I was new to the area and had no idea where I was. I ran blind. When I realized I was going the wrong way, I got off the road, stumbled through the woods toward distant lights, and reached town. Only then I wasn't sure where our house was. I was disoriented. Couldn't remember the street we lived on. After hours of walking, I finally got home."

Ben realized that he was now squeezing her hand. He tried to loosen his grip for fear of hurting her.

"I burst into the house, thinking my parents would go to the police and press charges against the boy. But, as always, my dad was drunk. He'd been waiting for me and building up steam. Before I could tell him anything, he started hitting me and calling me a slut. I was so banged up the next day, I couldn't go to school. And when my mother told my dad that it was the mayor's son who attacked me, they packed up and left that very morning. My dad wanted no part of pressing charges against a mayor's kid."

"Sweet Jesus." Ben's throat suddenly felt as if he'd guzzled drain cleaner.

"At the next school, there were other popular boys who asked me out. I was never dumb enough to accept again. To them, I was nothing. And that was pretty much true. I lived in shacks. My clothes were awful. My mom used some of her tips once to buy me makeup, and when my dad found out, he beat the hell out of her." She glanced up at Ben, her expression suddenly rebellious. "But being nothing doesn't mean I'm someone to be used."

Ben, gazing down at her precious face, couldn't believe she'd ever felt that way about herself, and it was even more mind-boggling to realize that she possibly still did. Before he could get a word out, she rushed on to say, "When I met you, I immediately tagged you as one of those popular boys. Well, not a boy, definitely a man, but I still used the same measuring stick."

Ben's heart twisted. He had been popular in school. Everyone in town had respected and admired his parents. At sixteen, he'd worked for his dad on the farm and earned enough money to buy a nice used pickup with his father's help. On the surface, he'd been the spoiled son of a pillar of the community.

"You come from a normal family. You not only got a good education as a kid but went on to university. What that boy said was true. My parents are white trash, and an apple never falls far from the tree."

Ben tried to protest, but Sissy cut him off. "You need to listen. The worst thing for me wasn't how the boys at school treated me. It was the way my father did. He couldn't keep a job because of his drinking, so when I was in my teens, my mom started working double shifts at a truck stop to keep a roof over our heads, booze in the cupboard, and at least some food on the table. About three months before I graduated, she started working the graveyard shift. One night, I woke up from a sound sleep to find my father on top of me."

Ben released his hold on her hands, not because he didn't want to comfort her, but because he knew he'd grip her fingers with too much force. He still didn't know her father's name, but he did know the man would crawl and beg for mercy if he ever found him. *Sissy.* He remembered when she'd given him the finger times five, and tears stung his eyes. Snotty, cold-shouldered Sissy with a smart mouth and an attitude he didn't understand. Now, though, he was starting to comprehend why she'd been wary of him for so long.

"My own father tried to rape me," she whispered raggedly. "He thought I was nothing, too. I hit him on the back of the head with my bedside lamp. He was already drunk. The blow knocked him out. At first I was afraid I'd killed him—but I hadn't."

Ben nodded. He knew that wasn't an appropriate response, but he couldn't speak.

"What were the chances that he'd remain unconscious until my mom got home? And, as always, we lived on a rough side of town, so I wasn't about to leave the house to hide from him all night, only to risk getting gang-raped. So

I ran out to his old beater pickup, grabbed the tire iron, and sat in the dark living room, waiting for the bastard to wake up."

Ben didn't ask what happened next. Sissy, who'd always guarded her secrets so fiercely, had now opened her floodgates. "When he staggered out of my bedroom, mad enough to hunt bear with a butter knife, I greeted him with the tire iron, and I was ready to use it. I told him that if he ever tried again, I'd kill him, and I meant it. He called me horrible names, but he didn't come near me. He finally got tired of yelling and went to my parents' room, where he passed out again on the bed."

Ben swallowed, trying to wet his throat so he could speak. "Did he ever try again?"

She shook her head. "I slept with the tire iron until I earned my diploma, and then, without a dime in my pockets, I moved out. Well, I grabbed what clothes I could carry and stole what was left of a loaf of bread. I've never contacted them since. I don't know where they are, and I don't care."

Ben stared down at her slender hand that he'd recently been holding. "You still wear your mother's mood ring."

She nodded. "My mom isn't bad, Ben. She's just crazy. That's my only explanation for her staying with him all these years. I despise my father. A part of me still loves my mother, even though I know she doesn't deserve that. She was the adult. She was obligated to protect me. Instead the only thing she ever did to make him stop pounding on me was to step into his line of fire and take the beating herself." She lifted her hand and stared at the ring. "The mood ring is symbolic to me. It changes colors, according to how the person wearing it feels. While growing up, I lived with a man whose moods predicted whether we had fair weather or foul inside our home. When I look at this ring, I don't think about how much I love my mom. I think about how I can avoid ever being anything like her."

Ben wished he could come up with something more to say, but he was fresh out of words. Sissy's former euphoria had been pushed aside by sadness and rage. He guessed that the narcotic could take a person either way. Only, in all honesty, he couldn't blame all this on the happy syrup. She had every reason to feel sad and outraged. Who wouldn't?

"So, after you left home, did you encounter any more jerks?"

"A trucker who pretended he had a spare set of tires that would fit my car if I'd meet him outside after my shift. Another trucker intervened, so except for a few bruises, I survived." She shrugged. "The bad guys were everywhere, and I had a talent for finding them. A couple of bosses who offered me better shifts to earn more tips, provided that I would go into the storage room with them every night and put out. Male waiters who busted ass to help do my work when it got busy and wanted favors in return." She smiled slightly. "I did meet a couple of good guys along the way, only it turned out the really nice one was gay, and the other one was already in love with someone else." She held up a finger. "And I can't forget my last boss, Gus. When he got mad, he threw pots around the kitchen, but he never laid a hand on his waitresses. And when I inherited the café, he spent hours on the phone with me, teaching me how to cook."

"I'm sorry that so many bad things happened to you." Ben flexed his shoulders and rubbed the back of his neck. "At least you're out of it now, a businesswoman who's worked hard for success." He gestured around them. "Just look at what you've done here! You've doubled your aunt's business. You're remarkable. Remember when I couldn't figure out my accounting program and I sent you my files? You figured it out after I'd been struggling with it for weeks. The apple *did* fall far from the tree in your case. You don't have to put up with any of that crap ever again."

Sissy surprised him by saying, "I know. After I got the café, I took online courses at night after working all day to improve my spelling, vocabulary, and math skills. Intellectually, I know I'm now just as good as anybody else is, when it comes to cooking, anyway." She pressed her fist over her heart. "But way deep down, Ben, that girl and young woman are still inside of me. Their voices still whisper inside my head. Not *really* voices, but feelings that remind me I'm *not* as good as everyone else. I try to chase them away, but they often sneak back in."

Ben took her hand again. "Maybe later, when things are back to normal, you should get some counseling."

"Maybe, but how could it help? When you're raised like I was, I think 'low-class' gets branded on your heart." She gave his hand a squeeze. "But, like you say, the bad times are behind me now. The problem is, I can't leave behind who I really am. My father is crazy. My mother is nuts. I've never met any of my relatives on either side, but I'm pretty sure I'll find a bunch of fruitcakes if I try to find them. I've got bad blood."

Ben's skin went cold. "You rose above it. Look at yourself now. There's nothing wrong with you."

"Law of averages. What are my chances?" She sighed as if talking so long had drained her. "At least you know who I really am now. I'm not from your world, Ben. As kids, we didn't even grow up on the same planet. Everywhere I ever lived, I was the daughter of the town drunk."

Ben struggled against his urge to gather her into his arms. "Sissy, will you do me a favor?"

"If you're about to ask me for sex, the answer is yes."

Ben laughed, and he couldn't quite believe he'd done it. Talk about bad timing. "I will ask for that sometime, but not tonight. The favor is this. I want you to brand something new on your heart in huge, bold print."

"What would that be?"

"Short and simple. 'Ben Sterling loves me.' "

Her eyes went shimmery and her mouth quivered. "Okay. I'll do that."

Ben stood and smiled down at her. "It's way past dinnertime. We both need something to eat. And while we eat, I want you to tell me about some happy things you remember."

"Okay. But first, I need my crutches. Ladies' room time."

Ben did a quick count of the hours since he'd carried her upstairs and wanted to kick himself for asking only once if she needed to use the restroom. Then he glanced at the coffee table, which sported no glass of water. All it had supported for most of the day and evening was his ass. She'd gone for hours without emptying her bladder. Hello, that meant she hadn't consumed enough fluids.

"Well, shit," he blurted. "I'm a rotten nurse."

Chapter
SEVENTEEN

For dinner, Sissy requested breakfast instead, crisp bacon, eggs over easy, and sourdough toast. As Ben cooked, the delicious aroma of the frying bacon began to make him hungry, but he also felt nauseated. He realized that he'd fed his patient earlier but not himself. While draining grease from the bacon onto paper towels, he cooked the eggs and made toast. He piled his plate with twice the amount of food he gave Sissy and didn't know if he could eat. Her story had made him feel half-sick.

Euphoric again, Sissy petted Patches, laughed at his antics as he played, and flirted with Ben. He enjoyed the latter but kept in mind that she was higher than a kite on happy syrup and he didn't take her seriously. Now that she'd spilled her guts, she'd moved on as if she'd never told him anything. He was still stuck in her past.

He propped her up with throw pillows this time so she could eat reclined on the sofa, her leg still elevated. Ben sat next to her on the coffee table. He forced himself to shove food in his mouth. Sissy took dainty bites and twice as long to clear her plate.

After she ate, he tidied the kitchen and then walked beside her to the bedroom to tuck her in for the night. He briefly considered finding her a fresh nightgown, but then thought better of it. If he got Sissy half-naked and she came on to him, he might lose his self-control.

After he'd gotten her situated on the bed with her leg elevated and the covers drawn over her, she looked up at him. In the golden glow coming from her bedside lamp, everything about her seemed to shimmer, especially her lush lips.

"Ben, will you kiss me good night?" she asked, her voice huskier than usual and slightly tremulous.

He managed a smile. "Sweetheart, I really don't think that's a good idea. I'd rather wait until you're clearheaded."

"Please?"

The note of appeal in her tone made it difficult for him to refuse. "Okay," he relented, "but only just once." And Ben meant to keep it friendly and quick.

Sissy had other plans. As his lips lightly grazed hers, she locked both arms around his neck, murmuring, "Make love to me, Ben. I need you to hold me."

Oh, how Ben wished he could accept that invitation, but the doctor had warned that sex was not allowed until he gave the go-ahead. So instead he slipped under the covers with her and gathered her into his arms. "I can definitely deliver on holding you." She tried to roll toward him. "No," he said firmly. "The leg stays on the pillow, and you stay flat on your back. Otherwise you'll fall asleep on your side and not elevate all night."

She released a grumpy sigh but lay back, pillowing her head on his arm. Ben splayed the fingers of his right hand over her midriff. It took all his self-control not to explore her breasts—and then journey lower.

"I love feeling your arms around me," she whispered. "It's like I've found my own little corner of heaven."

He smiled against her hair. "When you're off the happy syrup, maybe I'll show you some glimpses of how great heaven can be."

"Why can't you show me now?"

His grin deepened. "The syrup masks your pain. I don't want you wiggling around or arching your back by pressing down on the pillow with your leg."

"Why on earth would I arch my back?"

Ben moved in closer. "Just trust me on it. When you're sober, maybe you'll remember you shouldn't. Right now, I'm fairly certain you'd turn into a mattress gymnast."

She giggled and pressed her lips against his neck. "That'd be dangerous. I might knock you out with my brace."

Ben's groin throbbed with need. He yearned to thrust his hardness deep into her feminine wetness and find release. Instead he stroked her hip and kissed her hair until her body went limp and her breathing went shallow. When he felt certain she was asleep, he slipped cautiously from the bed so he wouldn't wake her. She'd plead with him to stay beside her. Ben wanted to do that, but he was afraid he might toss and turn during the night and accidentally jostle her leg.

He crept into the living room to find Patches. He tiptoed back to the bedroom and placed the sleepy kitten on Sissy's pillow. Patches curled into a ball against her cheek. Ben gazed down at them, smiling. Then he went through the apartment, shutting off lights before he stretched out on the sofa. He used his coat for a pillow and the sofa throw as a blanket. Not the best situation, but he'd work on improving it tomorrow.

Ben lay awake half the night. The sofa wasn't long enough to accommodate his height and his stocking feet hung over the cushioned armrest. Moonlight, which was supposed to be a gentle illumination, glared through the window glass. The wall heaters kicked on to keep the temperature up and then went off. When they were in off mode, their metal casings clicked as they cooled. When that stopped, he could hear a clock somewhere in the apartment ticking like a bomb. At one point, he also heard Snickers prancing over the keys of the electric piano.

The one thing Ben didn't hear was a single sound from Sissy. He was so thankful for that. It meant that her happy syrup was working. Eventually, though, she'd wake up, needing another dose. Only, she never called out to him, and she was long overdue for more medication.

At four, he crept into her room to see if she was stirring or tossing her head, a sure sign of pain. Standing still and being so quiet, Ben nearly parted company with his skin when Sissy asked, "What is it? Is something wrong?"

"You're awake?"

"It happens when you sleep a lot during the day."

Ben didn't recall her having slept that much, three hours at most. "Would you like some fresh water? Do you need to use the restroom? Anything?"

"No. I'm fine for now."

"What's your pain level?"

In the dimness, he saw her push up on her elbows, taking care not to disturb the sleeping kitten. "I've decided that I'm not taking any more medication."

Ben knew her pain level couldn't have dropped that much yet. "Why on earth did you decide that? The syrup eases your pain."

She sighed and let her head fall back, both the sound and gesture indicating to him that she thought his IQ had to be near the bottom of the chart. "Glimpses of heaven. Remember? You said I have to be off the drugs before it can happen."

Ben sat on the edge of the bed. He couldn't quite credit his ears. "Sissy, that's crazy. You're in severe pain right now. You need the medication to lessen the discomfort. I'll still be here in a few days to give you glimpses of heaven."

"I don't want to wait."

Ben had never been so touched, especially now that he'd heard the story of her life. She had every reason to never trust a man, and yet she had totally let down her guard with him. It was one of the most wonderful compliments he'd ever received.

"I don't want to wait, either," he replied. "But over the next couple of days, your tibia will start to heal, and your pain level will drop considerably. It isn't that long, honey."

An edge of crankiness rang in her voice when she said, "Easy for *you* to say. You've gotten more than glimpses of heaven. You've gone through the gates countless times! Well, I haven't! I'd rather lie here in pain, knowing I'll at least get some glimpses, than lie here drugged and still aching inside."

"Aching inside?"

"Yes, aching inside." Her voice had risen. "My muscles down there are throbbing. I'm not stupid, Ben. My body wants sex. And you won't even give me some appetizers because you're so damned determined to protect me."

Ben groaned. Bracing his elbows on his knees, he rested his head in his hands. From her point of view, everything she'd just said was absolutely true. He'd had sex with a number of women. Sissy was twenty-six, and her only normal experiences with men had occurred just recently—with him. Therefore, as much as her young body yearned for physical satisfaction, she didn't comprehend how distanced from reality she might get during the throes of an orgasm.

"Have you ever, um, satisfied yourself in bed at night?" He straightened to gaze at her through the moon-silvered gloom. "You know—like with your hand."

"No." She reclined on her pillow again, jostling Patches enough to make him emit a sleepy meow. "My only recourse is to eat Snickers bars. Remember?"

He couldn't help but smile. Sissy, the Snickers bar addict. "Well, when a woman climaxes that way, she almost always lifts her hips toward whatever or whoever is stimulating her down there. Could you try, right now, to lift your hips without using your injured leg?"

She tried, using only her left foot, but the brace that reached nearly to her thigh on her right leg weighed her down. She finally gave up with a groan of disgust and went limp on the mattress. "I hate you."

Ben squelched a chuckle. "I want nothing more than to crawl into that bed with you and give you everything you want. But if I do, you'll run a high risk of putting pressure on your fractured tibia. Are you willing to risk snapping it out of alignment and ending up with bolts in your bone? It'll leave you with scars for the rest of your life, and even worse, the tibia may not heal as nicely, which might mean you'll limp. Just say the word, Sissy. If you're willing to risk it, I'll climb in bed right now and give you everything you want, to hell with the doctor's orders."

"I'm not even sure what I want." In the dimness, her eyes sparked fire at him. "And that doesn't mean I'm so naive that I don't know anything about sex. When I was little, my father worked as a farmhand and we lived in a little shack on the property. I saw pigs do it. Horses. Even cows. And I've watched sex scenes on television as well. Did you ever watch reruns of *Star Trek*, where they beamed themselves from one place to another?"

"Yes, of course."

"Well, that's my knowledge about sex. I know how it starts, and I know how it ends, but I' hazy on all the stuff in between."

Ben took her hand and held it tight. "Luckily, I know what happens in between."

She squeezed his fingers. "I'll just bet you do. I don't really hate you. I'm sorry I said that."

"I know you don't. You're just frustrated, and I can't blame you."

She lay quiet for a moment. "I'm frustrated with you, too. Before I got hurt, I asked you when we'd do it, and you said I wasn't ready. Well, I *was*. So this is all your fault."

"Guilty." Ben wished now that he hadn't been so worried about going too fast with her. "I'm sorry. I made a really bad call."

She sighed. "Well, to be fair, you didn't know this was going to happen to me."

"True. And just for the record, if we had made love that night, you'd still be frustrated right now. Once you experience all the fun stuff that happens between the beginning and the end, you'll want it all the time, if I do my job right."

Her shimmery gaze clung to his. "You'll do it right. I can tell just by how you kiss me." She sighed again. "So, how long do you think we need to wait before I can see glimpses of heaven?"

"I think I should ask your doctor."

Sissy gasped. "You can't talk to him about *that*."

Ben bent over to give her a lingering kiss. When he lifted his head, he realized she had locked her arms around his neck. "Sissy," he warned. "Not until we talk to your doctor."

She released her hold on him. "Oh, God, how

embarrassing. I won't be able to look him straight in the eye."

Ben couldn't help but laugh. "He's a guy. I'm a guy. We'll do guy talk. He'll understand what I'm asking without me going into the details."

"What if he says no?"

Ben considered the question. "I'll think of some way to keep your hips anchored to the bed. As a rancher, I have tie-down straps long enough to do the job."

"I'm not about to be strapped down on the bed," she informed him. "Just get me a dose of syrup. I may as well feel happy while I'm miserable."

After Ben had given Sissy her medication, he tried to find a more comfortable position on the couch. She lay only a few feet away, and knowing how badly she wanted to be with him made him yearn for her even more. Why did the idea of a tie-down strap ruffle her feathers? He had one in the bed of his truck that would work. It was clear to him that the only reason the doctor had ruled out sexual activity was because he knew Sissy might use her injured leg to lift her weight.

God, how he wanted her. Did he live under a cursed star or something? She was so beautiful, and he was so in love with her. Wasn't it just his rotten luck that when she finally came around to wanting sex, he couldn't, in good conscience, accept the invitation?

That was Ben's last thought as he escaped the grasping fingers of consciousness and plunged into the black void of sleep.

"Ben? I need to go to the restroom, and I can't find my crutches."

Ben jerked awake so fast, he jackknifed to a sitting position and got a crick in his back. Holding a hand over the spot, he rolled to his feet. "I'm coming! Sorry."

He ran into Sissy's bedroom and spun to search the floor.

"Other side of the bed, I think. They must have toppled off the mattress while we were cuddling."

Ben could tell by the tension in her voice that her pain medication had worn off. She sat on the edge of her bed, looking like a tousle-haired fairy with elephantiasis in one leg. He hurried to get the crutches for her, then thumped the capped ends on the floor, one on either side of her feet.

"I'm right here," he said. "If you start to fall, I'll catch you."

She braced the rubberized tip of each crutch at an angle and leaned forward so the shoulder rests lent her support to struggle up onto her one good leg. "Got it," she said as she positioned the walking aids firmly under her arms. Then, with an agility that surprised him, she moved forward, wobbling slightly at the apex of her swing. Ben reached to steady her.

"The doctor says I can do this without help if I'm not drugged. And, hello, I am not drugged. My leg hurts so bad it feels like someone stabbed a knife through my bone."

She wobbled again and Ben almost grabbed her shoulder. But Sissy needed to do this by herself. At the beginning of their relationship, he hadn't understood her. Now, after hearing her life story, he finally did. Being able to take care of herself—succeeding in her business without help and being indebted to no one—was more important to her than it was for many people. He needed to reprogram his brain and think before he rushed in to help her.

At the bathroom door, she stopped to look up at him. "I really am going to be fine. You can leave and get some coffee on while I do all this. After I use the restroom, I'm going to find a fresh gown and then have a sponge bath. I'll take my medicine as soon as I'm done."

Ben wanted to rifle through her drawers to find her a nightgown. He wanted to stand beside her in the bathroom to steady her while she washed. Turning and walking out of the room was one of the hardest things he'd ever done.

After getting a pot of coffee on, he started breakfast, a rerun of the meal he'd made the night before, only this time he added fried cottage potatoes with caramelized onions. The wonderful smells flirted with his nostrils and made his stomach growl. He felt as if he'd dropped a good ten pounds over the last few days from not eating often enough.

As Sissy hobbled out on her crutches to sit at the table, looking adorable in a flannel gown with tiny roses on a white background, Ben had to remind himself that she was clearheaded and didn't need his help.

"The coffee's ready," he said. "And breakfast is nearly done."

She struggled with her crutches as she pulled out a chair. Then she sighed with relief as she sat down. "First I need my happy syrup."

Ben hurried to pour her a measure. Her hand trembled as she took the cup. Taking a sponge bath and dressing by herself had taken a toll on her. Ben wished she had asked him for help. But on the other hand, seeing her half-naked might have obliterated all his self-control.

"You've got orange juice and milk. Maybe a few sips will get the nasty taste out of your mouth and give you an energy boost."

"Orange juice, I think."

Ben poured her a glass and then returned to the stove. Everything was done. He switched off the burners and put lids on the pans to keep the food warm. After taking a seat across from Sissy, he said, "I'm sorry it hurts. If I could make it go away, I would."

"The syrup works fast. It's already helping a

411

little." She tipped her head and studied him. "I think you'd take my place if you could."

Ben couldn't deny it. "Yeah, if I could."

"Why do you love me so much?"

It was a question that came at Ben from left field. "My mother always says that love just runs up and bites you, no rhyme or reason to it. But I don't really believe that." He slowly trailed his gaze over Sissy's features. "This is going to sound self-centered. I've met a lot of women—nice ones, pretty ones, with great personalities—but I wasn't willing to change who I am to make it work with any of them."

"Why would you have had to change?"

Ben grinned. "That's one reason I love you, Sissy. You don't look at me as if I'm a work in progress. You don't see me as someone with the potential to be what you want."

"Women have said that to you? I don't get it."

Ben heard Patches meow and he went to get the kitten before it tried to jump off the bed. When he returned to the kitchen after setting Patches near his blanket and litter box, he resumed his seat.

"That's one of the reasons I love you," Sissy told him. "You care about my kitten. Not every man would."

Ben couldn't help but smile. "You nailed it. But some women don't like that about me. Well, they'd be glad if I liked their cats, but my world

412

revolves around other animals, too, and all the filth that comes with them. I briefly dated one gal who trained her cat to use the toilet. A litter box was too gross for her. As soon as I learned that, I walked. My ranch is one huge litter box."

"Your ranch is gorgeous. And so are all your animals. The horses are so beautiful."

Ben held up a finger. "That's another reason I love you. You didn't turn up your nose at all the things that define who I am. When I saw how much you care—about your chickens, Finnegan, and even old Christopher—I knew you had a huge heart. When I saw how hard you worked, putting in long hours and rarely taking time off, I knew you were someone who might get who I am. That you'd understand when I couldn't be with you because I was babysitting a mare about to foal. That you'd get it when I got home covered in mud, hay, or whatever else. You have an extraordinary work ethic. Ranching is sometimes grueling and consuming, but I think you'd be okay with its demand on my time." Ben ran a hand through his hair. "You didn't gag when you got horseshit all over your shoes. You weren't afraid to pet my orneriest cow. All very selfish reasons, when I look at them. But maybe all of us fall in love for selfish reasons. Real love and commit-ment is for life. How can you love or make a commitment to someone who doesn't like who you are?"

Sissy nodded. "I don't think anyone should try to change who they are in order to make a relationship work. It'd be a relationship built on lies. We can pretend that we've changed, but eventually who we really are will come out. It's foolishness. It isn't selfish of you to want someone who likes you as you are. It's honest and smart."

He couldn't help but grin. "With you, I don't have to pretend."

"Because I like you as you are."

"I'll never wear chinos and loafers. If it's a casual-dressy affair, I'll throw a Western sports coat over my jeans and shirt. If it's a dress-up affair, I'll show up in a Western-cut suit with a matching Stetson."

"And you'll look fabulous. The other men in regular suits will pale in comparison."

"Well, thank you."

He got up to serve them each some breakfast. He set the plates on the table and fetched flatware. Then he poured some coffee and sat across from her again. "I can't explain every reason I fell for you. But I think we're perfect for each other, that we can blend together as individuals and be life partners."

"Is there anything about me you'd like to change?" she asked.

"Not a single thing," he assured her. "If you changed, you wouldn't be Sissy."

"Our professions are worlds apart," she pointed

414

out. "I think your ranch is wonderful, but I love my café too much to ever be a partner who works at your side. I wouldn't mind helping you on my days off, though."

Ben smiled. "If you ever hire help so you can take days off."

"Oh, I'm going to. I'm stretched too thin and getting burned out. I really want to remodel, but if I work so hard to make it happen that I lose my love of cooking and waiting on my customers, what's the point?"

"That's why I hired Brett and why I'm thinking about hiring another helper. I love ranching. I love the smells. I love working with the animals and feeding them and tending to them if they're hurt. But it's hard work. And when I was doing it all alone, I found myself resenting that I had to go feed sometimes. Or grumbling because I had to go out in the rain. It was a warning sign that I needed some time off to relax and enjoy my life, and if I didn't make it happen, I might lose my love for ranching. Then where would I be? I definitely wouldn't be me." Ben swallowed a piece of bacon. "As for you working at my side, I don't expect that or even want you to. Helping me sometimes, sure. And in the reverse, I really enjoy helping you in the café. And for me, ending a long day at your café over a fabulous meal is perfect. I can continue to habitually eat out."

Sissy laughed and took a bite of potatoes.

"Hmm, delicious." After swallowing, she added, "I enjoy it when you help me in the kitchen."

An uncomfortable silence electrified the air between them. Ben finally asked, "So, have I satisfactorily explained why I love you?"

She dimpled her cheek at him. "For purely selfish reasons. And that works for me. You're saying that I suit you just as I am, and that's pretty awesome."

"I forgot to add that you turned me on the first time I ever saw you," Ben told her. "And you still do. Another purely selfish reason, I guess. But my dad would say, 'If you don't feel physical attraction, son, run like hell.' "

Sissy got a sip of coffee down the wrong pipe and coughed into her napkin. When she caught her breath, she said, "He sounds like a very wise man."

"He is. I think you'll like him."

Sissy pushed back her plate and sighed. "I think I need to elevate my injury. I can feel my leg swelling."

Ben shot up from his chair. "Shit. I forgot. The doctor said absolutely no sitting with your feet down."

"It's okay, Ben." She got up and balanced on one foot as she maneuvered the crutches under her arms. "But I think you'd better hang close while I go to the sofa. I'm feeling a little wobbly."

Ben wanted to pick her up and carry her there. But he'd meant it when he told her that he didn't want her to change. As long as she could do it herself, he had to let her. Moments later, she lay on the couch with her leg elevated on pillows. Patches jumped up to snuggle under her chin. Ben returned to the kitchen to clean up the breakfast mess, wolfing down another plate of food as he worked.

"You haven't asked me why I love you so much!" Sissy called out.

Ben started the dishwasher and went to sit on the coffee table. "Okay, let me hear it."

She grinned and said, "It won't take long. You're patient with me. You never push me to do something before I'm ready. You understand me when I don't understand myself." Her lashes fluttered closed. "You never give up on me."

Watching her drift to sleep, Ben thought, *And I never will.*

Believing that Sissy was totally out of it, Ben got a startle when she suddenly opened her eyes and said, "Just so you know, Ben, I won't be going into this with any expectations. No strings. I just want to be with you."

Ben didn't like the sound of that. *No strings?* He'd finally found the woman he wanted to spend the rest of his life with, and she wanted sex without commitment. He decided to let that ride for the moment. Over time, if he proved to her how much he loved her, she'd change her mind about that.

Chapter
EIGHTEEN

Sissy awakened from her nap to hear Ben speaking on his cell phone. A few words snagged her attention and her eyes popped open. Levering up on an elbow, she leaned forward to hear. From his side of the conversation, she deduced that he was talking to his mother and asking her to come stay with Sissy while he walked up the street to Nuts and Bolts for some fine mesh steel wool to plug all the holes that Snickers used to enter the building.

The moment Sissy felt sure he was off the phone, she said, "Ben, your mother doesn't have to come here to babysit me. She doesn't even *know* me. I'll behave. I promise. Don't bother her, please."

Ben gave an emphatic shake of his head. Sissy gulped. Why did he have to look so damned sexy all the time when he wasn't even trying? He leveled his gaze at her in that "dead serious" way of his. "Well, ma'am, it's like this. You won't be on the pain reliever forever. Probably only a few more days. But until you're off it, I'd rather follow the doctor's orders. The last thing you need is to fall while you're trying to reach the bathroom."

Sissy couldn't argue the point. She needed to heal with all possible speed. "You're right," she conceded. "But what on earth will your mom and I find to talk about while you're gone? I've never met her."

Ben laughed. "Trust me. You'll find plenty to chat about . . . if you can get a word in edgewise. My mom is a talker. One thing you should mention to her is all the trouble Drake Mullin is having. If he doesn't start getting some business, he'll go under."

Kate called in just under thirty minutes to let Ben know she was at the front door. As Ben hurried down the steep stairs, he vowed again to rip them out and start from scratch when Sissy renovated.

When he opened the door, his mother beamed a smile at him. She looked like a model in a Western fashion catalog for older women. She wore a wine-colored sweater over a plaid Western shirt with touches of burgundy in the pattern. Her jeans were tucked into a pair of chestnut Uggs, the boots folded over at the top to showcase the fur lining. Ben was surprised. His mom usually wore riding boots.

"Hey, gorgeous." Ben scooped her up in his arms and executed a half turn. "New boots?"

"No teasing me!" she warned as he released her. "Your father hates them. He took one look and said, 'What the *hell* is on your feet?' "

Ben drew her inside and closed the door. While locking it, he said, "They look great to me, perfect for snow."

"And great traction on ice. I fell a few winters ago, and my hip bothered me for weeks."

Ben dimly remembered his mother hobbling around. "I didn't know you fell. I thought it was arthritis flaring up."

"Bite your tongue. I refuse to have arthritis yet. That's for old people."

Grinning, Ben led the way upstairs to the landing. "Sissy's a little worried that you two will have nothing to talk about."

Kate giggled. "Well, that just goes to show she hasn't gotten to know me yet."

Ben was prepared to hang around until Sissy and Kate warmed up to each other, but within three minutes, Kate had Sissy chattering like a squirrel that had just found a cache of nuts. He excused himself to visit the hardware store, got two bags of steel wool, and used Sissy's flashlight to search for holes when he got back to the Cauldron. He found far more than he expected.

As he rounded the wall that divided the kitchen from the café, he stopped in his tracks. Snickers sat on his haunches near the cupboards. The rat had a small, silver measuring spoon, which he held gingerly in his tiny paws.

Ben couldn't help but smile. "You must be getting used to me. You didn't bother to hide."

Snickers squeaked at him in reply. Ben knew the rat would quickly depart for his nest with his new prize, and Snickers didn't disappoint him. Whirling around, the rodent nosed open the right cupboard door beneath the sink and vanished. Ben hurried to the backyard, hoping to see where Snickers exited the building.

The rat emerged from a crawl space ventilation hole in the ancient foundation. Making a mental note to cover it with new wire and check all the other openings, Ben kept his gaze fixed on Snickers. This might be his only chance to follow the rodent back to his nest.

The rat ran in a straight line for the shed in Marilyn Fears's backyard. Ben almost groaned. He opened the door and shone the flashlight inside. In the far left corner, he saw the nest—an impressive structure made of sticks and dry grass—and several rats scurrying to hide.

Disheartened, Ben stared at the back side of Marilyn's building. She'd have to be told and she would have to call pest control. That would break Sissy's heart. But this no longer involved only Sissy. Marilyn's building was probably being invaded.

Ben circled around to Marilyn's storefront.

When he walked in, she smiled and treated him to a flash of her merry blue eyes. "How is our Sissy doing?"

"Pretty well, considering. Mom is sitting with her while I do some chores."

"If need be, I can sit with Sissy in the evenings." Marilyn's gaze dropped to the two bags of steel wool tucked under Ben's arm. "You look like a man on a mission."

Condensing the story, Ben told Marilyn about Sissy's love affair with a pack rat and that Ben had just found the nest in Marilyn's shed. "I understand what you have to do," he told her. "It'll break Sissy's heart, but eventually she'll get over it."

Marilyn's gaze shot back to the bags of wool. "You're plugging all the holes in her building, I see. Would you mind taking care of mine as well?"

Ben mentally circled that. "If you call pest control, you really won't need your building to be ratproofed."

"Of course I will. Pack rats are a fact of life. So are other rodents. They can enter buildings if the owners don't take necessary precautions. I've been rather lazy about that."

"But their nest is in your garden shed."

"What nest?" She flashed another smile. "Nobody told me about any nest. Just warn everyone along this side of the street that pack rats have been seen. Word will travel. If people have any brains, they'll make sure no rodents can enter their buildings. If they don't, it's their problem, not yours." She shrugged. "I can't call pest control. Sissy loves that rat, and a pest eradicator won't care."

Ben tried his best not to smile. "It's very generous of you to care so much about Sissy's feelings, but I'm not sure it's the wisest decision you could make."

Marilyn laughed. "I'm getting too old to make wise decisions. Nowadays I live on the edge. Just ratproof my building."

"Won't you be afraid to go in your storage shed?"

She laughed again. "I'm a country girl. Besides, when was the last time you heard a news story about a pack rat attack?"

Another smile tugged at the corners of Ben's mouth. "Now that you mention it, I can't say I ever have."

"Exactly." Marilyn took a sip of bottled water. As she screwed the cap back on, she added, "I might get a little excited if you told me a female cougar with cubs had taken up residence in my shed, but I don't feel intimidated by anything I could step on—if I had to, that is. Besides, I love Sissy. In August when I got sick, she took care of me. She brought me special breakfasts and made me soups. This is my chance to repay her for her kindness."

●●●

For the next three hours Ben stuffed wool into every hole he could find in the two buildings. His thoughts kept circling back to the café. He needed to get the place open again, ASAP. Otherwise, Sissy would deplete her savings—which he was positive wasn't a lot—and have to work forever for the planned remodel. He might not win any chef-of-the-year awards, but maybe he could at least keep her customers coming in.

After warning other shop owners along West Main that pack rats had been seen, Ben returned to the Cauldron. At the top of the stairs, he heard Sissy and his mother talking. Kate was telling stories about Ben as a boy and singing his praises. He knew his mother, wondered what had already been blabbed, and felt his ears grow hot.

Opening the door, Ben asked, "When do you plan to nominate me for sainthood, Mom?"

Kate grimaced. "You aren't quite *that* perfect. But you're close to the mark."

Sissy, still on the couch elevating her leg, craned her neck to smile at him. In her eyes there was a soft glow he'd never seen, and he wondered if she was euphoric again.

Kate collected her sweater. "I need to get the pot roast in the oven. I made sandwiches before I left, but Jeremiah will be starving by six." Kate bent to give Sissy a hug, then wrapped her arms around Ben's waist. "I'll be back tomorrow."

"You don't have to do that," Sissy protested.

"Don't be silly!" Kate exclaimed. "I can't remember the last time I've enjoyed myself so much."

After Kate left, Ben sat on the coffee table and dangled the watch he'd retrieved in front of Sissy's nose. She stared at it for a moment, and then her face broke into a joyous smile. "You found Snickers's nest!"

Ben told her about Snickers leading him straight to Marilyn's storage shed. Then he related the conversation he'd had with Marilyn. "She says the nest can remain undisturbed. I warned everyone along the street. It'll be up to each shopkeeper to protect his building." With a shrug, Ben added, "Seems fair enough to me. Live and let live." He suppressed a grin. "That Snickers—he is pretty damned cute."

Sissy sighed and relaxed against the pillows. "Thank you, Ben. Most guys would rat Snickers out." She winced. "No pun intended."

Ben went to wash up. When he returned, Sissy patted the coffee table. "Can we talk for a moment?"

Ben resumed his seat. "Sure. What's up?"

She fiddled with the blanket that covered her to the waist. Then she nibbled her bottom lip. "I'm just thinking—well, maybe a tie-down strap wouldn't be so bad."

Searching her blue eyes, Ben knew it wasn't only the medication talking for her. She truly was eager to be with him in an intimate way. His gaze dropped to her chest. Against the rose-patterned flannel, her nipples jutted like rivets, one of them making a tiny flower look three-dimensional. A certain part of Ben's anatomy went rock-hard, and it took all his self-control not to carry her straight to the bedroom.

"I haven't talked with the doctor yet. We'll have to be very careful not to jar that bone."

She nodded. "I know. I can tell the brace is looser this afternoon. More of the swelling has gone down."

Ben moved to the opposite end of the table and unfastened the boot. The nightgown, which he'd pushed out of his way, drifted sideways over the couch cushion to reveal her upper thigh. He schooled his gaze on the brace, refusing to torment himself with glimpses of flawless skin. "Wow, the swelling has gone down." He drew each strap tighter. "I'm glad you said something. Your leg could have moved around in there too much."

Sissy sighed. "Maybe when I get a regular cast?"

Ben met her gaze again, understanding that she was still wondering when they might glimpse small corners of heaven together. "Actually, if all else fails, a tie-down strap works great for me."

Her brows lifted. "Really? Then run right down-stairs and get it."

Ben couldn't help it; he laughed. "I think I've come up with a better plan."

"What is it?"

He leaned forward to kiss her. "Let it be a surprise. And you have to remember one thing: What we do is going to be really tame, nothing like the sex we'll have once the doctor gives us the go-ahead. I don't want you to be disappointed because it isn't romantic-movie perfect."

"I'll be happy with less than perfect."

"First I need to give Drake some business. I won't be gone that long."

A warm twinkle lighted her eyes. "I'm craving Snickers bars like you wouldn't believe. Some-one I know once suggested that when I get these cravings, I may be wanting something else. I'm beginning to believe he's right."

Ben chuckled. "When I get back I'll do my best to make sure you never crave another Snickers bar."

"That's a tall order."

"I'm just the man for the job. And if you still want a Snickers bar afterward, I can run next door and get you one."

Sissy grew nervous after Ben left. The flannel nightgown she was wearing wouldn't do, but she had no sexy lingerie. Panties were out of the question. None of hers would fit over her brace. A T-shirt wouldn't be very attractive, but it was all she had that was stretchy enough for him to have access to all parts of her. She didn't want to miss out on an experience because he couldn't uncover something.

She was shaking as she sat on the bed to change. *What am I doing?* she wondered. *This is nuts.* Then, *I'll feel better when Ben gets here. He always makes me feel safe. He knows just what to say. He touches me so gently. Why am I letting myself have a panic attack? Oh, God, I need a shower, only I can't take one. I sponged off earlier, but that isn't the same as bathing. What if my armpits stink?*

What was taking him so long? She jumped as if she'd been stuck with a pin when she heard the apartment door open and close. The thump of Ben's boots hailed his arrival.

"Sissy?"

Voice quaking, she called, "I'm in here!"

He appeared in the doorway, holding a bright orange strap in one hand and a white sack bearing the Pill Minder logo in the other. "Just in case my plan doesn't work, I have a backup idea." He took in her T-shirt. She felt pretty sure he noticed that she was shaking. She expected— well, she wasn't sure what she expected, but it wasn't for him to ask, "Sweetheart, what the hell do you think you're doing?"

"Um—well, I tried to find something to wear." She plucked at the T-shirt. "I'm sorry it's not sexy, but it's stretchy. And then I was just waiting for you. I'm sorry I look so awful, but I don't own one stitch of sexy lingerie."

Ben's shoulders slumped. He tossed his purchases on the bed behind her. "You don't *need* sexy lingerie. It doesn't matter what you're wearing. Okay? Normally, whatever you put on will just come off. I want *you*. But for tonight, the T-shirt is a great choice. If my idea doesn't work and you start doing a hip dance, the strap is smooth nylon web. I had to look forever to find one that isn't rough on the edges. With the T-shirt, I don't have to worry about it abrading your skin."

Sissy's eyes had filled with tears. "So why did you yell at me?"

"I didn't yell. Okay, maybe I raised my voice. You're sitting with your feet down. How long have you been there?"

"Since you left."

He vanished and returned with her pillows. "Onto the bed. Get the pillow under your head. You're not allowed to sit with your feet down except to use the toilet. Otherwise, your leg is supposed to be above your heart."

Sissy pushed on the mattress with her hands to scoot backward and get her body fully on the bed. Ben gently lifted her leg and lowered it onto the pillows. Under his breath, he said, "I did not see that."

"You didn't see what?"

"It's nothing. Never mind."

Sissy looked toward her toes, saw that her T-shirt was stretched over her thighs to ride high on her uplifted leg, and knew what he'd seen. Only, he didn't seem to think he'd just glimpsed heaven.

"This isn't fun." She shot him an accusing look. "You aren't being romantic."

Ben placed his hands on his hips. "Your leg comes first, romance second." Then he rolled his eyes, tossed his Stetson onto her dresser, and bent his head. "I'm sorry. You're absolutely right. I'm not being romantic. It's just that right now, your well-being comes first, and you shouldn't have kept your feet down for a half hour." He raised his hands. "I suck at romantic when it comes to your injury." He sat beside her at an angle so they could be face-to-face. "You're high on drugs, and you came in here to change clothes on crutches without anyone to catch you if you got dizzy. One of us needs to think about the possibility of you falling and injuring yourself."

Sissy hated that she had tears in her eyes. "Well, that's just fine. But right now I don't care about my leg. I just want the romance."

A muscle in Ben's cheek started to twitch. "I understand. I really do. But I need to check how tight your brace is, and I need to put ice on your leg for no less than thirty minutes. We can talk while we ice. You're due for another dose of happy syrup, and I'll have a glass of wine. How's that sound? Getting relaxed together before we do anything. That can be romantic."

Sissy folded her arms over her chest. "I knew the T-shirt was a bad choice."

Ben stared at the ceiling. In the light coming through her upstairs window, he looked too sexy to be legal. "It's not the T-shirt. Right now, I love you too much to think about that." He gave her one of those direct, unwavering looks that told her he would have his way about this. "You *will* elevate for thirty minutes. You *will* endure icing your leg for an equal amount of time. If you argue with me, I'm tossing the strap and lubricant out the window, and you can just wait to glimpse bits of heaven until the doctor says you can. Got it?"

Sissy's heart felt as if it were melting. She had encountered men all her life who never cared about her. All they'd wanted was to use her. Ben already possessed her heart and was welcome to her body. But before he found pleasure with her, he wanted to be sure her leg was okay. He was so different from all the others, someone who actually loved her. "*That* is romantic," was all she could think to say.

He looked at her as if she were not a member of his species. *"What?"*

"It's romantic that you're willing to throw the strap out the window. It's romantic that you care about me more than you care about yourself."

He studied her for a long moment. His expression was a blend of total bewilderment and frustration. Finally, he said, "I don't get you, Sissy, but I sure do love you. And your leg is part of you. We're doing this against your doctor's orders. I have to be sure nothing we do jostles that bone. If you find that romantic, great, but to me, it's just practical. Do you understand?"

In that moment, Sissy believed she understood him even better than he understood himself. This wasn't about his needs and his desires. He was making it all about her.

That meant the world to her. Nobody else had ever put her first. Ben was doing that. It was an incredible feeling to know that she was loved. It was even more incredible that he'd just proved to her, beyond any measure of doubt, that she could trust him. A starburst of warmth filled her chest.

"So, let's relax together. While you sip a glass of wine and my happy juice starts working, we'll talk."

He left the room and returned moments later with a bag of ice, her dosage cup filled with syrup, and a goblet half-full of wine. She downed her pain medicine in one gulp. He pressed the ice around her brace. Then he sat beside her to sip his wine.

"I'm worried about the strap business," he said.

"Why?"

"A couple of reasons, the first being that I'm afraid it won't work. Anchoring your hips won't stop you from trying to push up."

"I'll just remind myself that I shouldn't."

His gaze locked on her face, and a tender expression softened his rugged features. "You have no idea, do you? When we do this, the last thing you'll be thinking about is your leg. In fact, you may not be thinking about much of anything. The French call the rush of physical pleasure during sex 'the little death.' Everything around you can go black, and all you see is your partner, if you can even see that. It's like the whole world evaporates, and your reality focus shrinks to a pinpoint. It becomes only about feelings and needs that build within you until you climax."

"That sounds amazing."

"It is."

"Thirty minutes is a long time," she told him. "Did you set the timer on your phone?"

He laughed and drew the device from his pocket. "Okay, all set."

"I hope you set it for twenty-nine minutes, because I know we've already spent one talking."

"Can you feel the cold through your brace yet?"

"No."

"Then thirty minutes on the timer works."

While they waited for the timer to go off, Ben told funny snippets about his childhood. Before she heard his device jangle, he smiled and trailed his fingertip lightly along her cheekbone and then traced the shape of her ear. Bending over her, he settled his mouth over hers, tantalizing her with light flicks of his tongue until she opened for him. He thrust deeply into her mouth, using a rhythm he'd never used before, yet Sissy instinctively recognized it and responded in kind. Her heart started to pound.

The broad canopy of his chest and shoulders sheltered and warmed her. She slid her arms around his neck, ran her fingers into his hair, and moaned as he trailed his lips to her throat to titillate her nerve endings by tickling her skin with his tongue.

"What—" Sissy gulped to find her voice. "What about the strap?"

"I told you. I have a better idea." He reached toward the nightstand to turn off a jarring ring-tone. "And my timer just went off."

He tugged on the neckline of her oversize T-shirt to bare her breasts. Her nipples went instantly hard, and he lightly grazed each of them with his teeth, making them even harder. Sissy felt electrified.

When he drew one of her nipples into his mouth and teased it with his tongue, she cried out with pleasure. Then he treated her other breast to the same tender ministrations.

She felt his hand, large and leathery, on her stomach as he pushed up her T-shirt. When her skin was bared, he moved down to taste it. Her whole body began to tingle with every touch of his mouth.

"Ben," she whispered.

"Lie still. If I feel you arch your back, I'll stop."

"No, please, don't stop."

He left no part of her torso unattended, and then he straddled her hips to kiss her fingertips, her palms, and then the sensitive flesh at the bend of her arms. *The little death.* Sissy had never felt like this. For her, nothing existed but the man above her.

Then he moved lower, tossing aside the bag of ice before he shoved her elevation pillows under her hips, and propped her injured leg on his left shoulder. Flashing a grin at her, he said, "You can push all you like with your other foot."

Before she could collect her scattered thoughts, he began kissing her inner thigh. Sissy felt as if her nerve endings had become harp strings being plucked by a maestro. Her muscles twitched. Her body quivered.

And then she felt the moist heat of his mouth at her most private place. Shocked, she pushed up on her elbows. "Ben, that's—" He flicked his tongue, and jolts of sensation shot through her belly. "Ben?"

All she could see were his shoulders and the top of his head. "Sissy, just trust me."

The vibration of his voice against that super-sensitive part of her sent rivulets of pleasure streaming through her. She fell back on the bed. He began teasing her there with light flicks of his tongue. A sense of urgency that soon became an ache of need made her arch up for more, using her good leg to push. He increased the pressure as he toyed with the flange of tender flesh. The ache within her became nearly unbearable. She felt her hips, as if of their own volition, pick up the rhythm. And then her muscles began to jerk, the pressure within her grew, and the next instant, it felt as if she shattered inside, every fragment exploding and electrifying her body.

Afterward Ben put the pillows beneath her braced leg again, tossed the strap and pharmacy sack on the floor, and then drew the other side of the coverlet over her. Still fully clothed except for his Stetson, he lay down and wrapped his arms around her. Sissy, feeling as if all her bones had dissolved, tried to roll toward him.

"No, honey. Leg on the pillow."

She sighed. "But I want to hold on to you. That was so wonderful. Unbelievable. I had no idea what I was missing, and now all I want is to get as close to you as I can."

"Next time, switch sides of the bed. You can roll toward me, put the pillows between your knees, and keep your leg up." He tightened his hold on her. "This is the best part, snuggling afterward. I like it."

His tone indicated that he'd never done it. Curious, Sissy asked in a sleepy voice, "You didn't know you liked it until now?"

She felt him smile against her hair. "No. Snuggling afterward isn't a part of my dating repertoire. Normally, I get dressed, talk a little so I won't seem rude, and then leave. It's just sex, and afterward it's awkward. Even with women I dated for a while, I never stayed. I didn't feel the inclination, and I don't think the women did, either. Kind of like when you go to watch the fireworks on the Fourth. When the show's over, you go home."

Sissy twisted her neck to look up at him. "Oh, Ben. You missed the show this time."

He kissed the tip of her nose. "This time was for you. Next time we'll worry about me."

"But it's not fair. Is that why you got lubricant?"

He grinned and nudged her head back down with his chin. "I don't need lubricant. I got it for you, just in case you were nervous and stayed dry down there."

"Oh."

Sissy relaxed again. Sleepiness crept over her like a warm, fuzzy blanket. Blackness came next.

For dinner that night, Ben made burgers and fries in the downstairs kitchen. *Trial by fire,* he thought as he turned on the fryer and then entered the walk-in freezer for some ground beef patties.

While he cooked, he talked with Sissy on his cell. She guided him, step by step. When he thought the burgers were done, he sent her a picture. She pronounced them perfect. He carried their meals upstairs on a tray. Ben perched on the coffee table to eat while she lay reclined.

He watched as she took the first bite of the burger. She looked doubtful, but then her expression transformed into pure bliss. She chewed enthusiastically, swallowed, and said, "Yum. The hamburger is perfect."

"Do you think I'm ready?" he asked.

Sissy almost choked on a fry. "To open the restaurant?"

"Joe's coming over in the morning to make out the first order."

"But it's more complicated than just making burgers and fries."

Ben told her about going over her menus and calculating the amounts of ingredients he needed. "I think I can do this. Will you let me at least try? I'd like to be open for dinner tomorrow night."

Sissy's eyes widened. "Bang, just like that, without even so much as a trial run?"

Ben studied her delicate countenance. "Okay, I can do a trial run. How about if I invite only friends and family and offer two menu selections?"

"That would be good. It will at least help you to familiarize yourself with the routine. It gets crazy in that kitchen."

"Speaking of trial runs, are you by any chance craving a Snickers bar for dessert?"

Her eyes darkened to a stormy blue. "Only if you get to enjoy it, too."

Ben could see her pulse kicking in the hollow of her throat. She was nervous because she wasn't sure how to make it good for him, but she was still game, and that made him love her all the more. He leaned forward, slipped a hand behind her head, and angled his shoulders to touch his lips to hers. Then he lifted her in his arms and carried her to the bedroom, depositing her on the left side of the mattress this time.

"For the snuggle session later," he explained. After getting the pillows under her leg, he began unbuttoning his shirt. He saw Sissy's eyes widen as he bared his chest. "Are you okay with this?"

She met his gaze. "I just want you to hurry so I can see the rest of you."

That was a request Ben couldn't deny.

"You're beautiful," she said softly when he was nude. As he joined her on the bed, she asked, "With my leg over your shoulder, why can't we do it for real this time?"

Ben curled an arm around her. "Because it might jostle your tibia. And also because you can't bend your brace. To get in the right position, I'd have you twisted like a pretzel." When he saw disappointment in her expression, he added, "We don't have to wait much longer. Besides, it gives us both something to look forward to."

After they'd both gotten satisfaction, Ben felt like a fallen log when he collapsed beside Sissy. Hands down, it had been the best sex he'd ever had. That blew his mind. They hadn't actually had sex in the traditional way. Yet with Sissy, it had still been extraordinary for him.

"Guess what," he said as he drew her into his arms, allowing her to roll toward him this time because her right leg could remain elevated. "I've developed a passion for Snickers bars."

She giggled. "Is that what we're now calling this activity?"

"Why not? It can be our code word."

The next day set a pattern for those that followed. Ben asked Joe Paisley to help him order supplies. While he waited for the deliveries, he called his family and some friends to tell them he was doing a practice run and would love it if they would come for dinner that evening, on the house. Once off the phone, he put a pot of chili on the stove, thinking he could use it over the next couple of days for Coney Island hot dogs. Then he tried his hand at making Sissy's chocolate cake and blueberry muffins. Shortly after he had the muffins on a cooling rack, a teenage boy arrived with fresh pastries from the Jake 'n' Bake. Ben felt as if he was officially open for business.

For dinner, he decided that his two offerings would be pot roast and hamburgers. He couldn't see how he could possibly screw up pot roast, and fries and onion rings were a snap.

Around lunchtime, people started coming in, which would have been great except they were not individuals Ben invited and it wasn't dinnertime yet. "We heard you reopened!" a man called out. "How is Sissy doing? And how are your nerves holding up? It can't be easy taking over for her."

Ben turned to see that the speaker was Charlie Bogart, owner of the sporting goods store. A large-boned but slender man, he wore a baseball cap bearing his business logo over his sandy-brown hair. His gray-blue eyes danced with amusement.

"I'm not actually open for business yet," Ben explained.

"You aren't? I got the word from a bag boy over at Flagg's Market." Charlie's mustache twitched.

"Are you forgetting what town this is? One person tells another person and—"

Ben cut him off. "I know how fast word travels. But somebody got the story wrong. Today I'm just practicing. I'm not ready to reopen."

Charlie swung up on a barstool. "Hmm." He glanced over his shoulder at the tables, which were filling up fast. "Well, start practicing. People are here to show support for Sissy. We want her to know we're behind her. Word is she'll be out of commission for a long time."

Ben forced a smile. "Well, I know she'll appreciate that. But I don't have anything cooked."

"Short order is fine. I'll have a grilled cheese."

Ben hurried into the kitchen to turn on the grill. Then he sent out a group text to all his family members. "Help! The restaurant is packed!"

Just then a deliveryman propped open the street door and began wheeling in boxes of produce. He'd barely finished unloading when the meat supplier showed up. Before Ben knew it, he was running through a maze of unpacked containers to make hamburgers, fries, onion rings, grilled tuna and cheese sandwiches, and his muffins were nearly gone. How in the *hell* had Sissy managed all this alone?

Jeb was the first family member to show up. He loved to cook, but he knew little about commercial equipment. His wife, Amanda, accompanied him and set up a playpen for their son in one corner of the dining room to keep him from running all over the place. Once a school cafeteria assistant, Amanda not only helped cook but also waited on and bused tables. Barney and Taffeta texted back to say they'd be along as soon as they both got off work. When Jeremiah and Kate arrived, Kate blew a kiss at Ben and went directly upstairs to watch after Sissy.

"I am so screwed," Ben whispered to Jeb in the kitchen. "The one thing I never learned to do is operate the damned cash register! And if I call Sissy to ask her how, she'll try to come downstairs on crutches."

Jeb burst out laughing. Then, to Ben's horror, Jeremiah stuck his head through the pass-through window and yelled, "Anybody out there know how to run a cash register?"

"Dad, keep your voice down to a dull roar, will you?" Ben said. "Do you want Sissy to hear you?"

Before Jeremiah could respond, Ma Thomas hollered back, "I do!" The next thing Ben knew, the older woman was at his elbow. "I also know my way around a commercial kitchen. I was once a cook at the Dewdrop Inn."

He didn't have time to hug her before she brushed past him and began to unpack all the boxes and crates stacked in the kitchen. Sooner than he dared hope, he actually had room to walk. He felt even more grateful when Ma unearthed some frozen packages of soup bases and soon had corn chowder bubbling on the stove beside the pot of chili.

"Salad. You need salad," she said. "Where's an apron?"

Ben knew that Ma had her own shop to operate. Yet here she was, helping Sissy. The next time her orders got mixed up, he'd be there to make sure she didn't have to go across the street and exchange sex toys for perfume.

Over the next hours, Ben came to understand how wonderful small towns could be. Many customers jumped in to help. Others ordered simple things like sandwiches or the soups of the day because they knew he couldn't serve them anything else. Ma Thomas taught him how to run the cash register and make change. Even Christopher Doyle proved his loyalty to Sissy by eating pot roast on his meat loaf night, and when Barney's little boy began to cry, Christopher held the child on his knee, wiped away the snot from his quivering mouth, and fed him Lynda VeArd's French fries.

Ben didn't know how he survived the fallout from everyone's love for Sissy. He did know he'd done a piss-poor job of filling in for her. But the customers hadn't seemed to mind. In fact, Ben had the feeling that eating at the Cauldron with him in charge had almost topped bingo night as entertainment.

After the café closed, all his family members

who could stayed to help Ben clean up and do breakfast prep. Jeremiah, busy laying strips of bacon out on racks, asked, "How the hell did she do all this by herself?"

Until today, Ben believed he'd understood how hard Sissy worked, but now he had a whole new perspective. "I don't know. I was wondering the same thing when I was tripping over boxes and trying to get the cash register open at the same time. She's amazing. A lot of it is preparing ahead. And she sticks to a meal plan for each day. But all in all, I think she sleeps very little and works a lot."

When the breakfast prep had been done and the kitchen was spotless, Ben bade his siblings and in-laws farewell, locked up behind them, and led the way upstairs so Jeremiah could collect his wife. They walked in to find Sissy and Kate playing canasta, Kate using the coffee table as her playing surface and Sissy using her blanket-draped abdomen.

"Don't interrupt us," Kate warned. "For the first time all night, I'm whipping her ass."

Kate Sterling never talked that way. Ben remembered Barney having to remind their mother once that the Virgin Mary had ridden into Bethlehem on an ass, trying to prove to her that *ass* was not a cussword.

Jeremiah arched an eyebrow. Kate shot her husband a merry grin. "This is a girls' night. On a girls' night I wear my girl hat."

"Oh." Jeremiah shrugged and turned to Ben. "You got anything to drink? We may as well have a boys' night."

The next morning, long before his cell phone alarm went off, Ben got a call that jerked him from a sound sleep. Startled and disoriented, he forgot he was sleeping on Sissy's sofa, grabbed for the device, and rolled over onto empty air. He hit the floor on his stomach, the phone still clutched in one hand.

"Hello, this is Ben," he croaked.

"Hey, bro. It's Barney. I'm heading your way. I can help in the kitchen until nine. I figure Dad will be awake by then, nursing his hangover with strong coffee and prancing like a rope horse in the box, wanting me to drive him to the café to get his truck. At ten, I go on duty."

Ben groaned and peered at his phone. "Damn it, Barney. It's only four thirty."

"Yep. While you were partying with Dad, I was in bed asleep. When he called for a ride home at eleven, I wanted to break your neck. Paybacks are hell. Why'd you let him drink that much whiskey?"

Ben rubbed his forehead. "It seemed like a fine idea at the time."

"Well, when you play you have to pay. I'll be there in thirty."

"Sissy's roosters haven't even gargled out a crow yet."

"I know. My roosters aren't awake yet, either. But you need to get ready, man. Breakfast is at seven."

Ben hung up and fished clothes from the pile of clean garments his mother had collected from his place. Soon he was standing under a hot shower. He hadn't tipped the Jack Daniel's jug as much as his dad had, but he hadn't gotten enough sleep to recover from the nonstop work he'd done yesterday.

After dressing, Ben mixed Patches a bowl of his mush and then administered a dose of medication to Sissy before giving her fresh ice water and her phone, which had charged in the kitchen all night.

"Call if you need me," he told her.

She fixed a bleary gaze on him. "Most men wouldn't do this, you know."

Ben shrugged. "I guess I'm not most men. Go back to sleep."

When Barney arrived, Ben was getting ready for the breakfast rush. He had a bucket of diced potatoes in water that would be drained before use. He'd gotten out packages of bread to make a variety of toast. Barney donned a sterile overcoat, found rubber gloves, and went to work as well.

"Thanks for calling," Ben said as they bypassed each other. "Sissy has this down to a fine art. I don't."

"Yep, and I have a feeling that half the town will show up for breakfast."

Four and a half hours later, as he fell into a chair with a pounding headache and a kitchen full of dirty dishes, not to mention a cash register full of money, Ben decided his brother was a prophet of no small ability.

Over the next few days, Ben got the hang of cooking. During slow periods at her store, Marilyn came over to help. If she saw customers going into her place, she ducked out to go wait on them. After the third day she put a sign on her door directing customers to come fetch her. Sissy's hens also started to lay, and the customers enjoyed farm-fresh eggs, even though the first ones were small. Ben compensated by serving three eggs instead of two. He still had plenty to spare. He silently saluted Sissy, though. She'd been smart to get all those chickens.

After that first week, Sissy had to be taken to St. Matthew's to get an actual cast put on her leg. Kate volunteered to be Sissy's chauffeur and arrived at the Cauldron with three pairs of over-size sweatpants with drawstring waistbands.

"She can't go out in a nightgown," Kate explained. "Where are some scissors?"

Ben found a pair and watched as his mother whacked off the right leg of each garment. "Her brace won't fit into them, even though they're stretchy," Kate said. "I cut them to hit just above the brace. Now she'll have bottoms to wear."

Ben reluctantly stayed at the café. Sissy's business was thriving. That was important to her. He worried the entire afternoon. His mother called him twice, once to let him know that Sissy's X-rays showed the bone was still in alignment and again to say that Sissy was in a treatment room, getting a cast put on her leg. Ben chopped vegetables, putting more force behind the blade than necessary because he wanted to be with Sissy. Would it be painful? Was she scared? It just seemed wrong that he wasn't there.

That night, when the dinner mess had been dealt with and the next day's breakfast was under control, he could finally go upstairs to see Sissy. He found her alone. She sat on the sofa with her leg elevated on the coffee table.

"Where's Mom?" he asked.

"I sent her home." Sissy smiled up at him. "The doctor says I can start cutting back on the pain medication. I won't be needing round-the-clock attendance now."

Ben studied her. "You're pale. That means you're hurting."

"A little. The good news is that it should hurt a little less each day."

Ben sat beside her. "That's a whopper of a cast." It was sky blue and reached to midthigh. "Is it heavy?"

"Not too bad. They use different stuff to make casts now. It's just as sturdy but not as weighty. I'll wear this one for a while. Then, if I'm lucky, get a walking cast."

Somewhere along the way, Ben had developed an ability to read Sissy better than he'd ever been able to read anyone. "You're upset about something. Give me the straight scoop."

She took a deep breath. "I can't have sex for another week."

Relief flooded him. She wasn't suffering any complications. "That's it? No other bad news, like you may limp for the rest of your life or you've contracted hydrophobia from Snickers?"

She giggled and slanted him a glance. "He wants another X-ray before he gives me the go-ahead."

Ben curled an arm around her shoulders and moved closer to draw her against his side. "Hey, it could be worse. He might have said a month. And, hello, I think those Snickers bars that we've been enjoying are phenomenal."

She looked up at him. "You're not upset?"

Ben considered the question. "Am I disappointed that it can't happen sooner? Yes. But I've learned something since I met you."

"What?"

"There are some things worth waiting for, and you're one of them."

Chapter
NINETEEN

By the middle of the second week after Sissy's fall, Ben could tell with only a glance when she was in pain and choosing to tough it out. He wanted to insist that she take a dose of medication, but he remembered how dearly she treasured her independence and realized he had to respect that. If she chose to be clearheaded rather than comfortable, that was her decision to make.

Ben didn't rest well on Sissy's sofa. If his head was settled on a cushion, his feet were dangling over the other end. If his feet were comfortable, his head and shoulders weren't, and his neck developed a crick. As for turning over, it required caution or he would end up on the floor. He still didn't trust himself to sleep with Sissy. He tossed and turned a lot, and he was afraid of hurting her.

One night when he'd been shifting around more than usual to get comfortable, he heard Sissy call him. When he went to see what she needed, she invited him to sleep beside her. "My leg is protected now. I don't think you'll injure me by turning over or thumping me with your knee."

Saint Ben flew out the window so fast that Ben didn't feel his exit. He and Sissy had been intimate, so it felt completely right to strip down to his boxers, slip between the covers, and hold her in his arms. She'd changed sides of the bed, even at night, so she was able to turn toward him and welcome him into her arms.

"You don't have to wear boxers," she told him as he settled cautiously on the mattress.

Ben kept them on anyway. "Think of them as behavioral modification tools."

She giggled.

The moonlight cast her upturned face into a silver-limned silhouette. He couldn't resist tracing the bridge of her nose. He liked the way it turned up slightly at the tip. "Have I told you today how much I love you?"

"Lots of times while you worked your butt off in my café. And when you forget to tell me, I remind myself of how worried you were when I got the cast put on. Your mom is a narc. She said you texted her twelve times while I was having it done."

"Of course I was worried. I even got mashed potatoes all over my phone."

"I just wish the doctor had said I can have actual sex. I'm twenty-six years old, I've found a man I love and trust, and I'm eager to experience the real deal."

Ben shifted closer to hold her against him. "It'll happen soon. Just be patient."

"Waiting sucks."

"So does a phone call from Barney at four thirty. He's coming again to help me out." Ben wanted to be buried deep inside of her as much as she wanted him to be there. She ran her hand over his chest and explored his belly. He nearly groaned. "Stop that," he warned with a smile in his voice. "I'll lie awake all night wanting you and end up back on the sofa in order to get some rest."

She drew back her hand. "Don't leave. I like having you beside me."

Ben lay awake long after Sissy fell asleep. He yearned to make actual love to her. But when he remembered how aloof she'd been in the beginning, he couldn't help but think how lucky he was to have even this amount of intimacy with her.

That thought remained with him as he followed her into dreamland.

When Sissy returned to Crystal Falls for her next X-ray, Ben closed up the restaurant for thirty minutes to walk to Flagg's Market on East Main and buy two bottles of mulberry wine. He planned to celebrate with Sissy that night and then seduce her. *Tonight,* he kept thinking. *Tonight I can finally make love to her.*

When Kate brought Sissy home from the appointment, he instantly knew by the glum expression on Sissy's face that she'd gotten bad news. He thought the worst and left Blackie and Ma Thomas waiting for their food while he helped Sissy upstairs, got her situated on the sofa, and then asked what the doctor had said. Sissy glanced at Kate, who was hanging her winter coat in the bedroom closet.

"I can't. Not for another whole week."

Ben, who'd been expecting to hear that her bone had gone out of alignment, nearly sank to the floor in relief. "So you're okay? Nothing's wrong? The doctor's sure about that?"

Sissy looked up at him as if he'd lost his mind. "Did you *hear* me?" She shot a warning glance at Kate's back and whispered, "I was so upset that I actually told him we were working our way around his mandate. He just laughed and said, 'Keep at it.' "

Ben sank onto the coffee table. Aware that his mother was nearby, he whispered, "I know it's hard. But the time will seem to fly by."

"No, it won't," she insisted. "I sit up here all day. You're busy. You have other things to occupy your mind. All I have is movies on television, and mostly they're love stories. Then, as we fall asleep at night, we fool around, but we never actually do it."

"Well, kiddos!" Kate chirped as she emerged from the bedroom. "It's lasagna night. I'd better get home and start playing with pasta."

Ben went to hug his mother. "Thanks, Mom. You're the best."

Kate drew away and flapped her hand. "Don't be

454

silly. We went out to lunch. Sissy says the food here is better, and she's right, but whenever I get to eat out, it's a treat." Kate went over to the sofa to pat Sissy's shoulder. "We had dessert as we drove home. Now she has me hooked on Snickers bars. I've never eaten two giant-size ones in my life."

Ben shot a wondering look at Sissy. She puffed out her cheeks with air and did her best to look fat. He tried to smother a laugh and snorted. Then he remembered that he had customers waiting downstairs. He needed to follow his mother out. Once on the landing, he cracked the door open to wink at Sissy. "That's adultery, you know. Twice. And all in one afternoon."

Sissy's gloomy expression transformed into a smile. "They were so good! After seeing that stupid doctor, I felt better after I ate them."

Ben was glad to see her laughing. But suddenly she stopped. "First it's a week. Then it's one more. What if you get tired of waiting?"

"Hell, no. I haven't gotten tired of waiting yet, have I? Watch another romantic movie, sweetheart, and remember during all the love scenes that I am going to outclass every Snickers bar you've ever eaten when I come back upstairs tonight."

Ben found Ma and Blackie indulging in their afternoon sweets. Ma grinned, wiped chocolate from her lip, and said, "I served us. Couldn't see any point in just sitting here when I knew how." She waved a hand at him. "And no need to worry about the inconvenience for me. I took an extra-large piece of cake and Blackie got two muffins."

"That sounds like a fair trade to me." Ben scanned the café, relieved to see no other customers. He had dinner prep done. He was learning the ropes. He could relax and visit with Sissy's customers for a moment. He rested his folded arms on the serving side of the counter, which put a crick in his back. "Sissy is bored out of her skull up there."

Ben didn't know where that had come from, but judging by the worried expressions on Ma and Blackie's faces, he wasn't wrong to feel concerned.

"Oh, poor thing," Ma said. "Of course she's bored. She's always been so busy. Now all she can do is sit with her leg up."

Blackie went *harrumph* and said, "Just bring her downstairs."

"I can't bring her downstairs," Ben said. "She has to keep her leg elevated."

Blackie polished off his first muffin and took a gulp of coffee. "You ever heard of a lawn lounge? It comes with cushions, sort of like a mattress."

"I know," Ben said, not getting Blackie's point. "My mom has a really nice one."

"Then, for God's sake, borrow it. Set it up for

Sissy down here. Bring down pillows to elevate her leg. You can find a place for it."

Ma clapped her hands. "Oh, Blackie, that's *brilliant.*"

Ben nodded. "She could be part of everything. Visit with people. Tell me every time I screw up. Throw me some Hail Mary passes when I get in trouble. She'll love it."

Sissy didn't understand why Ben awakened her at four thirty in the morning, told her to get dressed, and was now encouraging her to go downstairs on crutches for no good reason. "Has something gone wrong in the kitchen?"

"No, it's something good, not bad."

"At first I thought it would be easier going down. But it isn't. I'd blame it on being top-heavy, but I don't have any boobs."

Ben backed down the stairs in front of her, ready to grab her if she got overbalanced. "Your breasts are the perfect size for your build. And you *do* have some. Trust me, I notice things like that. Just get your butt downstairs."

"But *why?*"

"There's a surprise for you."

"Well, it had better be good," she grumped. "Sleeping in until almost noon makes the day seem shorter. You never get upstairs until at least ten."

Ben bit back a laugh. "As soon as you're well,

I'll return to my ranch, and then I can bitch at you for keeping odd hours."

Ben had already turned on the lights. When she got to the main floor, he expected her to notice the lounge, perfectly positioned for her to see the customers while they dined and also look into the kitchen. Instead she froze and said, "Oh, my gosh, who decorated for Halloween? Is it almost the end of the month?"

"My mom and sisters did it."

Black and orange garlands graced the walls, sporting witches and pumpkins. The tables and counter had been festooned with plastic pumpkins nestled in fall foliage, with battery-operated tea lights flickering inside the jack-o'-lantern globes.

"Oh, Ben. Thank you for bringing me down. I never had time to do much decorating. I did brighten things up for Christmas, mostly by stringing lights. This is just darling."

Seeing the decorations through Sissy's eyes, Ben had to admit they looked awesome. "They're pretty good. But if you hired help, you'd have more time, and seasonal decorating wouldn't be so overwhelming."

She relaxed her weight on the underarm cushions of her crutches. He knew how tender her armpits probably were. Swinging one's weight on the equivalent of two sticks bruised the flesh after a couple of days, but Sissy hadn't complained. "Well, it's just delightful," she told him.

"That isn't what I brought you down to see. Look to your left."

Sissy inched her crutches around and saw the lounge chair. "What's that for?"

"You. It's time for you to be part of the action down here again. I'll bring your pillows. Instead of watching television, you can visit with your customers and give me helpful tips when I get overwhelmed."

"Oh, Ben." Her face glowed with happiness. "You are *so* sweet."

"Actually, it was Blackie's idea. I just ran with it."

"You're both sweet. But you're the sweetest. Today will be so much fun."

Ben bent to kiss her—a quick kiss, because he had to get into the kitchen and prepare for the breakfast rush. "I tried to put this in the kitchen. God knows I could use you in there. But no matter how I positioned it, there wasn't room."

Sissy reclined on the lounge. Ben ran up to grab the pillows and a blanket. Then he handed over her cell phone, freshly charged. "I have lists made out for each supplier. Your first job of the day will be to call in your orders."

"A job? I get to do a job!" She sounded as excited as she might have if he'd just told her he was flying her to Paris for a weekend getaway. "It'll be good to feel useful again. And reconnected with the world. Halloween totally sneaked up on me."

"Until business hours you can talk to me and keep me company while I work."

She grinned up at him. "Get plenty of eggs out. They're easier to work with at room temperature."

The days sped by once Sissy began spending them downstairs. All her customers stopped to chat, and now Sissy had time to engage with them. They raved about the farm-fresh eggs. She heard about Ben's first days in the kitchen, how Ma had taught him to run a cash register and make change, and how many of the customers had pitched in to help. But what really blew Sissy's mind was that Christopher abandoned the booth he always occupied to move a table next to her lounge so he could visit with her while he ate.

As Halloween drew near, Sissy's excitement about the upcoming holiday mounted. It fell on a Monday, and she had an appointment with her surgeon that afternoon. That Friday, right before the holiday, Sissy, ensconced on her lounge, waited until no customers were in the café to remind Ben of her appointment. He grinned and winked at her. "Do I know a lady with her mind in the gutter?"

"No, I can't be accused of that. In all those movies I watched, the real deal gets blipped out."

Ben threw back his head and guffawed. When his mirth subsided, he said, "Maybe I should rent you some porn."

"Yuck. It'll be much more fun to let you surprise me."

He glanced toward the front door to make sure nobody was about to come in and leaned down to kiss her so hungrily that the toes of her left foot curled in delight. "Brace yourself. Our count-down has begun, and I may be full of surprises."

"Tell me," she whispered.

"Oh, no. I do my best telling with my actions."

"I can't wait."

When Halloween finally arrived, Sissy returned from her appointment in Crystal Falls so filled with excitement that she could barely contain herself. When she entered the café on crutches, Ben, working in the kitchen, looked out at her through the pass-through window. She loosened her hold on one crutch to jab her thumb in the air. His sun-burnished face creased in a broad grin. Then, apparently oblivious to the fact that the café was packed with customers wanting early dinners, he strode from the kitchen, grabbed Sissy up in a crushing bear hug, and twirled around with her in his arms. Her walking aids fell willy-nilly to the floor. And then, right there in front of God and everybody, he kissed her.

Shouts and whistles filled the dining area. Some customers even clapped. Christopher Doyle shouted, "You owe me fifty bucks, Charlie Bogart! I told you they were sparking!

What man in his right mind would do all this for a woman he didn't love?"

Drake Mullin, the new pharmacist who, with Kate's help, was finally operating in the black, laughed and said, "I knew he loved her when he brought her home from the hospital."

As Ben released Sissy and steadied her, Sissy felt her cheeks go fiery with embarrassment. Everyone *knew*. She wasn't sure how she felt about that until Ben straightened and got her crutches back under her arms. When she looked up at him and saw the love for her in his expression, she decided that she was the happiest woman on earth, and she didn't care who knew it.

Ben turned to face all the customers in the dining area. "Sissy got great news from her doctor. Her leg is healing well. It's a milestone for her, so I'm closing at eight tonight so we can celebrate!"

"Not to rain on your parade, Ben," Charlie yelled back, "but you can't close early! Every trick-or-treater in town will soap your windows."

Blackie slid off his barstool. "All that means is that we should start celebrating now! The first round of drinks is on me!"

Ben laughed, helped Sissy out of her coat and onto the lounge, and then hurried behind the counter to make drinks.

Sissy settled back on the cushions, anticipating the night to come. Through the front windows of the café, she saw that it was spitting snow outside. When darkness fell, small witches and goblins would enter the café. Ben had placed a large plastic tub of wrapped candies at the end of the bar. She noticed that several of the diners had cameras and wondered why they didn't take photos of the kids with their phones. She guessed that some older folks didn't think about their communication devices serving dual purposes.

Ben served her butternut squash soup and homemade bread with a crunchy crust for dinner. She enjoyed every bite. After he took her tray, he got her up on her crutches and moved the lounge closer to the front door so she could enjoy all the kids. She took out her phone, put it into camera mode, and chatted with customers while she waited for the first child to arrive.

Ben hadn't expected his whole family to show up for trick-or-treat night. Normally they stayed home to hand out candy. But tonight they'd left tubs of treats on their porches with a note that read, NO MORE THAN TWO PIECES. The thought made Ben smile. Not every kid in Mystic Creek could be trusted to abide by the honor system. His parents and siblings might go home to find their windows soaped and their bushes draped in toilet paper.

Even so, he was glad to have everyone dear to him at this impromptu Halloween party. The mood was festive. The customers seemed to love the special Halloween menu, especially the caramel apple pudding he'd made for dessert. Keeping an eye on Sissy as he worked in the kitchen to fill orders, Ben realized that she truly enjoyed seeing all the kids in their costumes. That made him wonder if Sissy had ever gone trick-or-treating, and his heart ached, because he felt certain she hadn't. She was the woman who'd never believed in Santa Claus.

Finally, nine o'clock came, and Ben was able to close up the restaurant. His family, all worried about Halloween tricksters, hadn't volunteered to help tonight. When everyone had left, he followed Sissy upstairs to make sure she had no mishaps during the ascent. Then he began after-dinner cleanup and breakfast prep.

Damn. He felt as nervous as a teenage boy as he grabbed a flashlight and made his nightly trek outside to lock up Sissy's chicken coop. Minutes later as he mounted the stairs to her flat, he had two bottles of mulberry wine in the crook of his arm, a ring in his pocket, and sweaty palms. As much as he yearned to make love to her, a part of him was afraid that he'd somehow muck up his well-rehearsed plans. *Ridiculous.* He wasn't an inexperienced kid. He'd been with Sissy in every intimate way they'd been allowed. The only difference tonight would be that they'd go all the way.

When he entered the flat, he found Sissy watching a flick on television. He caught only a glimpse of the screen before she blacked it out, but he felt certain she'd been deep into a love scene. He smiled, remembering the night they'd broken into the vet clinic and how she'd tried to prepare herself mentally to commit a crime. He couldn't help but wonder if he'd just caught her doing another mental prep.

She had her leg resting on pillows atop the coffee table where he usually sat while she reclined on the sofa. He put the wine in the kitchen, relieved that reds needn't be thoroughly chilled. He dried his palms on his jeans and strode toward the couch to sit beside her.

He came to an abrupt halt when he circled the end table and saw more of her than the blue cast and the back of her head. She wore one of those sexy, black slip things that reached only to the tops of her thighs. Ben couldn't remember what they were called, but he did know she was the most beautiful woman he'd ever clapped eyes on, cast and all.

"Are you still hungry? I didn't give you all that much for dinner." The moment he spoke, he wanted to kick himself. She was wearing a touch of makeup and very little else. Even from four feet away, he caught the flirtatious scent of her perfume. "I, um—dear God, Sissy, are you trying to give me a heart attack?"

She splayed the fingers of a slender hand over her breasts, which had been enticingly displayed by a V of black lace. "I—No, I'm not hungry. Are you okay? If you don't like this, I can find a gown or—something. Would nothing at all be better?"

"Not like it?" Ben's brains felt as scrambled as eggs whipped with a wire whisk. "You look fabulous. Beautiful. You just caught me by surprise. I didn't expect you to dress special." He glanced down at himself and felt like a street person who'd crashed a formal party. The toe of one boot sported a glob of what looked like dried butternut soup. And he didn't smell like flowers, more like garlic and onions. "I think I need to grab a shower—and shave."

Her blue eyes clung to his. "I've blown it. Haven't I?"

Ben shook his head. "The only thing you've blown is my mind. You're so beautiful I couldn't spit if you yelled, 'Fire.' " Now *that* was romantic. He raked his hand through his hair and wished he was wearing his hat. Only, a cook didn't wear a Stetson. A chef's hat, maybe. "I brought up wine. Mulberry."

She tipped her head to search his expression. "Ben, are you nervous?"

"Hell, yes."

Her mouth curved in a smile. "Oh, I'm so glad. Me, too. A glass of wine sounds perfect. Don't leave me to go shower. If I sit here all alone one

466

second longer, wondering how badly the first time will hurt, I'm going to chicken out."

Ben glanced at the wine he'd left on the table. "Can I leave you long enough to open a bottle and fill two goblets?"

She nodded. Ben hurried into the kitchen. He fished in a drawer for the opener. Then he bungled his first try to penetrate the cork with the screw. When he poured the wine, pieces of the stopper floated in the liquid. He thought, *What the hell?* and fished it all out with his finger.

When he returned to the living room, he handed Sissy one goblet and circled the coffee table to sit beside her. As he lowered himself onto the couch cushion, he slopped wine on his jeans.

"Son of a *bitch*."

Sissy giggled as he wiped at the denim with his hand. "I'm the one who's supposed to be in a dither."

Ben took a deep breath. "Yeah, I know. It's just—well, this is the most important night of my life. I want it to be perfect, and now I'm screwing it up."

She lifted her glass. "Drink. Maybe after a glass or two, we'll both calm down. And you haven't screwed it up." She took a dainty sip, savoring the taste. "In fact, you're doing everything so right. I wanted to be sophisticated and casual about this, so I ordered this camisole online especially for tonight." Her cheeks went pink, making her look even more beautiful. "Only, I don't know how to be casual and sophisticated." She lifted her glass again. "Wine for courage first. And then I want you."

Ben thought she already had more courage in her little finger than most people did. "Wine for courage," he agreed. "I can go for that." He took a large swallow. "I hope you aren't feeling pressured into this just because the doctor gave you the go-ahead today."

She shook her head. "You've never made me feel pressured. Well, maybe at the beginning I felt a little hemmed in, but it was nothing you did. I was carrying a lot of baggage." She set her wine on the end table and shifted to get more comfortable. The lacy hem of the camisole inched up. As usual, she wasn't wearing panties because they wouldn't fit over her Dumbo cast. Ben wanted her so badly that he nearly strangled on a swallow of mulberry. "I am feeling a little worried about tonight, though." Her cheeks went rosy again. "I have no protection on hand and couldn't get any because it was too icy outside for me to try going up the street on crutches. I absolutely could not work up the guts to ask your mother to go into the pharmacy to buy me condoms. Driving was out. In Aunt Mabel's SUV, there's a center console, making it impossible to get my right leg out of the way."

Ben could only smile. "I've been thinking about

making love to you for days. I knew today might be it, so I came prepared."

She glanced at the living room window, blackened by night. "The only thing to make tonight more perfect would be if we had a mulberry moon."

Ben would have treasured an opportunity to make love to her in a silvery wash of moonlight coming through the window. "Aw, but we have a new moon tonight. In a way, that's even better. A new moon and new beginnings. And any moon can be a mulberry moon if a couple is drinking mulberry wine."

She took another sip. "You may be right. I'm feeling less nervous now."

"Me, too. I do have one stipulation before I make love to you, though."

"A stipulation?" She looked up at him, her eyes filled with questions.

"I need to know, before we take our relationship to that level, that you'll be my forever lady."

She gazed up at him for what seemed to him a very long while. Then she shook her head no. "I can't promise that," she said. "Sooner or later, my parents will track me down, wanting to borrow money, if for no other reason. You don't comprehend just how horrible my father is, or how stupid my mother is for staying with him. If you still want this to be a forever thing after you meet them, I may consider saying yes."

"I don't care about your parents," he told her. "Bottom line, you may be linked to them by blood, but in every other way, you're your own person and separate from them. I meant what I just said. I can't do the casual sex thing with you. Been there, done that, and I'm finished with it. You're special to me. Everything about you is special. I love you. I've been searching for you all my adult life. If you refuse to make a commitment to me, I know I'll never find anyone quite like you again. You're it for me, the one and only woman I'll ever love."

"But—"

"No buts," he said, cutting her off. "You're precious to me. I want tonight to be the beginning of something beautiful and wonderful between us."

Tears shimmered in her eyes, and without her saying a word, he believed he'd won the argument. He set his wine goblet on the table, eased off the sofa, and went down on one knee beside her. He withdrew a small velvet box from his pants pocket. Holding it on his palm, he said, "This is one of the reasons I was so nervous earlier." He opened the box. The diamond ring glistened in the overhead light. "Will you marry me, Sissy?"

She looked at it, even stretched a finger toward it, and he knew she was tempted. But then she pulled her hand back and her expression changed.

"But, Ben, aside from the fact that my parents are crazy, I know absolutely nothing about my relatives. I've never met my grandparents. I must have aunts and uncles and cousins somewhere, but I know nothing about them. What if they're all nuts?"

Ben studied her face, memorizing every sweet line and angle of her features. "You aren't. That's all I care about. *You,* Sissy. Only about you."

"What if I'm the only sane one of the bunch?" she asked, her voice trembling. "What if we have a child and it's mentally off like my father?"

"We won't." Ben had never felt more certain of anything. "Children's characters are formed mostly by their parents. Studies have proven that. We'll raise our kids in a sane and loving environment, and they'll be products of what they're taught from the moment they're born."

"I wasn't raised in a sane environment."

"No. But you rose above it. As soon as you could, you left all the insanity behind you and began creating a normal life. You defied all the statistics. You're atypical, which is a remarkable thing. You're nothing like your parents. You're an individual and beautifully unique. And out of all the women I've ever met, you're the only one I've ever loved. Are you going to break my heart and say no?"

"I—don't know." Tears slipped over her lower lashes to create silvery trails on her cheeks. They yanked his heart out. He knew she wanted to say yes. He also knew this was a time to shut up and let her make her own decision without any more pressure. She looked again at the ring box, bit her lower up, and swung her gaze up to meet his. For nearly a minute neither of them moved.

Then a tentative smile lifted the corners of her mouth, and her eyes began to sparkle with something far deeper than tears. "Yes," she said. "Yes, yes, yes. Of course I'll marry you. For me, you're a dream come true."

Ben tugged the ring out of the box, grasped her left hand, and slipped the gold band onto her finger. Sissy stared down at it. "It's so beautiful, the most beautiful ring I've ever seen. How did you know my size?"

"It's not as beautiful as you are." Ben took her right hand in his and pulled the mood ring off her finger. "I slipped this off while you were sleeping one morning, drove to Creative Jewelry Designs, and got it sized. I slipped it on your finger again when I got back. You can keep the mood ring if you like, but you don't need to wear it anymore as a reminder of all the things you never want in your life again. You're not like your mother, and as long as I have breath left in my body, your father will never lay a hand on you again." He tucked the mood ring into the velvet box and closed the lid. "Tonight we're both saying goodbye to the past and hello to new beginnings."

Chapter
TWENTY

Ben carried Sissy toward the bedroom, convinced that he was now on familiar ground and wouldn't do anything else stupid. His only worry was that the penetration might hurt her. He'd never been with a virgin, so he had no idea how bad it might be for her. Holding her in his arms felt fabulous, though.

Then he forgot to turn sideways to wal through the door and whacked her cast against the doorframe. It rattled him so much he nearly dropped her. "Damn it. I'm sorry. Are you okay? Did I hurt you?"

"No." She tightened her arms around his neck. "Honest. It didn't hurt at all."

Ben turned sideways and inched through the opening, making sure this time that her cast connected with nothing. When he reached the bed, he laid her down as carefully as he could. Then he straightened and stripped off his shirt. The way Sissy stared at his bare chest made him feel like a Snickers bar she wanted to devour. He toed off one boot, then the other. "Are you still nervous about the pain?" he asked. "We don't have to go all the way tonight."

"A little nervous," she confessed. "But if you don't make actual love to me, I'll be very disappointed." She touched his navel and trailed her forefinger down the inverted triangle of hair beneath it until she encountered his belt buckle. "Remember the day you worked outside without a shirt, and I came out? You were so handsome that I nearly fainted. I've wanted to be with you, really with you, ever since."

Ben loosened his buckle and unzipped his Wranglers. As the pants puddled around his ankles, he started jerking off his socks. Sissy opened her arms, beckoning to him. He sank onto the bed beside her and bent to kiss her. From that second on, he totally forgot about possibly hurting her. His whole being was focused on the woman who was offering him the most beautiful gift he'd ever receive. Her skin taste as if it had been airbrushed with honey. Her mouth intoxicated him with the faint flavor of mulberry wine. The slight trembling of her body when he touched her was a telltale sign that she wanted him as badly as he did her, and he yearned to linger over her and give her so much pleasure that she would remember this night for the rest of her life. He just wasn't sure how long he would be able to wait.

Sissy felt as if she were floating on lightning-streaked clouds. Ben's mouth on her skin felt like warm, wet silk. When he drew on her nipples, the pleasurable sensations pulsed in ribbons to her lower abdomen and filled her with urgent need. *Ben*. His name became a song inside her head that increased in tempo as her desire mounted.

She couldn't easily move with the cast anchoring her to the mattress. But she arched to wrap her arms and one leg around him, to press herself so firmly against him that they became one. He kissed her and lightly teased her nerve endings with the tip of his tongue. Just below her ear, he found a spot that made her breath quicken with every stroke. Then he savored the bend of her arm, tasting and suckling on her skin as if she were, as she'd once dreamed of him being, an ice-cream cone.

And she felt as if she were about to melt. When she could bear it no longer, she said his name, and he shifted to lie beside her and trail his palm down her belly. She jerked when he ran a fingertip inside the aching cleft between her legs.

"Ben? Tonight's the real deal."

"Shhh," he murmured. "Trust me. I just need to get you ready."

Sissy trusted him as she had never trusted anyone. He found his target and gently teased her there until her body began to spasm with his every touch. Then sensation exploded through her, so intense that the world seemed to go black even as starbursts of brightness danced before her eyes.

Long after Ben withdrew his hand, her muscles continued to quiver. He kissed her neck and whispered that he loved her, gently bringing her back down to reality and him. She felt him shift his weight and heard a foil wrapper being opened. Then, after shifting the pillows that supported her cast, he moved between her thighs. In the dim light coming from the living room, she could see the defined musculature of his chest and abdomen. Tendons bunched in his shoulders as he pressed his fists into the mattress to support his weight.

The next instant, he thrust forward and impaled her. A sharp pain lanced through her, and she gasped at the shock of it.

"I'm sorry," he told her, his voice suddenly deep and gravelly. "But I got it over with fast, and it shouldn't hurt now."

He was right. Sissy felt only a stinging sensation deep inside where his hard shaft stretched her inner flesh and muscles to accommodate him. Then he withdrew and pushed forward again, wiping everything from her mind but the incredible feeling of having him inside of her. Pulsing, aching need filled her again. He quickened his rhythm, and she instinctively lifted her hips as best she could to meet his thrusts, dimly aware that she was digging the heel of her cast into the pillows to move. Now she understood why the doctor had refused to let her engage in this activity earlier in her recovery.

Someone shrieked. She suspected that she'd made the sound, but as the waves of mind-numbing pleasure crashed through her, she didn't care. Her wish had been granted.

They were one. Maybe only for this short period of time, but they were one, and she would never forget how it felt.

Afterward Ben maneuvered his way around her cast and managed to hold her in his arms. She nestled her head in the hollow of his shoulder, convinced that the indentation had been carved into his hard body just for her. He ran a hand lightly over her back, telling her without words how much he loved her. Sissy fell asleep wishing that all those fabulous feelings she had experienced could have lasted forever, but she consoled herself with the thought that being held close in his arms was almost as wonderful.

Ben woke around three in the morning with an erection. He saw no reason to waste it and began kissing Sissy, gently pulling her up from the depths of sleep.

"Hi," she murmured against his chest. He felt her lips curl in a smile. "Is it time to get up?"

"No, not yet. We have a whole hour and a half to play before I have to get ready for work."

She giggled. Then she reached up to run her

fingers through his hair, a gesture that he interpreted as an invitation. He dipped his head to possess her mouth with his. Then he began stroking her body. This second time was, for him, even better than the first, because no surprises awaited her this time, and he didn't have to worry about hurting her. He slipped on protection. Then he returned his attention to her.

He loved the way she responded to his touch, holding nothing back. He made love to her with a slow hand and lingering kisses until he felt her body start to quiver with need. Then he let go himself, bringing her to climax with his mouth. She cried out as the orgasmic pleasure snapped her slender body taut.

Ben waited until she lay lax on the bed, and then he pushed his throbbing erection deep into her feminine warmth and wetness. She revived quickly and worked her hips to meet his thrusts.

Giving her pleasure and receiving the same in return was one of the most incredible experiences of Ben's life.

Over the next few days, Ben and Sissy experienced the joy of being newly in love. Ben taught her the fine art of lovemaking. Sissy, without realizing it, taught Ben how incredibly beautiful sex could be when a man was with a woman he loved.

When Sissy got a walking cast, she began

helping Ben in the kitchen. He wouldn't allow her to stay on her feet too long and insisted that she elevate her leg frequently. But Sissy was so pleased to be back in her kitchen, even part-time, that she didn't mind the restrictions, especially when she had the late evenings with Ben to anticipate. He loved her, and she loved him. It seemed like a miracle to her. How could she be this lucky?

One afternoon Sissy's cell phone rang. During business hours, she got lots of calls, so she answered the same way she always did, saying, "Hello, this is Sissy at the Cauldron. How may I help you?"

Thumping her way toward the kitchen, Sissy stopped dead when a woman replied, "This is your mother, Sissy."

A dozen questions raced through Sissy's mind. The one she asked was, "How did you find me?"

"I hired a detective. I want to talk with you. To explain things. I've come to Mystic Creek. Right next door to your café, actually, in the Mexican restaurant. Will you please walk over and meet with me?"

"For what reason? If you need money, I'm a dead end."

"I'm not here for money. I'm here to try to mend my relationship with my daughter. I won't take much of your time. Please, Sissy?"

"Is that asshole you call your husband with you?"

"No, and he isn't my husband now. I left him four years ago. I've gone to counseling and straightened out my life. I went back to Homesville, the town where I grew up. I'm working there. I'm attending school. I've got my head on straight. All I want, all I need, is a chance to tell you how sorry I am for being such a horrible mother."

"Well, you just told me. I see no reason to meet with you so you can say it again."

"*Please,* Sissy. Think about it. Give me a chance. I've driven a long way. I'll wait here for an hour."

"I'll think about it." Sissy ended the call and went into the kitchen where Ben worked. "My mother just called. She wants me to meet with her. She wants to tell me she's sorry for everything. She's waiting nearby."

Ben stiffened. Then he carefully laid the chopping knife on the cutting board. "You owe her absolutely nothing. Not even a moment of your time. And what if your father is hanging around outside?"

"She says she left him four years ago."

"And you believe her?"

Sissy hugged her waist. "I don't know. I'm so stunned she called me, I can barely think." She dragged in a shaky breath. "But I think it ma do me good to see her. Maybe I'll get some closure, if nothing else."

Ben nodded. "It's your decision to make. I think it's a mistake, but I won't try to convince you not to go." He stepped to the pass-through and leaned out to look at the street windows. "My worry is that she lied about leaving your dad."

"José will be there," Sissy replied. "If my father walks in, he'll intervene and call the cops."

Stiffening her shoulders, Sissy went to the storage area to grab a jacket. Then, without looking at Ben, she made her way to the front door. She paused on her way out. "Wish me well?"

He winked at her. "Always. One word of advice, though. She wants to purge her soul, I'm betting. But don't let her do all the talking. Tell her how *you* feel. Get it off your chest."

In case it was icy, Sissy was cautious as she stepped out onto the sidewalk. She was only paces away from the front door. She made her way to the Straw Hat, paused to take a bracing breath, and walked in.

She'd known seeing her mother again wouldn't be easy, but when she saw her sitting in a booth facing the entrance, Sissy froze, feeling as if a hard fist had just connected with her solar plexus. Tears stung her eyes. Part of her wanted to hobble into the dining area at her top walking-cast speed to give Doreen a hug, but then she recalled all the times when her mother had failed her as a parent.

With as much grace as possible, she went to sit across from Doreen Bentley. "I've said it once, but I'll say it again. If you're here for money, you're wasting your time."

A timid hope faded from Doreen's tear-filled eyes.

Sissy felt ashamed of herself, but only for a moment. This was the woman who nearly gave birth to her only child under an apple tree. The woman who always put her husband first, no matter what he did. The woman who had allowed her daughter to be abused, not once, but countless times. Sissy knew her father had fractured her cheekbone twice when she was young because of dental X-rays she'd undergone as an adult. She hadn't been taken to a doctor either time, because questions would have been asked. Douglas Bentley might have been arrested for child abuse.

José came to take their orders. Doreen asked for coffee. Sissy looked up at her friend and said, "Nothing for me, thanks. I won't be here that long."

When José walked away, Doreen, with a lift of her chin, a chin that Sissy saw in her mirror every morning, said, "You and I need to talk. I deserve nothing from you but your contempt. The same goes for your father. But there are things I need to say."

"Then say them. And when you're finished, I have a few things to get off my chest as well."

"My divorce from your father is now final. All that's left is to clear up the financial mess. He fought me in court because he thought I was hiding assets. Oregon splits marital assets right down the middle. My legal fees went through the roof."

José served Doreen coffee. Sissy waited until he was out of earshot to ask, "So you really did divorce him?"

"After two years of duking it out with him in court, yes. He got an attorney who was willing to roll the dice to get a percentage of what money Doug could get from me. That's all over now, but it doesn't necessarily mean he's completely out of my life. At least I've been granted a divorce."

"What do you mean, he isn't out of your life?"

"He stalks me. Your father thinks of me as a possession that's been stolen from him." She shrugged. "Not that long ago I left class at night, and as I crossed the parking lot, he leaped out, grabbed my arm, and tried to drag me to his truck. He said he was taking me home where I belonged. I fought, and he beat the hell out of me. I now have a restraining order, and I haven't seen him since. But I know him. I'm more careful now. Like a bad penny, he'll always show up. Today as I drove here, I kept checking my rearview mirror. I never saw his old truck."

"Be more than careful," Sissy warned. "We both know he's violent when he's drunk."

Doreen shrugged. "He's beyond violent. But with the restraining order, I'm fairly safe. He doesn't want to go to prison. He beat me up pretty bad. The only time I'll ever have to see him again is when he signs an agreement, which my attorney drew up, saying that Doug has accepted

483

the money I'll give him and relinquishes his right to all other marital assets. Not that there's much. Doug's smart, in his way. He knows he can't draw blood from a turnip." Doreen stared into her coffee for a moment. "I'll be leaving town early in the morning, and I'll never be back unless you invite me, which you may never do. That makes me sad. You're my daughter, and I love you, but I understand that some mistakes a mother makes can never be erased with only an apology."

Sissy couldn't think what to say. "How do you plan to survive without the occasional income he brought in when he got desperate for booze?"

Doreen smiled. In the overhead light, touches of gray showed in her red hair. "Actually, Sissy, I was mostly Doug's sole means of support for years, not the other way around. Surviving on my own, without feeding him or buying his liquor, is a piece of cake." She lifted her narrow shoulders. "And I have a nice nest egg. After you were safely out of the picture, I started keeping half of my earnings and hiding it from Doug." She met Sissy's gaze. "I know I was a horrible mother, but at least I waited until you left before stirring that particular pot. He went berserk the first time I brought home cash instead of a check. He could no longer tell how much I'd actually been paid."

"He beat you."

"No more than usual, and by keeping half my money, I was giving him what he considered to be a reason." She winked at Sissy. "And, no, I never put the money in the bank. I worked, cashed my checks, and took home half. I kept my other earnings a secret in a safe-deposit box. Sometimes it was rough, but I could always eat at the restaurant where I worked, and he couldn't."

"At least he was the one who went hungry. But, Mom, what if he hires an investigator and discovers the safety-deposit box? Then he can take half your nest egg."

"Nope. I emptied it of money and put family mementos in it. Someone I trust is keeping the cash for me in another safety-deposit box in his name. He's sharp. He knows the law. Cash leaves no paper trail. He was so glad I wasn't stupid enough to open a bank account to put my money in. Doug could have taken half of it then."

Doreen glanced around the restaurant. "I peeked through the windows at your café. How are you doing financially? I know how difficult it can be to keep a small business afloat at first. If you need some cash, I owe you at least that much. I can postpone my own plans to open a business and replenish my savings over time."

Sissy thought for a moment that she needed to swab out her ears. Her mother was offering to give her money. "The Cauldron is financially stable. If you're fishing to see how well I'm doing, hoping to bleed me, you can forget it. I've saved to do a remodel, and every penny of that will go toward making my café more attractive to a younger crowd."

Doreen nodded. "I noticed that it's very shabby in there. And I'm not hoping to get any money from you. I have plenty to carry forward with my own plans."

"Which are?"

Doreen smoothed her hair. "You'll laugh. I hope to open a café. It's the farm girl in me, I suppose. The one thing I'm really good at is cooking, and God knows all my work experience has been in restaurants."

"You really plan to start a business?" Sissy couldn't keep a note of incredulity out of her voice.

"Mabel did it. Why shouldn't I? I'm still young. Having you at sixteen was pure hell at the time, but now I'm footloose, fancy-free, and only forty-three. Excuse me. It's my new motto since my recent birthday."

Though still feeling dazed by the changes in her mother, Sissy approved of her plan to open a café. "I'm proud of you, Mom. You're thinking outside the box."

Doreen laughed. "I've been thinking outside the box for nearly four years. The first year after leaving your father was rough. I went back to Homesville, for one, and had to face my family as a used-up, beaten-up, frantic person with no idea what I planned to do except get away from my husband." She paused and swallowed, making her larynx bob in her throat. "My whole family welcomed me with open arms."

"Oh, Mom." Sissy couldn't maintain the cool separation between her and her mother any longer. She reached out to grasp her slender hand, so much like her own. "I'm so glad you went home. Was it eventually a positive choice for you?"

"Positive? Not at first. Mama insisted that I needed counseling. She was terrified I'd go back to Doug."

"So did you go to counseling?" At the edge of her mind, Sissy thought that her grandmother had given Doreen sound advice.

"Oh, yes. The first time, she had to drag me, but I went. It was group therapy. I couldn't imagine talking with strangers about my life with Doug, and I expected to see a bunch of battered, pathetic, hopeless women exactly like me. But instead the group consisted of several professional women who'd remained members to be supportive of those of us who were new and give us a visual of how it might be for each of us after recovery." She waved her hand. "Not to say there weren't a lot of women like me. We were all a mess. But with the help of the therapist and those women who'd already been through the program, we began taking baby steps toward new beginnings."

Doreen fiddled with her napkin. "The funny part was, I didn't comprehend that I needed help.

None of us really did. We all ended up with men who convinced us that we were stupid and undesirable, and that everything that went wrong in the relationships was our fault." She passed her hand over her eyes and forced a smile. "That part of my life is behind me. I have nearly three years of college under my belt now. I'm three semesters away from having my bachelor's degree in business management and I've already completed two years at an accredited culinary arts school. I no longer believe I'm stupid. In fact, I'm excited about my future. So let's discuss yours instead."

Somehow their conversation went from strained to almost pleasant. Sissy revealed details about her plans for the café renovations. Doreen, judging by what she'd glimpsed of the café, approved. "It'll draw in young families and provide more seating, and you've even included a gas log fireplace. I think it'll be awesome."

Sissy agreed. "In order to save up the money, I haven't taken a single day off. Well, I did take one day, which was wonderful, and I couldn't work during my recovery after falling down the stairs. But a friend of mine took over for me." Calling Ben a friend made Sissy's heart catch. "Well, more than a friend. We're engaged. I'm madly in love for the very first time. Someday, maybe, I'll invite you here to meet him."

"But not today." Doreen nodded. "I was a horrible mother, a coward, and the enabler of a child abuser. You needn't avoid saying that to me. In group, I said it aloud plenty of times. As your mother, I sinned against you, Sissy. I'll ask for your forgiveness when I feel you're ready, but for now, I'm just grateful you're talking to me."

Now it was Sissy's turn to get tears in her eyes. "Mama, you were never the one who was cruel to me."

"Oh, yes. I didn't pack in the middle of the night and run to get you away from him. Looking back, I don't know where my head was. I felt unattractive, inept, and helpless. Men like Doug Bentley are experts at browbeating women. That's no excuse for my behavior, I know, but I didn't believe I had it in me to feed you and keep a roof over your head if I left him." She reached for her coat, which lay beside her on the seat. "While I drive home, I'm going to pray with every roll of the tires that what I've told you may help you to forgive me. I'm going to pray that our talk today may be a new beginning for us. And if it's not, I'm going to pray that you have a wonderful life with that nice young man of yours. Please watch for the signs. Having grown up with your father, you should know them well."

Sissy searched her mother's face. "Ben isn't a Doug Bentley. He's smart, patient, caring, generous, and never says mean things to me or anyone. He's so wonderful I can't begin to list all his attributes."

Doreen smiled. "So what are his flaws, Sissy? They're there. None of us is perfect. Be sure you're seeing him through clear lenses."

Sissy laughed. She hadn't expected to do that during this meeting. "Oh, he has them. He's stubborn. When he set his sights on me, I couldn't get rid of him."

Doreen nodded. "He knew a good thing when he saw it. Go on."

Sissy thought a moment. "He's a little too protective. He used to jump in and do everything for me. Or decide what was best for me. But he's a caring man, and I think he came to realize that I need to make my own choices and feel independent. For instance, when you called me he didn't approve when I decided to walk over here. He said that I owe you nothing, and he was afraid you might have lied about being divorced from my father."

Doreen chuckled. "But he allowed you to come. I haven't seen a man peering through the windows to check on you."

"He didn't *allow* me to come, Mama." Sissy paused, amazed that she'd addressed her mother twice as she had as a kid. "Ben isn't my boss. He doesn't rule me. He's working his ass off right now to keep my business afloat, so maybe he's still a little protective of me, but in a good way. Without him, I'd be in hurt city financially right now."

"Does he drink?"

Sissy almost laughed again. "Yes. A little. We'll have a glass or two of wine. I imagine he enjoys a beer now and then with his brothers. But I've never seen him drunk."

Doreen, slender enough to slip on her jacket while seated in the booth, said, "I'm proud of you. At least I taught you one good thing. Look closely at a man before you leap." She slid from the seat to gaze down at Sissy. Looking up at her, Sissy couldn't help but note how alike they were in appearance except for their coloring. "Remember those prayers I'll be saying as I drive home. And be happy with Ben. It sounds as if you've found a winner. There's nothing more wonderful than a healthy relationship."

Sissy raised her eyebrows. "You've met someone." It wasn't a question.

"Oh, yeah." Doreen grinned. "And he's everything Doug isn't. I played it smart this time."

Sissy struggled up from the booth. Doreen slid her gaze from the top of Sissy's head to her feet, one still in a cast. When she looked back up, she said, "You are a beautiful woman. Remember that. I know you aren't ready for a hug. But blowing you a kiss good-bye should work."

Sissy could have sworn she felt the kiss, as if it had somehow drifted through the air and landed on her cheek. It wasn't until her mother left the restaurant that Sissy touched her lips to her palm and blew a kiss back.

491

When she hobbled into the Cauldron seconds later and reached the kitchen, Ben asked, "So, how did it go?"

"She's divorced my dad. I *think*. My mother isn't above lying. But I actually believe she left him."

"Good for her."

"I think she'd like to see me again, but I'm wary. I don't want to invite that kind of craziness back into my life."

Ben kept chopping onions. "Good for you."

After visiting with her mom and remembering so many things she didn't wish to about her father—how domineering and cruel he'd been, in particular—Sissy loved Ben even more. As caring as he was, he didn't want to run her life. He'd disagreed with her decision to see her mother, but he also appreciated that Sissy needed to make her own decisions. If she made mistakes, he'd be there to comfort her. If she made the right choices, he'd be there to pat her on the back. She was still calling her own shots, and it was a fabulous feeling.

Shortly before Thanksgiving Ben's whole family came to the café to celebrate Ben and Sissy's engagement. Sissy had expected to feel nervous, wondering if she was being sized up as to her suitability, but she enjoyed being with Ben's loved ones. While watching them, she learned what it could be like in a normal family, with brothers and sisters teasing one another while the parents looked on with indulgent smiles.

Ben waited until the café was crowded with his relatives and customers before he drew Sissy up from the lounge and yelled to be heard over the roar of conversation, "I have an announcement to make!"

A sudden hush fell over the dining room. Sissy felt her cheeks go warm, not with embarrassment, but pleasure. This man, whom she'd come to love so deeply, was about to tell the world that he wanted to make her his wife.

"As all of you may have guessed, I am madly in love with this beautiful lady." He grinned down at Sissy. "And though it may seem a little too soon to some of you, we've spent so much time in each other's company that we both feel we know each other better than we've ever known anyone. So I asked Sissy to marry me." Ben grasped Sissy's left hand and held it up so everyone could see her engagement ring. "She accepted, and I feel like the luckiest guy in the world."

People clapped their hands. Some of the men stomped and whistled. Sissy found herself being hugged, first by members of Ben's family and then by customers. While lying on the lounge, she'd had time to grow acquainted with practically all her regular patrons, and she now counted them as her friends, loving them almost as much as she did Blackie, Christopher, Marilyn, and the VeArds.

After all the congratulatory hugs and hand-shakes, Ben went behind the counter to serve drinks on the house. Even Christopher indulged in a glass of wine, saying, "If one glass kills me, I'll die a happy man. My honorary granddaughter has found herself a damned good husband."

Everyone cheered and a few people patted the stooped old man on the back. Charlie Bogart yelled, "Bottoms up, Chris. Walk on the wild side tonight. Did she adopt you, or did you adopt her?"

Christopher raised his glass. "I adopted her. I'm her grandpa now, whether she likes it or not."

Sissy limped over to Christopher and gave him a gentle hug. "I'm going to call you Gramps. Whether you like it or not."

Sissy still tired easily, and her leg had begun to ache, so she lay on the lounge with her cast propped up on pillows to enjoy watching every-one party. Both Ben's family and many customers stayed long after the usual closing time. She knew many of her older patrons were staying up late in order to celebrate their engagement. She had finally found love and a place she could call home.

Studying the Sterling men, she noticed how greatly they resembled one another, yet each of them had different character traits that made them special. Sarah and Adriel, Ben's younger sisters, had taken after their mother, with slight builds. Sissy didn't often meet women who were as energetic as she was, but she realized that she'd met her matches in Kate and her daughters.

That thought made Sissy more impatient to get her cast removed. The doctor had made it clear that she'd need weeks of physical therapy, but she looked forward to even that. She would be able to go for her triweekly treatments in Mystic Creek. It would hurt at first. But it would be worth whatever she had to endure in order to be active again.

When Ben had finally bade everyone good night, locked the front door, and put up the CLOSED sign, he lifted Sissy from the lounge and ascended the stairs sideways to reach the flat.

"Don't you still have breakfast prep to do?"

He deposited her on the sofa. "That's one of the beauties of entertaining family. They helped in the kitchen. They started early, and I'm done for the night." He quickly went back downstairs to retrieve her pillows. As he reentered the flat, he went on talking as if there hadn't been a lull. "You know what that means. I can spend the rest of my evening making passionate love to my future wife."

Sissy's weariness vanished, and Ben followed through on his promise, making love to her three times before they fell asleep in each other's arms.

Chapter
TWENTY-ONE

The next evening, right after the last customer left the café, Ben got a phone call as he locked the front door. When he came into the kitchen, he said, "That was my dad. He's been training two horses that were brought to me. Apparently, he's been looking high and low for a special bit and hasn't been able to find it. I can't remember where I put it, but it's for sure not in the tack room where it belongs. I've got to go find it so he'll have it come morning." He glanced at the counters, laden with dirty cookware and dishes. "I won't be long. If your leg's bothering you, take a rest, and we'll knock it out together when I get back."

Sissy's leg ached only a little. "I'm fine," she assured him as she followed him to the back door. "Don't drive too fast on the curves. It may be icy out."

He bent to kiss her. It was a long, leisurely exploration of her mouth that left her feeling breathless. "Do you really believe I'd drive like a maniac with a beautiful woman like you waiting for me? If I got in a wreck, I might miss out on happy hour later."

Sissy giggled. Then she sobered. "I'm no longer on crutches. I miss Finnegan. He's a part of our family, and it doesn't seem right without him here. Could you run by Barney's and pick him up on the way back?"

"He could still trip you."

"He won't. He's smart, Ben. He'll realize I'm hurt and be extra careful."

"All right, I'll bring him home, but not tonight. It's late. We've got cleanup and prep to do. And Barney may already be in bed."

"But you'll get him tomorrow?" she pressed.

Ben sighed. "Against my better judgment, yes, I'll bring him home tomorrow."

Sissy locked up behind him, listened for the familiar thump of his boots going down the steps, and then leaned against the door for a moment, smiling. He hadn't said he would bring Finn *here*. He'd said he would bring Finn *home*. That made her feel so secure and—well, just happy.

Hobbling on her cast, Sissy made her way toward the kitchen. She'd just entered the café proper when Ben's distinctive and never-changing knock, three raps with long pauses in between, resounded up the hallway from the back door. She smiled and retraced her steps.

As she turned the key in the lock to disengage the mechanism, she said, "What did you forget?"

The door burst open with enough force to knock her backward and off her feet. Her head smacked the wall, making bright spots appear before her eyes.

When her vision cleared, she saw the man of her nightmares standing over her. He smiled as if seeing her sprawled at his feet amused him. Sissy glanced past him and saw that he'd closed the door. She had no doubt that he had locked it, and she could tell by his glazed eyes that he was either drunk, stoned, or both.

Sissy refused to call him Dad. He didn't deserve the title. "What are you doing here?"

He grabbed her arm in a brutal grip and jerked her to her feet. "I came for what's ours. The money. Mabel never stopped loving me. She almost married me. Your mom and I should have inherited this dump and all her money. If you behave yourself for once in your miserable life, maybe that's all I'll take. You don't have that tire iron now, sweet cheeks."

Sissy almost fell again as he released his hold on her arm and shoved her up the hallway. She lurched against the wall, throwing all of her weight on her injured leg. She managed to keep her footing, but only just barely. She remembered how he'd mimicked Ben's knock, and knew that he'd been watching her and waiting to strike. He was like a rattlesnake . . . except he gave no warning.

"Is my mother in on this?" she asked over her shoulder. "Did she tell you where I am?"

"Yep. What d'ya think, that she had a sudden personality change? You know her as well as I do. She never turns up her nose at free money. And she was mad as hell when we found out Mabel left you this place. Doreen thought she should have inherited it, not you. I'm here to take what I can of what should've been ours."

Even though fear reigned supreme within Sissy, she felt a stab of pain in her heart. Her mother had betrayed her.

Ben had already counted down the till and put the day's proceeds in the safe.

He had been making regular deposits at the bank for her, but he only did it once a week, on Monday. This was Friday. Five days of profit sat in the safe. Sissy had already lost enough money after her accident while the café was closed. There was no way she would open that safe and let her father take nearly a week's income.

Ben had worked so hard here to keep Sissy's restaurant operating in the black. In a way, her father would be stealing Ben's sweat. The thought infuriated her.

Sissy's mind raced. Douglas Bentley was a big, ham-fisted man. Physically, she was no match for him. Her only hope was to outsmart him.

Once he'd pushed Sissy into the café dining

room, he seized her arm again and dragged her to the cash register. "Open it."

Sissy knew that he'd realize she had more money stashed somewhere if she gave in too easily. All that remained in the till was the next morning's startup cash. "No way!" she said, forcing defiance into her voice. "My whole week's profit is in there. I'm not going to let you walk out of here with it."

Doug Bentley drew back his arm and slapped her. Even as Sissy staggered backward and nearly fell under the force of the blow, she knew she'd gotten off lucky. In the past, he'd always used his fists.

"Open it, or I swear to God I'll bust that leg of yours again and make you a cripple for the rest of your life."

Feigning reluctance, Sissy fished under the counter for the register key, which she always kept hanging on a nail where few people would think to look for it. "You're a bastard. Do you have any idea how badly it'll hurt me financially if you take a whole week of my profit? Look at this place. It's a dump. I'm barely making ends meet."

Doug sneered at her. "Frankly, my dear, I don't give a shit."

Sissy opened the drawer, hoping that she had played her role convincingly enough to make her father believe he was making off with every dime she had in the building. "Help yourself, then. Ruin your daughter financially. You may find the checks difficult to cash, and a lot of people use credit cards, but you can take everything else."

Her father shuffled through the bills in each divider. Then, without any warning, he snarled and backhanded Sissy across the mouth. The blow sent her stumbling backward, and she fell against the shelving. Pain streaked up her leg.

"Do you really think I'm that stupid?" he asked. "This is only the opening money for tomorrow."

Looking up at her father's glaring eyes, Sissy knew that he might kill her if she refused to open the safe. No amount of money was worth dying for, especially not when she was so happy for the first time in her life. *Ben.* A future with him, getting married and raising a family with him. To her, that was the true treasure. Giving her father even as much as a dime stuck in her craw, but as she regained her feet, she assured herself that this would be the last time she'd ever have to deal with him. The moment he left, she'd dial 911. He would be arrested before he left town. And she wouldn't hesitate to press charges. He'd do hard time for robbery, breaking into her building, and assaulting her.

For once in his life, Douglas Bentley would get what was coming to him.

Sissy hobbled to the safe in the kitchen pantry,

detesting the man who followed behind her. He'd injured her leg. It didn't feel as if it was broken again, but it did hurt when she put weight on it. What bothered her was that he didn't care. If she ended up being a cripple for the rest of her life, he'd never feel a moment's remorse. There was something missing inside of him, that part of a person that allowed him to experience compassion and love.

Sissy was so furious that her hand didn't shake as she turned the dial to unlock the safe. When she heard the click, she pulled open the door and stepped back. He grabbed an empty money bag. Ben had stacked each denomination of bills and secured them with paper clips.

Sissy watched her father grabbing money, filling the bag as full as he could get it. He couldn't close the zipper. Sissy knew he'd just relieved her of about seven thousand, maybe more. That had once seemed like a lot to her. Now she thought of it as working capital, which would quickly deplete when she paid for supplies. The café provided her with a comfortable living, but it would never make her rich.

Her father placed the money back on the shelf and said, "Well, now, I've got nearly everything I came for."

He lashed out so fast to grab her by the hair that she couldn't move quickly enough to evade him.

"I've been waiting ten years for this moment, ever since you turned sixteen and got tits."

Sissy's skin went icy. She knew what he intended to do, and she also knew she couldn't stop him.

"I'm your daughter," she reminded him.

"You aren't my kid. Before you were born, I got thrown in jail for six months, and when I got released, Doreen was three months gone with some other man's brat."

Sissy knew he was lying. She hadn't taken after her father in build, but she had his dark hair and blue eyes. She also had a little bump on her right earlobe that her mother had told her ran in his family. She shifted her gaze to the side of his head and saw it. He was a piece of trash. "I wish I weren't yours! I'd give up an arm not to have your blood in my veins. But that's your fairy tale, not mine. You're a bastard who's about to rape his own daughter."

He doubled his fist and really hit her then. Sissy had endured blows from his bunched knuckles enough to know that he might have fractured her cheekbone. If so, it wouldn't be the first time. His grip on her hair kept her from falling. She glared up at him. She was frightened. Somewhere behind her rage the fear clawed at her stomach like icy talons. She knew she couldn't fight him off. He looked soft, but under the layer of flab, he packed a lot of muscle. If he got her underneath him, he would be able to pin her with his weight alone.

Sissy was going to come out the loser in this battle. Ben wouldn't return in time to save her. The physical closeness between them had been sacred, or something very close to it. What her father planned was just the opposite, a sacrilege.

Her mouth was dry. But she tipped back her head, despite the sting of her hair follicles, and with all the force that she could muster, she spit in her father's face.

He roared with anger, and with one powerful swing of his arm, he threw Sissy so hard that she hit the lower cabinets of the kitchen before she landed on the floor. Dimly, she realized that her cast had broken. Through the pain that radiated over her body, she also knew she couldn't try to run, not without anything to brace her leg. She could break her tibia again.

Her father snarled and sprang at her. For an instant, it seemed to Sissy that he floated on the air with his arms spread. And then he landed, all two-hundred-plus pounds of him flattening her against the floor with such impact that all the air in her chest gushed from her mouth. She tried to scream, but instead she could only gasp with lungs that refused to inflate. Black spots danced before her eyes. She felt her blouse rip. Felt her father's beefy hands on her bare skin.

Finally, she was able to drag in a jagged breath. Her vision cleared. With horror, she felt the waistband of her sweatpants down around her hips. She turned her head to look for a weapon. She had fallen near the open shelving that housed her cooking pots. The small cast-iron fajita skillets lay just beyond her reach.

Her father was grunting above her and tearing at her bra. Sissy strained to reach the handle of a fajita skillet. It wasn't large, but if she could grasp the handle, it would be light enough for her to swing it with all her might. She managed to shift her shoulders closer to the shelf. Her father was so intent on pulling up her bra that he'd lifted some of his weight off her.

Sissy touched the tip of the handle with her fingers. She still couldn't get a solid grip. She pushed with her good leg, trying to inch closer. Finally, she was able to curl her fingers around the stout handle. At the edge of her mind, she realized her father had bared her breasts and was pinching her nipples. Her stomach heaved with revulsion.

My father, she thought. And then, with all the strength she had left, she swung the skillet at his head. Then she swung again.

He went limp, his weight still pinning her to the floor. She lay beneath him, keeping a death hold on the cast iron, prepared to bonk him again if he came around. She didn't care if she killed him. All she cared about was getting him off of her, being free of his stench.

She squirmed sideways. He was so heavy he was crushing her. She pushed with her uninjured leg and gained another inch. He was round at the belly and rolled slightly. She pressed both hands against his shoulders and shoved with all her might. He didn't topple off of her, but his weight shifted, enabling her to wiggle out from under him.

Every intake of air whined against her eardrums. She turned onto her stomach, still holding the skillet, and belly crawled to put distance between them. When she reached the corner of the cupboards, she sat up and rested her back against the door. She stared at her father, lying on the floor, possibly dead, but more likely, still breathing. She needed to call the police, but her phone had fallen from her sweatpants pocket when he'd been knocking her around.

Remembering his hands on her breasts, she gagged and purged her stomach. Lumpy liquid landed on her top. It stank, but not as badly as her father.

Terrified that he might regain consciousness and knowing she didn't dare try to run, she did the only thing she could. She screamed.

As Ben parked in Sissy's backyard and opened the door to get out of his truck, he heard her screaming. This time, it wasn't pain he heard in her cries, but terror. He hit the ground running, cursing the fact that he'd never had a duplicate of her key made. He felt as if he were racing against a headwind, every step taking a lifetime. Across the yard, up the steps. He smacked the back door with such force that he took out the frame again.

Sissy's screams came from the kitchen. The hallway seemed to be a mile long. When he reached the dining room, he heard her sobbing. Following the sound, he burst into the cooking area and almost tripped over a man sprawled on the floor. He saw Sissy huddled in the corner of the cup-boards. Blood trickled from her nose and puffy lower lip. Her cheek was bright red. The front of her blouse hung open, revealing her bra, pushed above her breasts.

Ben wanted to kill the man on the floor with his bare hands, but he was either already dead or out cold. There was a deep gash on his temple, which he suspected had been put there by the skillet Sissy still held. He hurried over to her. "Sweet-heart, are you okay?"

When he reached toward her, she flinched away. "D-don't. Please don't t-touch m-me."

Ben snatched his cell phone from his pocket and dialed 911. A female dispatcher answered. "This is Ben Sterling at the Cauldron. Some man broke in and attacked Sissy Bentley. I

507

believe she hit him on the head with a skillet and knocked him out. She may be badly hurt, and he's unconscious."

"I've dispatched the call, sir. Help is on the way. Would you like me to remain on the phone with you until the officers and paramedics arrive?"

"No," Ben said. "Ms. Bentley needs attention. I have the situation under control."

Ben pocketed his phone and gazed down at Sissy. Never had he felt so helpless.

"My father," she said, her voice still shaking. "He's my f-father. And my mother is in on it."

Ben's stomach rolled. He wanted to plant a boot in the bastard's face and then grab him by the hair and pound his already-injured head against the floor. He'd tried to rape Sissy. Maybe he'd succeeded. Judging by the way she'd shrunk away from Ben's touch, she appeared to be in shock.

Ben crouched beside her. "Did he—?"

"N-no. B-but almost. I b-bashed him on the head to kn-knock him out." She released her grip on the skillet, and it clanked on the floor. "He br-broke my c-cast. I c-couldn't run. I was so scared he'd wake up."

Just then, she jerked and her eyes widened with renewed terror. Ben pivoted in a crouch and surged to his feet just as Bentley rushed him. Ben had no time to react. The other man's body slammed him with such force that Ben fell against the grill behind him.

Ben's recent rage, diminished by concern for Sissy, returned, licking through his bloodstream. He clenched his hands into fists. Bentley was fair game now, awake and in attack mode. Ben drew back and hit the son of a bitch squarely in the face with all his strength. The older and heavier man reeled backward, but he remained standing. Something primal overtook Ben. He strode across the floor and punched the bastard again, one more time in the face and then with an uppercut blow to his belly.

Sissy, he thought. *Not much to her,* Drake had said. And it was true. Yet this bastard, her own father, had harmed her. Broken her cast. Possibly, if her tibia had been damaged, crippled her. Ben wanted to beat him to death.

Bentley crashed to his knees. Ben drew back and planted his boot in the man's ribs.

"Ben, stop! You'll kill him and go to jail!" Sissy screamed. "Stop! Please, stop!"

Sanity returned, and Ben, fists still clenched, stared down at Bentley, who lay huddled in a fetal position. "Count your lucky stars, you asshole. I've never wanted to kill a man before, but I'd gladly put you six feet under."

Chapter
TWENTY-TWO

Sissy stared at her father as he writhed on the floor. She felt soiled in a way that soap and water would never remove. Douglas Bentley wasn't only a piece of trash. He had something haywire in his brain. She couldn't believe alcohol alone had turned him into such a monster.

And his blood flowed in her veins.

She heard the faint sound of sirens, and with every beat of her heart, they grew louder. Then she heard the screech of tires as speeding vehicles came to a sudden stop.

"I'm not leaving you to let them in," Ben said. "Not with him conscious."

Sissy listened for the sound of shattering glass, but somehow the emergency response team gained access to the building without breaking a window.

"In the kitchen!" Ben called.

Barney Sterling was the first person to charge into the kitchen. He glanced at Sissy, determined she was in no immediate danger, and then straddled Doug Bentley and jerked his arms behind his back to cuff him. "You have the right to remain silent and refuse to answer questions. Anything you say—"

"Go fuck yourself. You think this is the first time I ever heard my rights?"

As if Bentley hadn't spoken, Barney continued. "Anything you say may be held against you in a court of law."

For Sissy everything after that happened in a blur. Paramedics rushed in. She was checked over and lifted onto a gurney. Before she knew it, she was in an ambulance headed for Crystal Falls. Though her cheekbone still throbbed, she didn't feel badly hurt, except for her leg, which she prayed wasn't serious. Emotionally, however, she felt wounded in a way that no doctor could ever heal. She thought of Ben and closed her eyes to ward off an urge to sob. He was such a wonderful man and came from an equally wonderful family.

Sissy was the daughter of a mentally ill drunk and a woman who'd offered her child up tonight as a sacrifice to get her hands on some money. Because of Doug Bentley, people had looked down on her all her life. She remembered that football player who'd called her white trash. Well, he'd been right. They'd all been right. Her feelings of inferiority had always run deep, and they flooded back to the surface now. Her father was sick, beyond sick. She'd seen the knot on his ear. No matter what he said, she was his child.

Once in the ER, Sissy was examined and under-went X-rays. Her mental anguish was so intense that the process didn't bother her nearly as much as it normally would. She'd been lucky, they told her. No new bones had been fractured. Her surgeon was called in. He said Sissy's tibia held fast even after the cast broke. In his estimation, the pain in her leg was due more to the atrophy of her muscles and tendons. He applied a new cast with a walking heel, told Sissy to baby the leg for two days, and released her to go home. Despite bruises and lacerations, she required no hospitalization.

The moment Sissy limped out of the ER, she saw Ben in the waiting room. He surged to his feet and strode toward her. She knew that he intended to drive her home and believed they could pick up where they left off. Sissy's heart felt as if it were breaking. She would always love Ben. What woman wouldn't? But what had happened tonight could never be erased from her mind. Ben Sterling deserved a whole lot better than what Sissy could offer him. Undoubtedly, her father would be locked up, but for how long? After tonight he'd be out for revenge as well as money.

The man was crazy. She'd seen madness in his eyes tonight. But his genetics, latent though they seemed to be in her, could still be passed on to her kids. Ben wanted to have babies. They had never discussed it, but the intense manner in which he had argued that children were products of their environment had been a telltale sign that he yearned to have a family. And he deserved to have that, to be a father. But he needed to do that with a woman whose genetic makeup didn't include a violent, insane man and a woman who would set her daughter up to be robbed and raped.

When Ben reached Sissy and tried to grasp her arm, she said, in a flat, unemotional tone, "One of the Mystic Creek deputies is giving me a ride back to the café."

Ben couldn't believe he'd heard correctly. There was an empty, glassy look in her eyes, and she avoided his gaze. Something was going on in her head. He just wasn't sure what. Even so, all his instincts told him to back off. Her own father had just tried to rob and rape her. And her mother had been complicit in the attempt. She had to be feeling emotionally shattered. A smart man didn't press a woman at a time like this.

"All right," he told her, even though those were some of the most difficult words he'd ever uttered. He wanted to hold her against him and comfort her. He wanted to put ice on her swollen cheek and puffy lip. "All right."

Ben turned to leave the ER. With every step, he prayed she'd call out his name. He waited inside his truck in the parking lot until Sissy

513

emerged from the building. He clenched his hands over the steering wheel as he watched her climb into a taxi. Deputy, hell. She'd called a cab. The fare to Mystic Creek would be astronomical. Yet she preferred to pay out the nose for a ride rather than allow him to take her home.

When Sissy returned to the café, she shuddered. Whether she imagined it or not, the stench of her father still lingered there, and everywhere she looked, she remembered his brutality and the crazed look in his eyes. He'd tainted her building with his presence, and now she just yearned to be alone. The sheriff and two deputies were still taking pictures and dusting the surfaces of her cash register and safe. She locked the front door and approached Sheriff Adams, a stoutly built older man with the beginning of an impressive beer belly.

She briefly told the law officer what had occurred.

"I have that figured out," he replied. "He has a criminal record. One of my deputies already took a few of what we believed were his prints and ran them. A few must have been Ben's, but we found a match on the others in no time. His prints are on the door of the safe and all over the money bag. It's a clear robbery attempt." He studied Sissy's bruised face. "And judging by the state of your clothing, he also sexually assaulted you."

Sissy had closed her blouse as best she could, but it was still clear to anyone who looked that someone had tried to rip the garment off of her. She swallowed. "Yes. He tried to rape me."

The sheriff cleared his throat. "I know he's your father. It's difficult to press charges against a close relative."

Sissy looked him squarely in the eye. "It won't be difficult. I hope he spends the rest of his life behind bars, and if I can make that happen by pressing charges, I will. And, for your information, he physically assaulted me *before* he tried to rape me. I want to press charges against him for breaking and entering, assault, attempted rape, and attempted robbery. He also told me my mother is his accomplice. She came to visit me, all nice and lovey, saying she left him four years ago. She lied. She wanted to get the lay of the land, tell him where I am, and get the money he tried to steal in her greedy little hands."

Adams beckoned her toward the bar to fill out the paperwork. Sissy shook her head. "Can I do that upstairs? My injured leg took some punishment tonight, and I'd like to elevate it for a while."

"Certainly."

The sheriff followed Sissy up the stairs. "Wow, no wonder you broke your leg in a tumble down these. They're mighty steep."

Sissy trusted the sheriff. She wasn't nervous about being upstairs alone with him. That was a gift to her from Ben. He'd taught her that some men in the world were decent and caring individuals.

"Barney Sterling has Nate Ramsey from Nuts and Bolts replacing your back door. You'll be able to lock up tonight."

"Oh, thank you," Sissy said as she sank onto the sofa and rested her throbbing leg on the coffee table. "It'll be fun explaining to my insurance agent why I've had door damage twice in such a short period of time."

The sheriff sat beside her on the sofa, but not so close that she felt her space was invaded. "We have all the evidence we need to nail him. All you have to do is sign the documents."

He handed her a clipboard. As Sissy signed to press charges against her father, she pushed down harder with the pen than she normally would, wanting her signature to show clearly on the pink copy. She'd hang it on her wall. She never wanted to forget that she'd been the one who finally put her father behind bars for possibly years. It'd be just her luck that he'd do only six months. Regardless, Doug Bentley deserved every day of the time he was imprisoned.

"How is he?" she asked.

"A pretty deep gouge on his temple. A mild

concussion. At this moment, he's in the Mystic Creek jail."

"Good. He can't hurt anyone in there."

After the sheriff left, Sissy locked up after him. Then she resumed her seat on the sofa, held Patches close, and cried her heart out.

When Ben knocked on her apartment door and called to her, she wasn't surprised. He loved her. She didn't doubt that. In fact, she knew he would lay down his life for her. It was so hard not to unlock the door and invite him in. She wanted so badly to feel his arms around her that she ached. But that would be unfair to Ben.

A cold feeling coursed through her as she recalled her father's hands groping her body. *Sick.* Sissy had never met any of her dad's family. They could all be batshit crazy. Her mom had seemed so sincere when she said she'd pray with every roll of the tires driving home, and the whole time she'd been plotting to get her hands on Sissy's money. Sissy had observed their operation for years. She'd been stupid to believe her mom had changed. The woman she'd spoken with at the restaurant had been an illusion, someone playing a role.

They were sick. *Sick.* Sissy had always preferred to think Doreen was just spineless. But in her own way, she was as treacherous and deadly as her husband.

Desperately hoping she was wrong, Sissy got out her laptop and used the search term *mental illness genetics*. The screen popped up with bold blue headers, leading to sites that said in the brief descriptions that five major mental disorders had been proven to have genetic roots. Even the Mayo Clinic affirmed what Sissy feared the most—that she could pass on mental illness to her children.

She shoved the computer on the floor. Patches crawled onto her lap. Sissy cuddled him against her neck, began rocking back and forth, and sobbed her heart out once more. She loved Ben too much to taint his life with all the baggage she carried from her parents. On threat of death, she'd *never* do that to him.

"You're my one and only," she whispered raggedly to the kitten. "I can love you all I want and never hurt you."

When Sissy didn't answer Ben's knock, he decided to give her some space and time to think. Through the door, he said, "I love you, honey. You'll never know how much because I can't put it into words. I know you've been to hell and back tonight. I understand how upset you must be right now. So I'll go and leave you alone to sort your way through all this. I found your spare key in the pantry. I'll lock up as I leave and return the key when I come back in the morning to work."

"No!" Ben heard her cry. "I'm healed enough now to handle everything here."

Ben frowned. She *wasn't* healed enough. If she tried to run the café without help, especially after what she'd been through tonight, she'd put too much stress on the leg. "That's where we're going to butt heads, sweetheart."

"I'll hire help. I'll call the employment department tomorrow. I'll put an ad in our weekly paper. I can also put up an ad on Craigslist."

"And it may take you days to find someone. Then you'll have to train that person. I'll be here in the morning. You don't have to speak to me. I won't speak to you unless it's necessary. But I'm helping until you no longer need help."

"I won't let you in."

Ben sighed. "Fine. I'll just come through the front door like customers do."

He turned and started down the stairs. He heard Sissy calling his name. Sadness welled within him. She was trying to cut him out of her life. *Why?* Things had been so perfect between them. Why in the hell would she want to end it with him?

Ben's hope that a night's rest would change Sissy's mind was futile. When he arrived the next morning she didn't utter a syllable. She had bruises on her face and arms. A split lip. How could she still look so beautiful? But to him, she did. Fortunately, they'd worked together so much in the café that they didn't need to communicate. It reminded Ben of those early days when Sissy had given him the cold shoulder.

Ben worked at the café the next day and the day after that. As long as he could work with Sissy, he had hope.

He wasn't sure what was going on with her. But he damned sure meant to find out. By midmorning of the third day, he decided that he'd give Sissy no choice. She *would* talk to him tonight after they closed the café. He loved her too much to take no for an answer.

Only, Sissy beat him to the punch by finally breaking the silence. "Tonight after closing, we need to talk."

Ben nodded. "I was going to ask you, actually. We've got to figure this out."

She turned away. "Great. We're both on board. And just for the record, I've already figured it out." Her tone suggested that the conversation she had in mind was going to be the opposite of great.

It seemed to Ben that the remainder of the day lasted far longer than usual. But finally Sissy locked the front door and closed the café. Normally, they adjourned to the kitchen to do cleanup and breakfast prep. But tonight she beckoned for him to take a seat at the bar. As he straddled a stool, she circled the counter and stood across from him.

"I want to thank you for all you've done, and also tell you that you needn't be here in the morning. I've hired a helper. She has plenty of experience. I really like her. She'll be perfect." Other than sounding firm, her voice was completely expressionless.

Ben gazed at her face. He knew that look. Sissy had erected the walls around her heart again, particularly the wall between herself and him. She reached into her chef coat pocket and brought out the diamond ring that he'd put on her finger not long ago. She carefully set it on the counter.

"I'm ending our engagement," she said, her tone still flat. "I'm sure Blackie will give you a fair price for the ring. It's so beautiful. You'll be able to recoup a large portion of what you paid for it."

"Sissy—"

"No, Ben. We have nothing more to say to each other. It's over."

"I've figured out why you're pushing me away," he said, acting as if she hadn't spoken. "You've always worried about your family. You're afraid mental illness runs in your bloodline. But there are ways around that, sweetheart. We can still have babies. As many as you'd like to have. We'll just adopt."

Her eyes went misty, but her expression didn't change. "No," she said. "You want children of your own, and I don't blame you for that. You have such a great family. On Halloween night, I watched you with your dad and brothers. The family resemblance is so strong that even strangers who saw all of you together would know you're related. An adopted son would bear no resemblance to you, his uncles, or his grandfather." She shrugged. "I won't do that to you, Ben. You might feel content at first with adopted children, but there would always be an empty place within you."

"We could hire a surrogate to carry my child, then." Ben wasn't sure where that idea had come from. He actually wanted a little girl that resembled Sissy. But now that the idea had slipped into his brain, he believed it might be an option Sissy would consider. "Then the kid would have my genes."

"You see? You *do* yearn for your own children."

"That *isn't* how I meant it. You're wrong. I'd be perfectly happy to adopt kids. Jeb adopted Chloe. Barney adopted Sarah. Those little girls are their daughters in every way that matters. You're three days out from being sexually assaulted by your father. You're upset, conflicted, and not thinking straight."

"Why should I be thinking straight?" she fired back. "Do you think my father has a rational thought in his head? Or that my mother does? No sane woman would stay with a man like him."

She pushed the ring closer to him. "Take it, Ben. I love you. I love you too much to let you mess up your chances to have the kind of life you deserve. I'm not going to change my mind. Just go. Don't make this any more painful for either of us than it has to be."

She turned away and headed into the kitchen. Ben noted that her limp was less pronounced than it had been since her father's attack. That meant her leg was healing.

Now if only he could find a magical remedy for his heart.

"I'm leaving the ring," he said, knowing she could hear him because of the pass-through. "I bought it especially for you, and I don't want it back."

On legs suddenly shaking and unsteady, Ben walked out.

The next morning, Ben awakened with renewed determination roiling within him. He bypassed his usual silent hour and went straight to his computer to sign up and pay a membership fee for a site that promised a user could learn anything about anyone. He began with Mabel Rushwater, now deceased, and soon he found the names of her parents and siblings.

Ben was about to investigate Sissy's grandparents when someone knocked on his kitchen door. He sighed, feeling frustrated. He still knew so little about Sissy's family. He left Finn asleep by the desk and found Barney on his porch.

"Hey, bro," Barney said. "I need to talk to you."

"Terrific. I'm kind of busy. What is it?"

Barney pushed his way inside. "I just thought you'd like to know that Sissy's mother is back in town."

Ben's heart skipped a beat. "Is she here to bail him out of jail?"

"She did bring him money."

"That figures. Sissy says her mom will stand by her crazy bastard of a husband, no matter what. Does she know that he tried to rape her daughter?"

Barney, in uniform for work, went to pour himself some coffee. As usual, he forgot to remove his Stetson. Ben forgot half the time, too. "Oh, yeah, she knows. But you're wrong about her standing by her man. She left him. Not sure when, but I get the feeling it's been a while even though the divorce only recently became final. The money she brought Doug is his legal half of their assets, a directive from her attorney." Barney grabbed a jug of creamer from the fridge and added a dollop to his mug. "I heard her tell him that if she ever sees him again, she'll say hello with a loaded twelve-gauge and aim for his balls." He glanced up. "Considering what he'd done to her daughter, we searched her for weapons when she came in, afraid she might shoot him."

"And?"

"She was carrying. I think she was so upset about what he'd done to Sissy that she meant to put a bullet between his eyes. She didn't admit that. She claimed she has a permit to carry concealed and just forgot to take the pistol out of her pocket. Adams checked, and she is licensed to carry. He also discovered that Bentley assaulted her a few months ago and she has a restraining order against him. He could have arrested her for bringing a weapon inside the building. Instead he took possession of it and gave it back to her as she left."

Ben gave his brother a shocked look. "Really? Sissy describes her mom as a spineless wimp."

Barney shrugged. "I'm not questioning Sissy's opinion of her mother. But abused women can get counseling. Her name is Doreen. She now uses her maiden name. At the jail, she made her ex-husband sign a notarized document prepared by her attorney that releases her from any further financial obligation to the jerk. I was one of the witnesses. Adams was the other one. The notary came in from the bank."

"Wow." Ben's mind was racing. "Good for her. And she tried to sneak in a weapon? I'm liking her better and better." Ben pressed a hand to his forehead. "I didn't mean that. And yet I do. I wanted to kill him when I saw what he'd done to Sissy. I can totally get how Doreen must feel if she loves her daughter."

"Sissy resembles her in build and facial features, only her mom is a redhead and fair skinned with freckles. You can definitely tell they're related. Doreen is staying at the Dewdrop Inn. Room forty-three. Checkout is at eleven. If you want to meet her, you'd better hurry. She could leave early."

Ben grabbed his hat and jacket. "She's leaving town even though she knows her daughter was almost raped by her father? What the hell? You'd think she'd at least stop by the café."

Barney leaned his hips against the counter. "Cut her some slack, Ben. Do you really think Sissy wants to see her?"

Ben sighed. "No. I get you." He opened the door and whistled for Finn, still asleep in the office. The dog came running. Ben tipped the brim of his hat to his brother. "I'm headed for the Dewdrop. Cross your fingers. I really want to talk to her."

Chapter
TWENTY-THREE

That night, Sissy was about to close the café when a slender woman walked in and took a stool at the counter. Only two other customers remained in the café, Lynda and Tim VeArd. Sissy nearly dropped a pan when she recognized her mom. She stared at her, wondering how she dared to show her face.

She stomped from the kitchen on her walking cast and faced Doreen over the counter. "Get out!"

"Oh, God, your face. If he gets out with a slap on his hand, I swear to God I'll find him."

"I said 'get out.'"

"Unless I'm physically forced, I'm not leaving. Your father lied. I played no part in what he did. You can call the cops to carry me out of here, but all you'll learn from them is that I tried to sneak into the department this morning with a loaded gun. I wanted to kill the son of a bitch for what he did to you."

Sissy, still furious, stared hard into her mother's eyes. "How'd you know he was in jail unless he called you?"

"He did call. He needed money, and I still

owed him his half of our marital assets. I knew he was in jail here. I thought maybe he'd been arrested for stealing a car. But when I pulled into town, I stopped at a café for breakfast at the edge of town. The place was abuzz with all the sordid details of how Sissy Bentley's father broke into her café, beat the hell out of her, then tried to rob her and rape her." Doreen's larynx bobbed. "When I heard that, my whole reason for coming changed. I wouldn't need a signed and notarized release from a dead man."

"It's illegal to enter a public building with a loaded gun," Sissy countered back.

"I got the permit to carry concealed after the bastard attacked me the last time. I normally keep the weapon in the glove box unless I feel threatened by him. But this morning, I put it in my coat pocket before I went into the sheriff's office. When a deputy found it, I told the sheriff I forgot I had it in my pocket, so he gave me a pass."

Sissy could no longer believe a word her mother said. "Wow, I'm so impressed. Suddenly mama bear comes out. Where was she when he beat the hell out of me countless times as I was growing up? Where was she the night he tried to rape me right before I graduated from high school?" Sissy didn't care if her customers heard. They were her friends. Everyone in town already knew her parents were no good. "Don't come in here with another bullshit story. Trick me once, shame on you. Trick me twice, shame on me. I won't fall for it."

Doreen's face went white, her mouth slack with shock. "In high school? He tried to rape you in high school? Why didn't you tell me?"

Sissy crossed her arms and looked up at the ceiling. "Jeez, let me think. Maybe because he broke my cheekbone twice and you never did a thing about it, including taking me to a doctor? Maybe because you let him throw me against walls? Maybe because you let him kick my puppy to death for peeing on his piece-of-crap rental floor? Maybe because all you ever did when he beat me was to sometimes throw yourself in his line of fire to take the punishment yourself?"

Doreen bent her head. Her thin shoulders shook with silent sobs. Sissy stared at her, feeling nothing. *Nothing.* Her mother had betrayed her for the last time.

Then, when Doreen regained her composure, she looked up, her eyes aching with regret and pain that ran so deep, not even Sissy could fail to see it. "You're right," she said so loudly that Sissy winced because the VeArds remained in the café. "My name is Doreen. I married an abusive man. I bore him a child, a beautiful little girl, and I didn't have the courage to protect her when he turned on her. I didn't have the courage to protect myself. I believed I was stupid, ugly, worthless, and helpless."

Sissy's heart caught. This sounded like a speech her mother had made many times in front of others, a confession for which there was no absolution. Doreen slid off the stool and turned toward the two individuals who remained in the café. "I deserve nothing from my daughter but her con-tempt. Nothing I ever say or do can make up for how I failed her."

Counseling, group counseling, Sissy thought. Her mom had told her that there was nothing Sissy could say to her that she hadn't already said aloud countless times to people in her group. Sissy felt as if a huge, cruel hand of steel was crushing her heart.

"Mama," she cried.

Doreen whirled to face her. She reached into her pocket and slapped several folded sheets of motel stationery on the bar. "I came to bring you this, a list of all your relatives on both sides with details about all of them. Read it. Contact them. Go meet them. You come from good stock."

Sissy gasped. "Ben talked to you!"

"Of course he did. The man loves you and is trying to save the relationship. There's not a thing wrong with you genetically. And if you love him and lose him because you're an idiot, it's on you. You're an adult. The stupid choices you make now are on your shoulders, not mine." As

Doreen walked out, she added, "I included my phone number. If you'd ever like to speak with me about all this, I'll be grateful if you call." Just as the door was nearly closed, Doreen pushed it ajar to add, "I did watch my rearview mirror all the way here the day I came to see you. I never saw your father's truck, but a little red sports car was behind me all the way into town. I'll bet Doug stole it. Have the sheriff follow up on it. Maybe Doug will be charged with car theft along with everything else, which will keep him behind bars longer. He shouldn't be on the streets."

Silence descended on the café. Tim and Lynda sat at their booth as if they were statues. Sissy practiced deep breathing to calm herself. With a horrible, chilling wave that surged through her body, she realized her father had lied. Her mom truly had left him and gotten a divorce. She'd turned her life around after years of counseling. And Sissy had not only rejected her but also humiliated her.

So upset her gaze was fixed on nothing, Sissy jumped with a start when Lynda's warm hand grasped hers. Sissy realized Tim was standing at the counter as well. Her friends. Lynda, the fiery one with a huge heart, said nothing. Tim, who was just as caring, said, "Sweetheart, I think you just made a huge mistake. I heard about your mother going into the jail with a gun. Everyone's talking about it, saying she meant to kill him for what he did to you. Nobody said anything in front of you, I'm sure, for fear of embarrassing you. But I happen to believe your mom meant to take him out, and I can't blame her."

Lynda piped in with, "Neither can I. If Tim did that to our daughter, I'd pull the trigger and ask questions later." She elbowed her husband. "Not that he ever would. But when he served in the navy and was away for months on end, I lived on base, in military housing. My friend next door was just like your mom, dealing with an abusive husband. She got beaten down until she believed she was ugly, stupid, and good for nothing. Then her husband got transferred. I never saw her again. But a few months ago I got a letter from her. I have no idea how she found my address. She told me she stayed with her husband for years before she found the courage to leave him. She went home to her family. She's mending her relation-ships with her kids. After two years of counseling, she got a good job and now has a new husband. She's finally happy."

Sissy realized Lynda's story about her friend closely resembled the one Doreen had told her at the Straw Hat.

"It sounds like your mom failed you a lot of times," Tim said.

Sissy nodded. "Yes, but now I think she's finally

got her head on straight. I shouldn't have been so awful to her."

"It can be fixed with a phone call." Tim looped an arm around Lynda and led her toward the door. "Dinner was great! We'll see you tomorrow."

Sissy was left alone to stare at the folded stationery that her mother had left on the counter. She finally sat at the bar, opened the notes, and began to read. A tremulous smile touched her mouth and deepened more as she perused each entry. At the end, she saw her mom's phone number and dialed it.

"Hello," Doreen said. She sounded as if she were speaking on a car phone.

"It's me," Sissy said. "I'm sorry I was so horrible to you, Mama. My father told me you were in cahoots with him and knew he was here."

"No. I told you he's been stalking me. I think he stole that red car to follow me that day, and that's how he found you. I'm sorry I didn't pick up on it then. It wouldn't be the first time he's stolen a car. Normally he didn't drive them any distance, though. Too risky."

Sissy toyed with the papers. "Thank you for the notes about my relatives. They sound like such wonderful, stable people."

"They are. You need to meet them."

"Mama, can you drive back? Maybe spend

533

the night so we can talk and mend our fences?"

"I'll come back another time and look forward to it. But right now you have a far more important relationship to mend, Sissy. Ben is a wonderful young man. I don't want you to lose him. When you're with him again, I'll drive back for a slumber party."

After ending the call, Sissy stared down at her phone. It took all her courage to do it, but she dialed Ben's number. He answered so fast she suspected he'd been waiting for her to call.

"Hi," he said, his deep voice pitched low. "You pissed at me for talking to your mom?"

Sissy squeezed her eyes closed. If he was worried about her being angry with him, maybe they still had a chance to put the pieces back together. "I was miffed at first." Her smile returned. "But unless my mom lied, I know so much more about my relatives now. My paternal grandfather is a minister married to an English teacher. My dad has a sister who's a vet! She was awarded Vet of the Year in that county three years running. And on my mom's side, my two uncles are professionals, one an attorney and the other one a dentist. I can't believe it."

"Believe it. Your father was an apple that fell far from the tree. And your mom—well, shit happens. She married him when she was so young. They eloped, she used fake identification to lie about her age, and he immediately started browbeating her and physically abusing her."

"I'll never understand why she stayed with him."

Ben sighed. "Sissy, go online and read about emotionally and physically abused women. You'll find answers there."

Sissy clung tight to her phone. "I need to visit Homesville and meet both sides of my family. Maybe then, I can get everything into perspective."

"Would you like some company? Moral support?"

"I think this is something I need to do alone, Ben. I called to ask if you'll bear with me and wait until I get back."

"Wait? Wait for what, Sissy?"

She groped for an answer. "I need you to give me a chance to meet my other relatives. If everything my mom says is true, there'll be no reason for me not to marry you."

"You have no reason right now," he said, with a new edge of firmness in his voice. "So, no, I won't wait. You've already put me through enough hell."

Sissy's heart sank. "So no matter what I find out in Homesville, you're finished with me?"

"That isn't what I said. I said I won't wait for you to go there and convince yourself that you're genetically sound. Have you ever heard about people taking a chance on love?"

"Yes, but this has nothing to do with love."

"I disagree. I need to know that you'll love me, no matter what. I need to know that you'll stand beside me. No buts, no conditions. We can adopt children. Couples do it all the time."

Sissy wondered what had happened to the sane and logical conversation she'd planned to have. Somehow it had turned around on her. "But you want your own children."

"I want you more, and over the last few days, I've had nothing to do but think. I had to prove myself to you, over and over, before you could trust me. Now I'm asking you to prove yourself to me. Do you love me? Or maybe I should ask if you love me enough. When you go to Homesville, I want you to go with my ring on your finger. I want a commitment from you. Will you love me no matter what? I'm a forever kind of guy. I've been up front with you about that. What if I'm sterile or have a low sperm count? What if I get genetic marker testing and find out I have a high risk of getting leukemia, or colon cancer, or any other scary thing? Are you going to bail out on me?"

How could he believe she might walk away from him? "No, of course not. I'd still love you."

"Well, right back at you. Excuse my French, Sissy, but you breaking our engagement over your possible genetic flaws was a bunch of bullshit. It still is a bunch of bullshit. You think about that, and then you get in touch with me. And, by the way, if you decide you're truly committed to this relationship and want to reinstate our engagement, this time you can ask me to marry you."

Sissy was too flabbergasted to respond. Her mouth was dry. She waited, but all she heard was flat silence at his end. She licked her lips. "Ben? Are you there?"

There was no answer. Sissy went to stare out at the dark street. No matter how she circled it, she had screwed up, big-time. Ben was right. Breaking their engagement for the reason she had was absolute bullshit. What if he were genetically predisposed to get certain kinds of cancer? How would she feel if he backed out of their relation-ship because he might pass that propensity on to their children? Two people who truly loved each other stayed together, no matter what. They faced all the storms and rough patches together. Real love was unconditional. She didn't come with any guarantees and neither did he.

Ben was in his recliner, trying to concentrate on an episode of a series he'd started watching after Sissy broke up with him. Then he heard a knock coming from the entryway. Nobody who frequently visited his home went to the front door. They knew he used only the side entrance.

Finn sprang up from his nap and emitted a joyful bark. A slight smile curved Ben's mouth. Finnegan loved members of Ben's family, but only one person incited him to react with that much excitement. And of course Sissy wouldn't know to use the side door. She'd been to his house only once. He was damned glad she'd found a good kitchen assistant, because that part of their relationship had to change. He needed to be with her more when she wasn't working, and as long as she put in fifteen hours a day, seven days a week, that couldn't happen. He wanted to take her out to dinner a couple of nights a week. He wanted to prepare her a meal here, where they could sit at *his* table. Going to see a flick together again would also be nice.

He strode to the door and opened it, flipping on the rarely used porch light as he did. She looked so cute standing on his doormat—cute but very stressed-out. He guessed that he'd gotten his point across. For the very first time since he'd met her, she wore a dress. Her heavy winter parka, a fluffy blue thing, detracted from the outfit's impact, as did her thigh-high cast, but, to Ben, no woman on earth had ever looked quite so beautiful as she did, bruised face and all.

"I expected you to just call."

Her large blue eyes dominated her features, and they were filled with anxiety. "I—um—

didn't think it was a good idea to ask you to marry me over the phone. Marilyn gave me a ride."

Ben stepped back to invite her inside. After closing the door, he helped her take off the parka. The dress was silky black and skimmed what was, to him, a perfect figure.

Finn was so happy to see her that he wiggled from head to toe, but he didn't jump up. Sissy had called it right. The pup seemed to realize that he couldn't be his usual rambunctious self around her now. Sissy bent to rub Finn's back, ruffling his fur. "Hi, sweet boy. I've missed you, too." She straightened and said to Ben, "I've missed you even more."

Before he could take her coat to the closet, she plunged a hand into the right pocket and drew it back out in a fist. He suspected that she'd just retrieved her engagement ring. Despite what he'd said to her on the phone, he intended to be the one who slipped it back on her finger. But first, he'd let her sweat a little.

She glanced beyond the entry hall into the huge living room, which Ben had created by taking out two bedrooms, leaving him with five after he knocked out a couple more walls to create a huge master suite with a walk-in closet and bathroom.

"Oh, Ben, your house is lovely. Compared to this, I live like a pauper."

"After you propose to me, I'd like to raise a houseful of kids here."

She turned to look up at him with those fathomless eyes. It was like staring into the clear blue water of a lagoon. "Ben, I'm so sorry for how I've acted."

"Actually, I did what you suggested and looked up mental illness. I read some pretty scary stuff and sort of get where you were coming from." He couldn't help but smile. "But you treated me *awful*. I love you with all my heart, and I felt like you were cutting me out of your life with a surgical scalpel. No emotion from you. Hell, until you officially ended our engagement, you wouldn't even speak to me while we worked together."

She nodded. "I *couldn't* talk to you. I knew, if I opened that door, I'd lose my resolve and throw myself into your arms. I realize how wrong it was now—to end things between us over something I wasn't even sure was true. But at the time, it seemed like the only thing I could do without being completely unfair to you."

"Well, if you expect me to marry you, you'd better be ready to go with the flow and take whatever comes. I think the term is *for better or worse*."

Her eyes went bright with tears. "I felt that I fell into the 'worse' category, that you deserve so much more."

"More." Ben tasted the word as it rolled slowly over his tongue. "More? You're *it* for me, Sissy, my one and only. There isn't anyone who can offer me more."

A single tear slipped down her cheek, and she wiped it away, as if impatient with herself. "Do you realize that I never, *ever* cried before I met you? It's embarrassing to me now, how easily I cry."

"Do you know why that is?" Ben asked softly.

"No. If I did, I'd fix it."

"Crying washes away all the pain. It's healing. That's why you're suddenly crying a lot, because inside where no one can see, you've been badly wounded."

"Yes, I guess I have."

"I had to get to know you to see behind the mask. At first, I only caught glimpses of the sweet person you really are. Otherwise, you came off as a cold, haughty witch."

She smiled and made a face at the same time. "A cold, haughty *witch?*"

"Hey, if the shoe fits?"

"It does, and I'll wear it. At first, you scared me to death."

"Are you scared now?"

"No, not at all. Well, sort of. If I ask you to marry me, you may say no."

"Try me and find out."

She smiled and took a deep breath. After exhaling, she asked, "Ben Sterling, will you please become my husband? For richer or poorer. In sickness and in health. For better or worse, whether or not we're genetically flawed, crazier than loons, or predisposed to have any kind of cancer?"

She unfolded her fist and presented her open palm, upon which sat five thousand of his hard-earned dollars and his heart. "I'll never let you down again. I'll never cut you out of my life. If you get leukemia, I'll take care of you and pray the treatments work. If they don't, and you die, I'll want to die with you."

Ben closed the distance between them. "If I say yes, will you have unprotected sex with me tonight and risk getting pregnant?"

She kept her gaze fixed on his. "Yes. Afterward, I'll even lie flat on my back with my hips propped on pillows so your swimmers have every opportunity to make a home run."

Ben plucked the ring from her palm. "Are you sure?"

She nodded.

"Then, yes, Sissy, I'll marry you." He lifted her left hand and slipped the diamond back on her finger. "For better or worse, and if my swimmers hit a home run, which is a mixed metaphor, by the way, I'll be the happiest man alive."

Being back in Ben's arms was, without question, the happiest moment of Sissy's life. As he trailed kisses down her flat belly, she hoped, even in the throes of passion, that he planted his seed in her womb.

Moments later, when he impaled her without protection, she loved the feeling of being flesh-to-flesh with him, with nothing separating them from being truly one.

"Oh, dear *God*." He groaned out the words. "This is beyond fabulous. I've never been with anyone like this."

"Me, neither. Oh, Ben. I love you." Moments later as he went taut above her and pumped heat deep into her center, she clung to him and cried out with the unimaginable pleasure of it as she climaxed with him. "Oh, my God!"

Afterward they lay skin against skin, with only her cast to hamper them. Ben's muscular arms cradled her against his chest. She found that special place in the hollow of his shoulder that she believed had been designed especially for her head to rest.

Drowsy with indescribable contentment, she murmured, "At the Halloween party, I thought that I'd finally found a home. But I was wrong."

"How's that?" he asked in a voice thickened by recent arousal.

"Home isn't a town or building." She kissed his neck. "My true home is right here, Ben, in your arms."

"And mine is in yours," he murmured. "Don't

ever run away from home again, Sissy. I swear I'll track you down."

She giggled even as tears of gladness slipped down her cheeks and pooled on his sweaty skin. "Promise?"

"I'll swear it before God and witnesses. You're mine, and I'm yours. And don't feel wimpy because you're crying. It's time, sweetheart. You've gone through so many things that wounded you. They'll cleanse your heart."

"I hurt you," she whispered. "You're not crying."

Ben tightened his arms around her, buried his face in her hair, and replied, "Oh, yes, I am." His voice went even thicker. "I thought I'd lost you. Don't ever do that to me again."

Just then, one of Ben's tears slid off his chin and plopped on her eyebrow. "I won't. I swear to you and to God that I won't."

And Sissy meant it with her whole heart.

Epilogue

At their evening wedding on the Mystic Creek Bridge during the full moon of September, almost exactly a year since her chickens had paraded up Main Street, Sissy could barely wait to say the vows that would bind her to Ben for the remainder of her life. Her maternal uncle George, a successful Portland attorney, was giving her away. Sissy had tears in her eyes as he guided her up the long and steep ascent to the crest of the natural bridge where her groom waited. She was walking, step by step, toward the only man in the world she would ever love, and she knew, without a doubt, that marrying him was the best decision she'd ever made in her life.

All of Ben's family were present, but Sissy had a crowd from her side as well, people who'd known of her existence all her life and had greeted her with open arms when she had visited Homesville many months ago. She'd met amazing, well-adjusted people, and for Sissy, it had been a healing experience. Since that visit, she and Ben had returned to Homesville several times to get better acquainted with her family, and they had come to Mystic Creek as well, making Sissy very glad that Ben had such a large house. Her relatives had been comfortable at his place, and Sissy, who'd moved in with Ben, had been able to spend much more time with them than she could have if they'd stayed at a motel.

Sissy's mom stood on the bride's side with her family and Doug's, and, more important, with her boyfriend, a great guy named Greg who'd lost his wife to ovarian cancer five years ago. He still mourned for her, but he also felt ready to move forward now. Doreen, whose first marriage had given her a wealth of knowledge, told Sissy that Greg's lingering sense of loss was one of the things she loved most about him.

Greg was a math teacher from Homesville who had applied for a teaching position in Mystic Creek for the current school year and had been hired to replace a retiring educator. He had relocated because he wanted to be with Doreen, who had invested a large sum of money into remodeling the Cauldron to become Sissy's partner. Together, they had planned the downstairs alterations, which were completed, and now they were gutting the upstairs to turn it into a private, reservations-only dining area, complete with an elevator. Sissy had developed a close relationship with her mother now and was extremely proud of her. Like a phoenix, she had risen from the ashes of her life with Doug, and, by putting one foot in front of the other, had become the woman she always could have been if given the chance. With the talents she had garnered during her culinary arts education, she was teaching Sissy to be an even better cook.

Sissy no longer worked full-time at the café. She and her mother had hired plenty of help so they could both enjoy their personal lives. Sissy treasured every moment of her time off with Ben. Over the last many months, they'd been able to actually date, going to see movies, dining out, and driving the curvy mountain roads around Mystic Creek to have romantic picnics at incredible viewpoints. Ben still invaded the café kitchen occasionally to help with meal prep. In turn, Sissy often helped him at the ranch. She particularly enjoyed the horses, but she liked the cows, too. She'd also taken over the ranch bookkeeping. Ben hated the computer accounting software and had often called Sissy into his office to help him make sense of it. It made her feel good to take that responsibility off his shoulders.

Though she and Ben used no form of birth control, she still hadn't gotten pregnant. Sissy wasn't worried. If she didn't conceive soon, they could both get checked out. She'd take fertility drugs if necessary, or Ben could take medication to help him create more swimmers. If everything failed, they had agreed to adopt. Ben had grown up in a large family, and he wanted six kids. Sissy, who'd never had a real family, couldn't wait for the first one to arrive. When she worked at the café, she'd take their baby with her.

Patches, who'd relocated with Sissy to Ben's ranch, loved living there. Ben had built a huge network of protected outdoor kitty tunnels, and the cat enjoyed going outside, even when it was snowing. Kate had made him waterproof boots so the cold wouldn't make his stubs ache.

Sissy had hoped for good weather for their wedding, but bits of snow drifted down onto her veil as Ben stepped forward from the pinnacle of the bridge to grasp her hand. The rush of the water below them sang in the chilly evening air, a magical, romantic song, which seemed fitting.

Ben led Sissy to stand in front of her paternal grandfather, Otis Bentley, an ordained minister. He smiled often and had a gentle manner about him. He also had the Bentley bump on his ear. His wife, still teaching English, grieved over her youngest child's sentence to twenty years in prison, but both she and Otis seemed to accept that Doug's problems weren't their fault. Their son's alcoholism, combined with drug use, had altered his personality, turning him into someone they didn't recognize.

Sissy sighed as she glanced up at the sky. The mulberry moon, streaked with pink and crimson, was a replica of the mulberry moon a year ago that had first brought her and Ben together. As Sissy stood beside Ben, saying that she would honor and cherish him for the rest of her life, she couldn't help but wonder if the ancient Native American legend, about two people being destined to fall in love if they stood together beneath a mulberry moon, was only a hokey story, after all.

She and Ben had stood together during a mulberry moon, and now they would share a love for each other that ran so deep it would last a lifetime.

It had taken Sissy twenty-six years to get here, but she finally believed in happy endings. How could she not when she'd met and fallen in love with the man of her dreams?

About the Author

Catherine Anderson is the author of more than thirty *New York Times* bestselling and award-winning historical and contemporary romances, including *New Leaf, Silver Thaw, Walking on Air,* and *Cheyenne Amber,* mong others. She lives in the pristine woodlands of Central Oregon.

<u>Connect Online</u>
catherineanderson.com
facebook.com/catherineandersonbooks

Center Point Large Print
600 Brooks Road / PO Box 1
Thorndike, ME 04986-0001 USA

(207) 568-3717

US & Canada:
1 800 929-9108
www.centerpointlargeprint.com